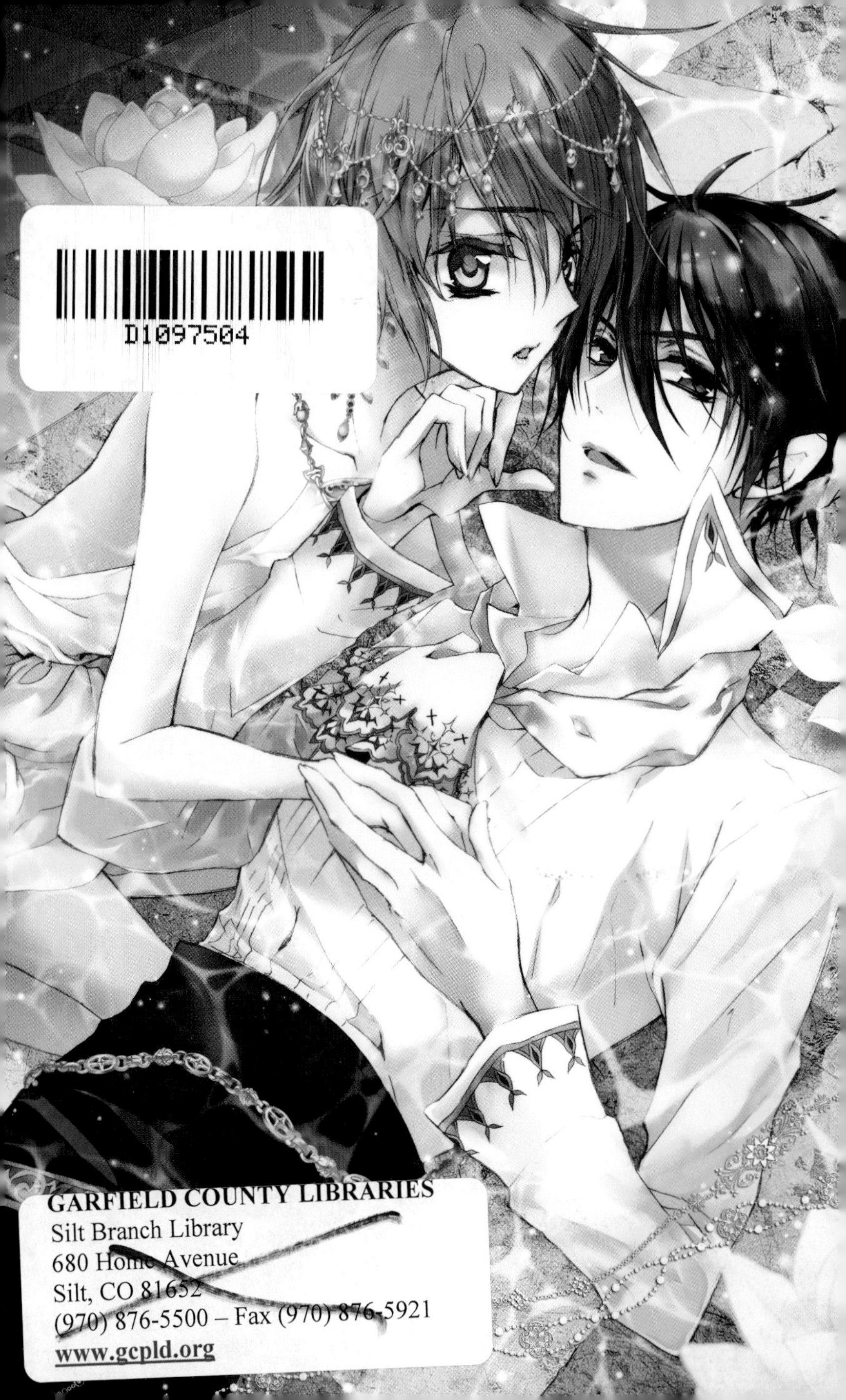

c o n t e n t s

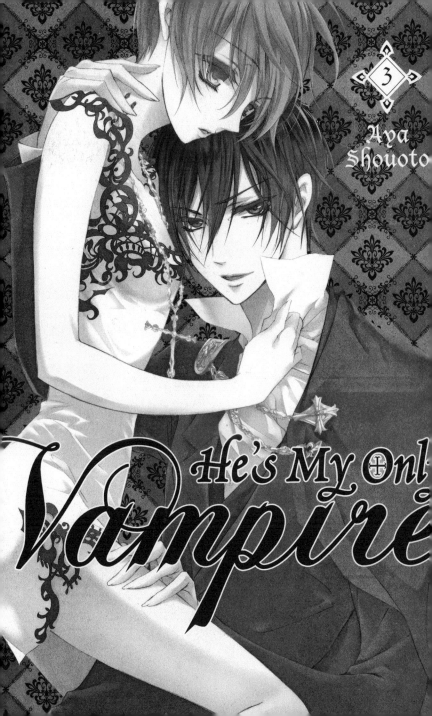

3

Aya
Shouoto

He's My Onl
Vampire

Characters and Story

"Thrall"

One who is ageless and deathless and shall surrender the entirety of their being to their vampire master for all of eternity...

When Kana, a student at St. Agatha Academy, is caught up in a fatal traffic accident, her life is saved by the vampire Aki. However, by feeding her his blood, Aki has also turned Kana into his "thrall."

Aki's goal is to be the victor of the game to gather the seven stigmas and gain the power to awaken his younger brother, Eriya. Jin Shiranui, who owes his life to Kana and Aki, has now joined forces with the pair to help Aki win.

In order to gather information on the seven stigmas, the three form a school club called the "Curious Events Club." Having successfully solved a case brought to them by the student council president, their club is now officially recognized by the academy. However, their celebration is short-lived, as a mysterious girl appears before them declaring that she is Aki's fiancée...

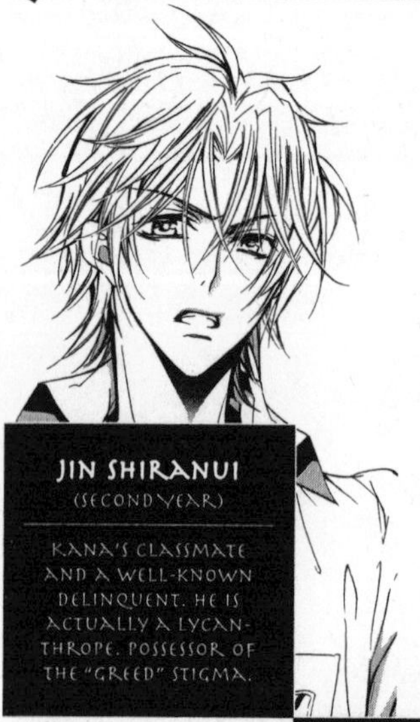

Jin Shiranui
(Second Year)

Kana's classmate and a well-known delinquent. He is actually a lycanthrope. Possessor of the "Greed" stigma.

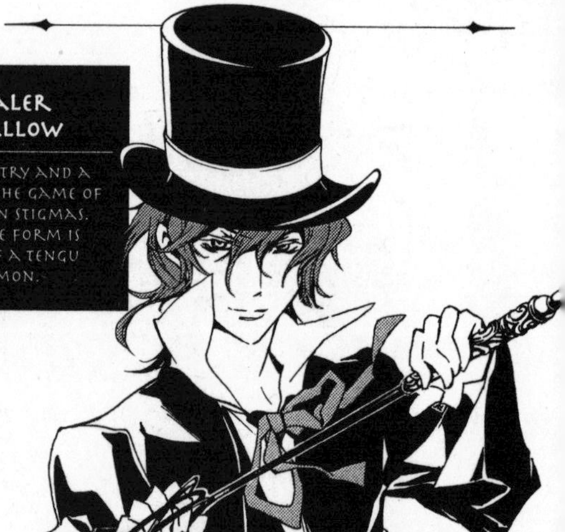

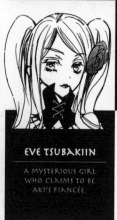

Dealer Swallow

Aki's sentry and a judge in the game of the seven stigmas. His true form is that of a tengu demon.

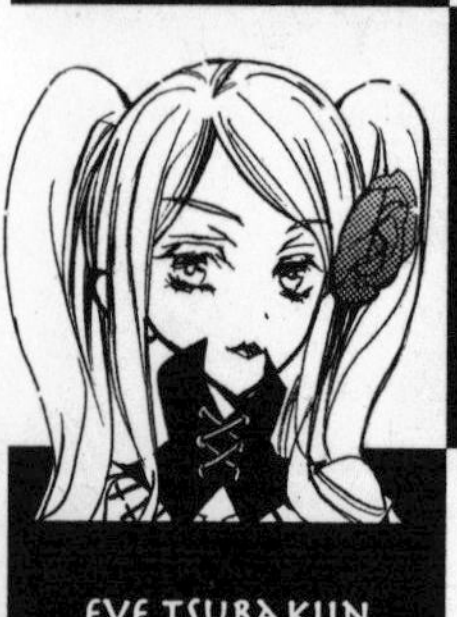

Eve Tsubakiin

A mysterious girl who claims to be Aki's fiancée.

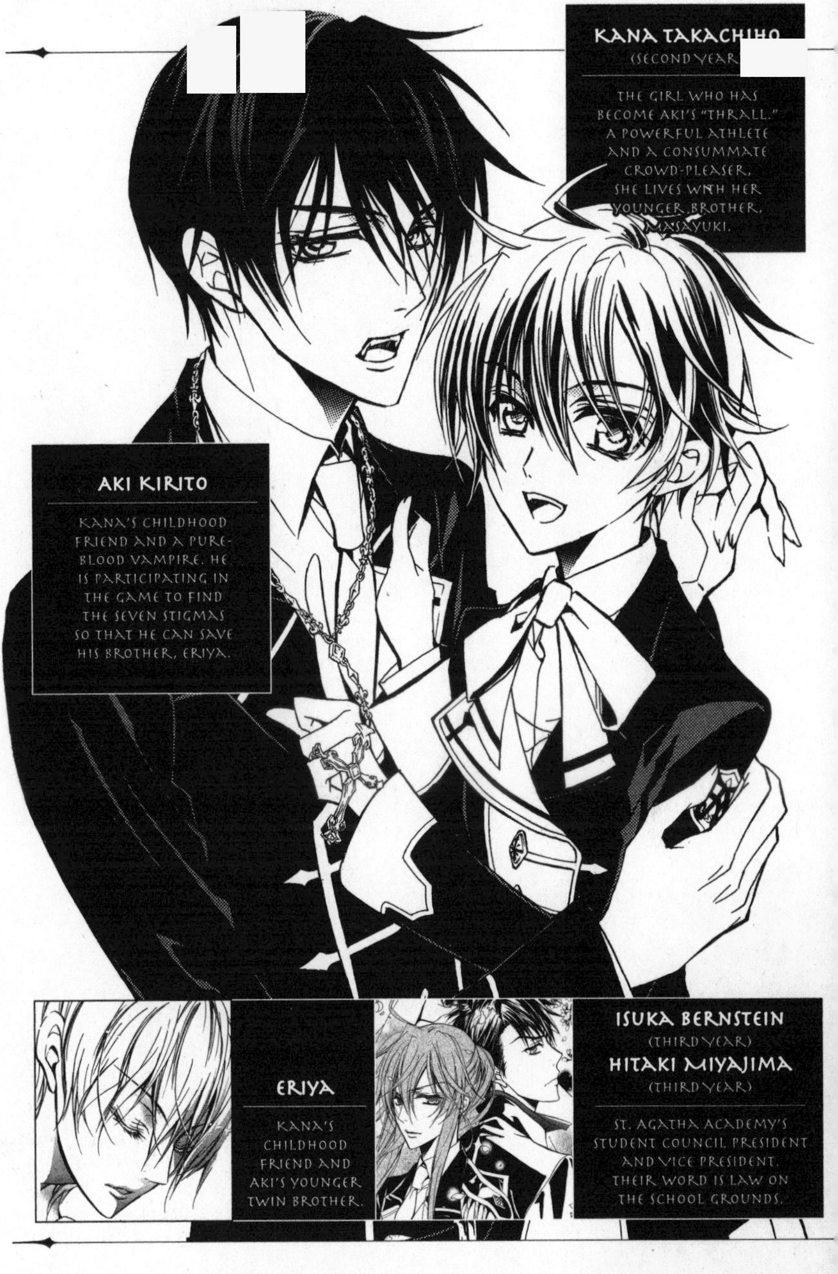
KANA TAKACHIHO
(SECOND YEAR)
THE GIRL WHO HAS BECOME AKI'S "THRALL." A POWERFUL ATHLETE AND A CONSUMMATE CROWD-PLEASER, SHE LIVES WITH HER YOUNGER BROTHER, MASAYUKI.
AKI KIRITO
KANA'S CHILDHOOD FRIEND AND A PURE-BLOOD VAMPIRE. HE IS PARTICIPATING IN THE GAME TO FIND THE SEVEN STIGMAS SO THAT HE CAN SAVE HIS BROTHER, ERIYA.
ISUKA BERNSTEIN
(THIRD YEAR)
HITAKI MIYAJIMA
(THIRD YEAR)
ST. AGATHA ACADEMY'S STUDENT COUNCIL PRESIDENT AND VICE PRESIDENT. THEIR WORD IS LAW ON THE SCHOOL GROUNDS.
ERIYA
KANA'S CHILDHOOD FRIEND AND AKI'S YOUNGER TWIN BROTHER.

He's my only vampire
Aya Shouoto

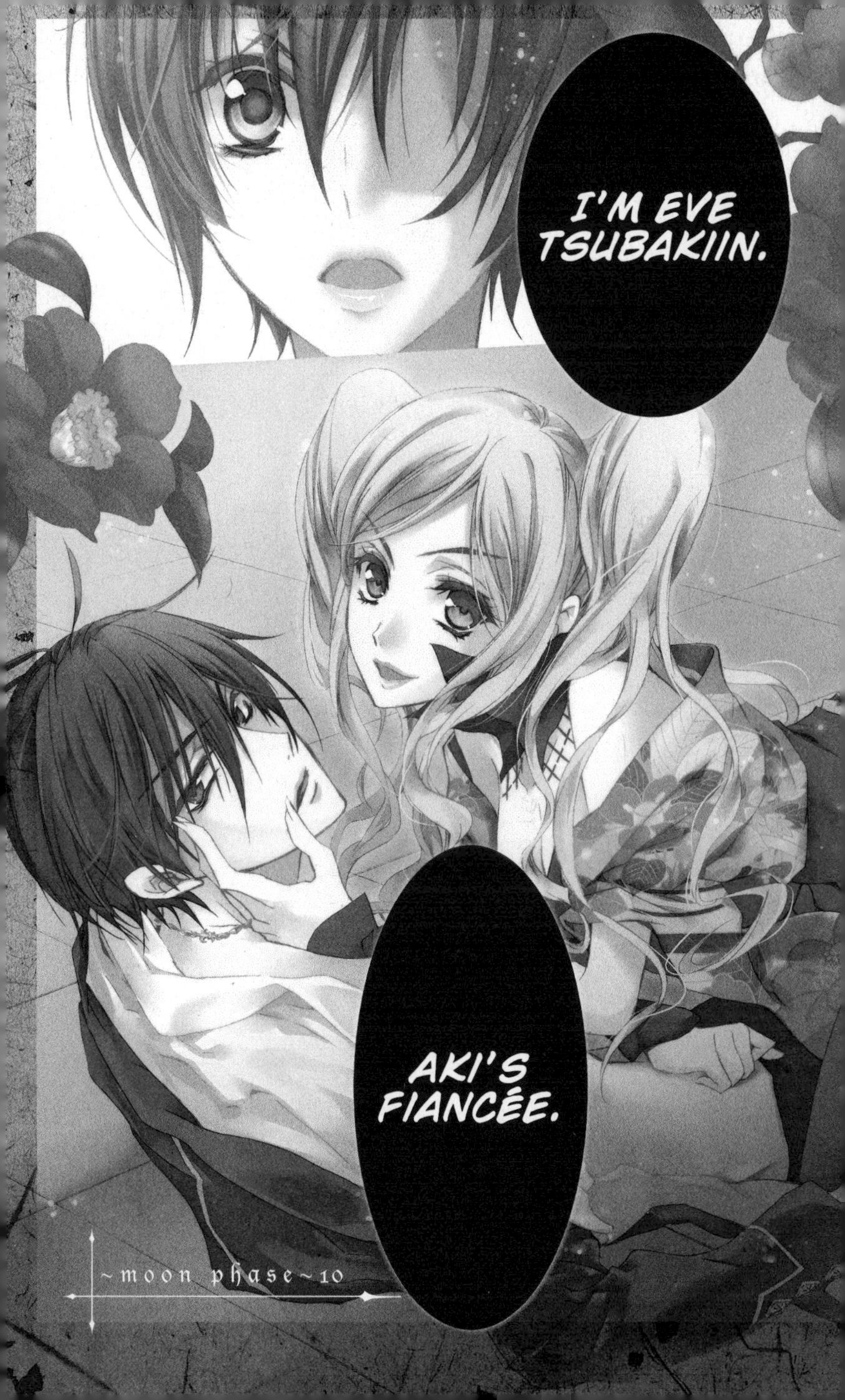
I'M EVE TSUBAKIIN.
AKI'S FIANCÉE.
~moon phase~10

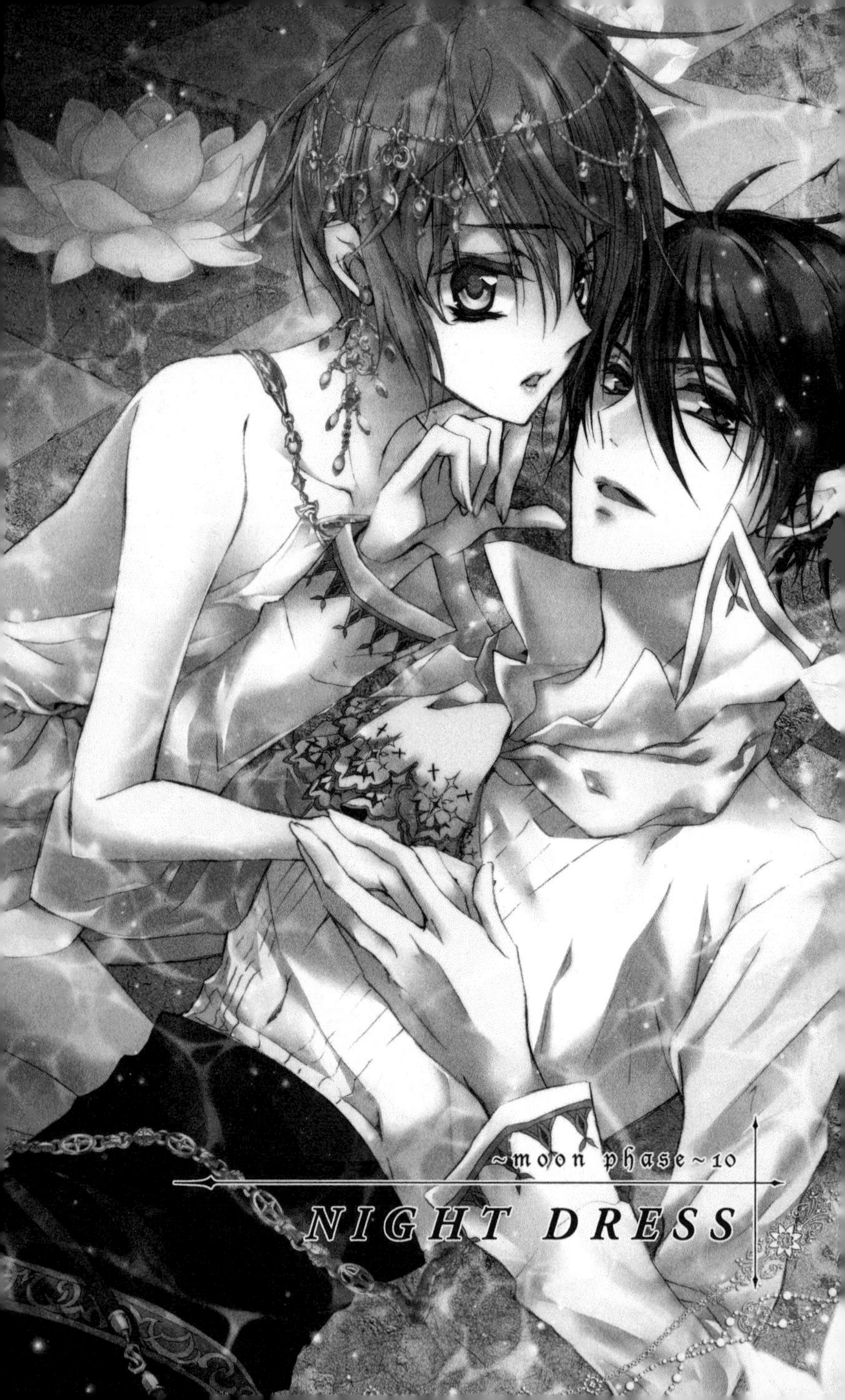
~moon phase~10
NIGHT DRESS

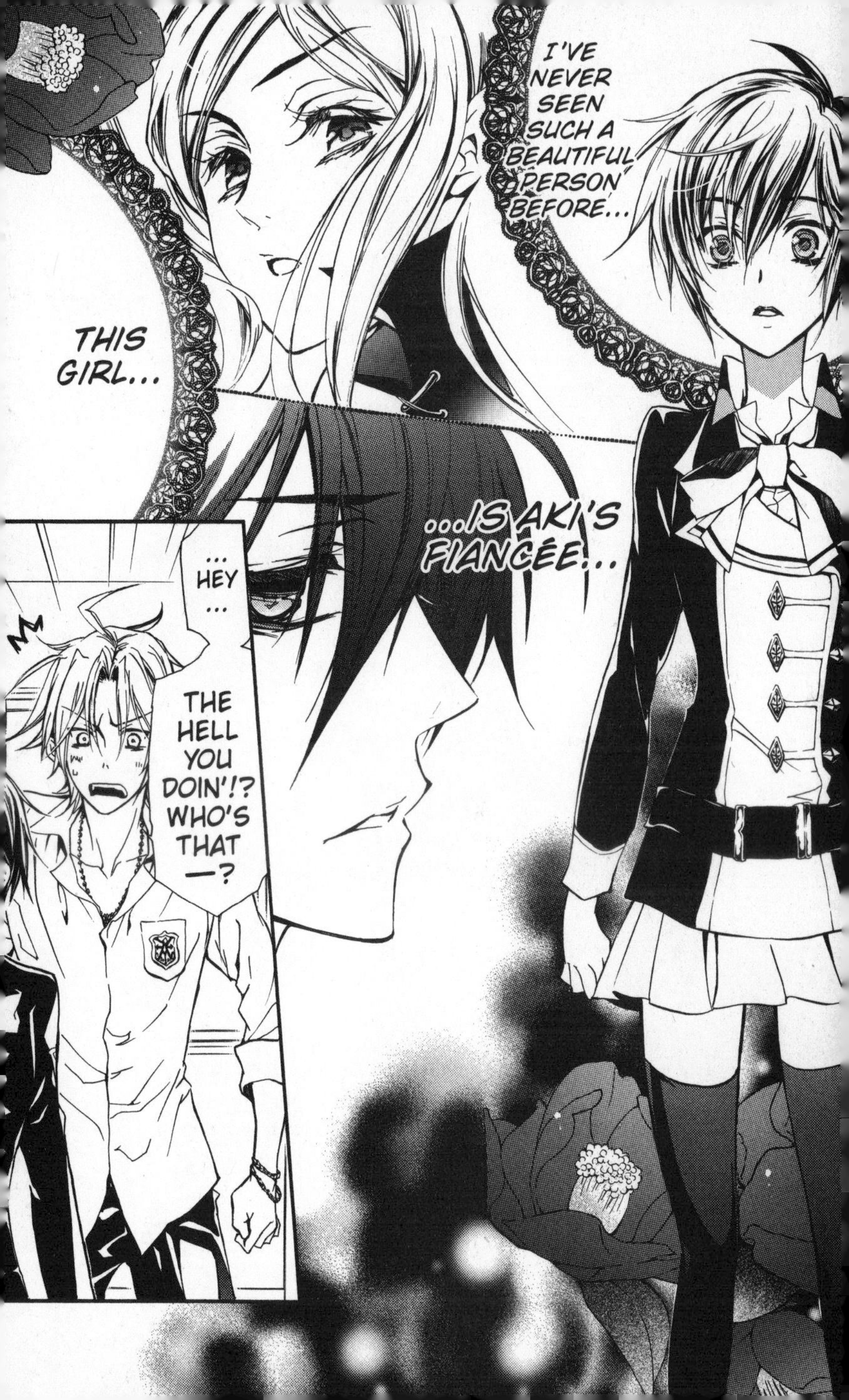
I'VE NEVER SEEN SUCH A BEAUTIFUL PERSON BEFORE...
THIS GIRL...
...IS AKI'S FIANCÉE...
...HEY...
THE HELL YOU DOIN'!? WHO'S THAT—?

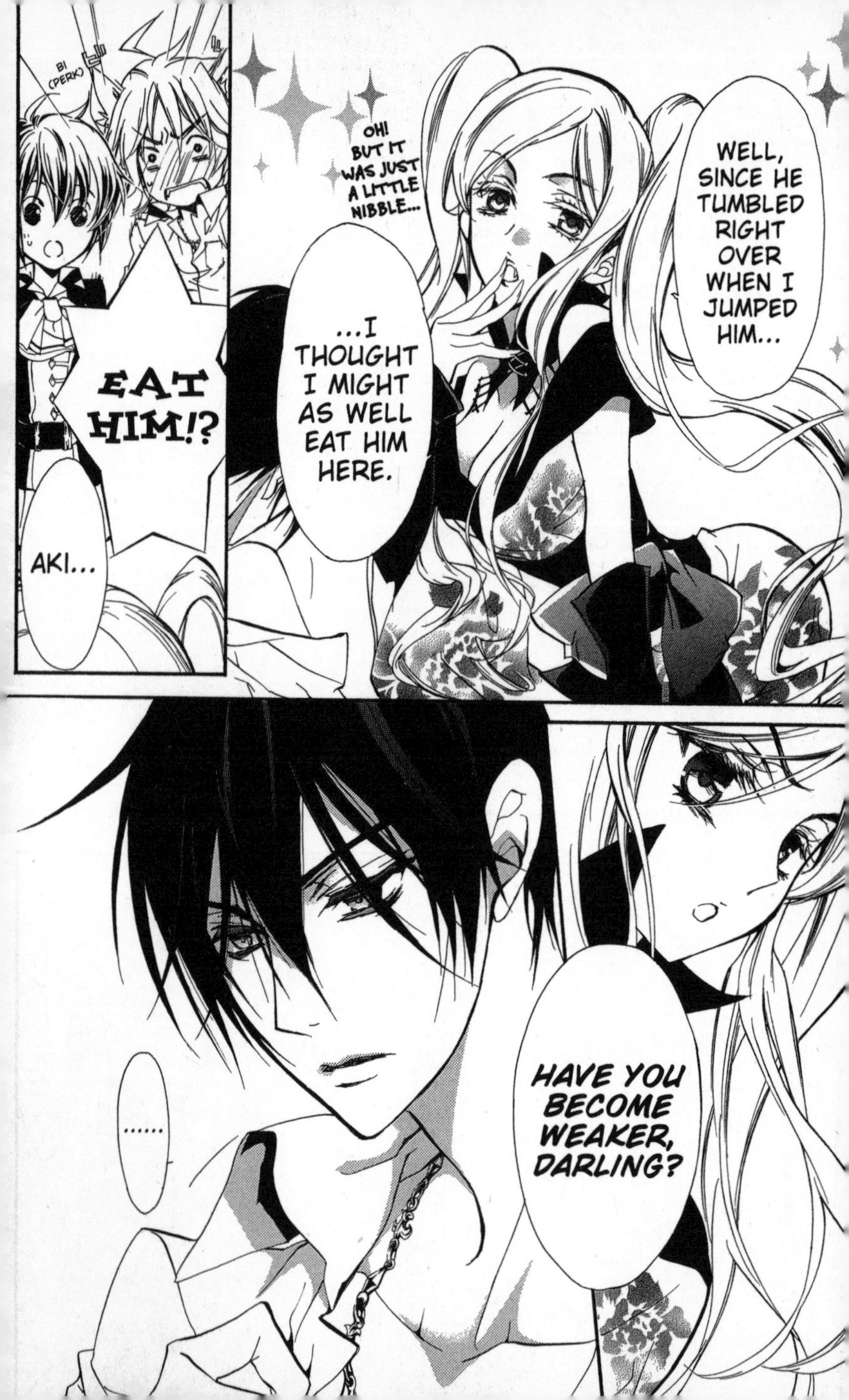
WELL, SINCE HE TUMBLED RIGHT OVER WHEN I JUMPED HIM...
...I THOUGHT I MIGHT AS WELL EAT HIM HERE.
OH! BUT IT WAS JUST A LITTLE NIBBLE...
BI (PERK)
EAT HIM!?
AKI...
HAVE YOU BECOME WEAKER, DARLING?
......

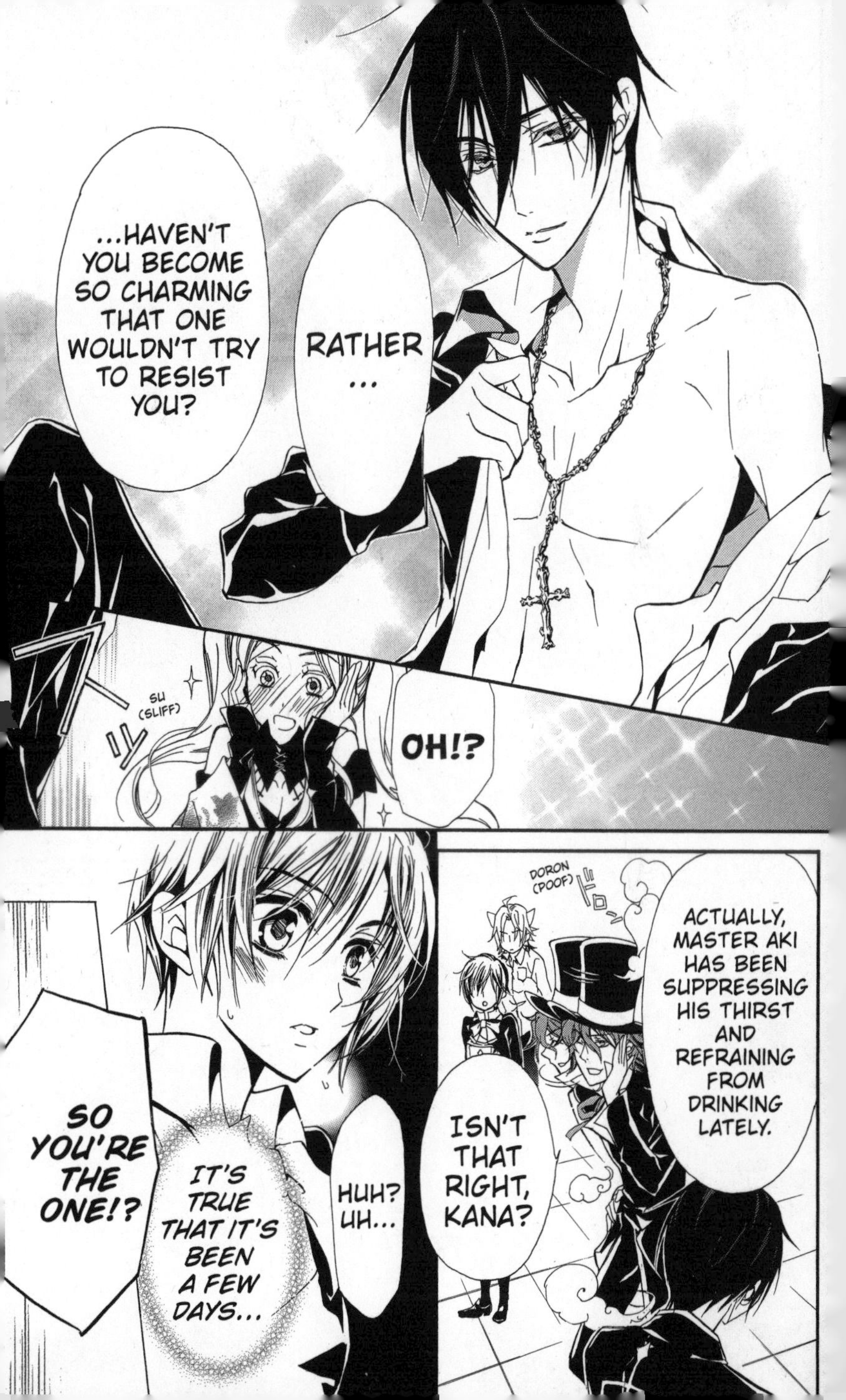
RATHER ...
...HAVEN'T YOU BECOME SO CHARMING THAT ONE WOULDN'T TRY TO RESIST YOU?
OH!?
SU (SLIFF)
ACTUALLY, MASTER AKI HAS BEEN SUPPRESSING HIS THIRST AND REFRAINING FROM DRINKING LATELY.
DORON (POOF)
ISN'T THAT RIGHT, KANA?
HUH? UH...
IT'S TRUE THAT IT'S BEEN A FEW DAYS...
SO YOU'RE THE ONE!?

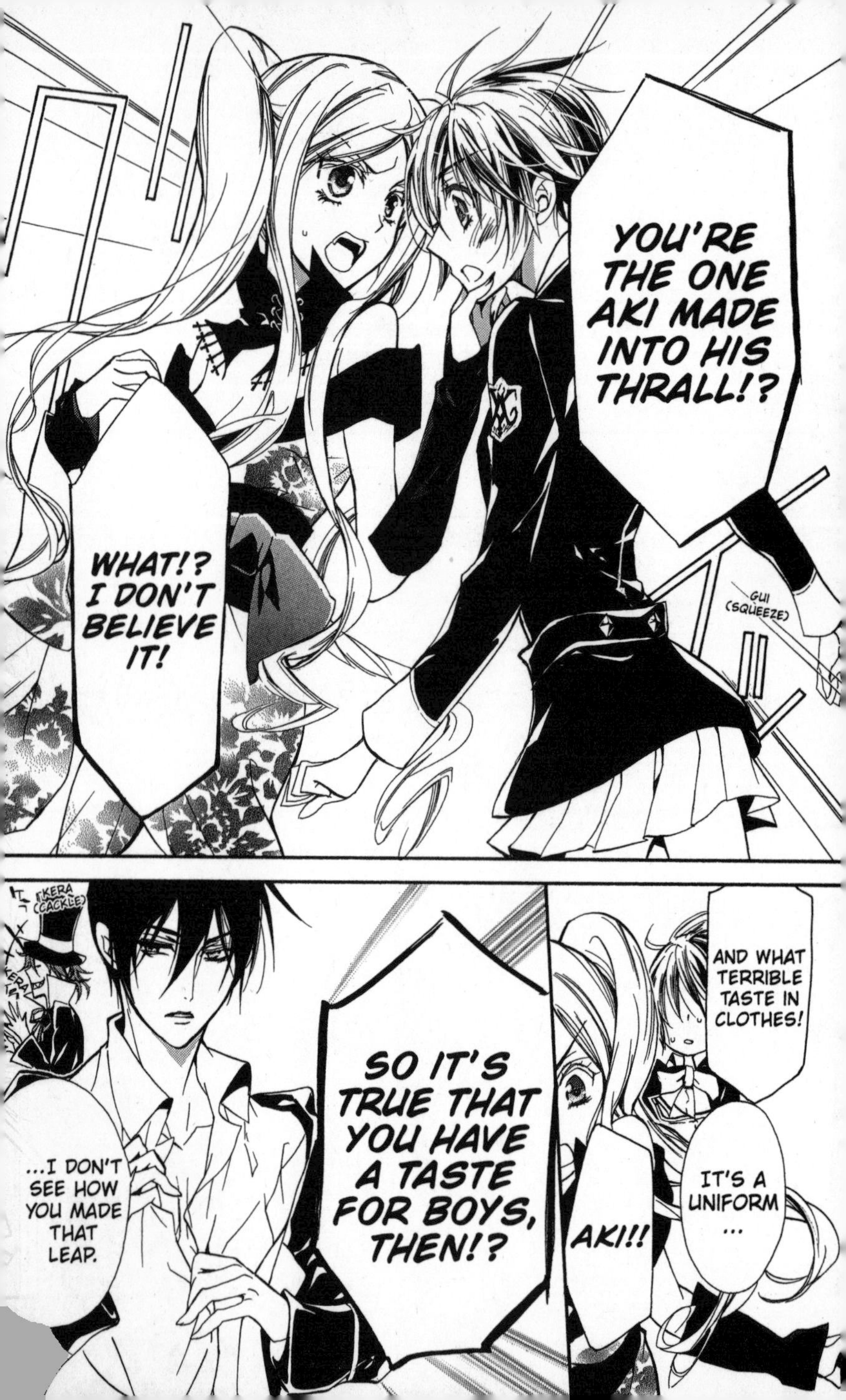
YOU'RE THE ONE AKI MADE INTO HIS THRALL!?
GUI (SQUEEZE)
WHAT!? I DON'T BELIEVE IT!
AND WHAT TERRIBLE TASTE IN CLOTHES!
IT'S A UNIFORM ...
AKI!!
SO IT'S TRUE THAT YOU HAVE A TASTE FOR BOYS, THEN!?
KERA (CACKLE)
...I DON'T SEE HOW YOU MADE THAT LEAP.

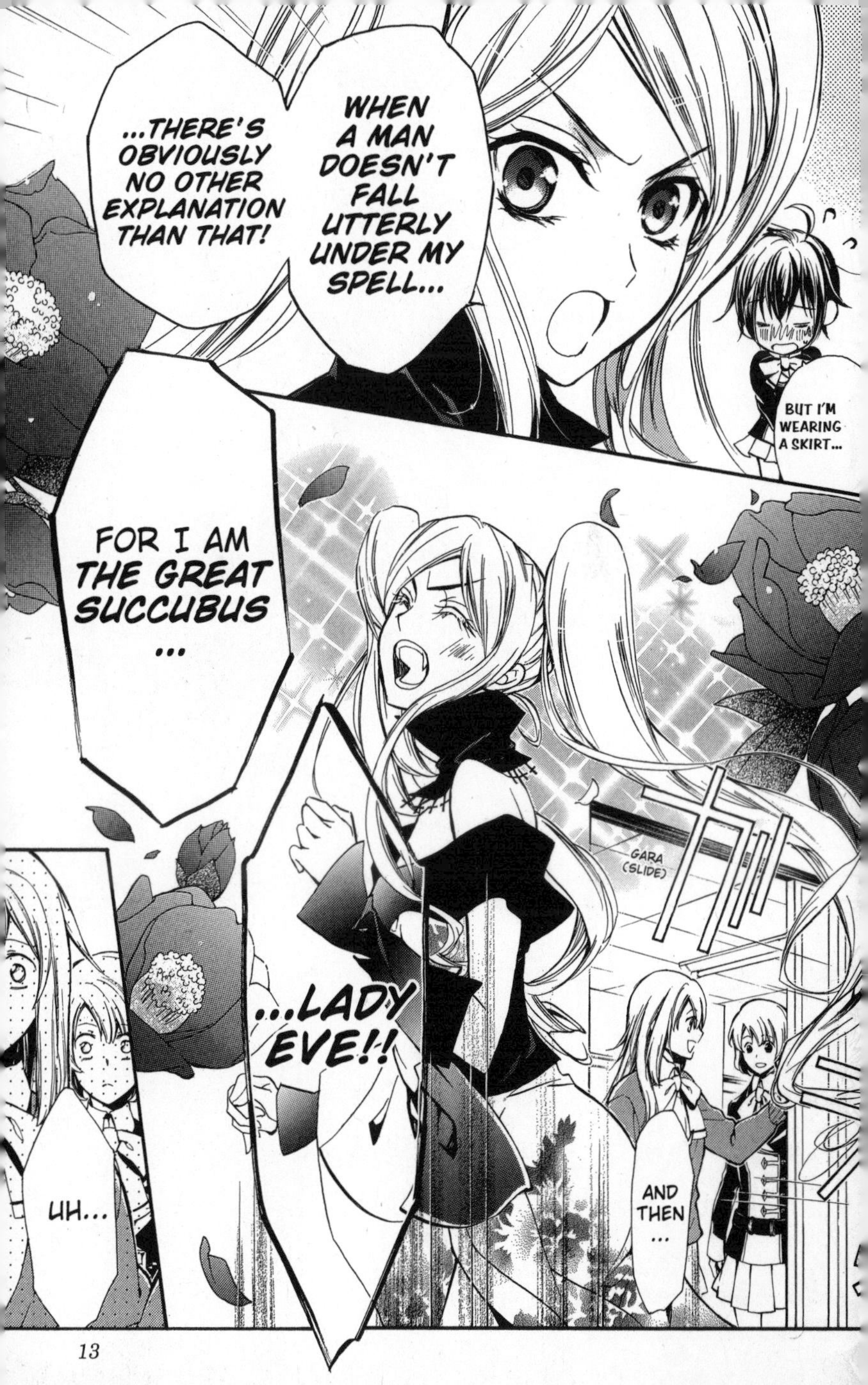
WHEN A MAN DOESN'T FALL UTTERLY UNDER MY SPELL...
...THERE'S OBVIOUSLY NO OTHER EXPLANATION THAN THAT!
BUT I'M WEARING A SKIRT...
FOR I AM THE GREAT SUCCUBUS ...
...LADY EVE!!
GARA (SLIDE)
AND THEN ...
UH...

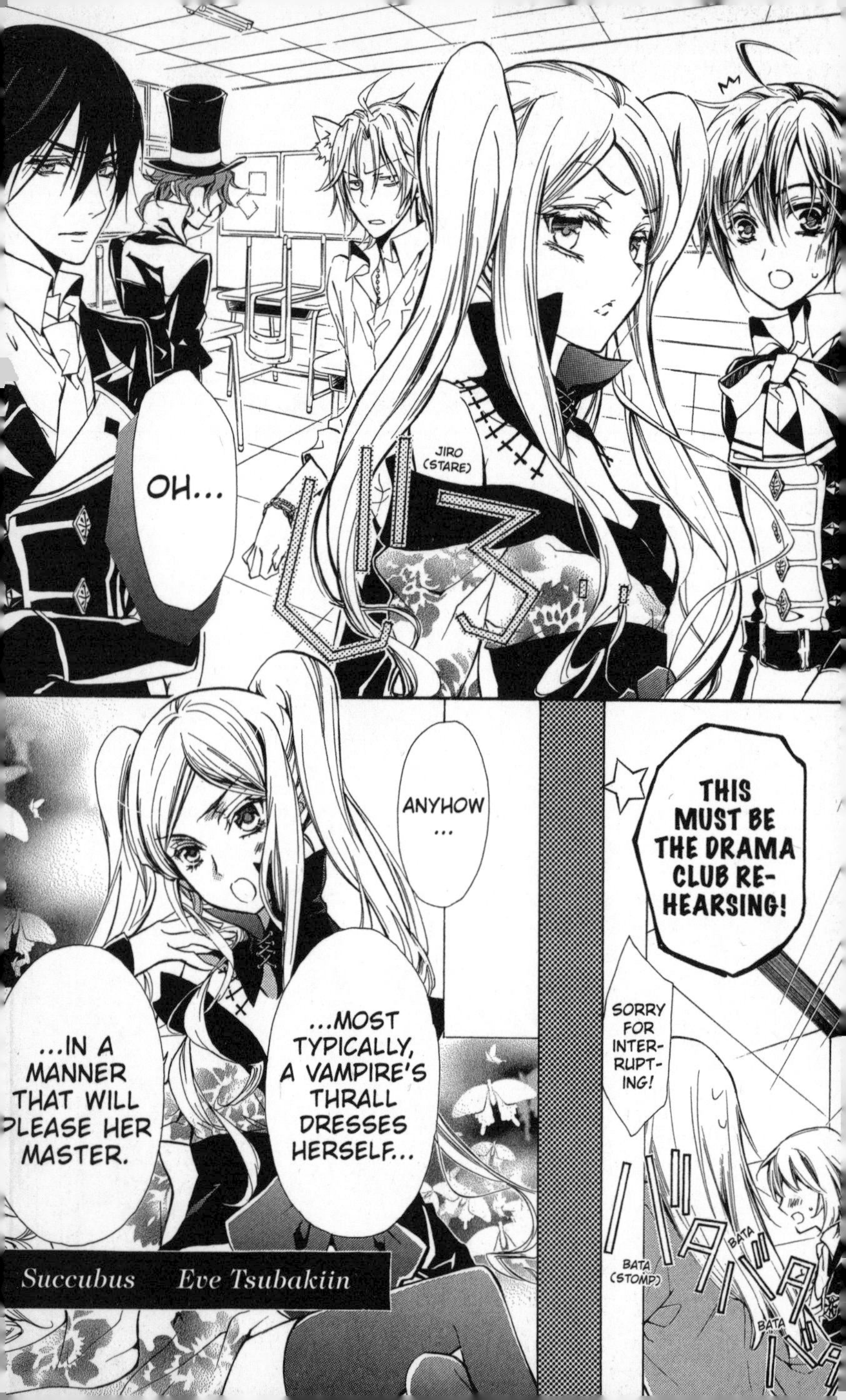
JIRO (STARE)
OH...
THIS MUST BE THE DRAMA CLUB RE-HEARSING!
SORRY FOR INTER-RUPT-ING!
BATA
BATA (STOMP)
BATA
ANYHOW...
...MOST TYPICALLY, A VAMPIRE'S THRALL DRESSES HERSELF...
...IN A MANNER THAT WILL PLEASE HER MASTER.
Succubus Eve Tsubakiin

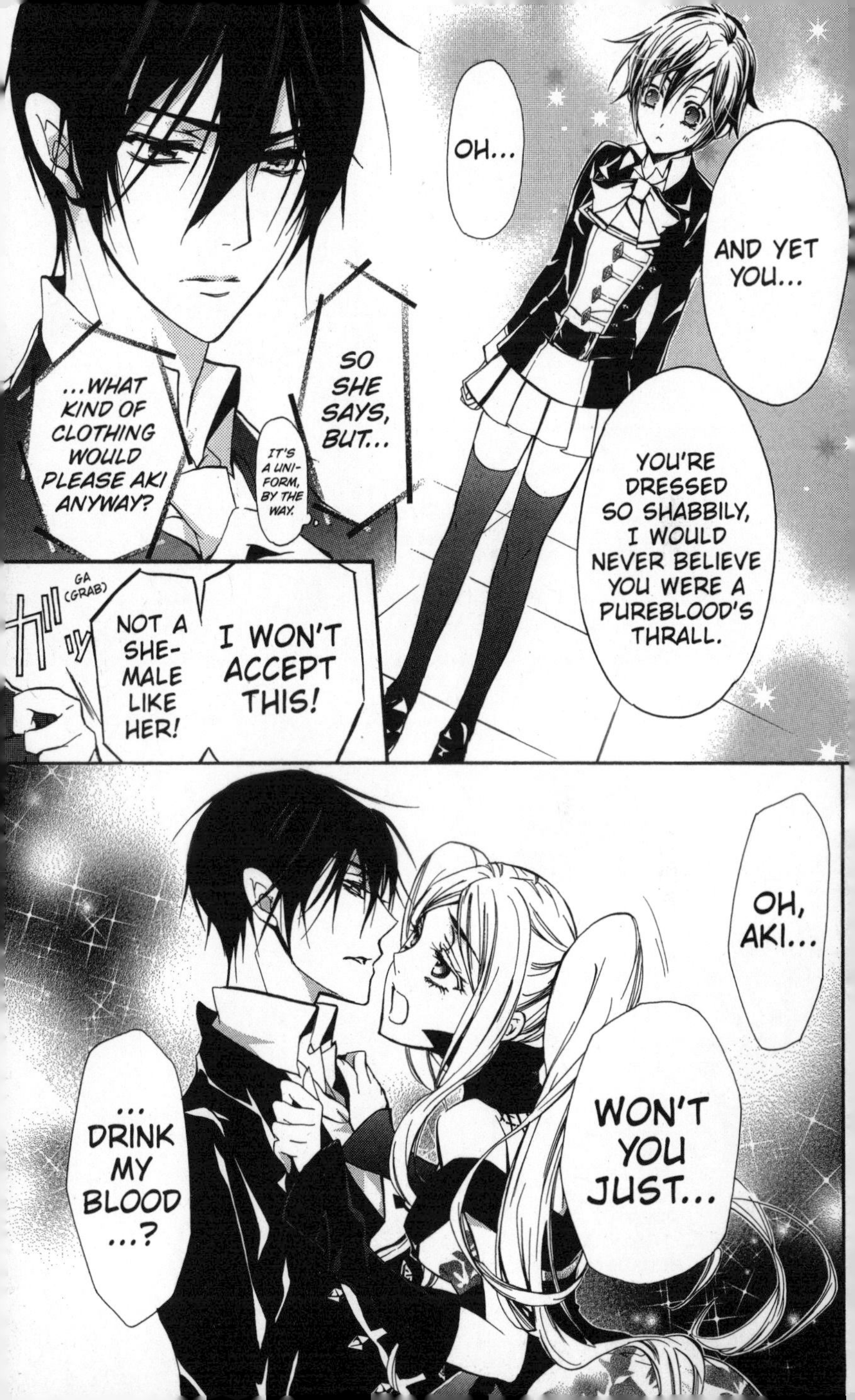
OH...
AND YET YOU...
YOU'RE DRESSED SO SHABBILY, I WOULD NEVER BELIEVE YOU WERE A PUREBLOOD'S THRALL.
SO SHE SAYS, BUT...
IT'S A UNIFORM, BY THE WAY.
...WHAT KIND OF CLOTHING WOULD PLEASE AKI ANYWAY?
GA (GRAB)
I WON'T ACCEPT THIS!
NOT A SHE-MALE LIKE HER!
OH, AKI...
WON'T YOU JUST...
...DRINK MY BLOOD...?

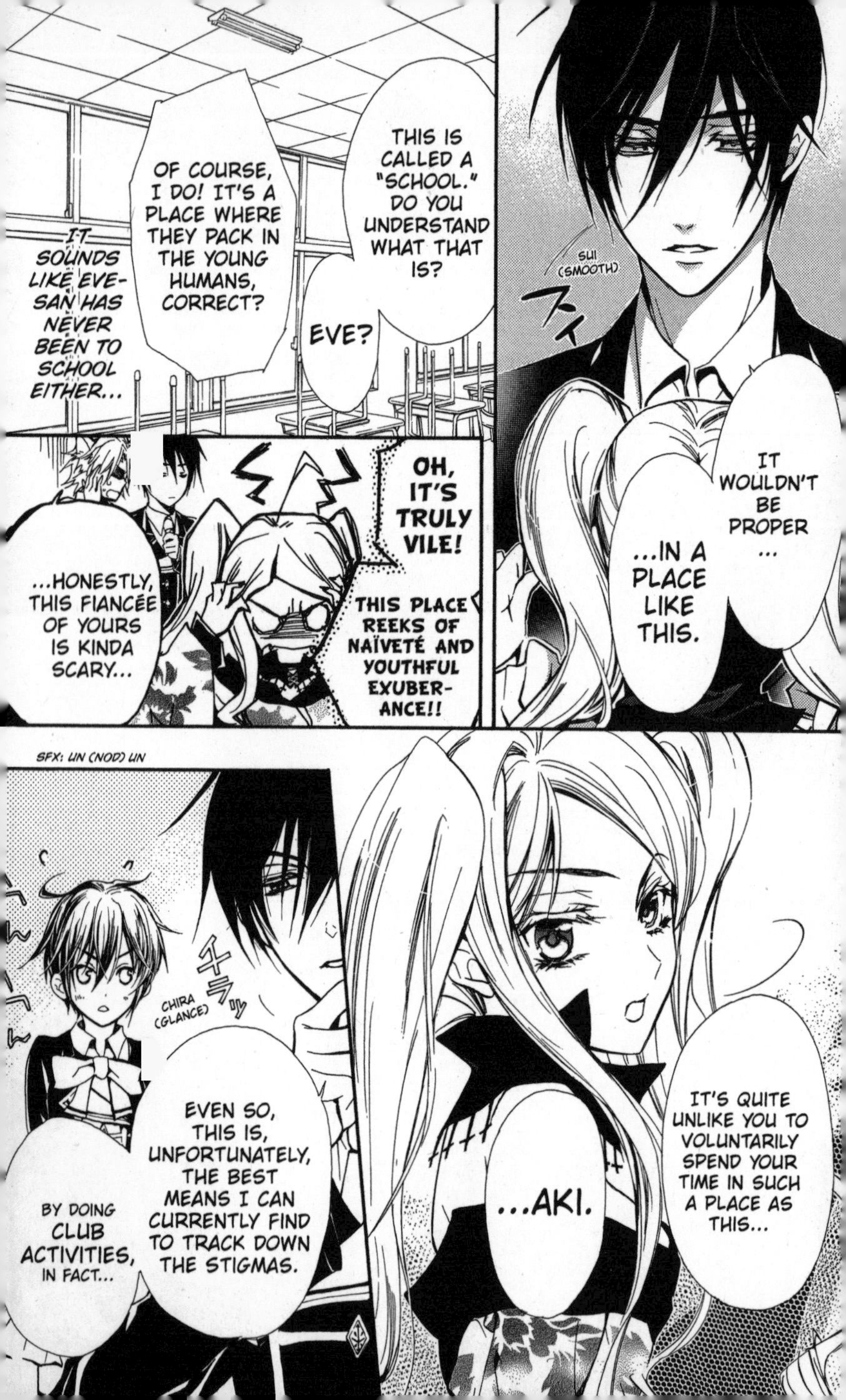
SUI (SMOOTH)
IT WOULDN'T BE PROPER...
...IN A PLACE LIKE THIS.
THIS IS CALLED A "SCHOOL." DO YOU UNDERSTAND WHAT THAT IS?
EVE?
OF COURSE, I DO! IT'S A PLACE WHERE THEY PACK IN THE YOUNG HUMANS, CORRECT?
IT SOUNDS LIKE EVE-SAN HAS NEVER BEEN TO SCHOOL EITHER...
OH, IT'S TRULY VILE!
THIS PLACE REEKS OF NAÏVETÉ AND YOUTHFUL EXUBERANCE!!
...HONESTLY, THIS FIANCÉE OF YOURS IS KINDA SCARY...
SFX: UN (NOD) UN
IT'S QUITE UNLIKE YOU TO VOLUNTARILY SPEND YOUR TIME IN SUCH A PLACE AS THIS...
...AKI.
CHIRA (GLANCE)
EVEN SO, THIS IS, UNFORTUNATELY, THE BEST MEANS I CAN CURRENTLY FIND TO TRACK DOWN THE STIGMAS.
BY DOING CLUB ACTIVITIES, IN FACT...

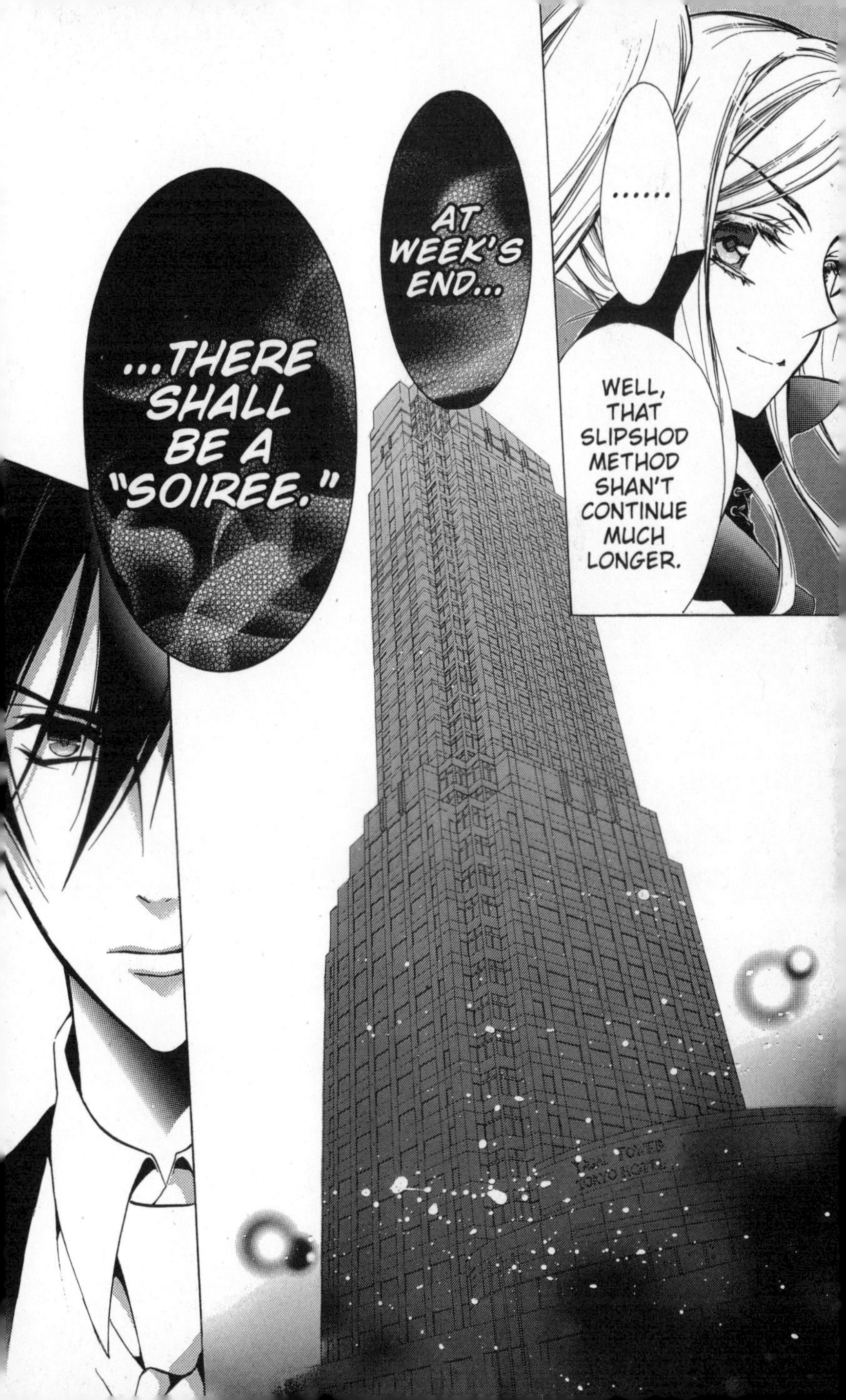
......
WELL, THAT SLIPSHOD METHOD SHAN'T CONTINUE MUCH LONGER.
AT WEEK'S END...
...THERE SHALL BE A "SOIREE."

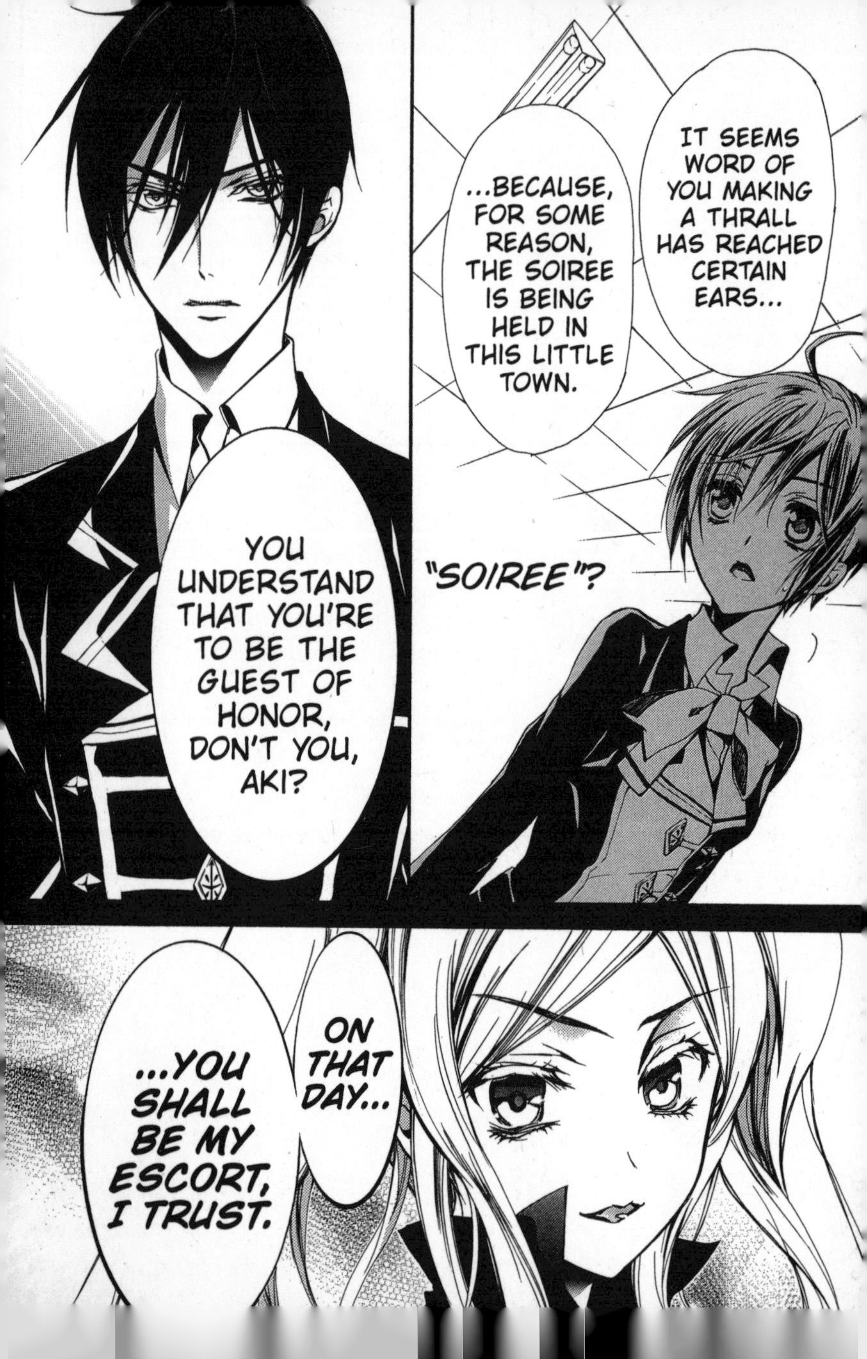
IT SEEMS WORD OF YOU MAKING A THRALL HAS REACHED CERTAIN EARS...
...BECAUSE, FOR SOME REASON, THE SOIREE IS BEING HELD IN THIS LITTLE TOWN.
"SOIREE"?
YOU UNDERSTAND THAT YOU'RE TO BE THE GUEST OF HONOR, DON'T YOU, AKI?
ON THAT DAY...
...YOU SHALL BE MY ESCORT, I TRUST.

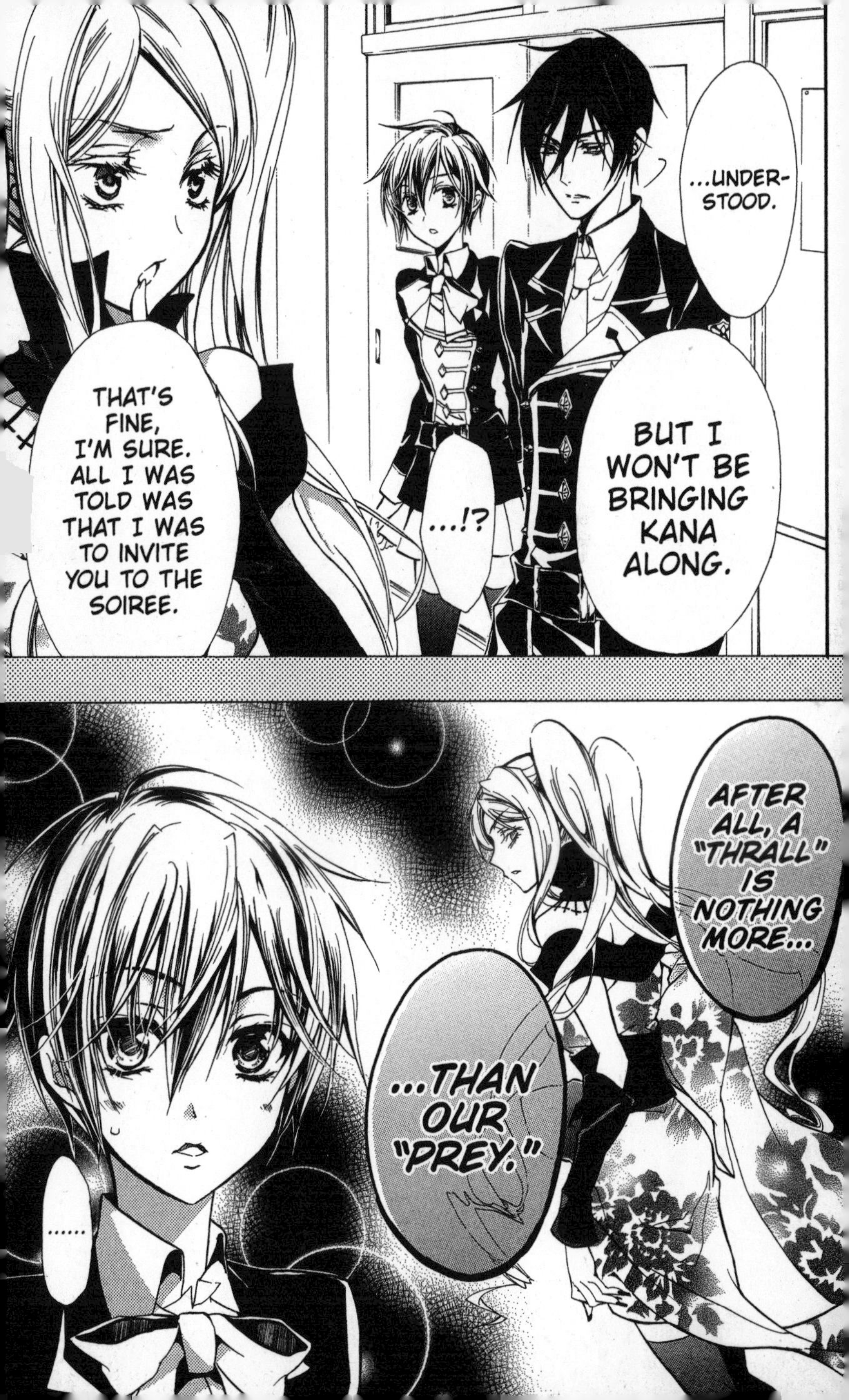

...UNDER-STOOD.
BUT I WON'T BE BRINGING KANA ALONG.
...!?
THAT'S FINE, I'M SURE. ALL I WAS TOLD WAS THAT I WAS TO INVITE YOU TO THE SOIREE.
AFTER ALL, A "THRALL" IS NOTHING MORE...
...THAN OUR "PREY."
......

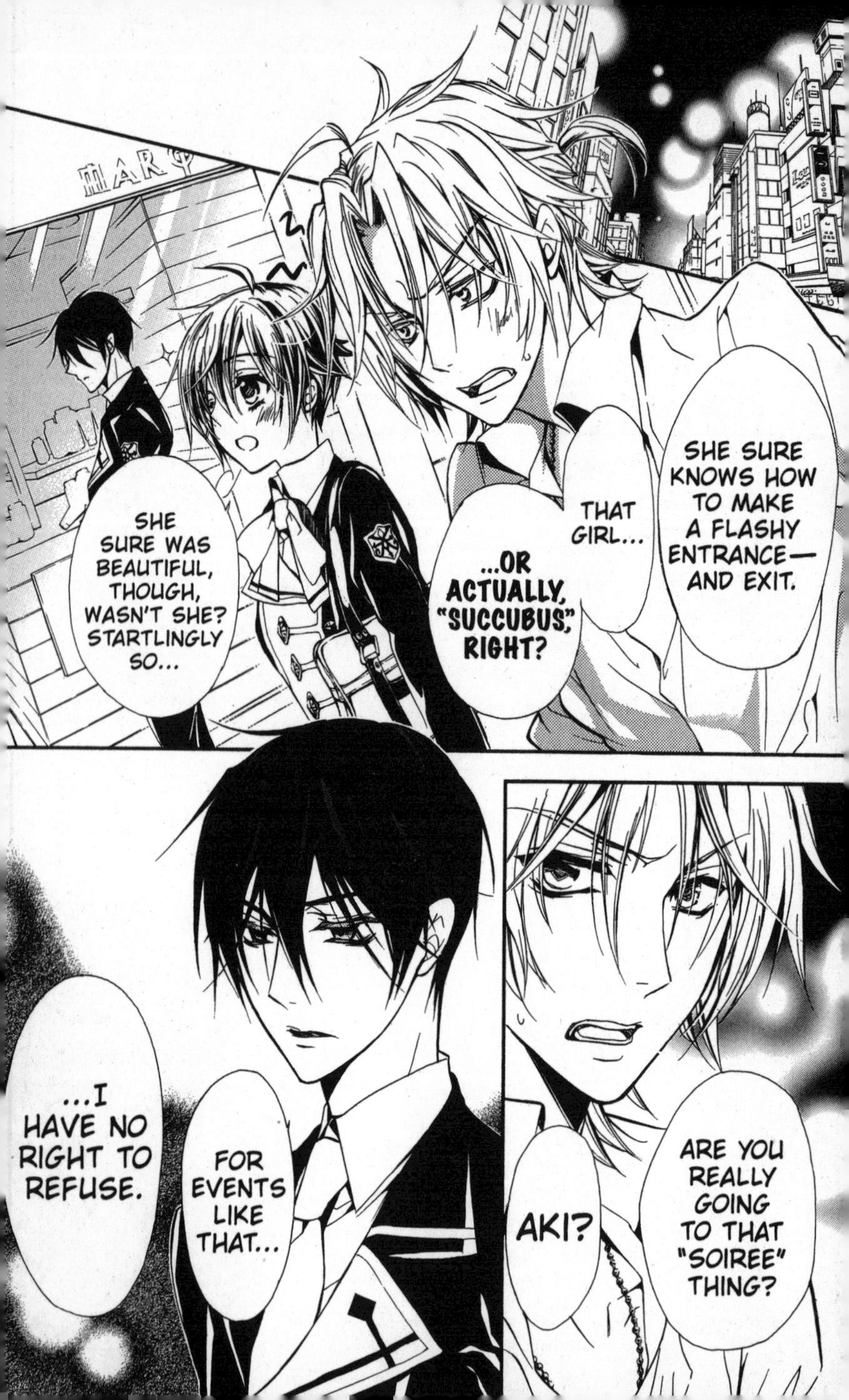
SHE SURE KNOWS HOW TO MAKE A FLASHY ENTRANCE— AND EXIT.
THAT GIRL...
...OR ACTUALLY, "SUCCUBUS," RIGHT?
SHE SURE WAS BEAUTIFUL, THOUGH, WASN'T SHE? STARTLINGLY SO...
ARE YOU REALLY GOING TO THAT "SOIREE" THING?
AKI?
FOR EVENTS LIKE THAT...
...I HAVE NO RIGHT TO REFUSE.

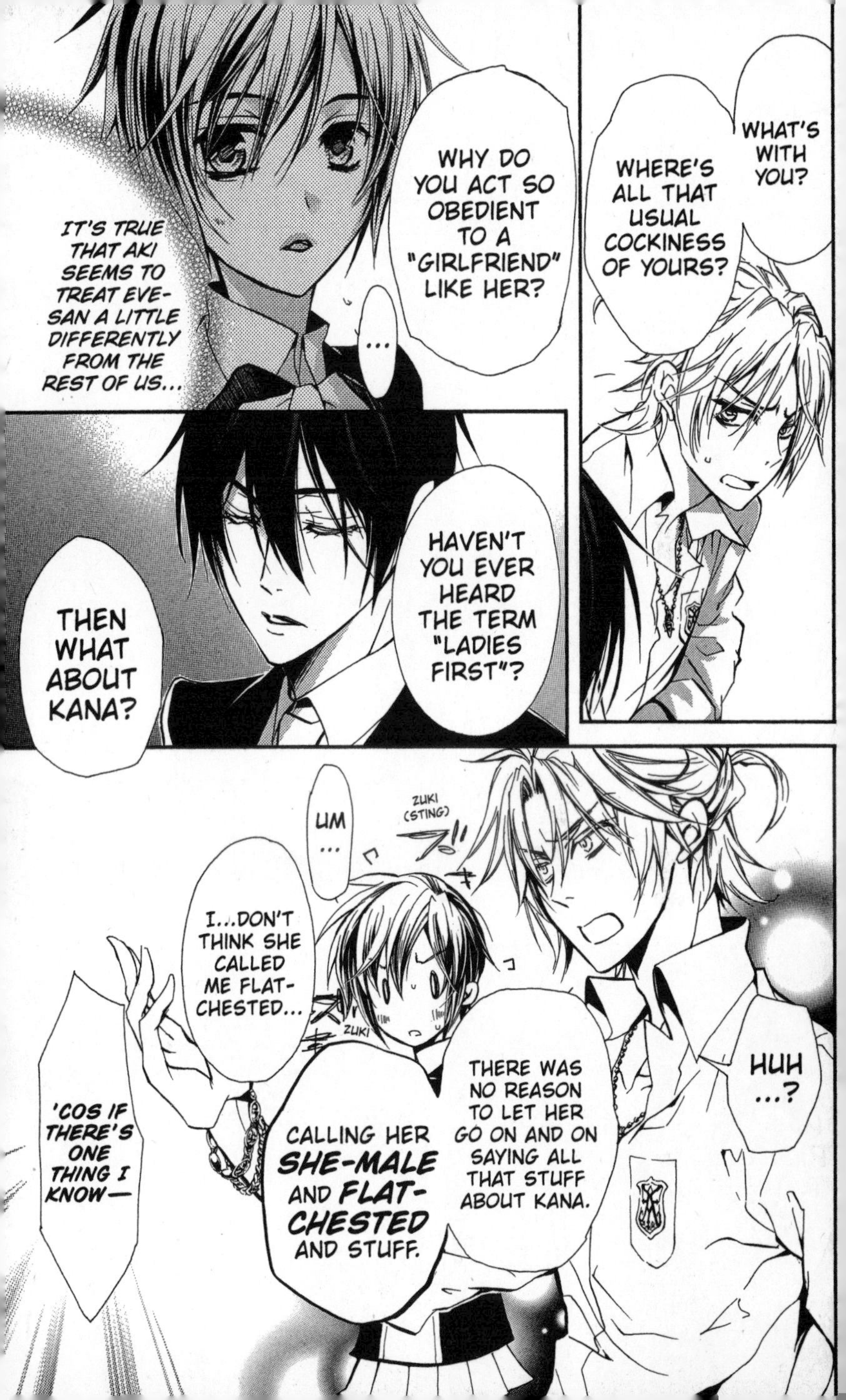
WHAT'S WITH YOU?
WHERE'S ALL THAT USUAL COCKINESS OF YOURS?
WHY DO YOU ACT SO OBEDIENT TO A "GIRLFRIEND" LIKE HER?
...
IT'S TRUE THAT AKI SEEMS TO TREAT EVE-SAN A LITTLE DIFFERENTLY FROM THE REST OF US...
HAVEN'T YOU EVER HEARD THE TERM "LADIES FIRST"?
THEN WHAT ABOUT KANA?
HUH ...?
THERE WAS NO REASON TO LET HER GO ON AND ON SAYING ALL THAT STUFF ABOUT KANA.
CALLING HER SHE-MALE AND FLAT-CHESTED AND STUFF.
ZUKI (STING)
UM ...
I...DON'T THINK SHE CALLED ME FLAT-CHESTED...
ZUKI
'COS IF THERE'S ONE THING I KNOW—

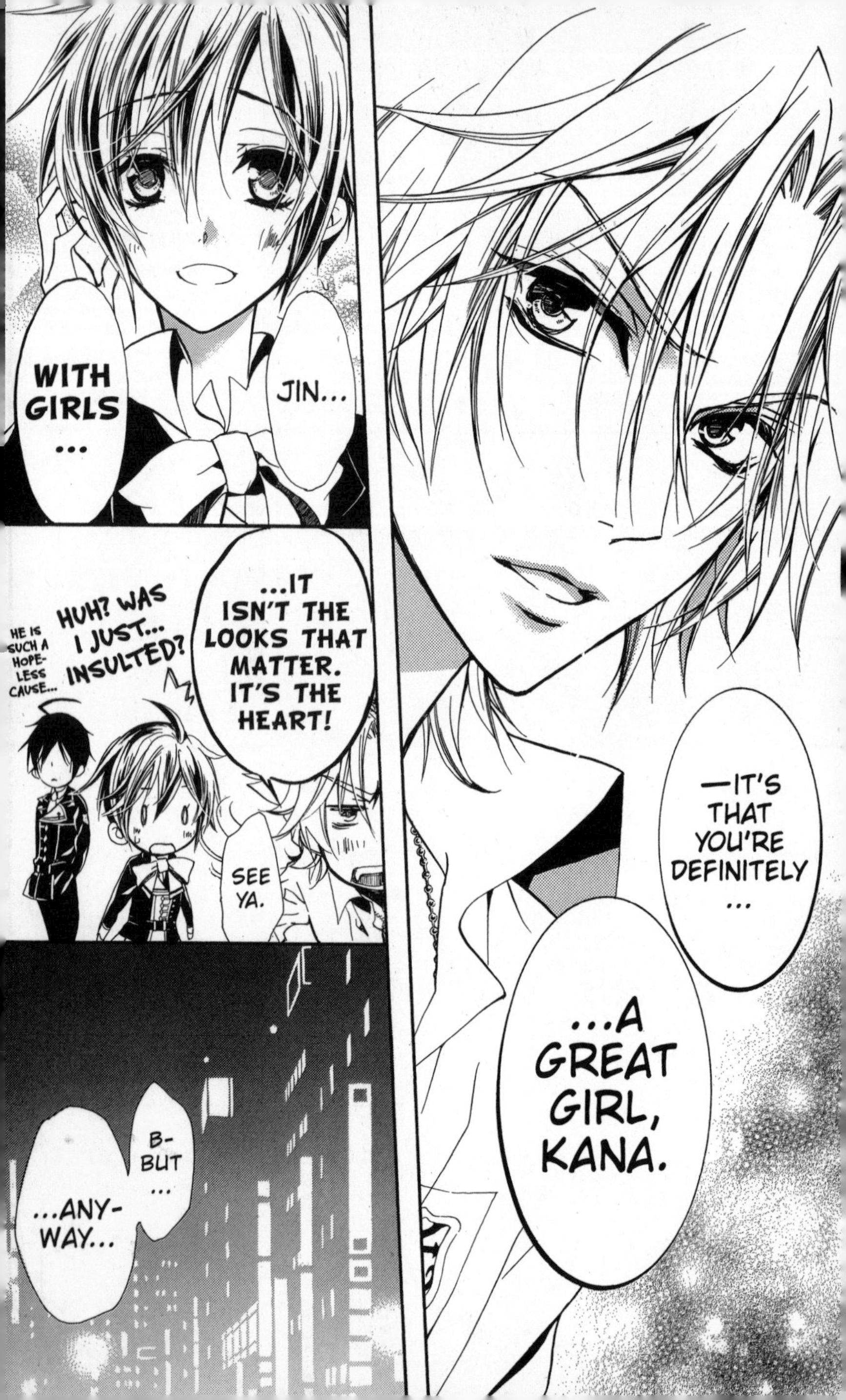
—IT'S THAT YOU'RE DEFINITELY...
...A GREAT GIRL, KANA.
JIN...
WITH GIRLS...
...IT ISN'T THE LOOKS THAT MATTER. IT'S THE HEART!
HUH? WAS I JUST... INSULTED?
HE IS SUCH A HOPE-LESS CAUSE...
SEE YA.
B-BUT...
...ANY-WAY...

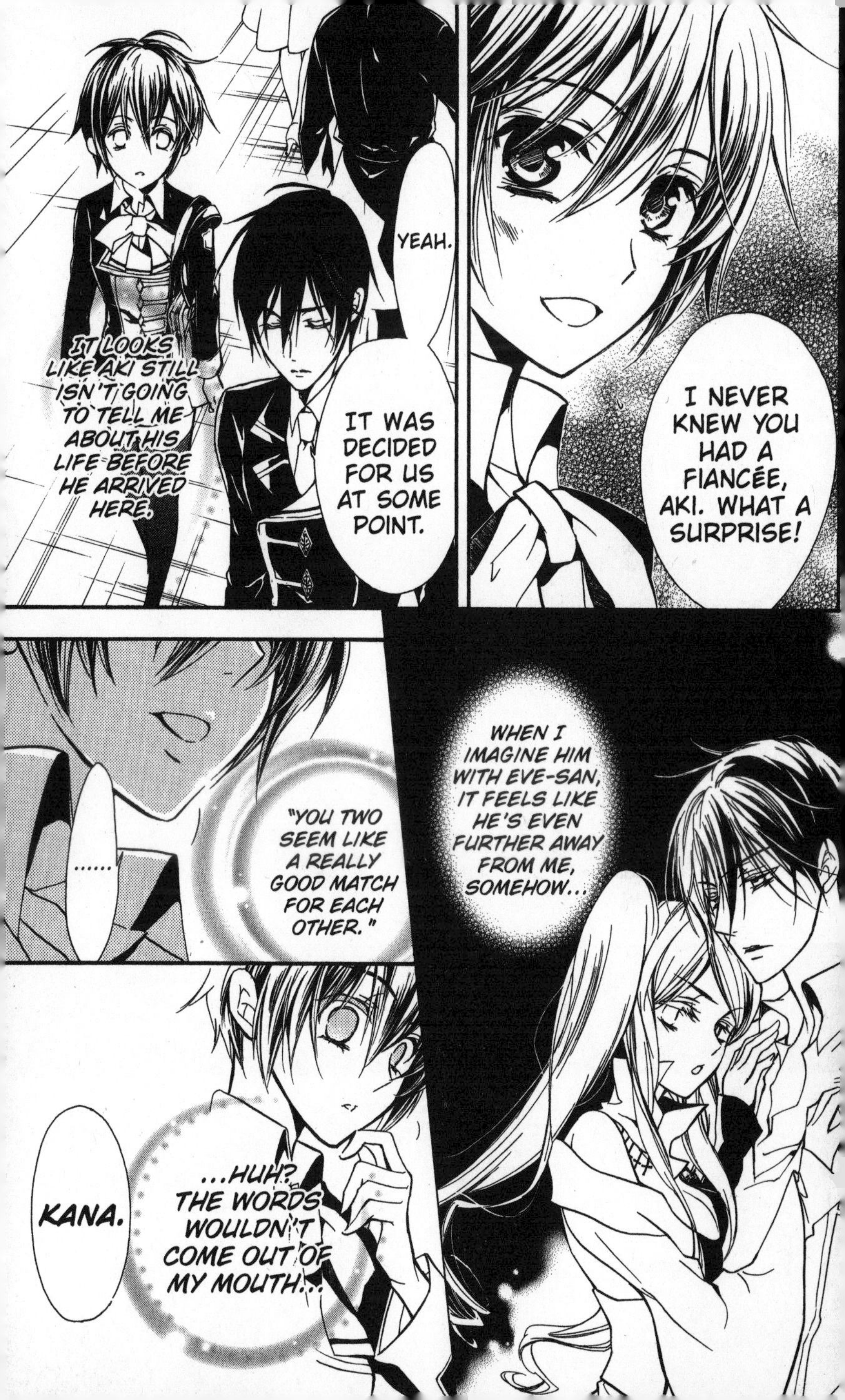
I NEVER KNEW YOU HAD A FIANCÉE, AKI. WHAT A SURPRISE!
YEAH.
IT WAS DECIDED FOR US AT SOME POINT.
IT LOOKS LIKE AKI STILL ISN'T GOING TO TELL ME ABOUT HIS LIFE BEFORE HE ARRIVED HERE.
WHEN I IMAGINE HIM WITH EVE-SAN, IT FEELS LIKE HE'S EVEN FURTHER AWAY FROM ME, SOMEHOW...
"YOU TWO SEEM LIKE A REALLY GOOD MATCH FOR EACH OTHER."
......
...HUH? THE WORDS WOULDN'T COME OUT OF MY MOUTH...
KANA.

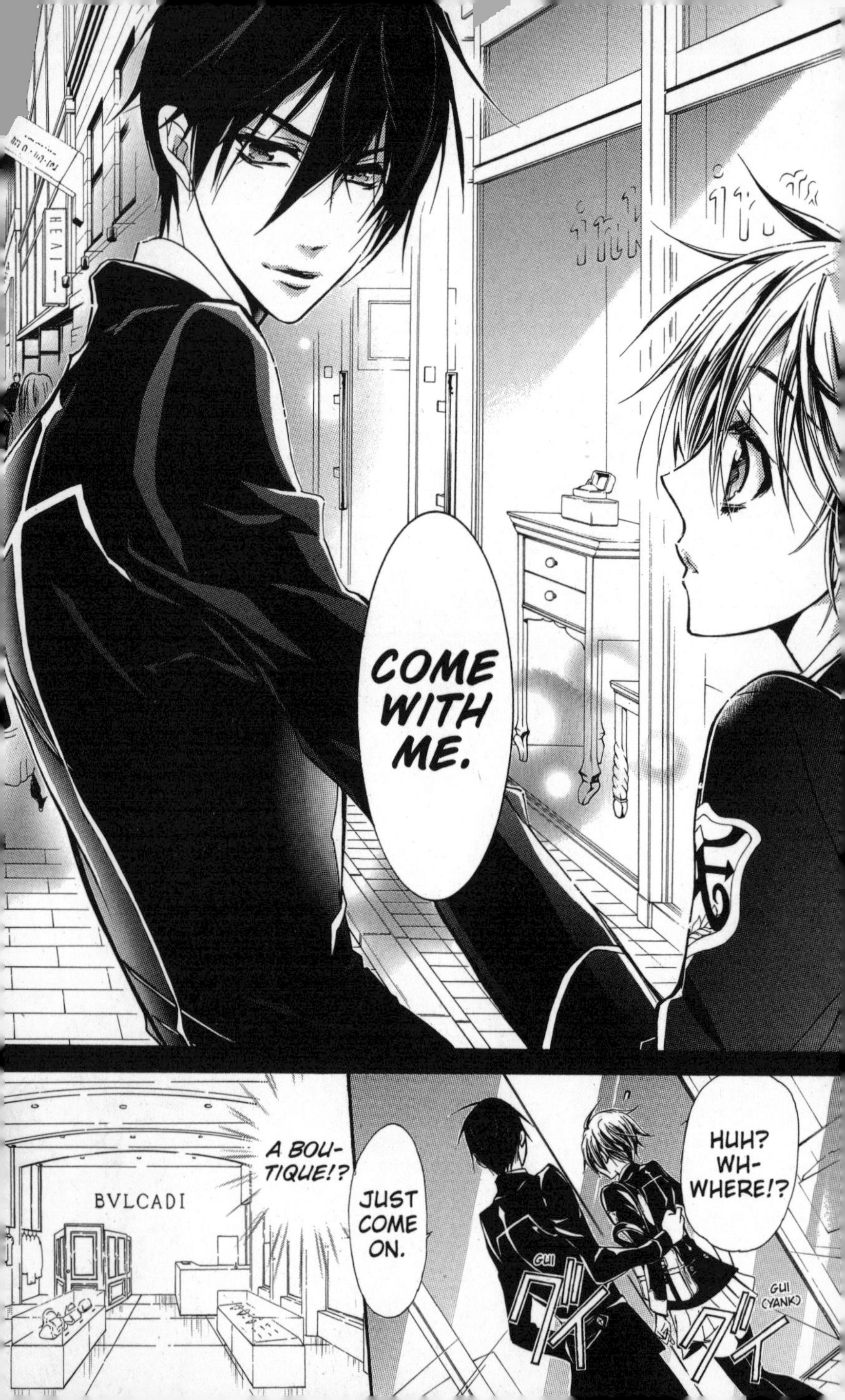
COME WITH ME.
HUH? WH-WHERE!?
GUI (YANK)
GUI
JUST COME ON.
A BOU-TIQUE!?
BVLCADI

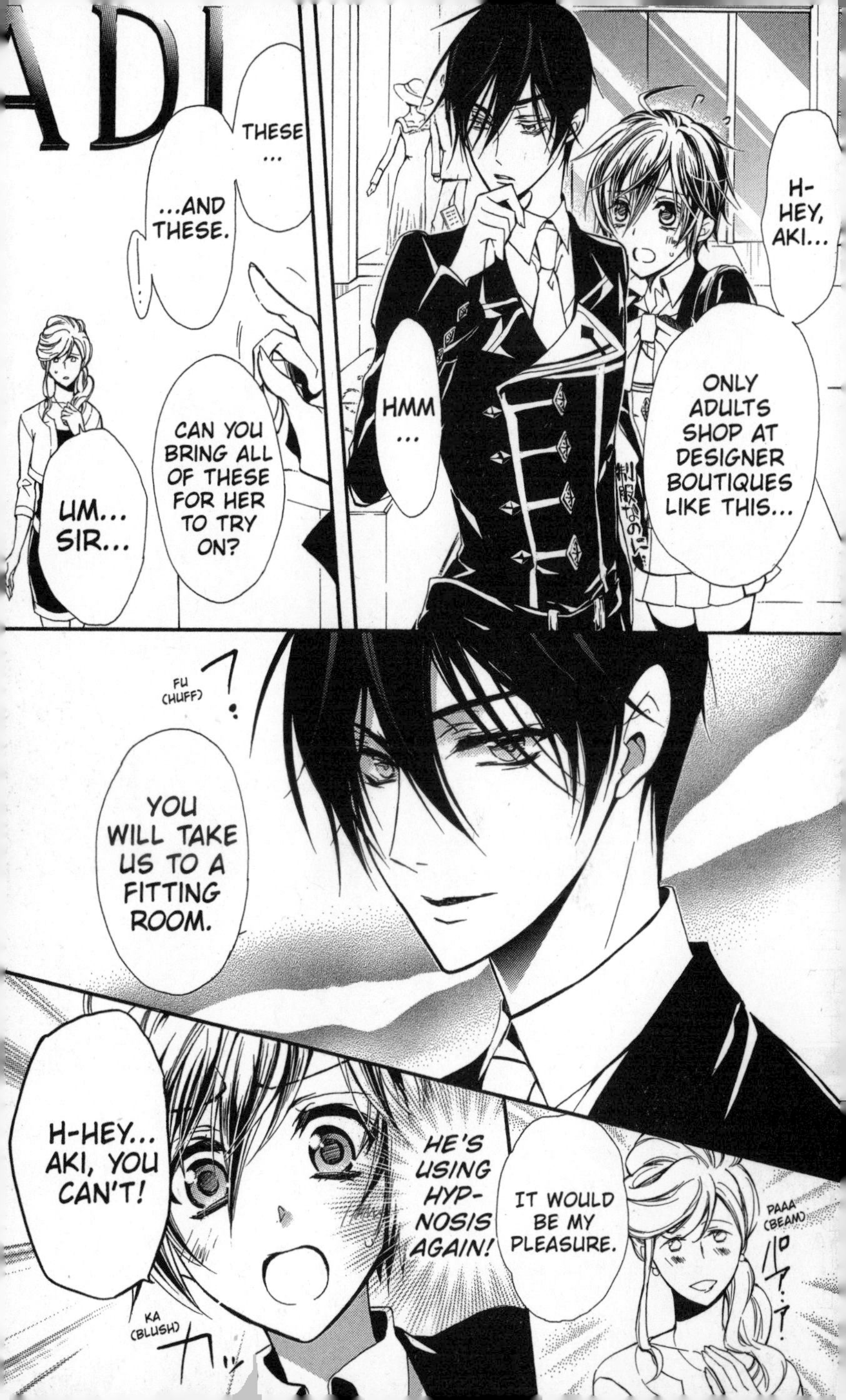
H-HEY, AKI...
ONLY ADULTS SHOP AT DESIGNER BOUTIQUES LIKE THIS...
HMM...
THESE...
...AND THESE.
CAN YOU BRING ALL OF THESE FOR HER TO TRY ON?
UM... SIR...
FU (HUFF)
YOU WILL TAKE US TO A FITTING ROOM.
PAAA (BEAM)
IT WOULD BE MY PLEASURE.
HE'S USING HYP-NOSIS AGAIN!
H-HEY... AKI, YOU CAN'T!
KA (BLUSH)

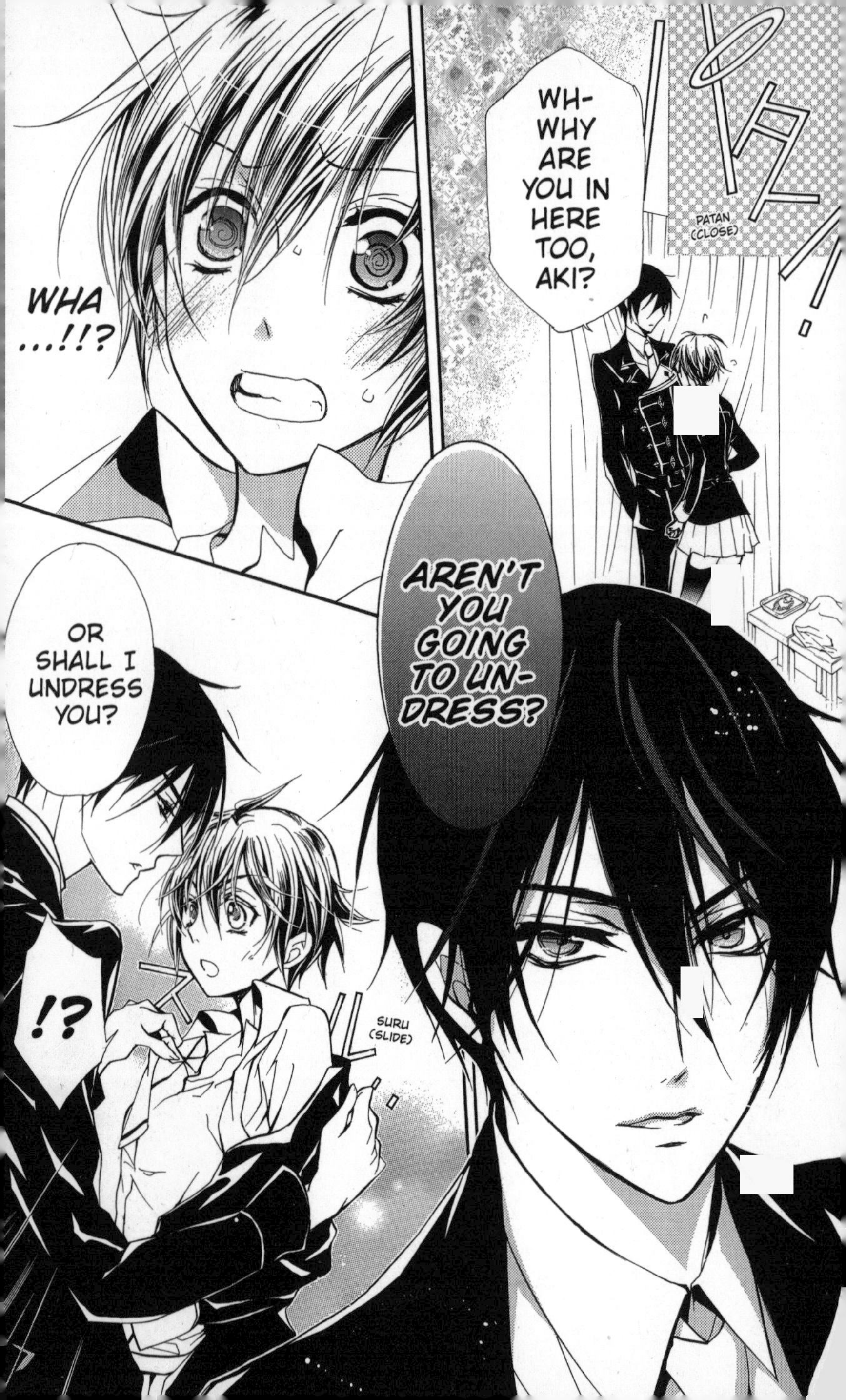
WH-WHY ARE YOU IN HERE TOO, AKI?
PATAN (CLOSE)
WHA ...!!?
AREN'T YOU GOING TO UN-DRESS?
OR SHALL I UNDRESS YOU?
SURU (SLIDE)
!?

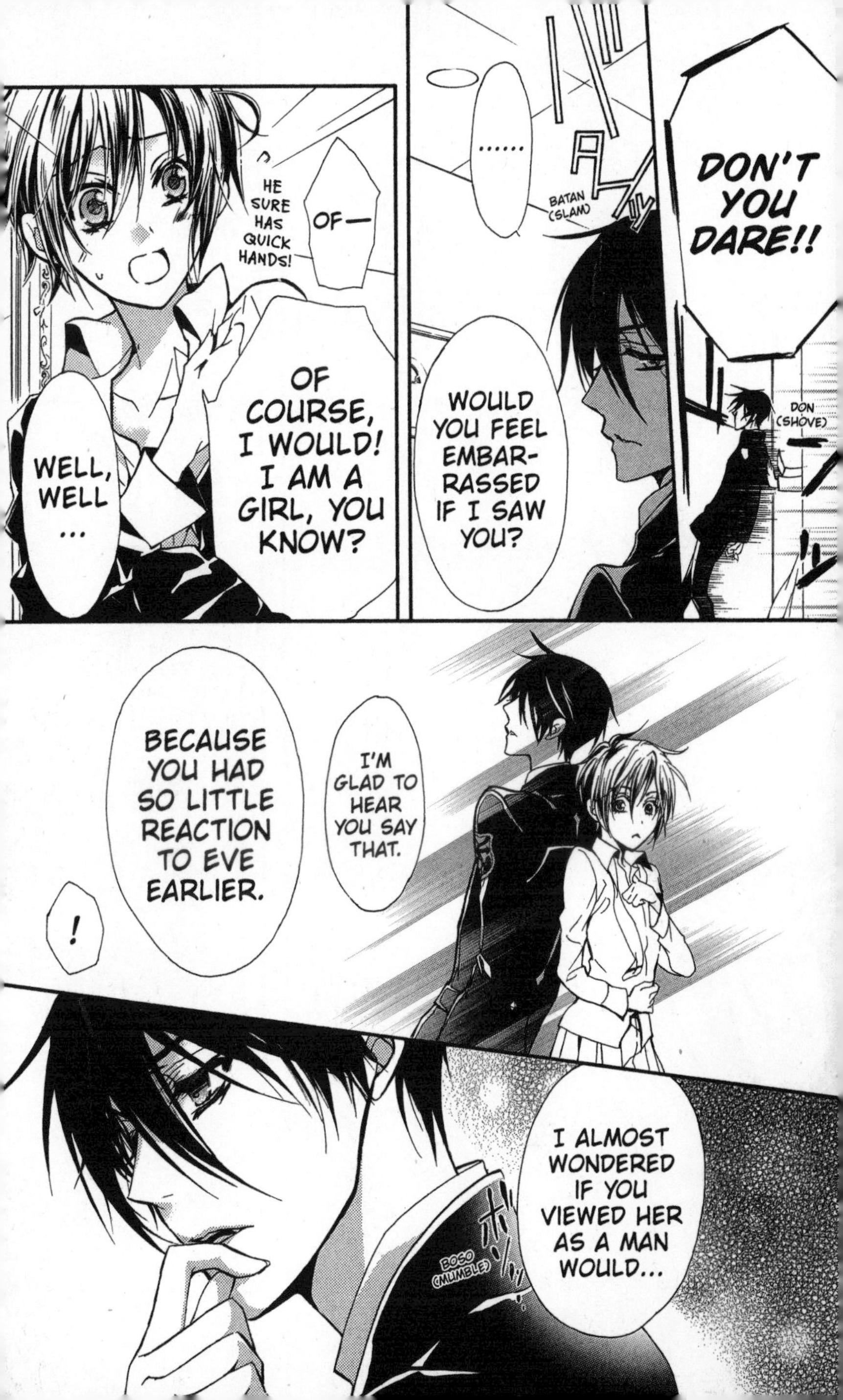
DON'T YOU DARE!!
DON (SHOVE)
BATAN (SLAM)
......
WOULD YOU FEEL EMBAR-RASSED IF I SAW YOU?
OF—
HE SURE HAS QUICK HANDS!
OF COURSE, I WOULD! I AM A GIRL, YOU KNOW?
WELL, WELL ...
I'M GLAD TO HEAR YOU SAY THAT.
BECAUSE YOU HAD SO LITTLE REACTION TO EVE EARLIER.
!
I ALMOST WONDERED IF YOU VIEWED HER AS A MAN WOULD...
BOSO (MUMBLE)

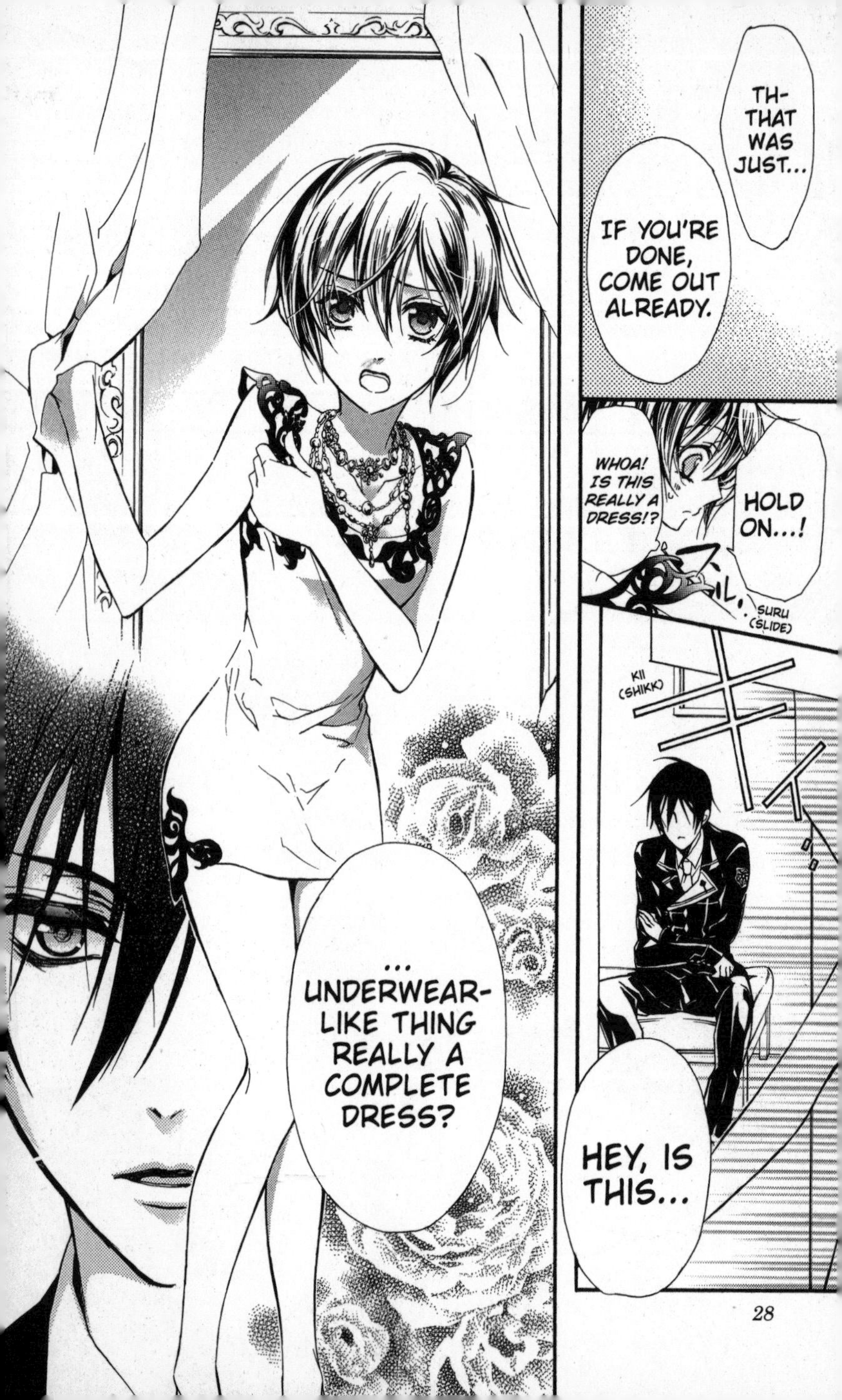
TH- THAT WAS JUST...
IF YOU'RE DONE, COME OUT ALREADY.
HOLD ON...!
WHOA! IS THIS REALLY A DRESS!?
SURU (SLIDE)
KII (SHIKK)
HEY, IS THIS...
... UNDERWEAR-LIKE THING REALLY A COMPLETE DRESS?

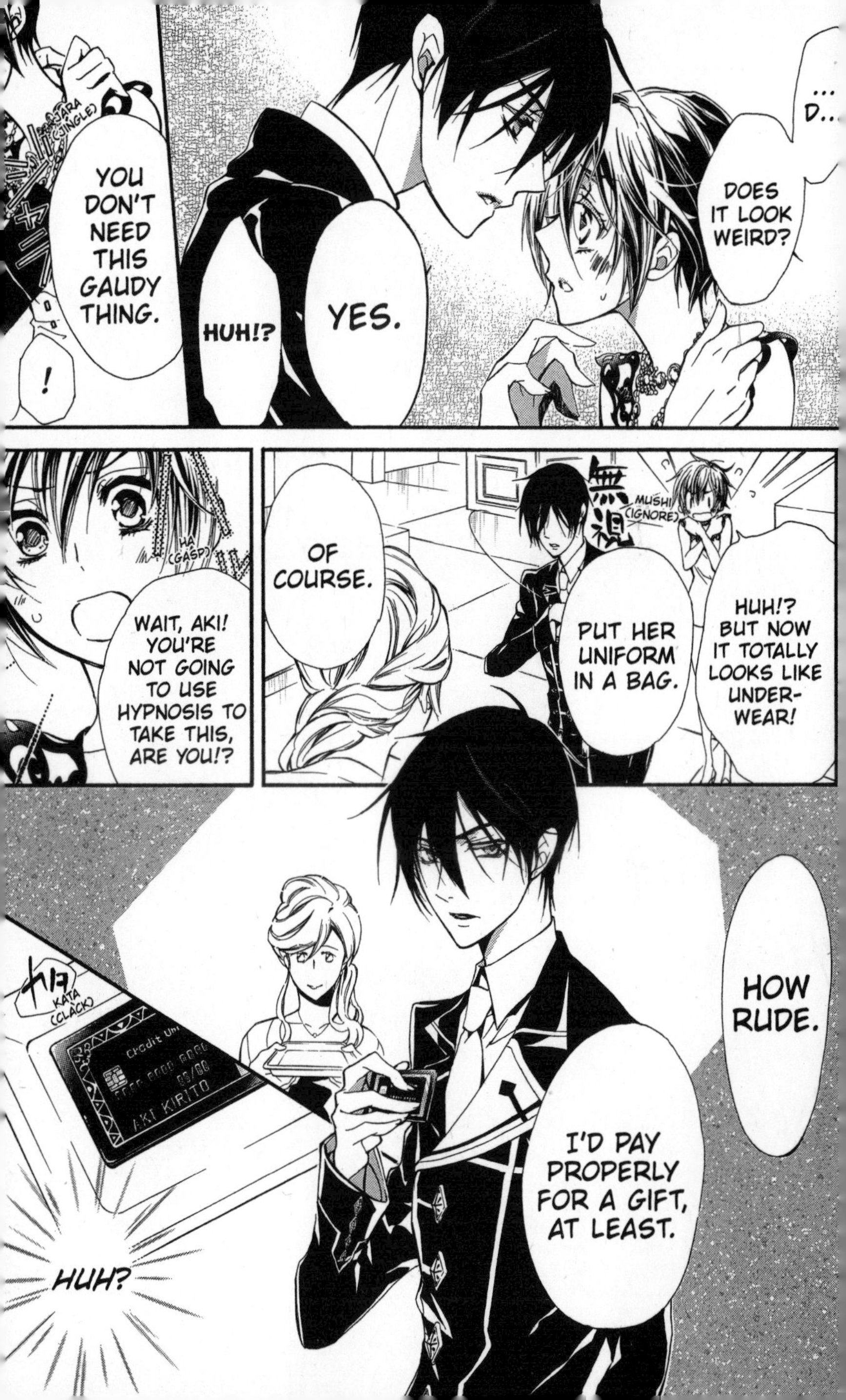
...D...
DOES IT LOOK WEIRD?
YES.
HUH!?
JARA (JINGLE)
YOU DON'T NEED THIS GAUDY THING.
!
HUH!? BUT NOW IT TOTALLY LOOKS LIKE UNDER-WEAR!
MUSHI (IGNORE)
PUT HER UNIFORM IN A BAG.
OF COURSE.
HA (GASP)
WAIT, AKI! YOU'RE NOT GOING TO USE HYPNOSIS TO TAKE THIS, ARE YOU!?
HOW RUDE.
I'D PAY PROPERLY FOR A GIFT, AT LEAST.
KATA (CLACK)
AKI KIRITO
HUH?

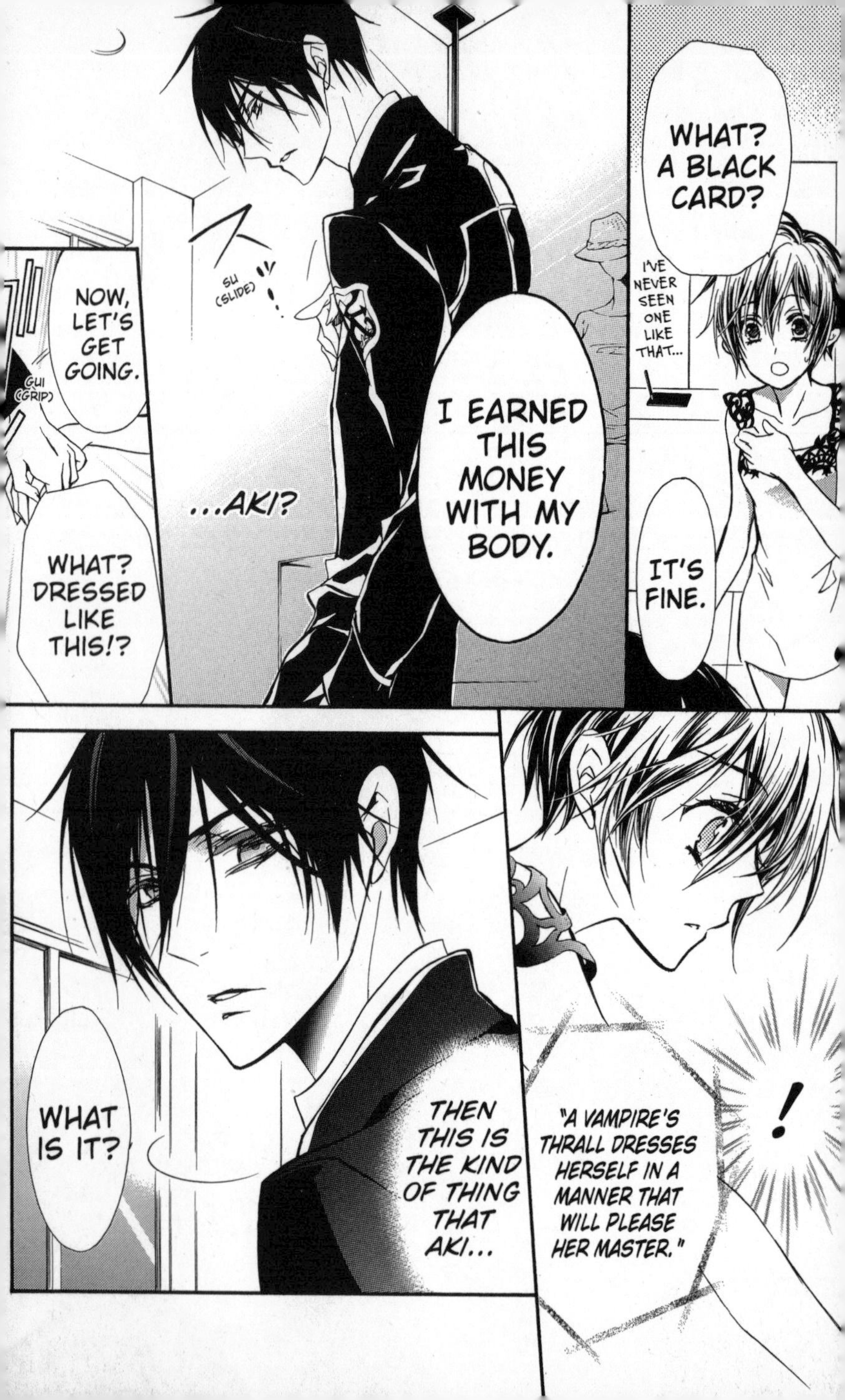
WHAT? A BLACK CARD?
I'VE NEVER SEEN ONE LIKE THAT...
IT'S FINE.
SU (SLIDE)
I EARNED THIS MONEY WITH MY BODY.
...AKI?
NOW, LET'S GET GOING.
GUI (GRIP)
WHAT? DRESSED LIKE THIS!?
!
"A VAMPIRE'S THRALL DRESSES HERSELF IN A MANNER THAT WILL PLEASE HER MASTER."
THEN THIS IS THE KIND OF THING THAT AKI...
WHAT IS IT?

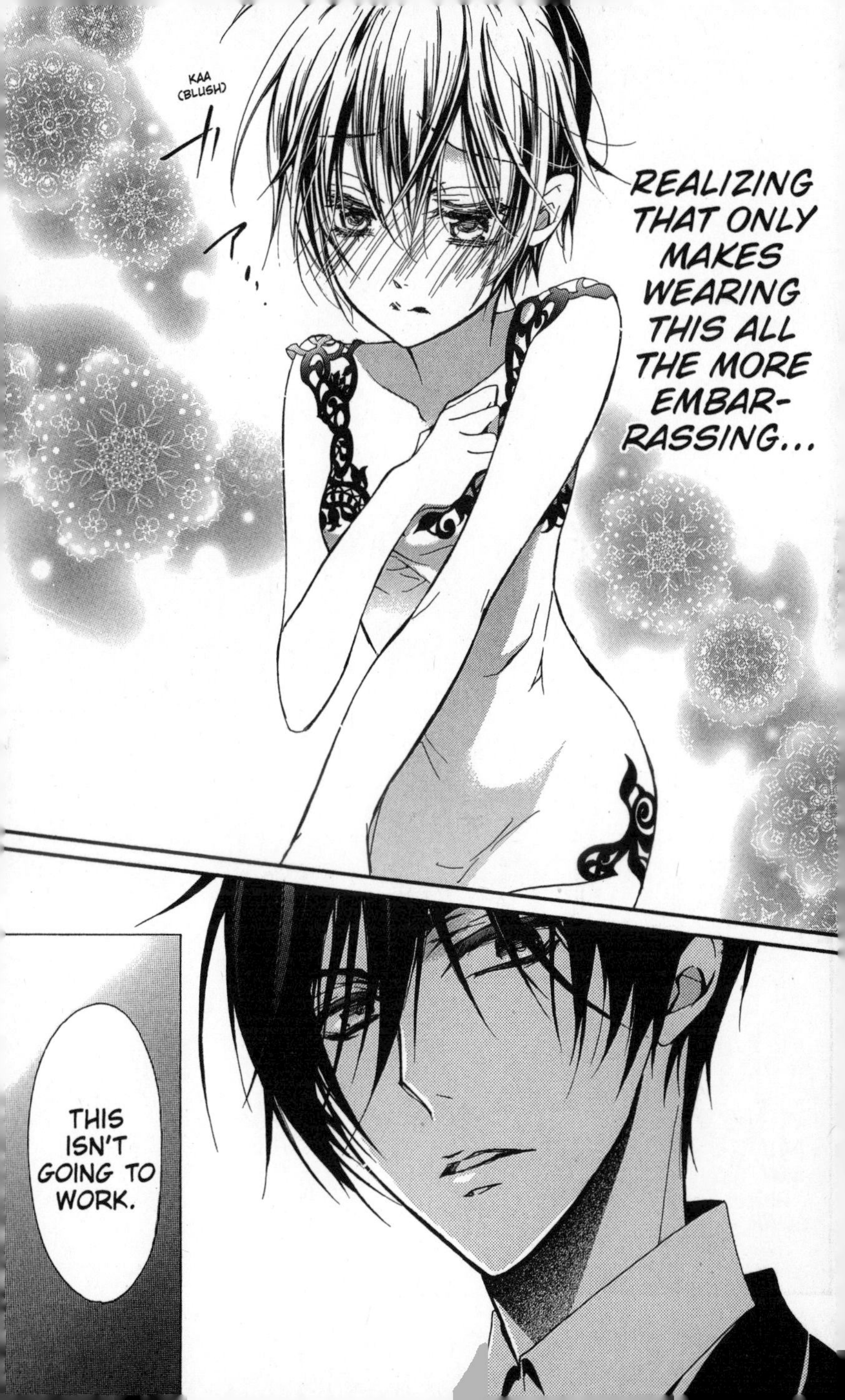
REALIZING THAT ONLY MAKES WEARING THIS ALL THE MORE EMBAR-RASSING...
KAA (BLUSH)
THIS ISN'T GOING TO WORK.

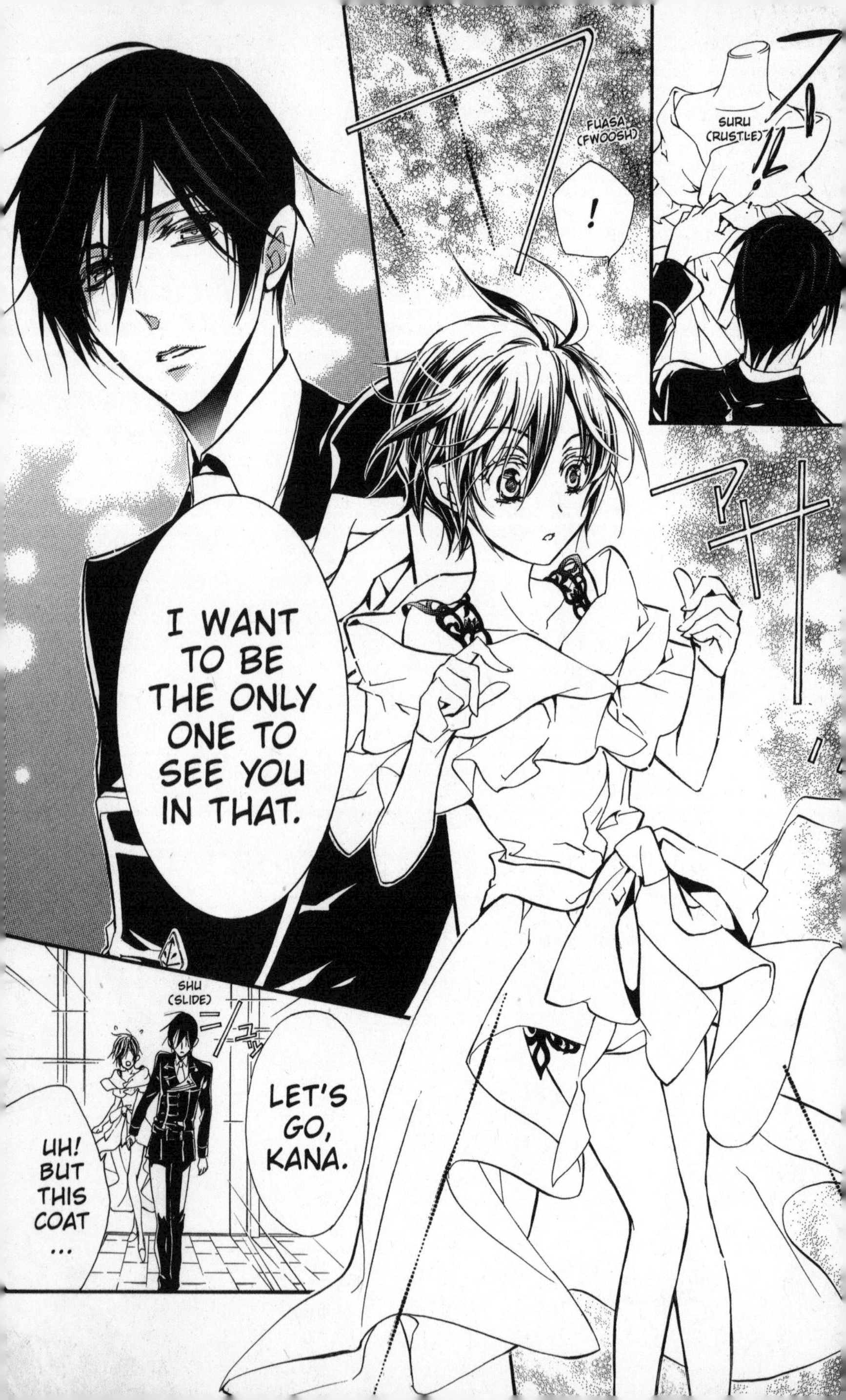
SURU
(RUSTLE)
FUASA
(FWOOSH)
!
I WANT TO BE THE ONLY ONE TO SEE YOU IN THAT.
SHU
(SLIDE)
LET'S GO, KANA.
UH! BUT THIS COAT ...

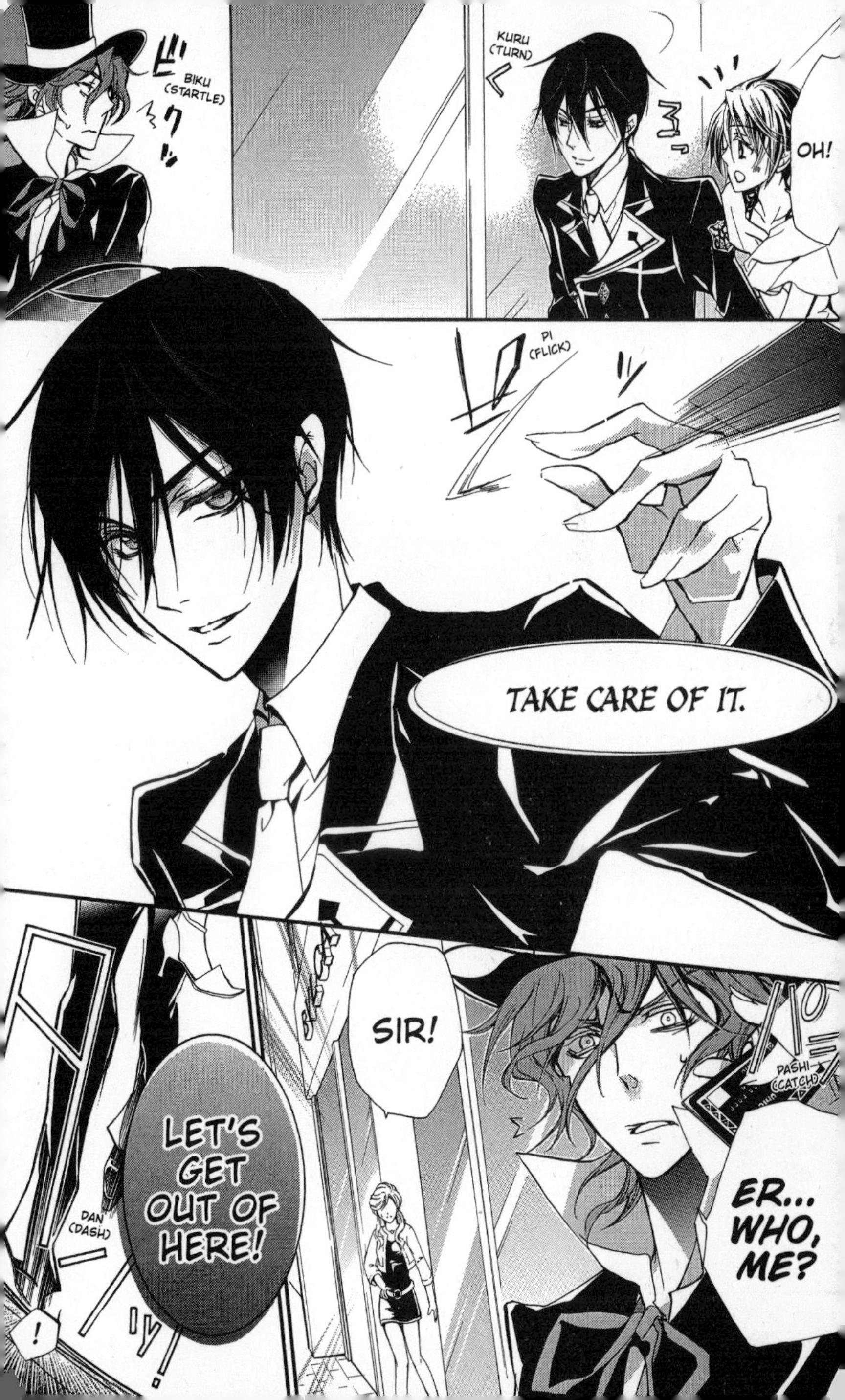
OH!
KURU (TURN)
BIKU (STARTLE)
PI (FLICK)
TAKE CARE OF IT.
PASHI (CATCH)
ER... WHO, ME?
SIR!
LET'S GET OUT OF HERE!
DAN (DASH)
!

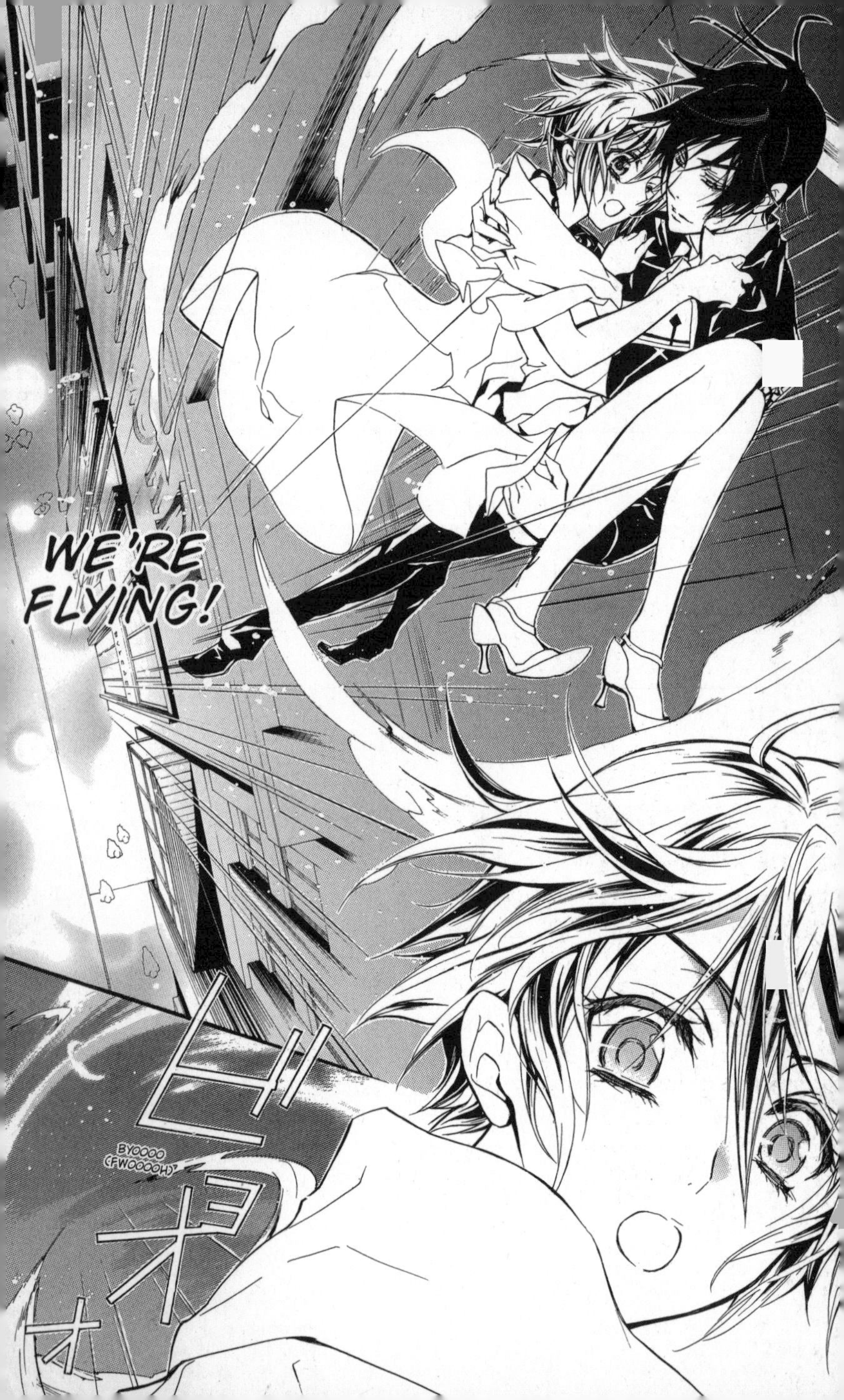
WE'RE FLYING!
ビョオオ
BYOOOO (FWOOOOH)

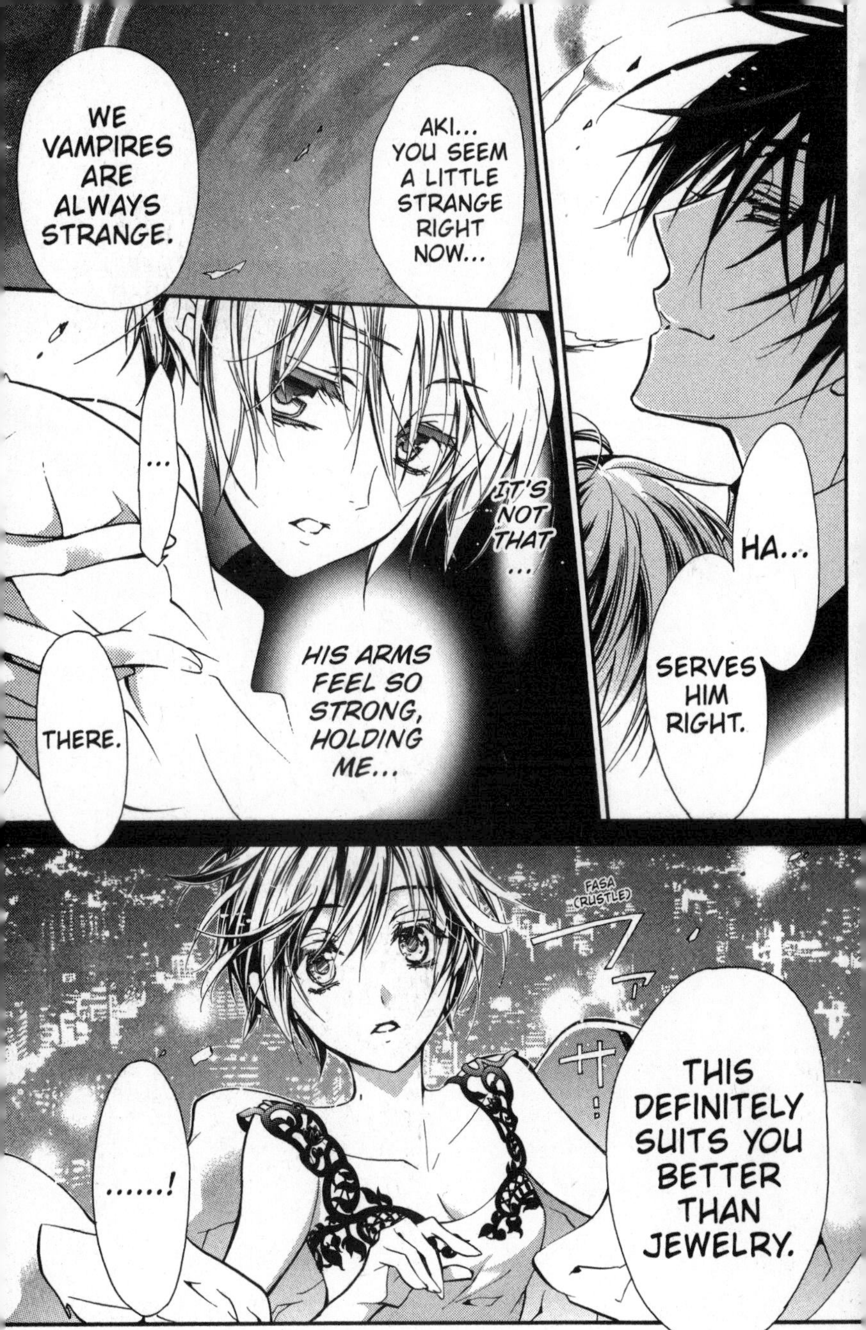
HA...
SERVES HIM RIGHT.
AKI... YOU SEEM A LITTLE STRANGE RIGHT NOW...
WE VAMPIRES ARE ALWAYS STRANGE.
...
IT'S NOT THAT...
HIS ARMS FEEL SO STRONG, HOLDING ME...
THERE.
FASA (RUSTLE)
THIS DEFINITELY SUITS YOU BETTER THAN JEWELRY.
......!

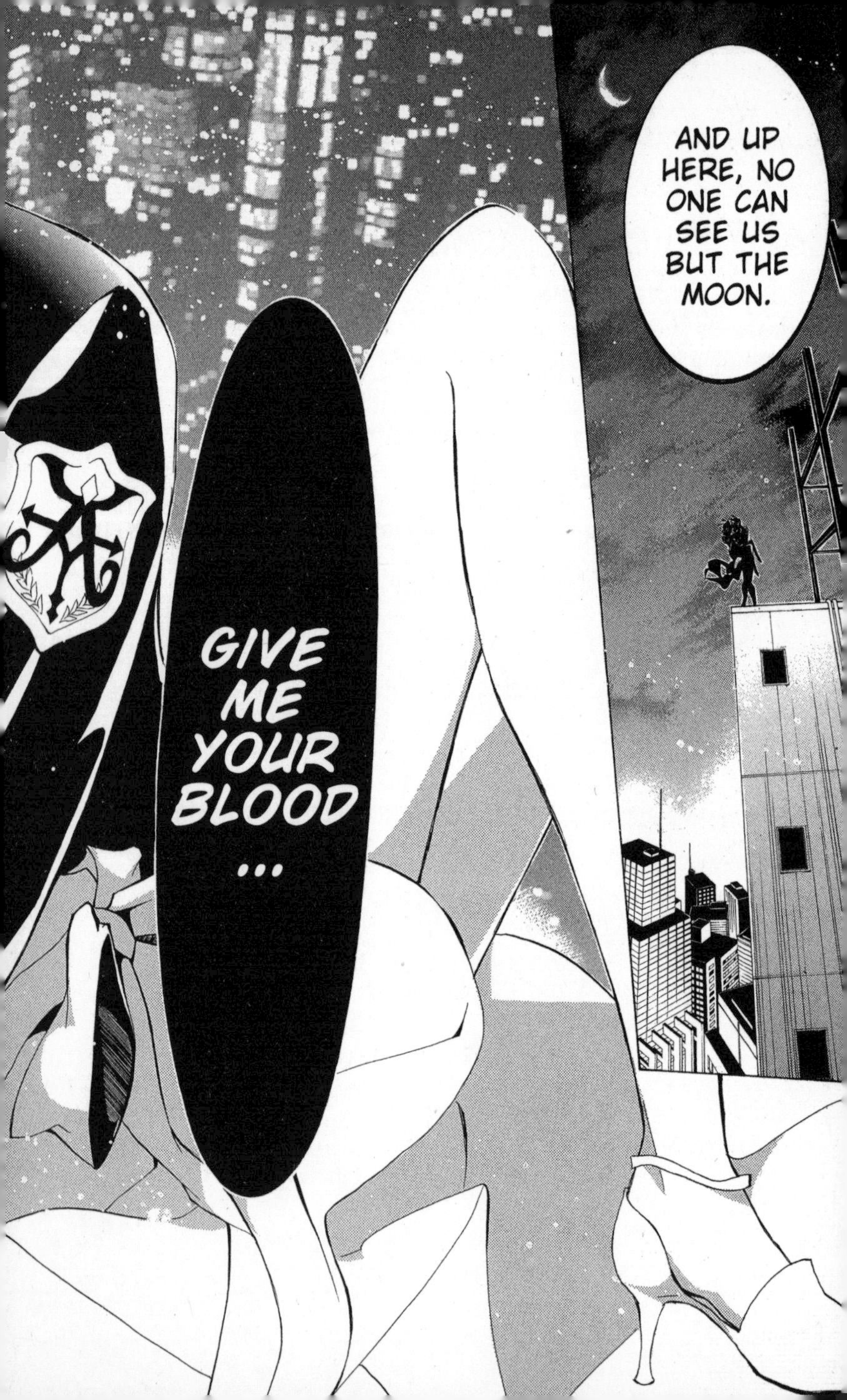
AND UP HERE, NO ONE CAN SEE US BUT THE MOON.
GIVE ME YOUR BLOOD ...

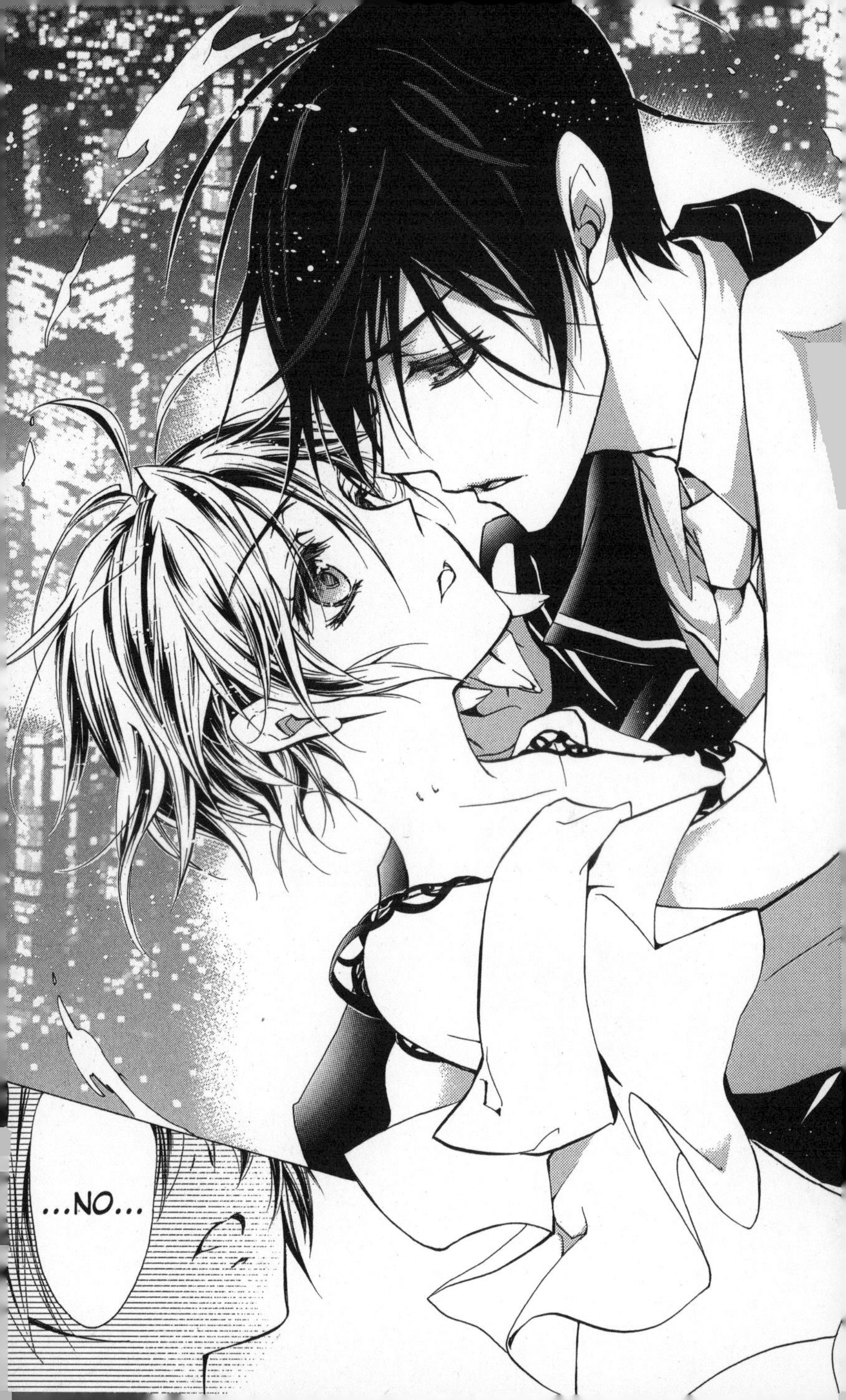
...NO...

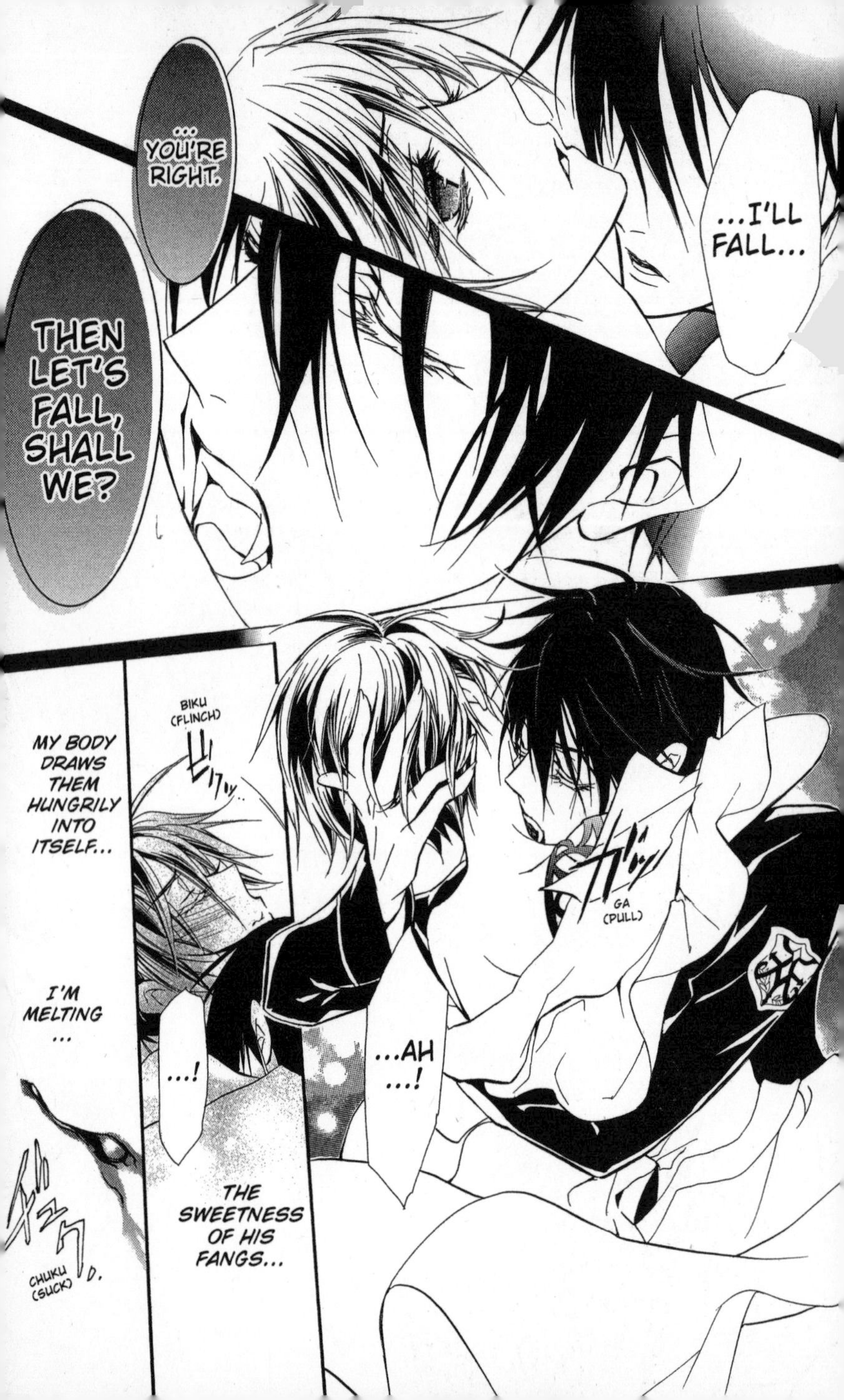
...I'LL FALL...
...YOU'RE RIGHT.
THEN LET'S FALL, SHALL WE?
BIKU (FLINCH)
GA (PULL)
...AH ...!
THE SWEETNESS OF HIS FANGS...
MY BODY DRAWS THEM HUNGRILY INTO ITSELF...
I'M MELTING ...
...!
CHUKU (SUCK)

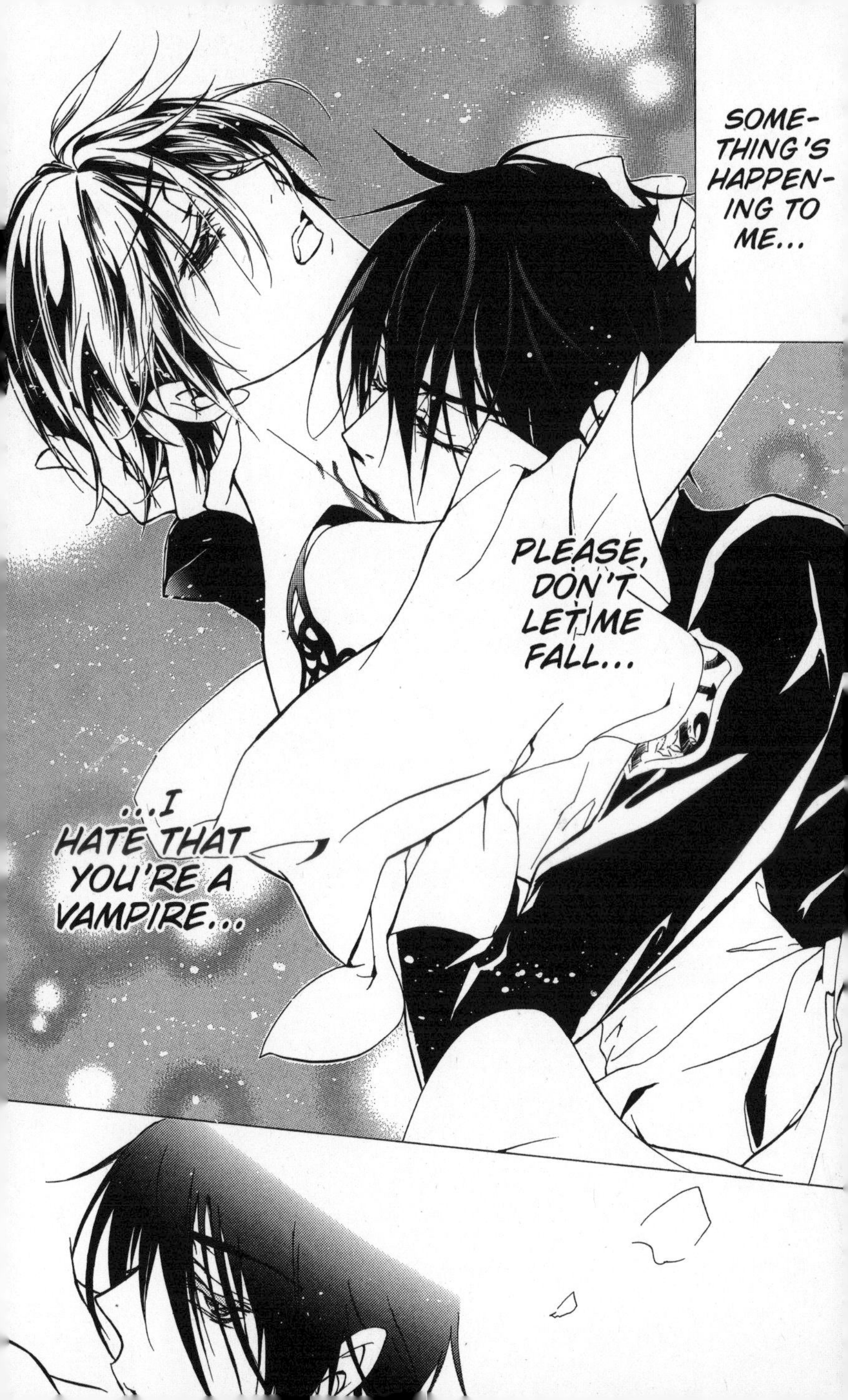
SOME-THING'S HAPPEN-ING TO ME...
PLEASE, DON'T LET ME FALL...
...I HATE THAT YOU'RE A VAMPIRE...

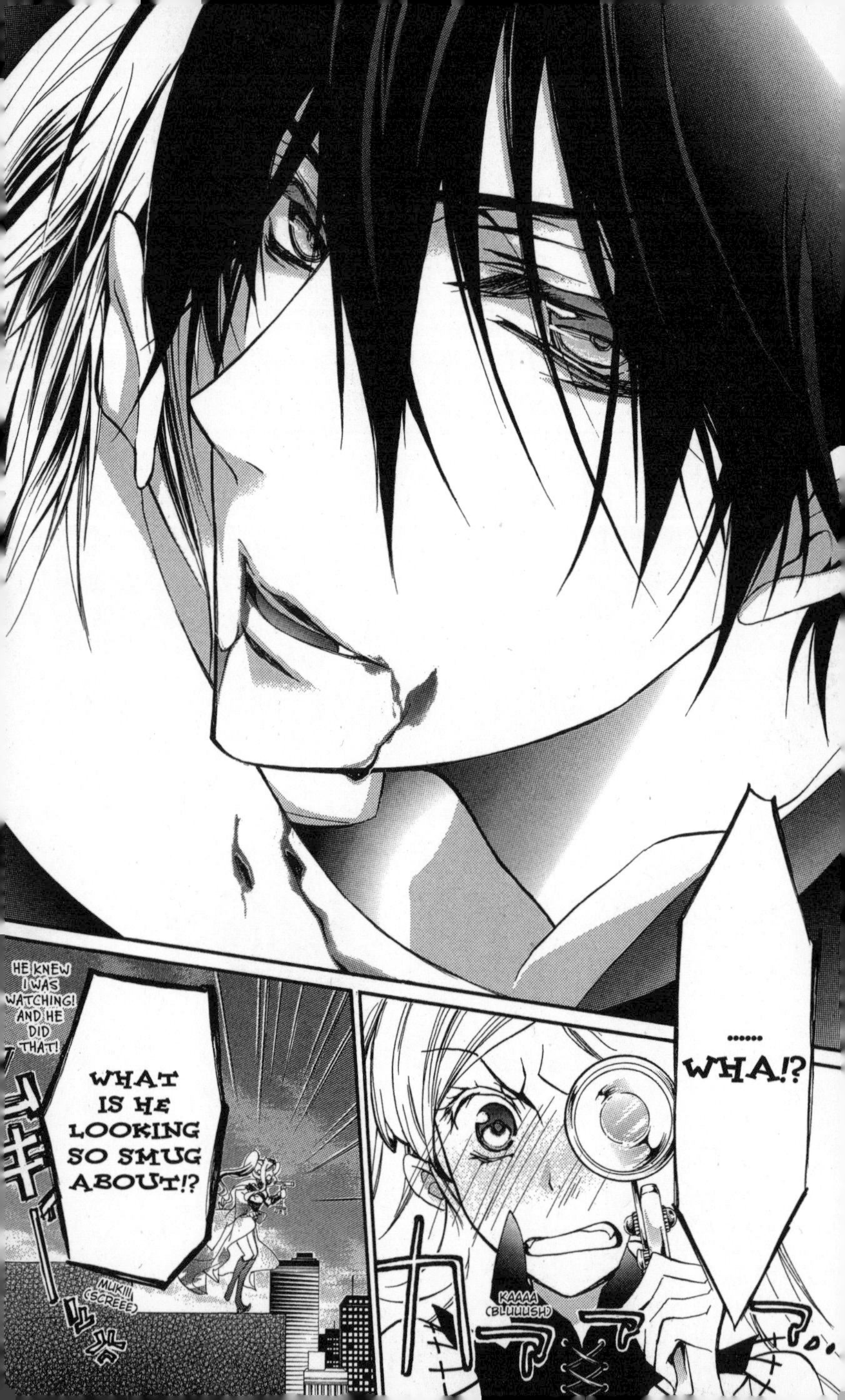

......
WHA!?
KAAAA (BLUUUSH)
WHAT IS HE LOOKING SO SMUG ABOUT!?
HE KNEW I WAS WATCHING! AND HE DID THAT!
MUKIII (SCREEE)

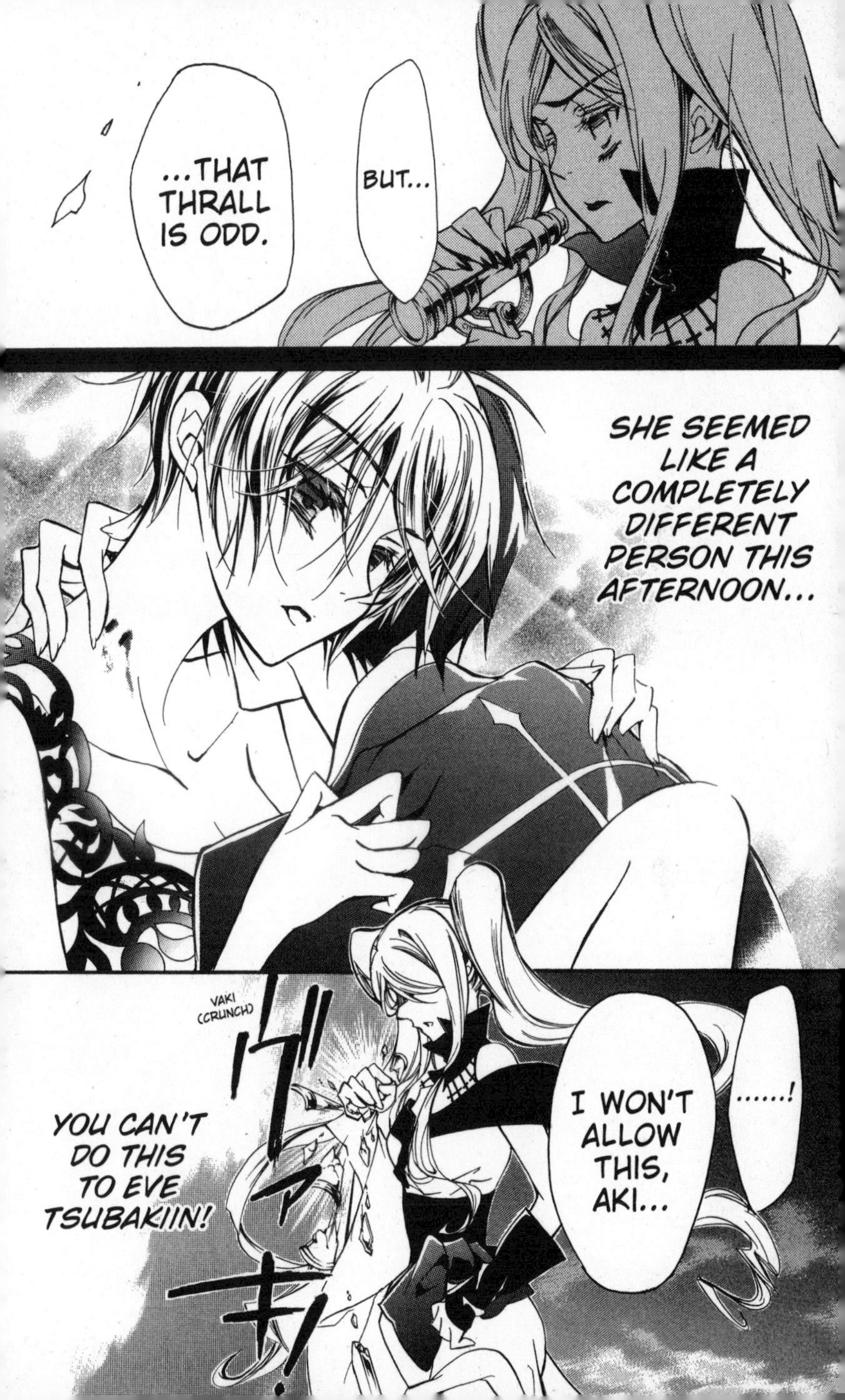
BUT...
...THAT THRALL IS ODD.
SHE SEEMED LIKE A COMPLETELY DIFFERENT PERSON THIS AFTERNOON...
......!
I WON'T ALLOW THIS, AKI...
VAKI (CRUNCH)
YOU CAN'T DO THIS TO EVE TSUBAKIIN!

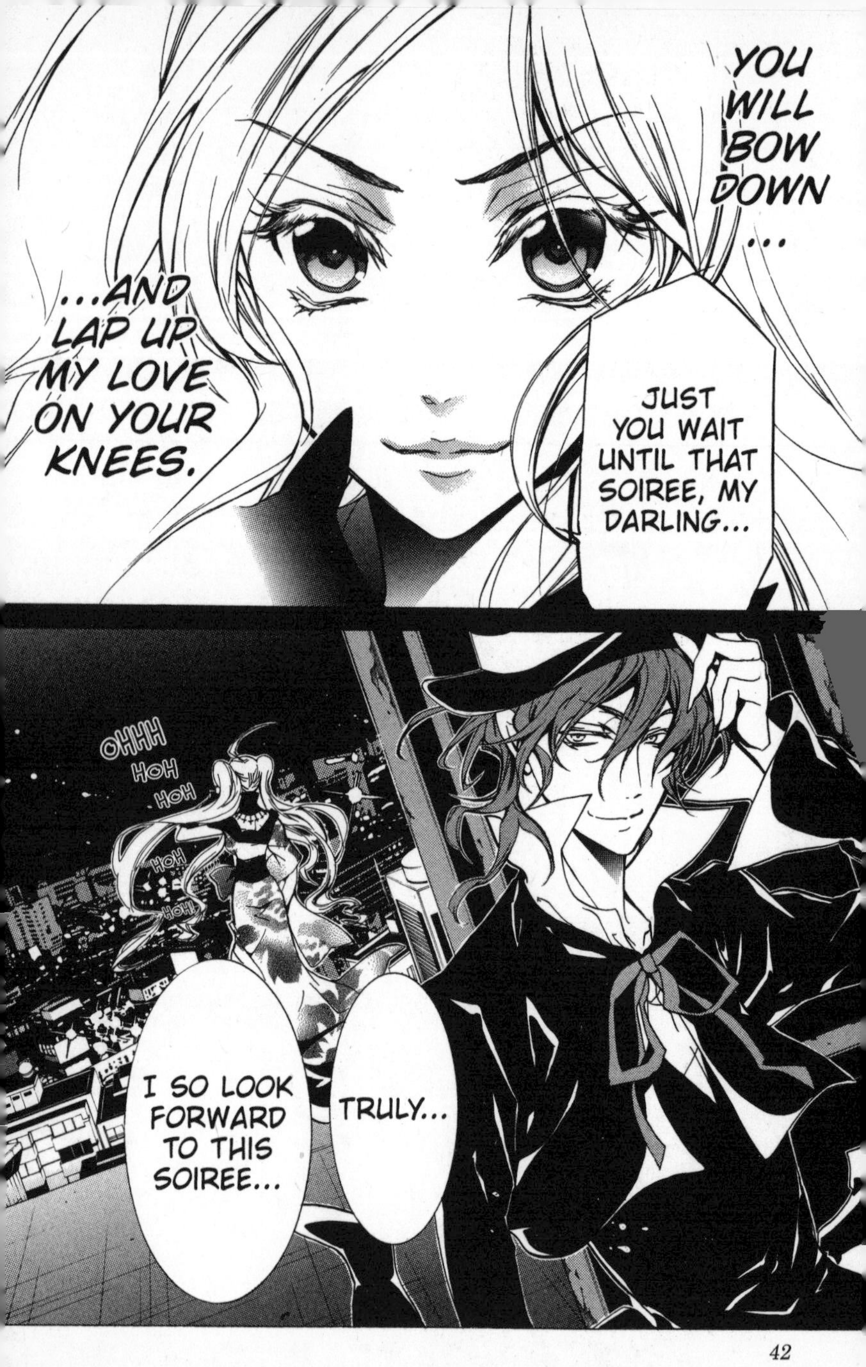
YOU WILL BOW DOWN...
JUST YOU WAIT UNTIL THAT SOIREE, MY DARLING...
...AND LAP UP MY LOVE ON YOUR KNEES.
TRULY...
I SO LOOK FORWARD TO THIS SOIREE...
OHHH HOH HOH HOH HOH

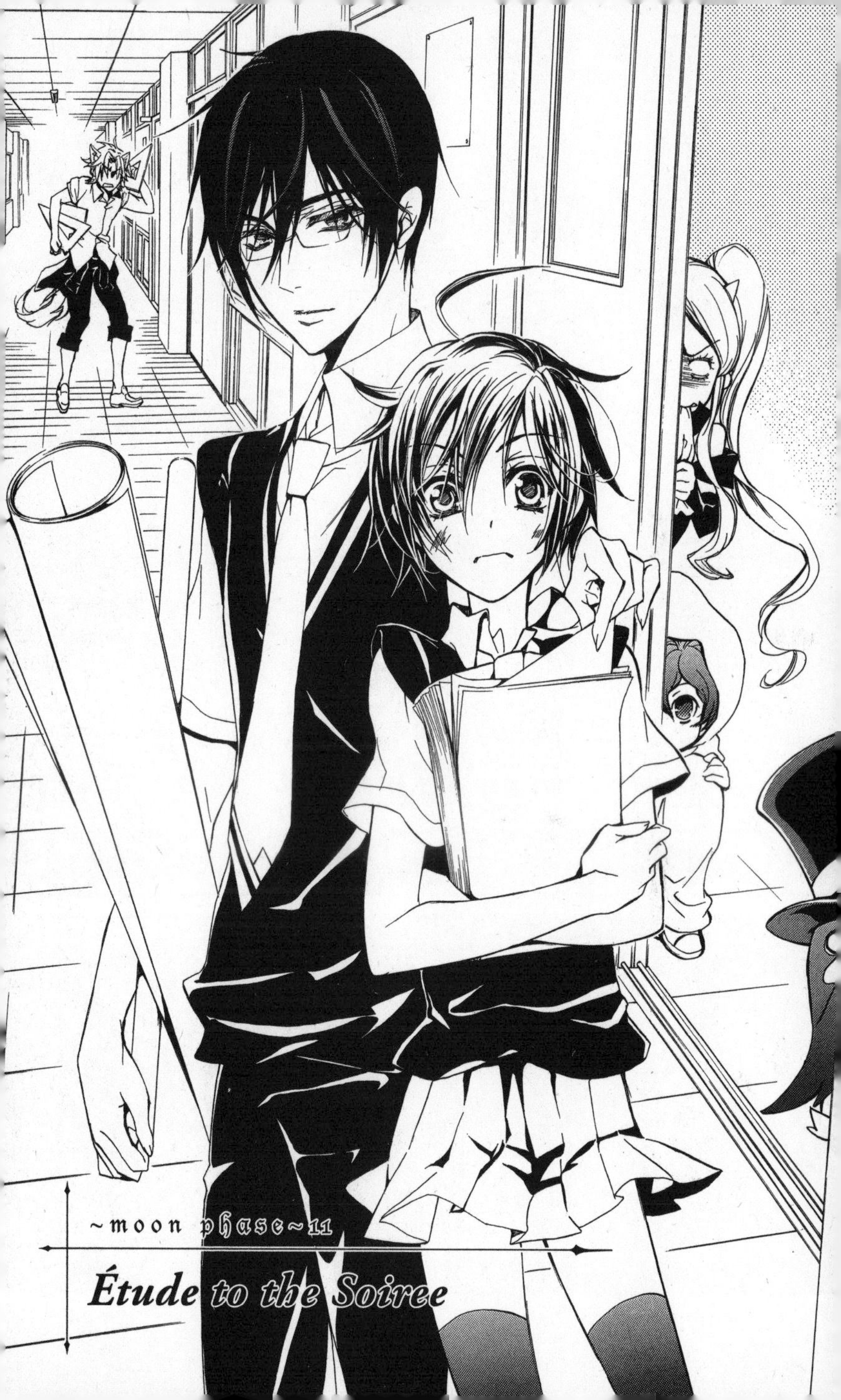
~moon phase~11
Étude to the Soiree

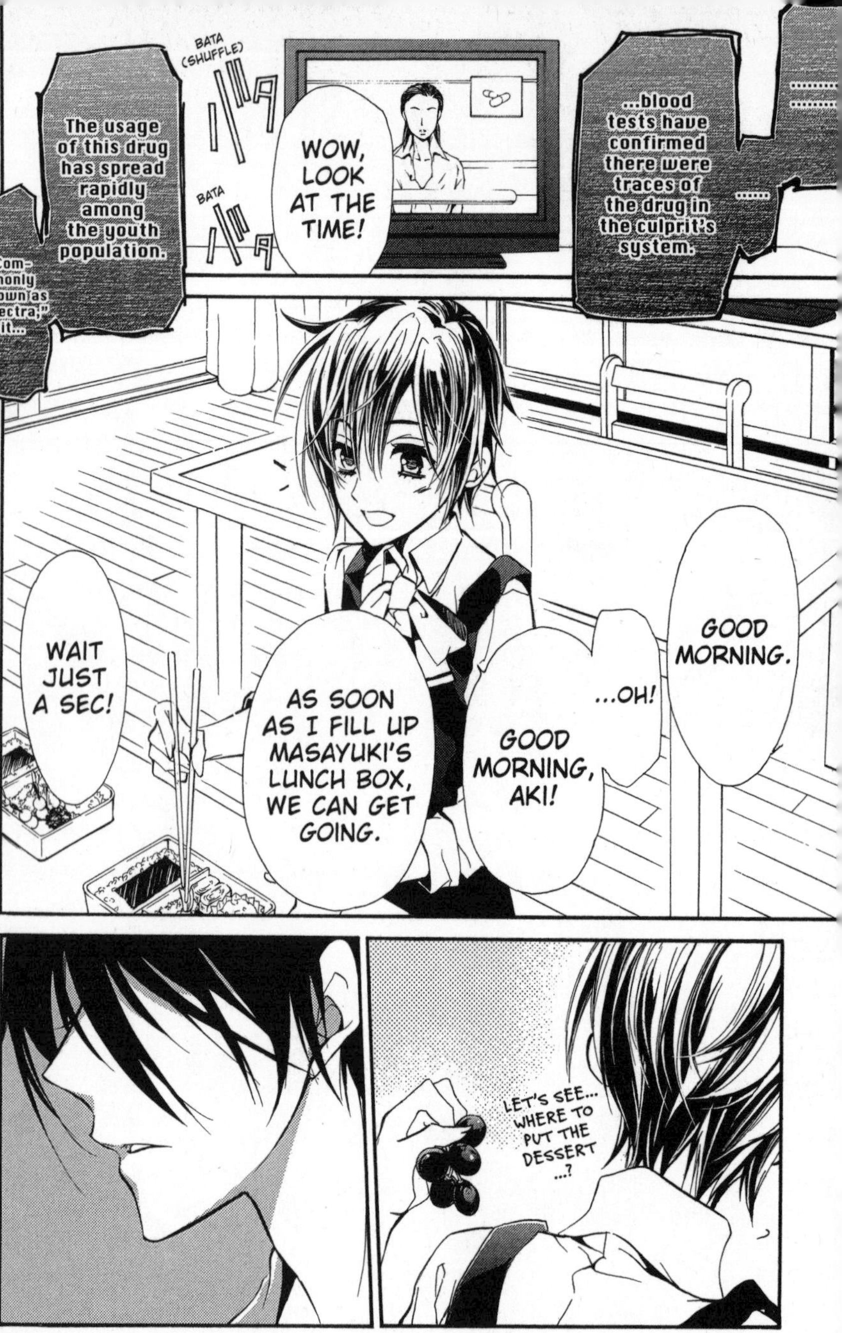
......
......
...blood tests have confirmed there were traces of the drug in the culprit's system.
......
WOW, LOOK AT THE TIME!
BATA (SHUFFLE)
BATA
The usage of this drug has spread rapidly among the youth population.
Commonly known as "Electra," it...
GOOD MORNING.
...OH!
GOOD MORNING, AKI!
AS SOON AS I FILL UP MASAYUKI'S LUNCH BOX, WE CAN GET GOING.
WAIT JUST A SEC!
LET'S SEE... WHERE TO PUT THE DESSERT ...?

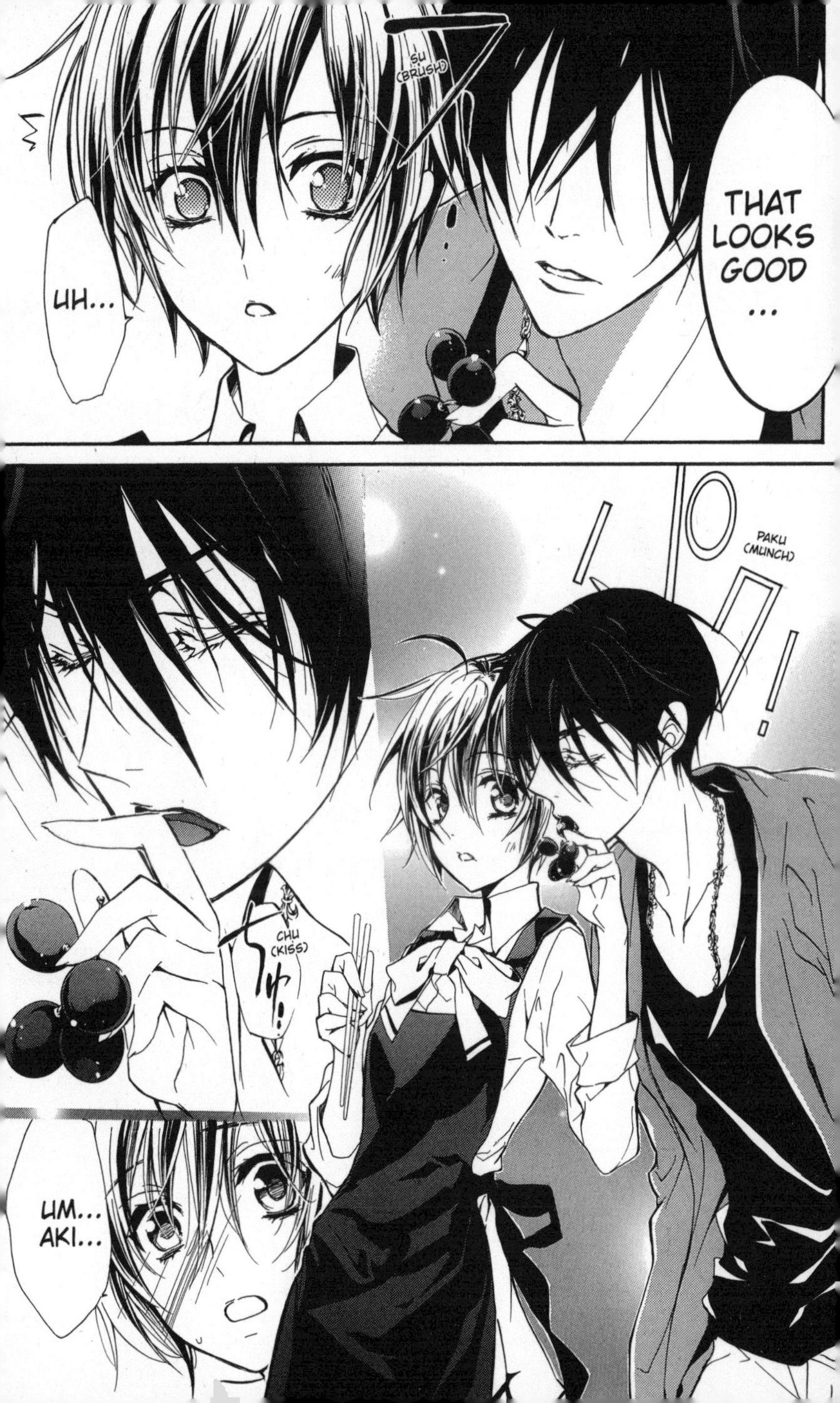
THAT LOOKS GOOD ...
SU (BRUSH)
UH...
PAKU (MUNCH)
CHU (KISS)
UM... AKI...

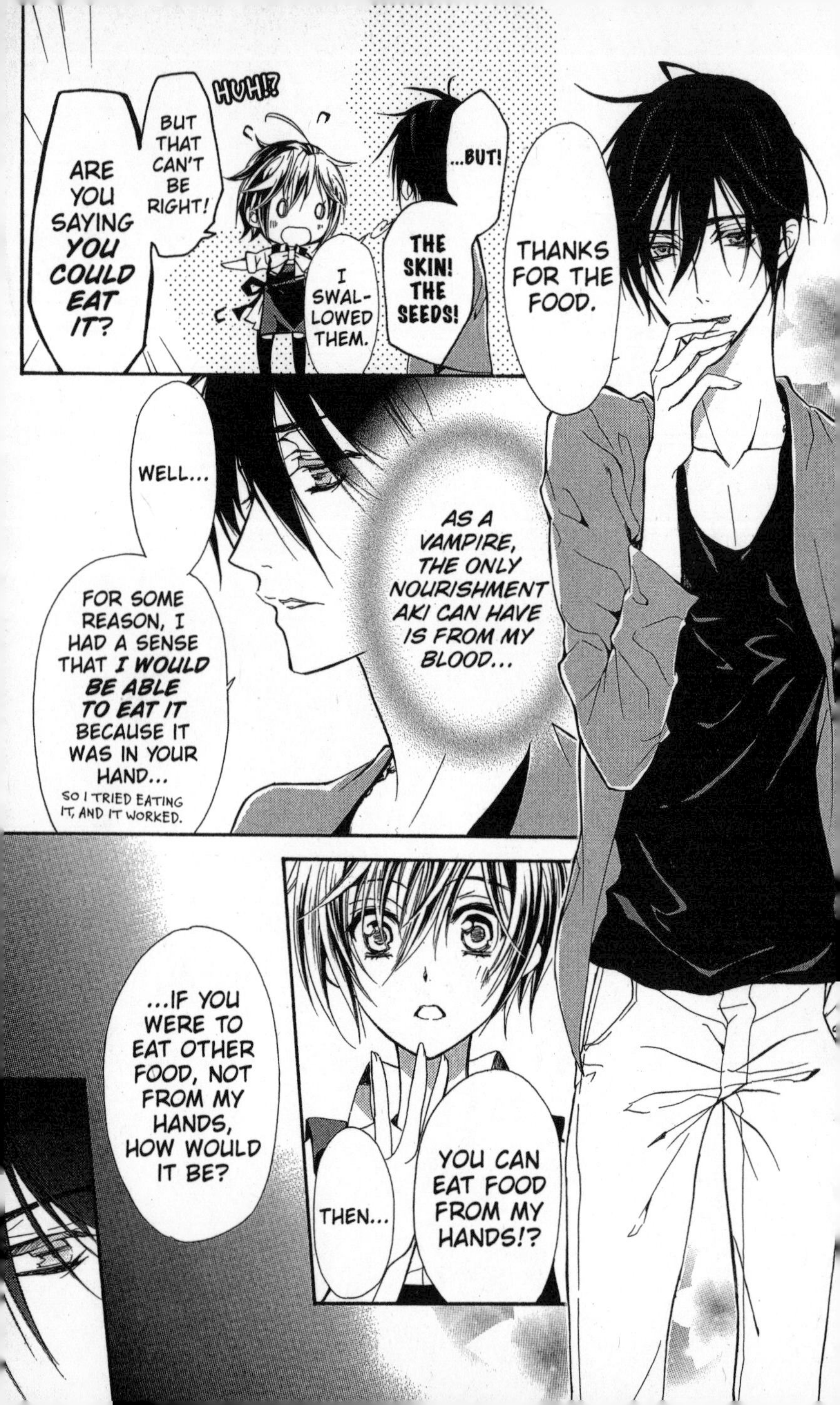
THANKS FOR THE FOOD.
...BUT!
THE SKIN! THE SEEDS!
I SWAL-LOWED THEM.
HUH!?
BUT THAT CAN'T BE RIGHT!
ARE YOU SAYING YOU COULD EAT IT?
AS A VAMPIRE, THE ONLY NOURISHMENT AKI CAN HAVE IS FROM MY BLOOD...
WELL...
FOR SOME REASON, I HAD A SENSE THAT I WOULD BE ABLE TO EAT IT BECAUSE IT WAS IN YOUR HAND...
SO I TRIED EATING IT, AND IT WORKED.
YOU CAN EAT FOOD FROM MY HANDS!?
THEN...
...IF YOU WERE TO EAT OTHER FOOD, NOT FROM MY HANDS, HOW WOULD IT BE?

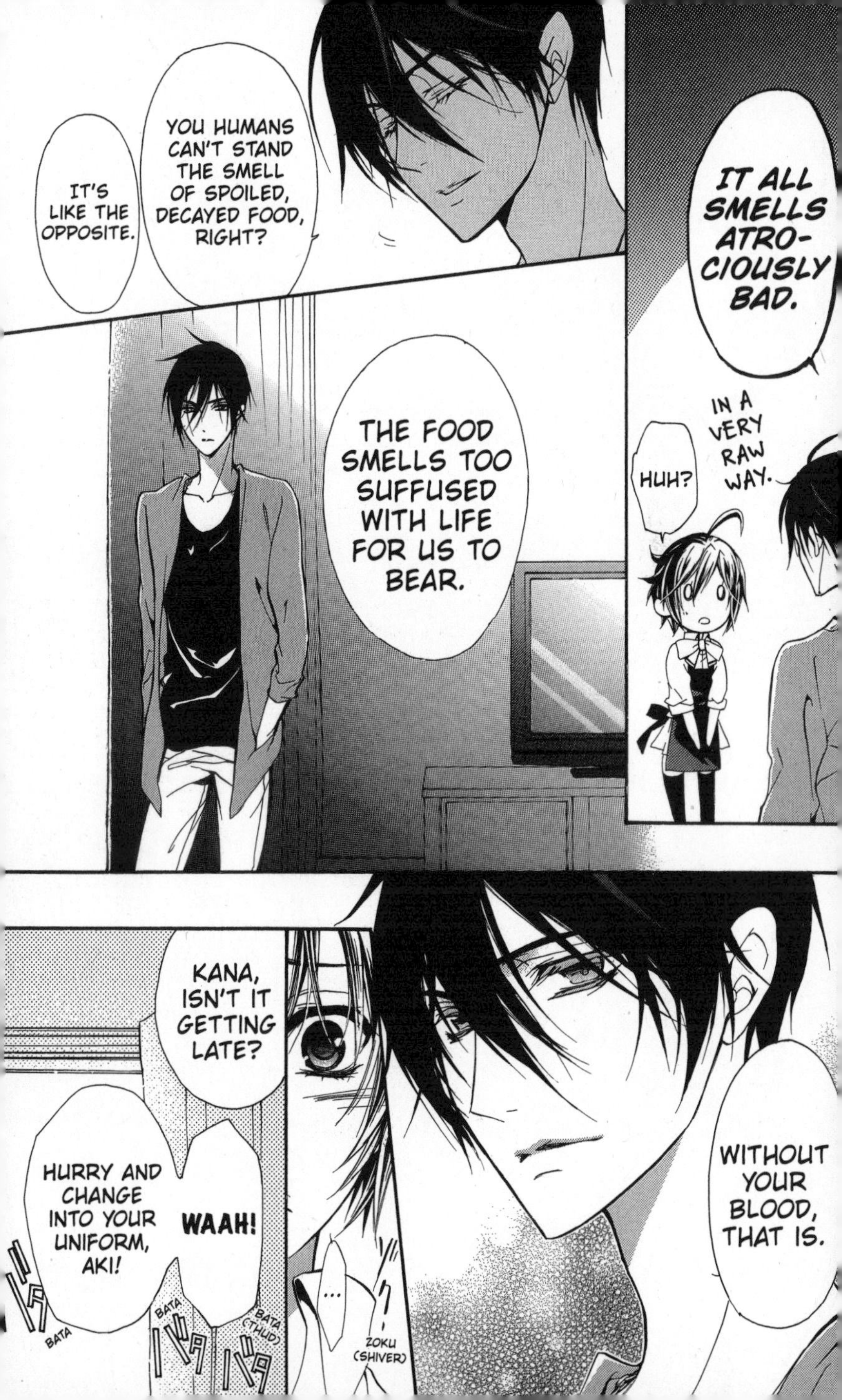
IT ALL SMELLS ATROCIOUSLY BAD.
IN A VERY RAW WAY.
HUH?
YOU HUMANS CAN'T STAND THE SMELL OF SPOILED, DECAYED FOOD, RIGHT?
IT'S LIKE THE OPPOSITE.
THE FOOD SMELLS TOO SUFFUSED WITH LIFE FOR US TO BEAR.
WITHOUT YOUR BLOOD, THAT IS.
...
ZOKU (SHIVER)
KANA, ISN'T IT GETTING LATE?
HURRY AND CHANGE INTO YOUR UNIFORM, AKI!
WAAH!
BATA (THUD)
BATA
BATA

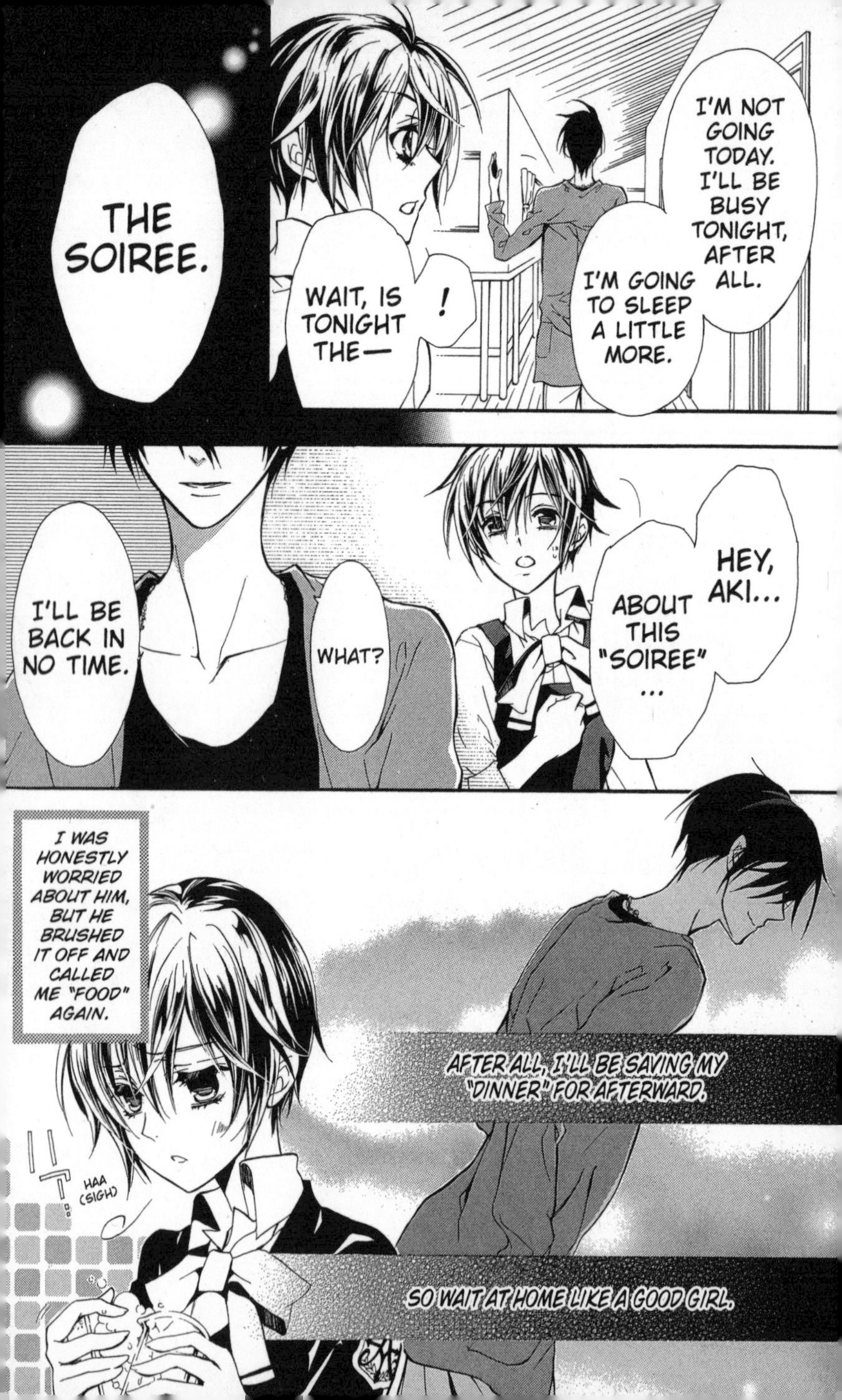
I'M NOT GOING TODAY. I'LL BE BUSY TONIGHT, AFTER ALL.
I'M GOING TO SLEEP A LITTLE MORE.
!
WAIT, IS TONIGHT THE—
THE SOIREE.
HEY, AKI...
ABOUT THIS "SOIREE" ...
WHAT?
I'LL BE BACK IN NO TIME.
I WAS HONESTLY WORRIED ABOUT HIM, BUT HE BRUSHED IT OFF AND CALLED ME "FOOD" AGAIN.
AFTER ALL, I'LL BE SAVING MY "DINNER" FOR AFTERWARD.
HAA (SIGH)
SO WAIT AT HOME LIKE A GOOD GIRL.

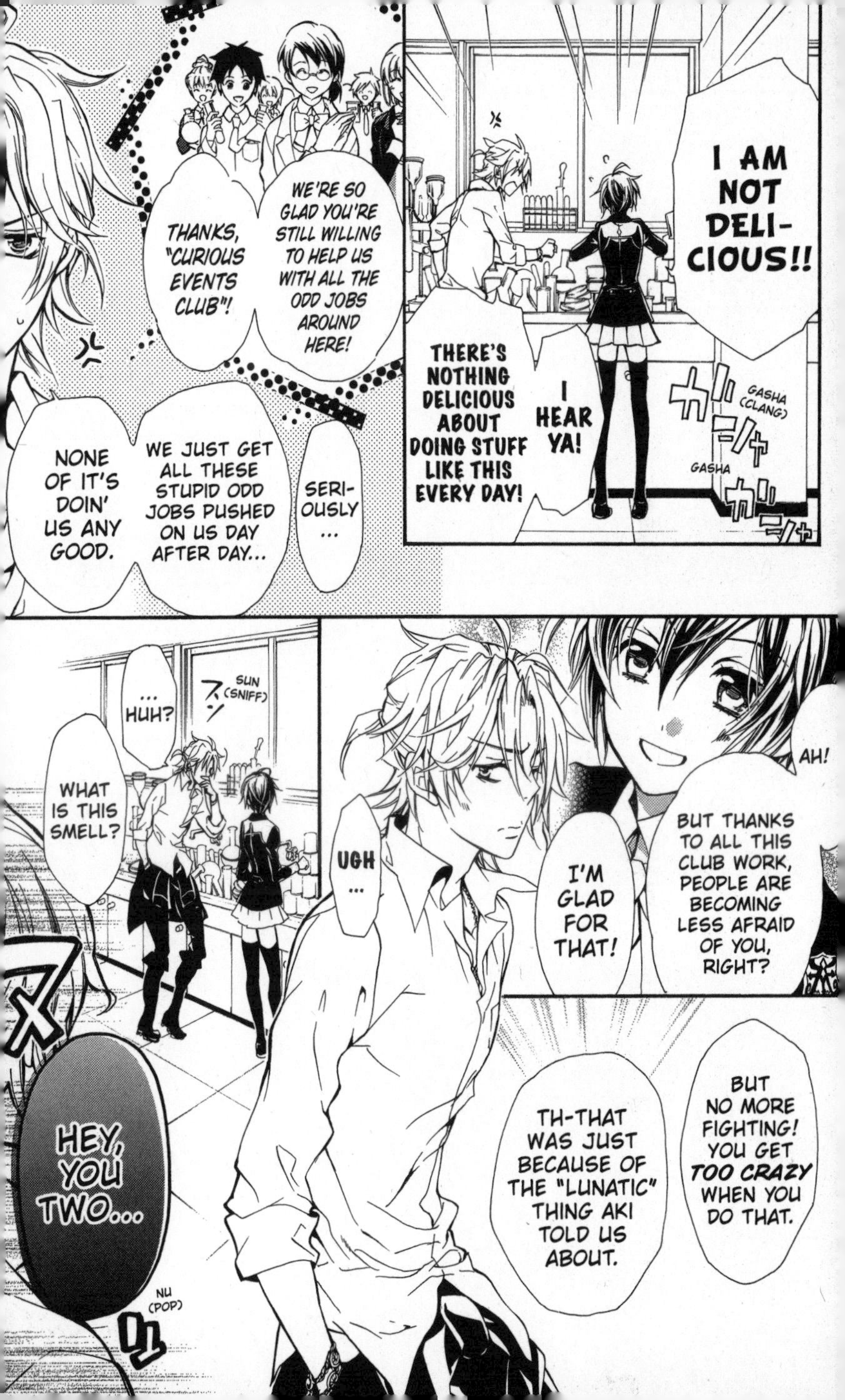
I AM NOT DELICIOUS!!
GASHA (CLANG)
GASHA
I HEAR YA!
THERE'S NOTHING DELICIOUS ABOUT DOING STUFF LIKE THIS EVERY DAY!
WE'RE SO GLAD YOU'RE STILL WILLING TO HELP US WITH ALL THE ODD JOBS AROUND HERE!
THANKS, "CURIOUS EVENTS CLUB"!
SERIOUSLY...
WE JUST GET ALL THESE STUPID ODD JOBS PUSHED ON US DAY AFTER DAY...
NONE OF IT'S DOIN' US ANY GOOD.
AH!
BUT THANKS TO ALL THIS CLUB WORK, PEOPLE ARE BECOMING LESS AFRAID OF YOU, RIGHT?
I'M GLAD FOR THAT!
UGH...
BUT NO MORE FIGHTING! YOU GET TOO CRAZY WHEN YOU DO THAT.
TH-THAT WAS JUST BECAUSE OF THE "LUNATIC" THING AKI TOLD US ABOUT.
...HUH?
SUN (SNIFF)
WHAT IS THIS SMELL?
HEY, YOU TWO...
NU (POP)

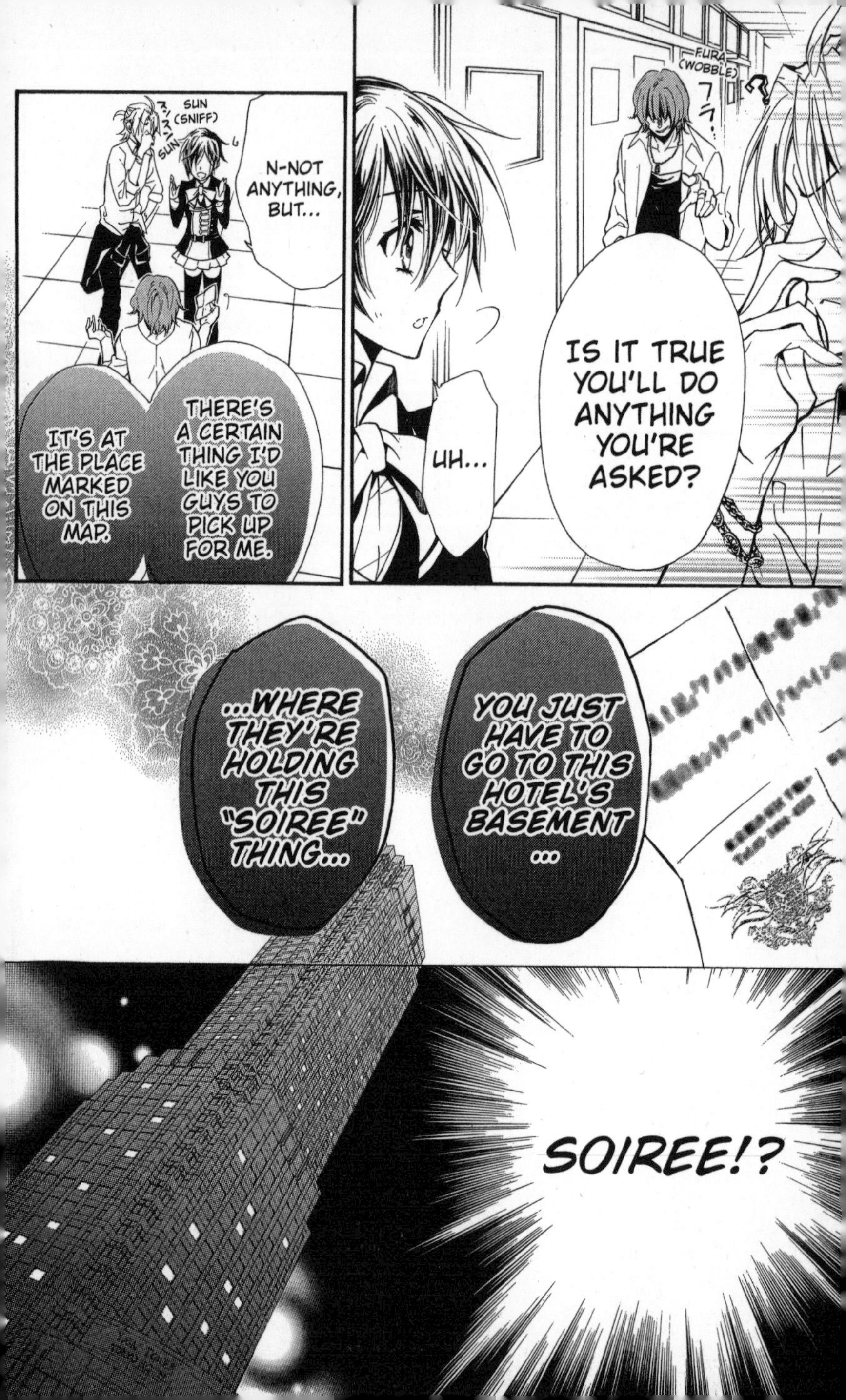
FURA (WOBBLE)
IS IT TRUE YOU'LL DO ANYTHING YOU'RE ASKED?
UH...
N-NOT ANYTHING, BUT...
SUN (SNIFF)
THERE'S A CERTAIN THING I'D LIKE YOU GUYS TO PICK UP FOR ME.
IT'S AT THE PLACE MARKED ON THIS MAP.
YOU JUST HAVE TO GO TO THIS HOTEL'S BASEMENT...
...WHERE THEY'RE HOLDING THIS "SOIREE" THING...
SOIREE!?

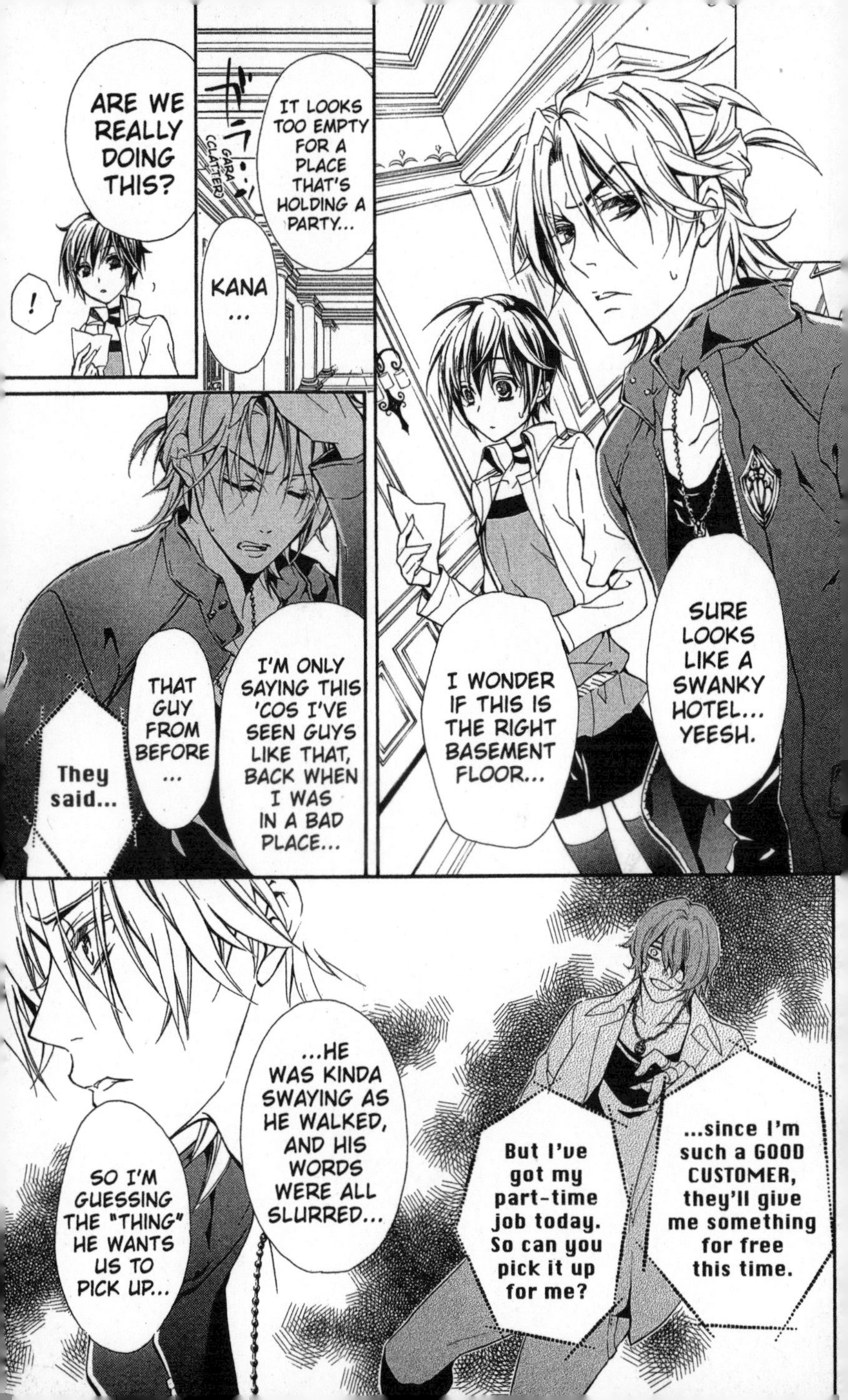
SURE LOOKS LIKE A SWANKY HOTEL... YEESH.
I WONDER IF THIS IS THE RIGHT BASEMENT FLOOR...
IT LOOKS TOO EMPTY FOR A PLACE THAT'S HOLDING A PARTY...
GARA (CLATTER)
KANA...
ARE WE REALLY DOING THIS?
!
I'M ONLY SAYING THIS 'COS I'VE SEEN GUYS LIKE THAT, BACK WHEN I WAS IN A BAD PLACE...
THAT GUY FROM BEFORE...
They said...
...since I'm such a GOOD CUSTOMER, they'll give me something for free this time.
But I've got my part-time job today. So can you pick it up for me?
...HE WAS KINDA SWAYING AS HE WALKED, AND HIS WORDS WERE ALL SLURRED...
SO I'M GUESSING THE "THING" HE WANTS US TO PICK UP...

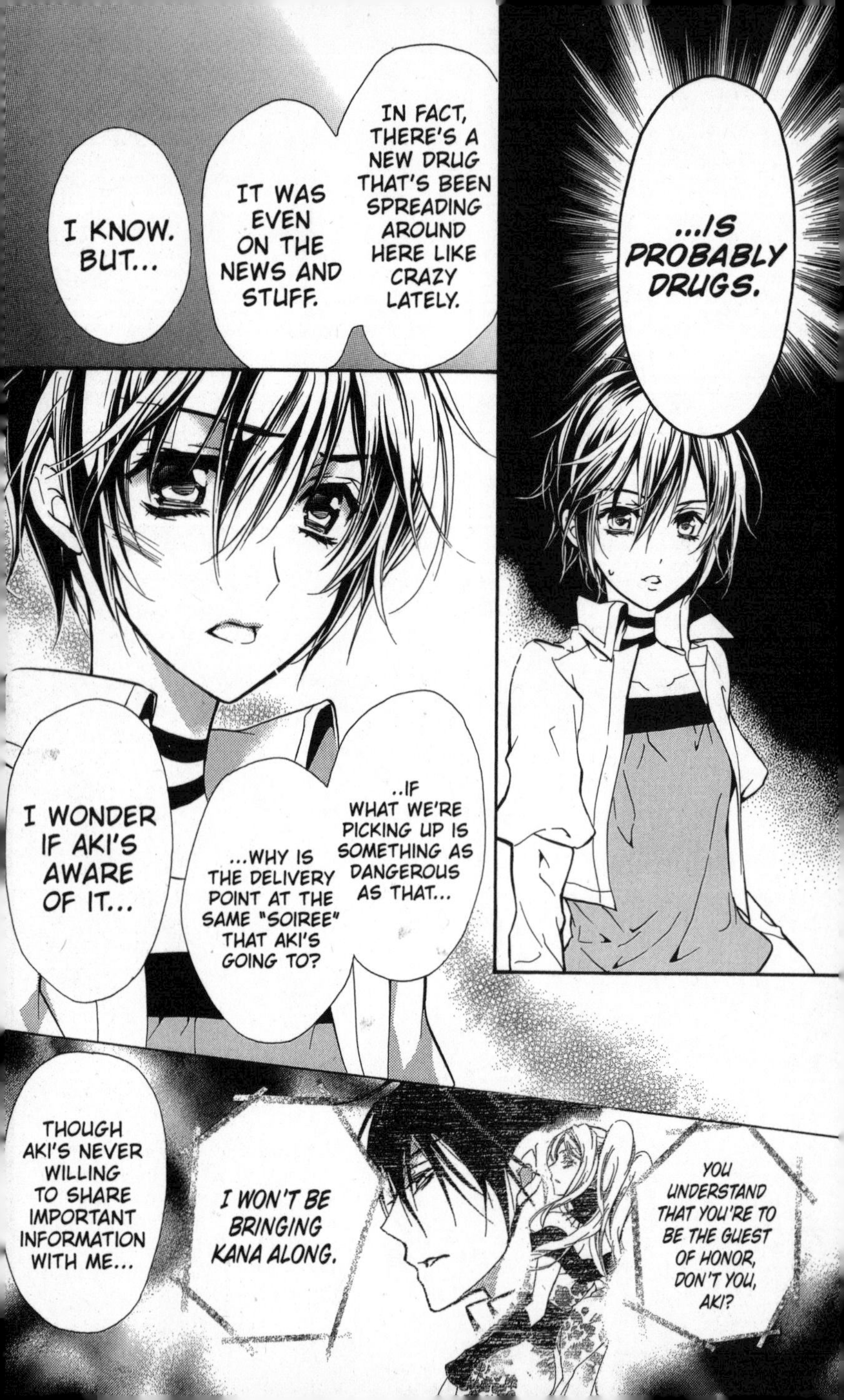
...IS PROBABLY DRUGS.
IN FACT, THERE'S A NEW DRUG THAT'S BEEN SPREADING AROUND HERE LIKE CRAZY LATELY.
IT WAS EVEN ON THE NEWS AND STUFF.
I KNOW. BUT...
..IF WHAT WE'RE PICKING UP IS SOMETHING AS DANGEROUS AS THAT...
...WHY IS THE DELIVERY POINT AT THE SAME "SOIREE" THAT AKI'S GOING TO?
I WONDER IF AKI'S AWARE OF IT...
YOU UNDERSTAND THAT YOU'RE TO BE THE GUEST OF HONOR, DON'T YOU, AKI?
I WON'T BE BRINGING KANA ALONG.
THOUGH AKI'S NEVER WILLING TO SHARE IMPORTANT INFORMATION WITH ME...

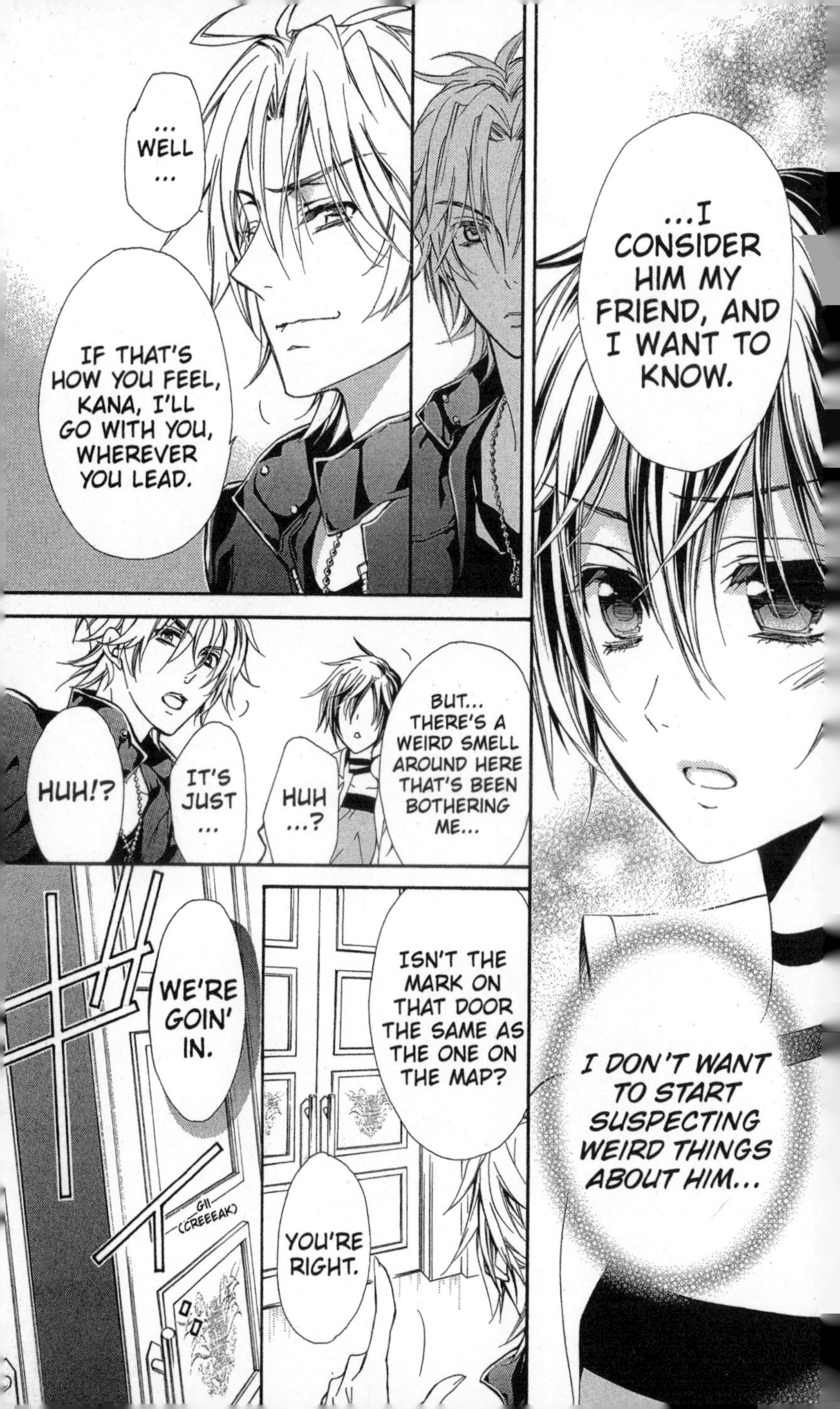
...I CONSIDER HIM MY FRIEND, AND I WANT TO KNOW.
I DON'T WANT TO START SUSPECTING WEIRD THINGS ABOUT HIM...
...WELL...
IF THAT'S HOW YOU FEEL, KANA, I'LL GO WITH YOU, WHEREVER YOU LEAD.
BUT... THERE'S A WEIRD SMELL AROUND HERE THAT'S BEEN BOTHERING ME...
HUH...?
IT'S JUST...
HUH!?
ISN'T THE MARK ON THAT DOOR THE SAME AS THE ONE ON THE MAP?
YOU'RE RIGHT.
WE'RE GOIN' IN.
GII (CREEEAK)

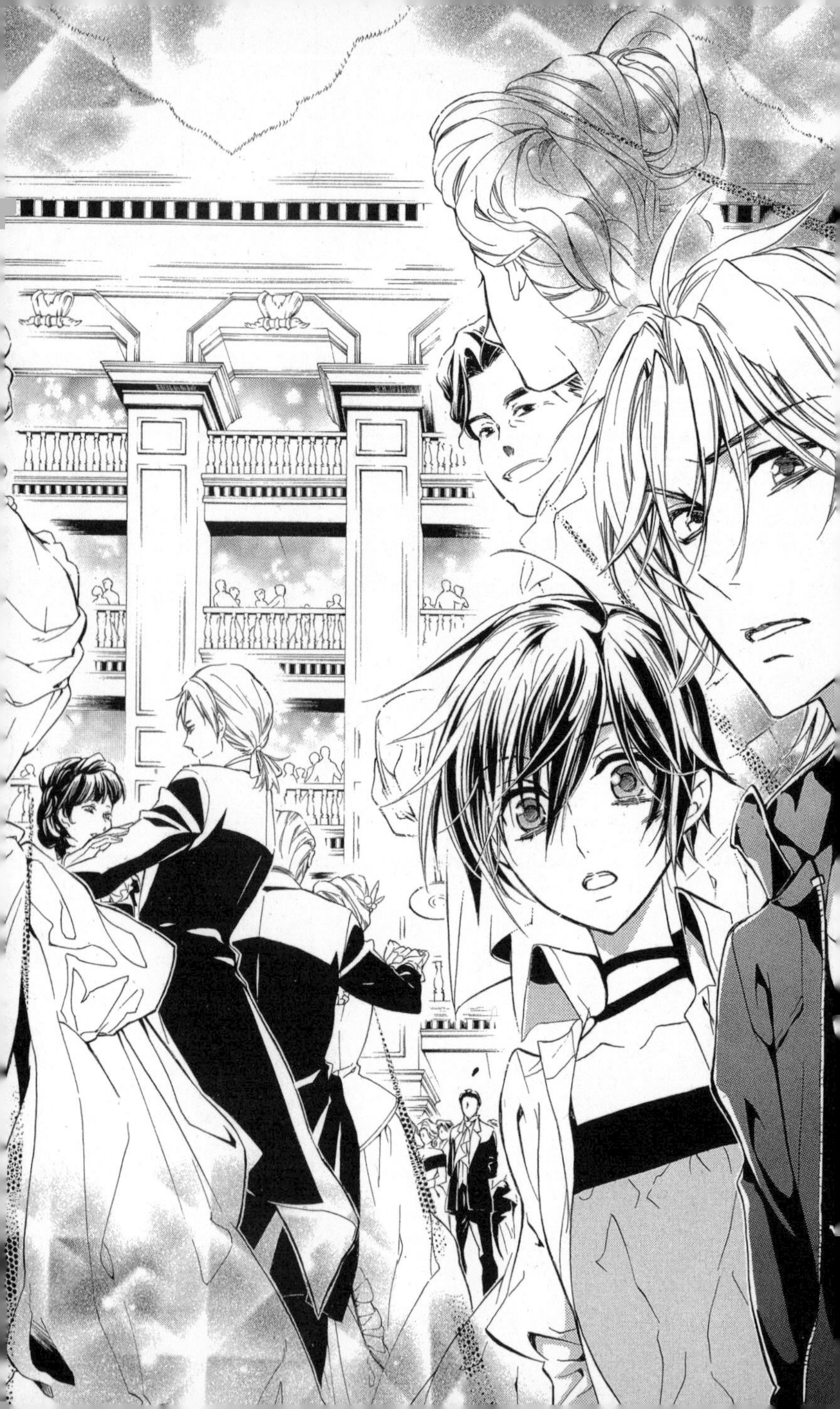

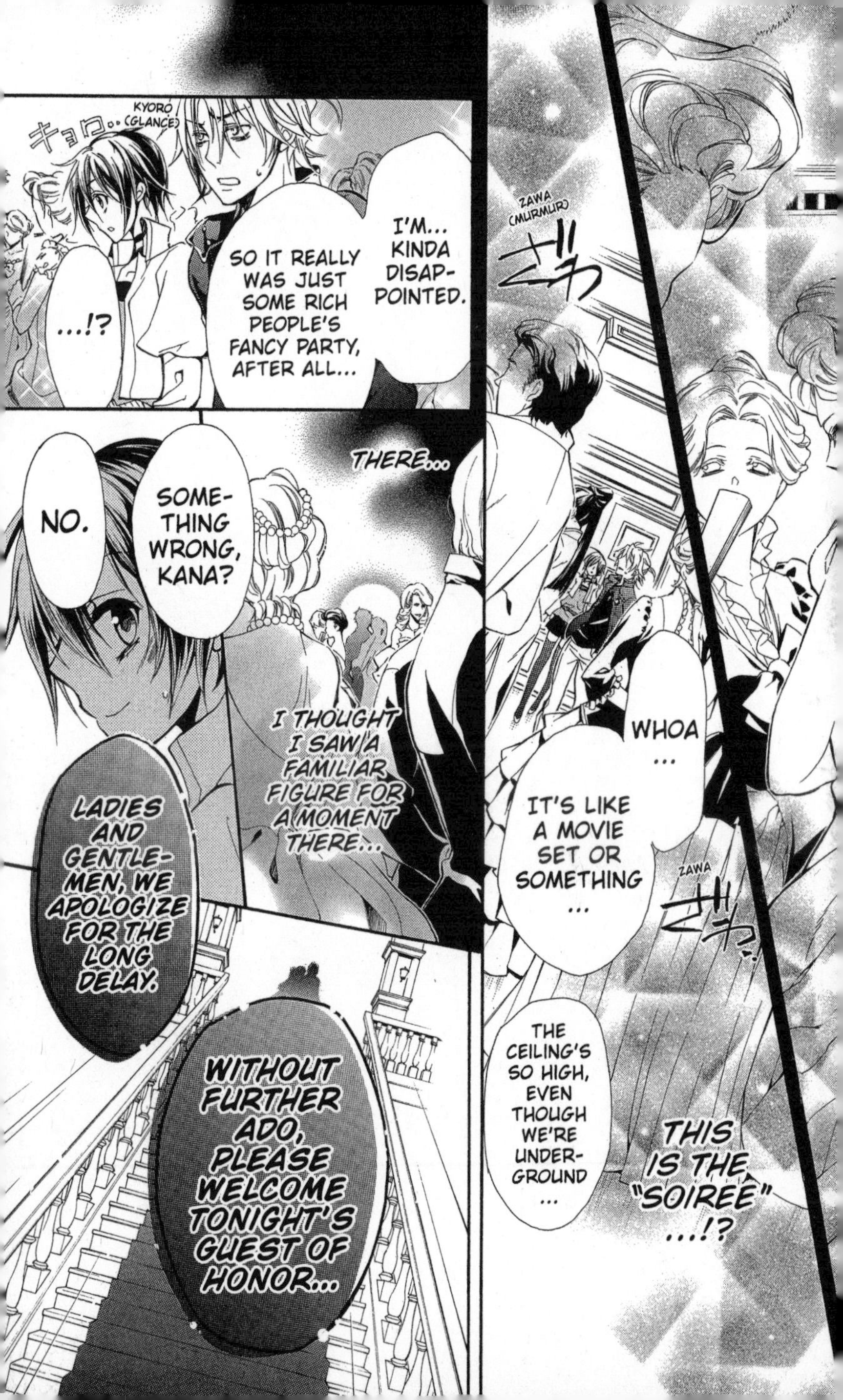
ZAWA (MURMUR)
ざわ
WHOA...
IT'S LIKE A MOVIE SET OR SOMETHING...
ZAWA
ざわっ
THE CEILING'S SO HIGH, EVEN THOUGH WE'RE UNDERGROUND...
THIS IS THE "SOIREE"...!?
I'M... KINDA DISAPPOINTED.
SO IT REALLY WAS JUST SOME RICH PEOPLE'S FANCY PARTY, AFTER ALL...
KYORO (GLANCE)
キョロ..
...!?
THERE...
SOMETHING WRONG, KANA?
NO.
I THOUGHT I SAW A FAMILIAR FIGURE FOR A MOMENT THERE...
LADIES AND GENTLEMEN, WE APOLOGIZE FOR THE LONG DELAY.
WITHOUT FURTHER ADO, PLEASE WELCOME TONIGHT'S GUEST OF HONOR...

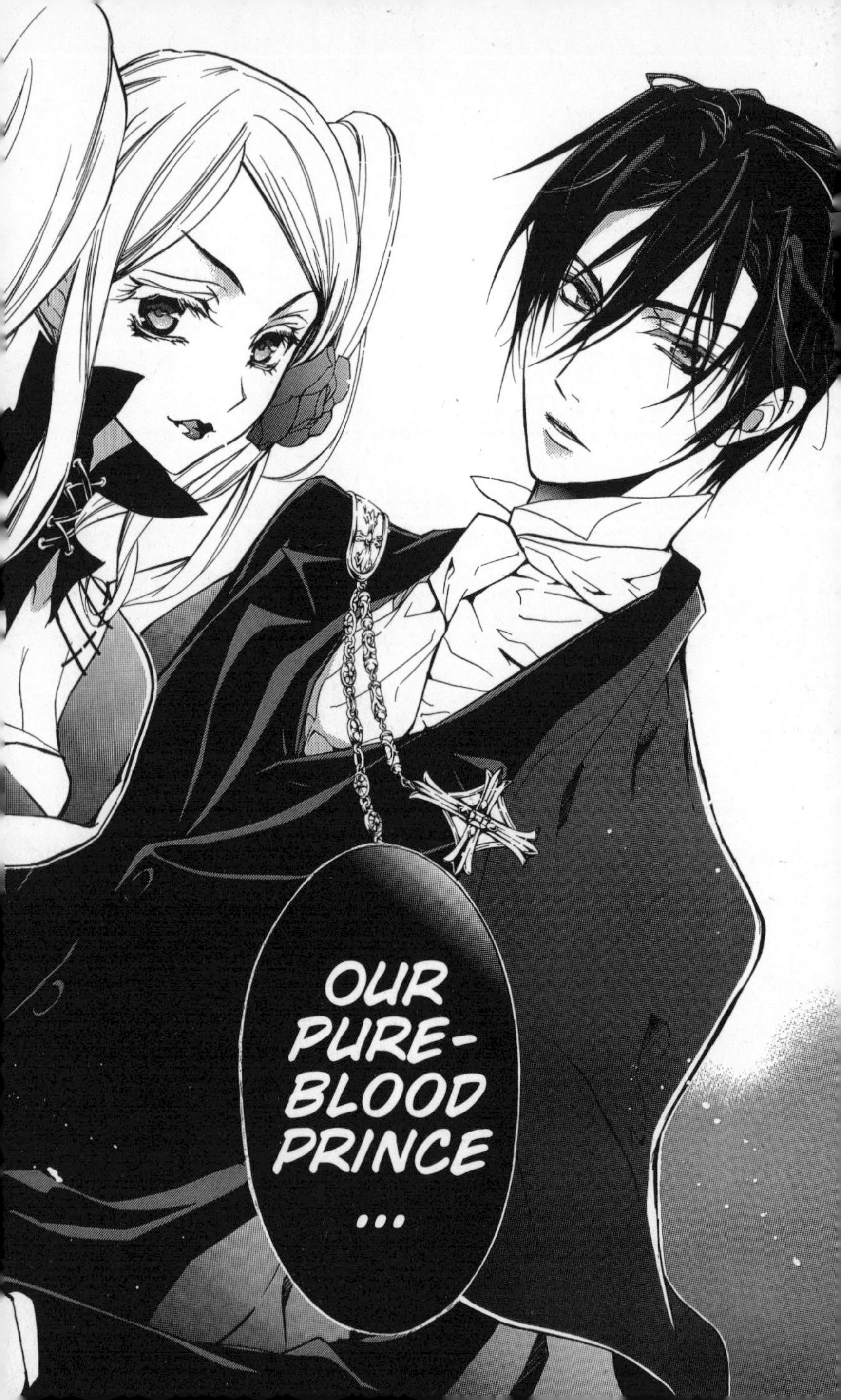
OUR PURE-BLOOD PRINCE ...

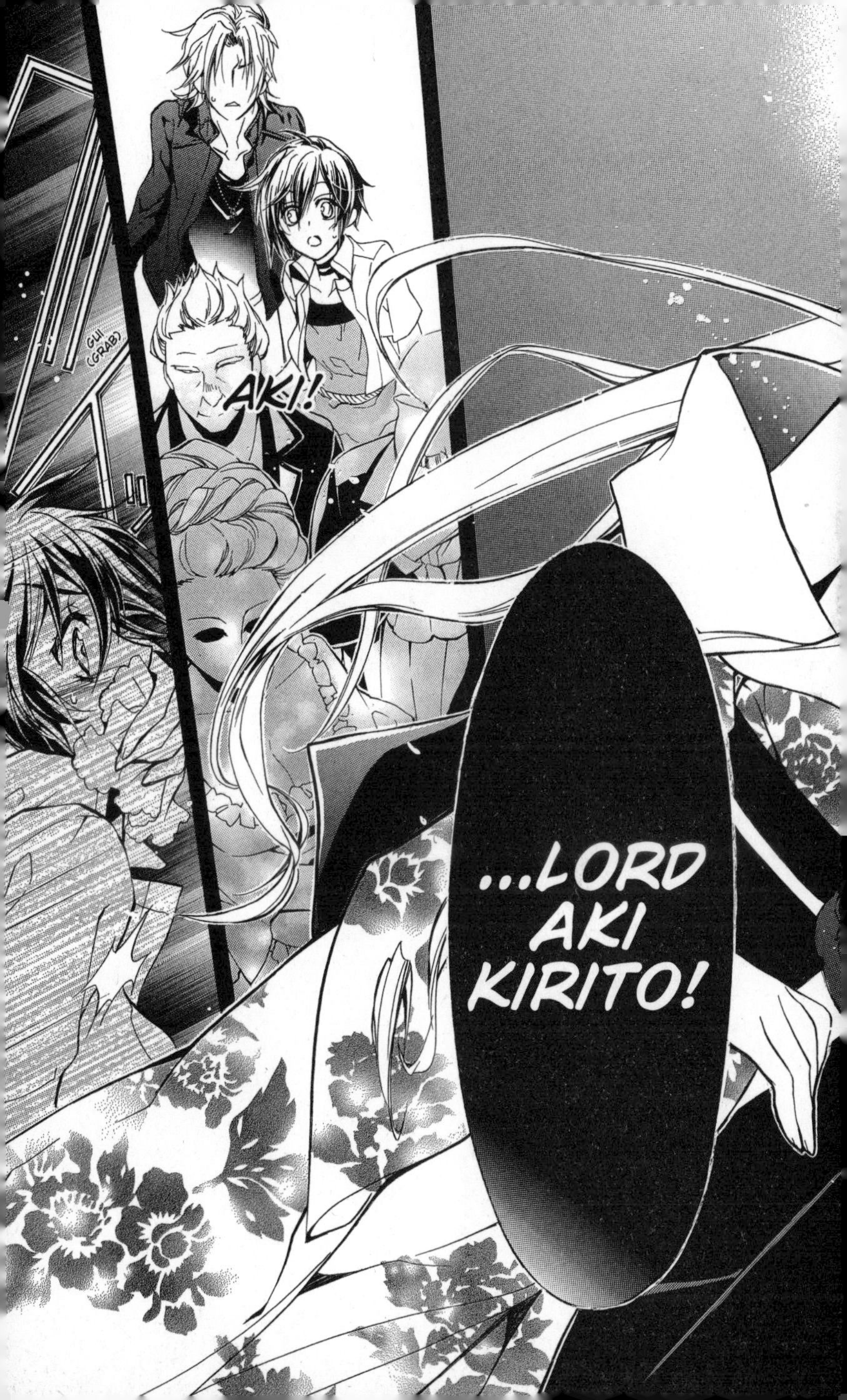
...LORD AKI KIRITO!
AKI!
GUI (GRAB)

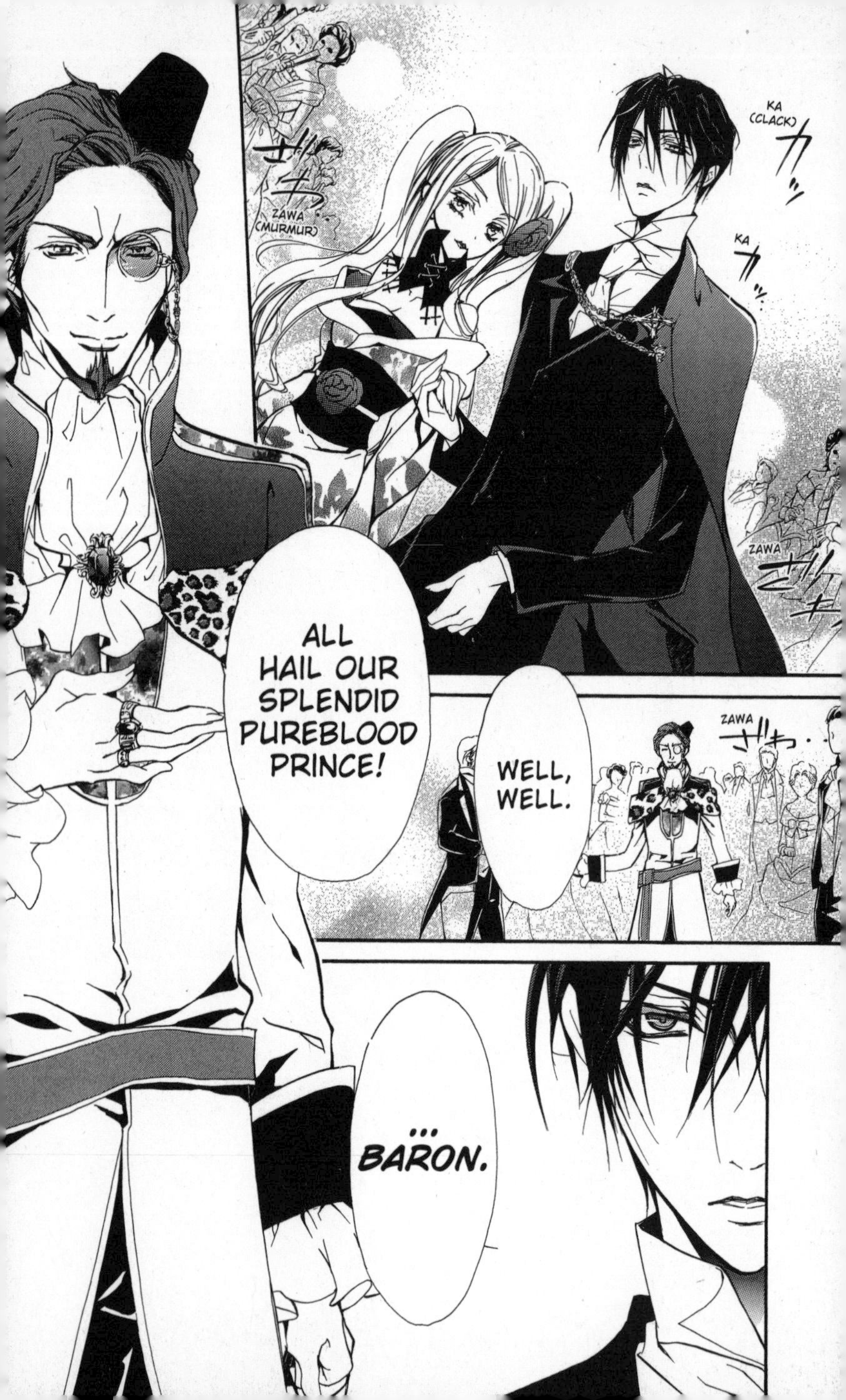
KA (CLACK)
KA
ZAWA
ZAWA (MURMUR)
ALL HAIL OUR SPLENDID PUREBLOOD PRINCE!
ZAWA
WELL, WELL.
... BARON.

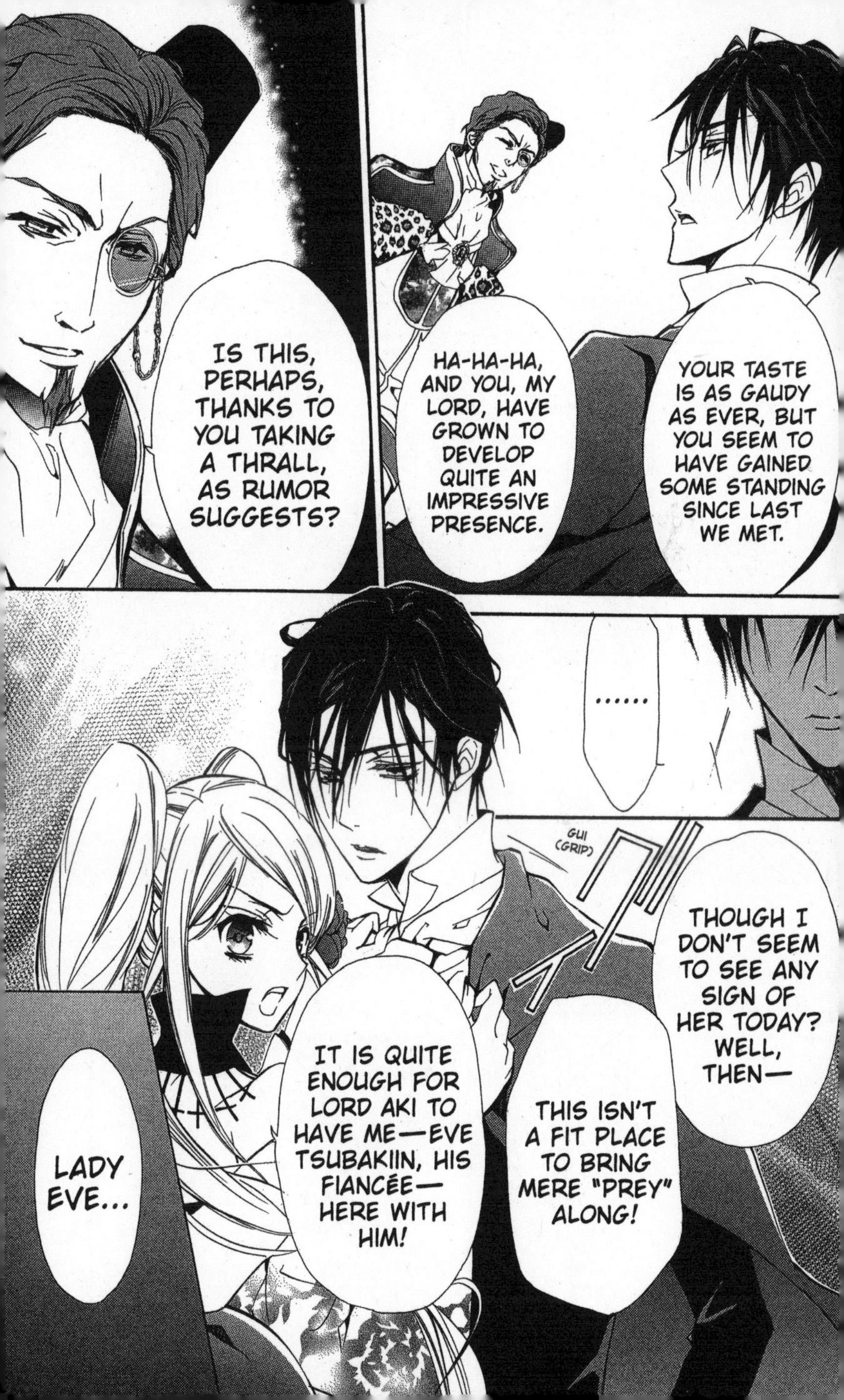
YOUR TASTE IS AS GAUDY AS EVER, BUT YOU SEEM TO HAVE GAINED SOME STANDING SINCE LAST WE MET.
HA-HA-HA, AND YOU, MY LORD, HAVE GROWN TO DEVELOP QUITE AN IMPRESSIVE PRESENCE.
IS THIS, PERHAPS, THANKS TO YOU TAKING A THRALL, AS RUMOR SUGGESTS?
......
GUI (GRIP)
THOUGH I DON'T SEEM TO SEE ANY SIGN OF HER TODAY? WELL, THEN—
THIS ISN'T A FIT PLACE TO BRING MERE "PREY" ALONG!
IT IS QUITE ENOUGH FOR LORD AKI TO HAVE ME—EVE TSUBAKIIN, HIS FIANCÉE—HERE WITH HIM!
LADY EVE...

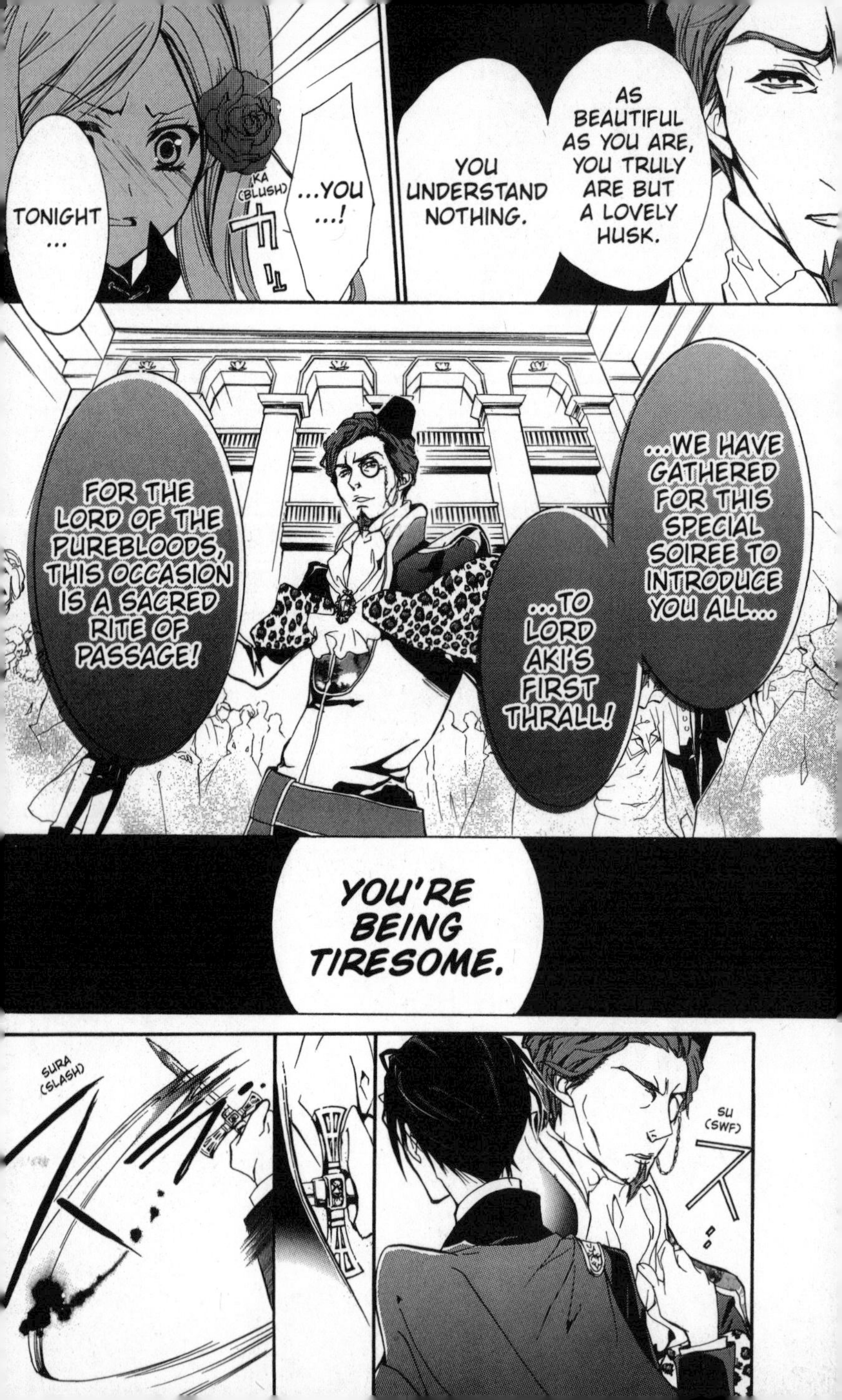
AS BEAUTIFUL AS YOU ARE, YOU TRULY ARE BUT A LOVELY HUSK.
YOU UNDERSTAND NOTHING.
...YOU ...!
KA (BLUSH)
TONIGHT ...
...WE HAVE GATHERED FOR THIS SPECIAL SOIREE TO INTRODUCE YOU ALL...
...TO LORD AKI'S FIRST THRALL!
FOR THE LORD OF THE PUREBLOODS, THIS OCCASION IS A SACRED RITE OF PASSAGE!
YOU'RE BEING TIRESOME.
SU (SWF)
SURA (SLASH)

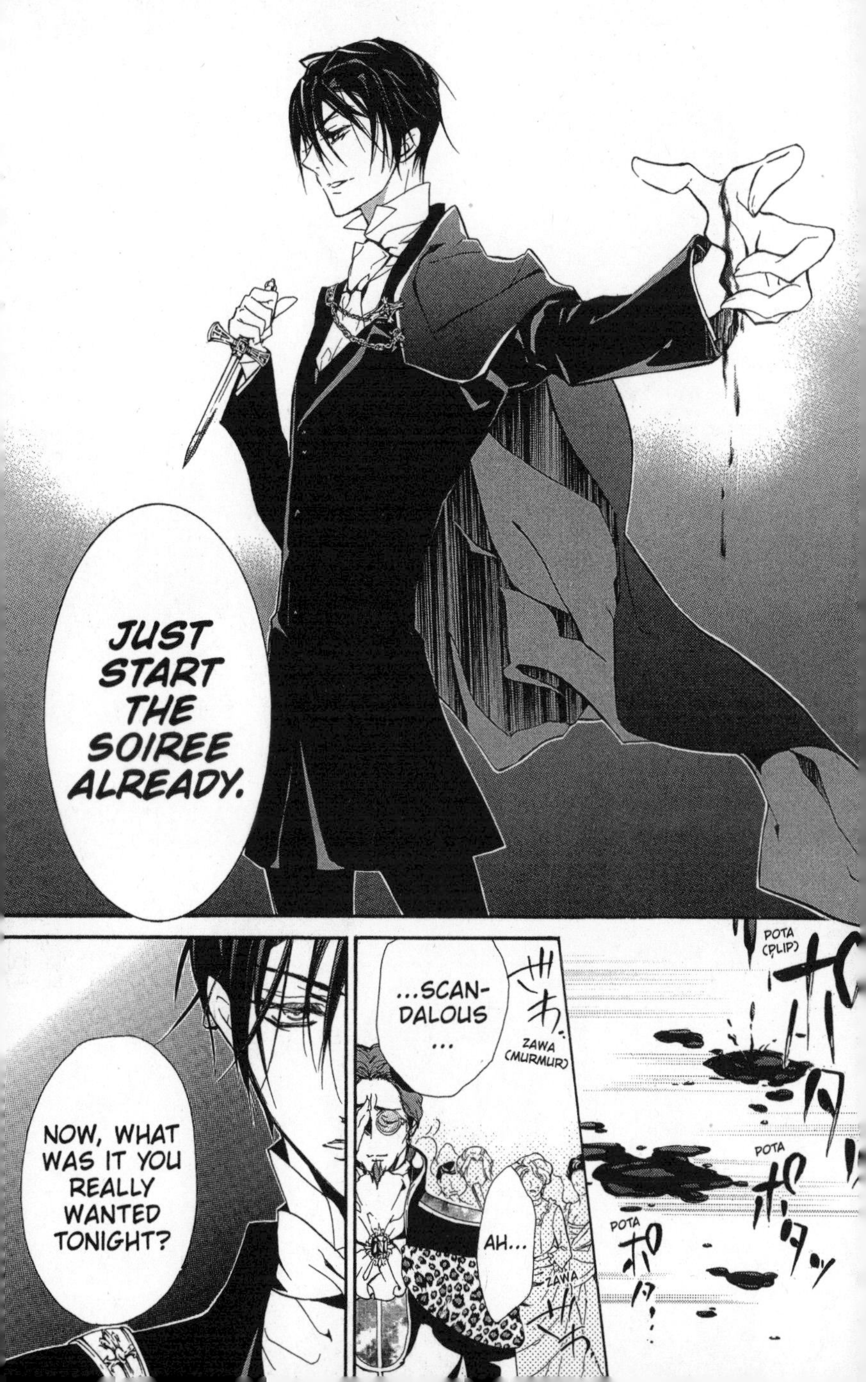
JUST START THE SOIREE ALREADY.
POTA (PLIP)
POTA
POTA
...SCAN-DALOUS...
ZAWA (MURMUR)
AH...
ZAWA
NOW, WHAT WAS IT YOU REALLY WANTED TONIGHT?

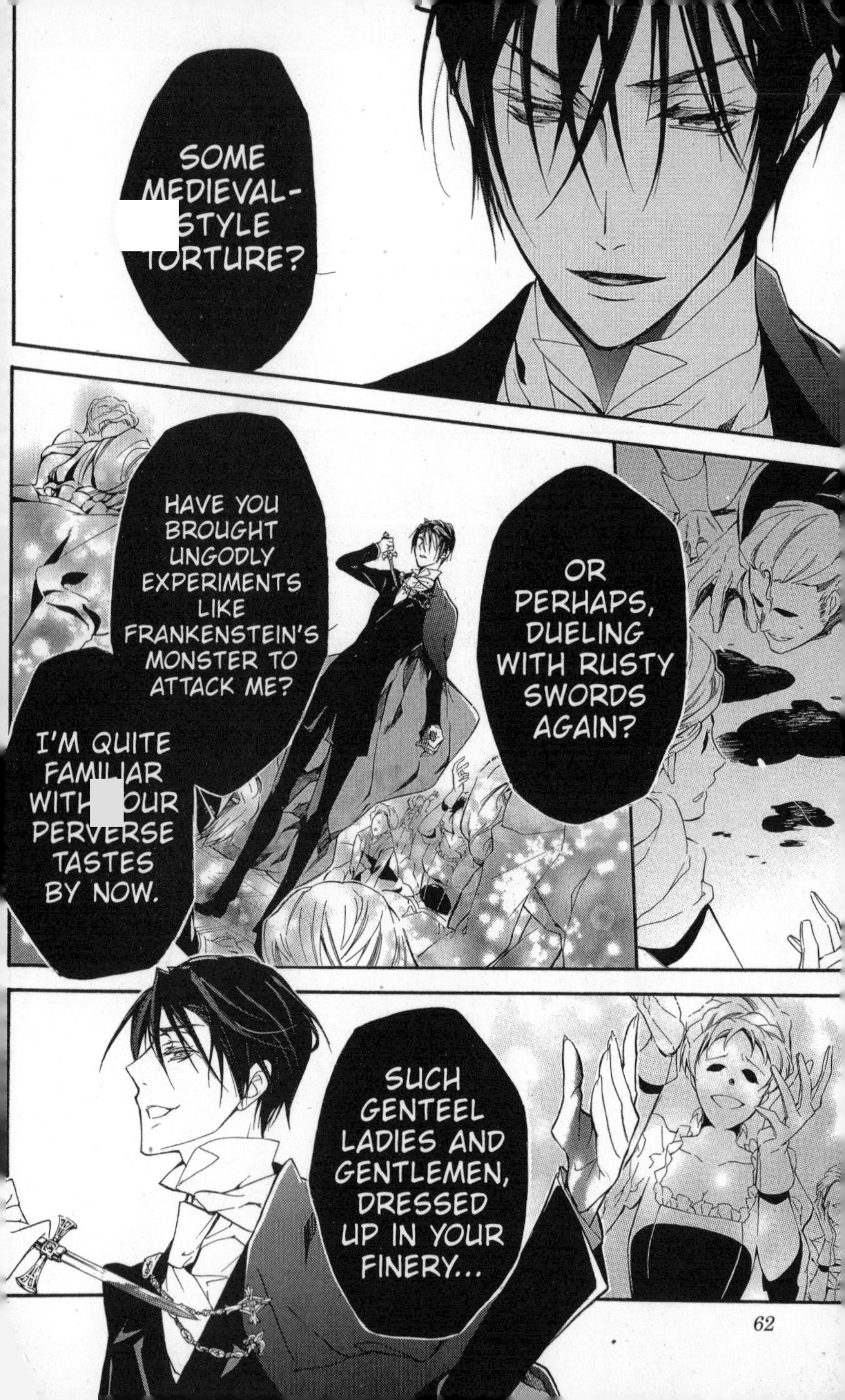
SOME MEDIEVAL-STYLE TORTURE?
OR PERHAPS, DUELING WITH RUSTY SWORDS AGAIN?
HAVE YOU BROUGHT UNGODLY EXPERIMENTS LIKE FRANKENSTEIN'S MONSTER TO ATTACK ME?
I'M QUITE FAMILIAR WITH YOUR PERVERSE TASTES BY NOW.
SUCH GENTEEL LADIES AND GENTLEMEN, DRESSED UP IN YOUR FINERY...

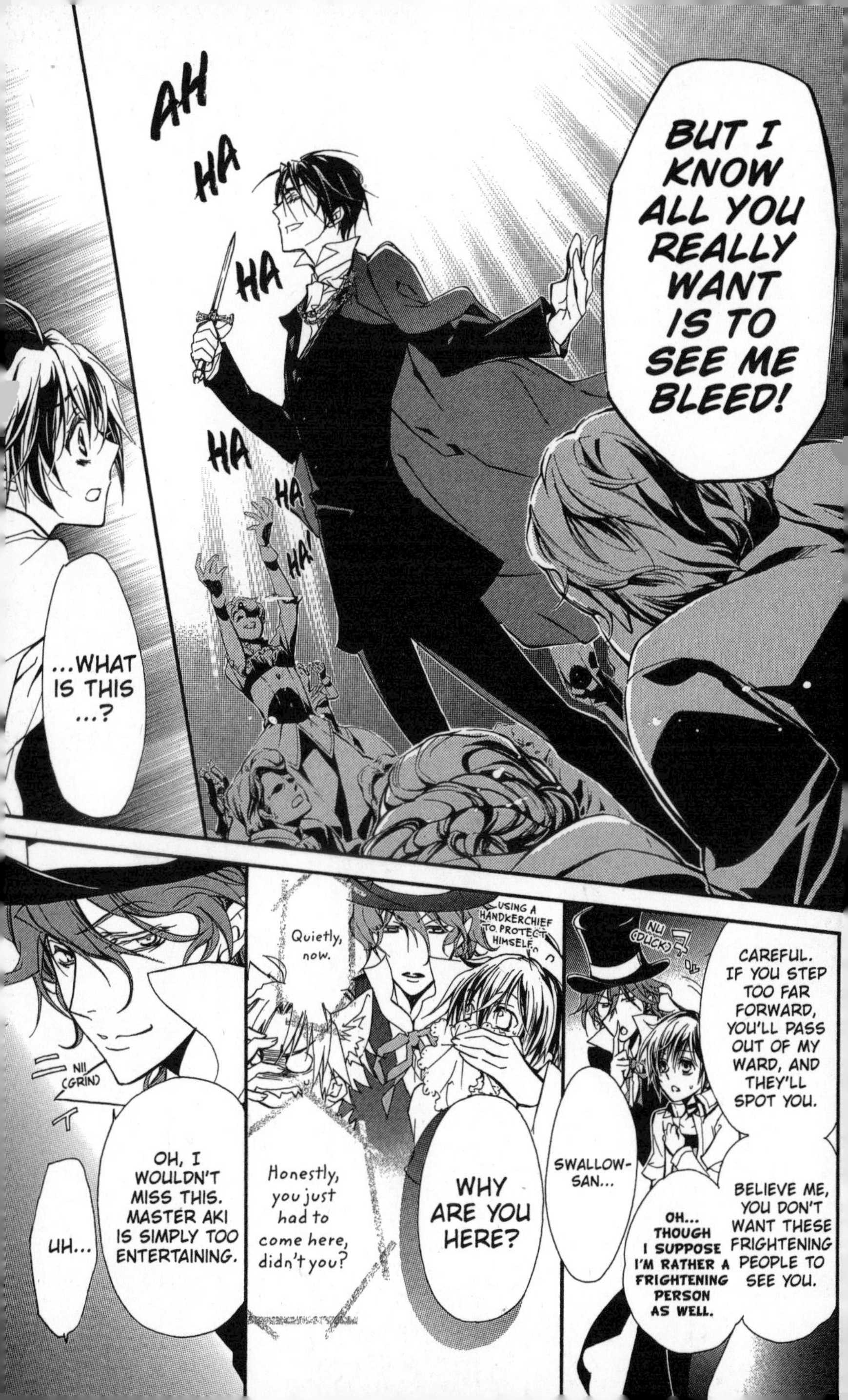
BUT I KNOW ALL YOU REALLY WANT IS TO SEE ME BLEED!
AH HA HA HA HA HA!
...WHAT IS THIS ...?
NU (DUCK)
CAREFUL. IF YOU STEP TOO FAR FORWARD, YOU'LL PASS OUT OF MY WARD, AND THEY'LL SPOT YOU.
SWALLOW-SAN...
BELIEVE ME, YOU DON'T WANT THESE FRIGHTENING PEOPLE TO SEE YOU.
OH... THOUGH I SUPPOSE I'M RATHER A FRIGHTENING PERSON AS WELL.
USING A HANDKERCHIEF TO PROTECT HIMSELF
Quietly, now.
WHY ARE YOU HERE?
Honestly, you just had to come here, didn't you?
NII (GRIND)
OH, I WOULDN'T MISS THIS. MASTER AKI IS SIMPLY TOO ENTERTAINING.
UH...

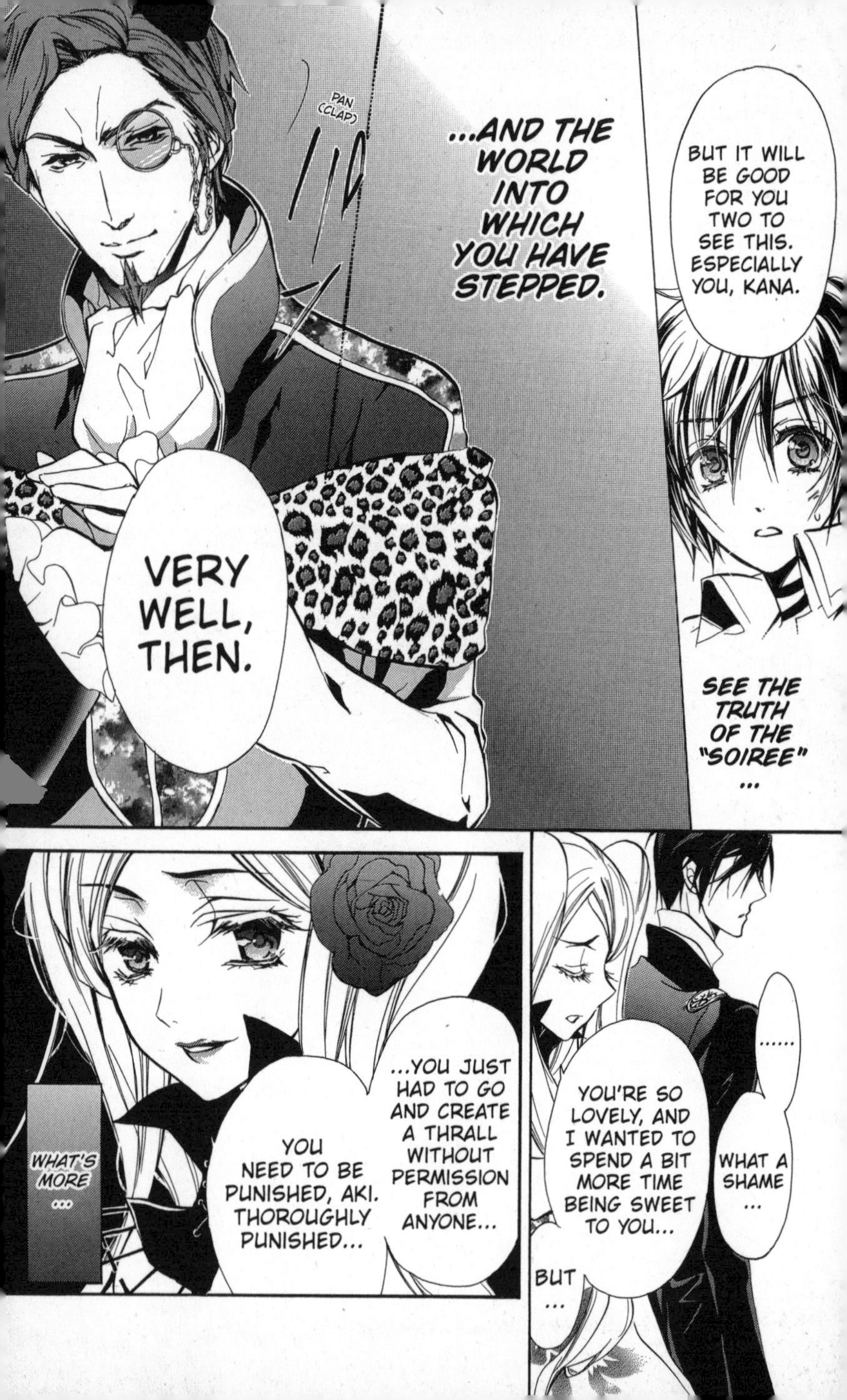
BUT IT WILL BE GOOD FOR YOU TWO TO SEE THIS. ESPECIALLY YOU, KANA.
SEE THE TRUTH OF THE "SOIREE"...
...AND THE WORLD INTO WHICH YOU HAVE STEPPED.
PAN (CLAP)
VERY WELL, THEN.
......
WHAT A SHAME...
YOU'RE SO LOVELY, AND I WANTED TO SPEND A BIT MORE TIME BEING SWEET TO YOU...
BUT...
WHAT'S MORE...
...YOU JUST HAD TO GO AND CREATE A THRALL WITHOUT PERMISSION FROM ANYONE...
YOU NEED TO BE PUNISHED, AKI. THOROUGHLY PUNISHED...

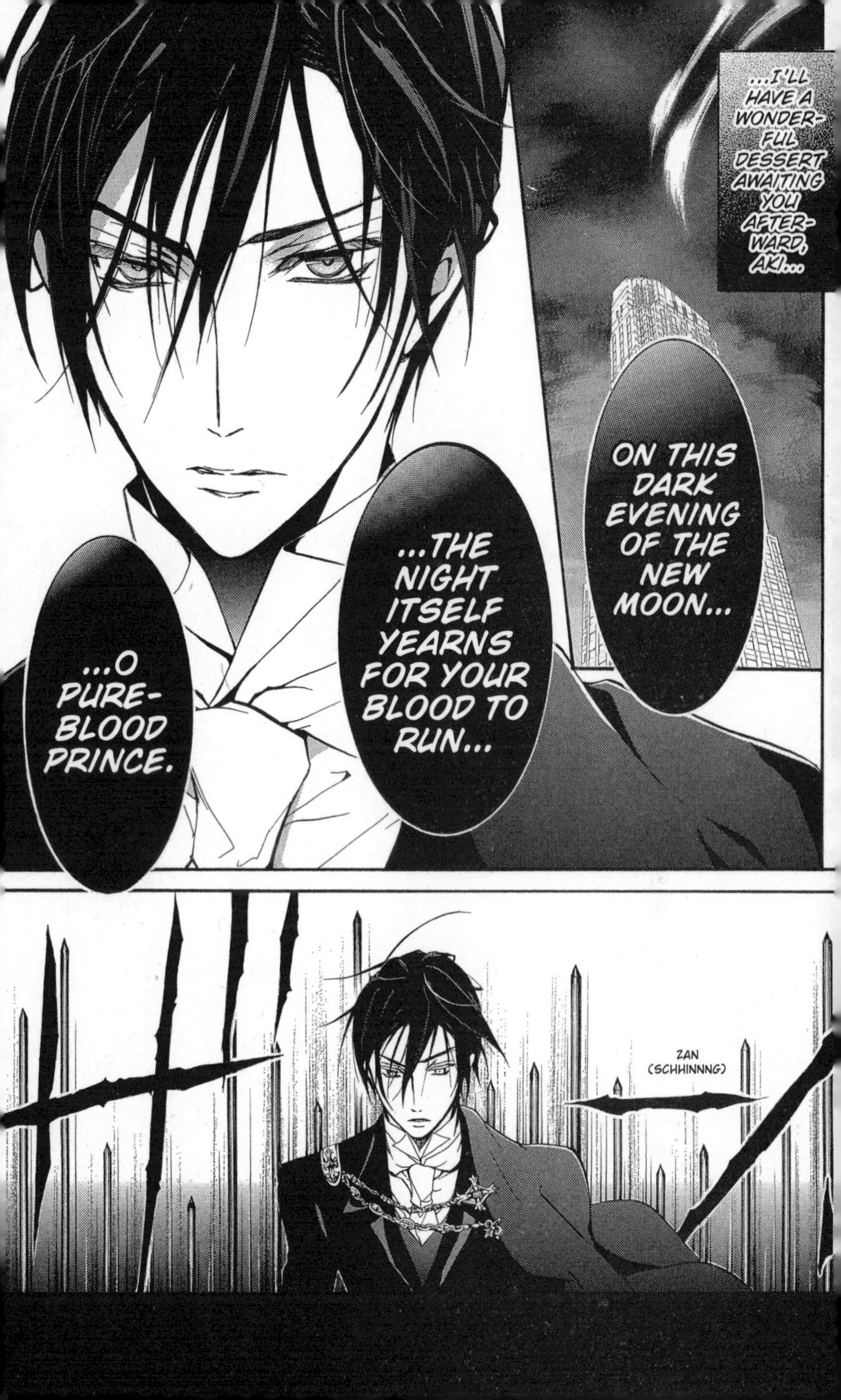
...I'LL HAVE A WONDER-FUL DESSERT AWAITING YOU AFTER-WARD, AKI...
ON THIS DARK EVENING OF THE NEW MOON...
...THE NIGHT ITSELF YEARNS FOR YOUR BLOOD TO RUN...
...O PURE-BLOOD PRINCE.
ZAN (SCHHINNNG)

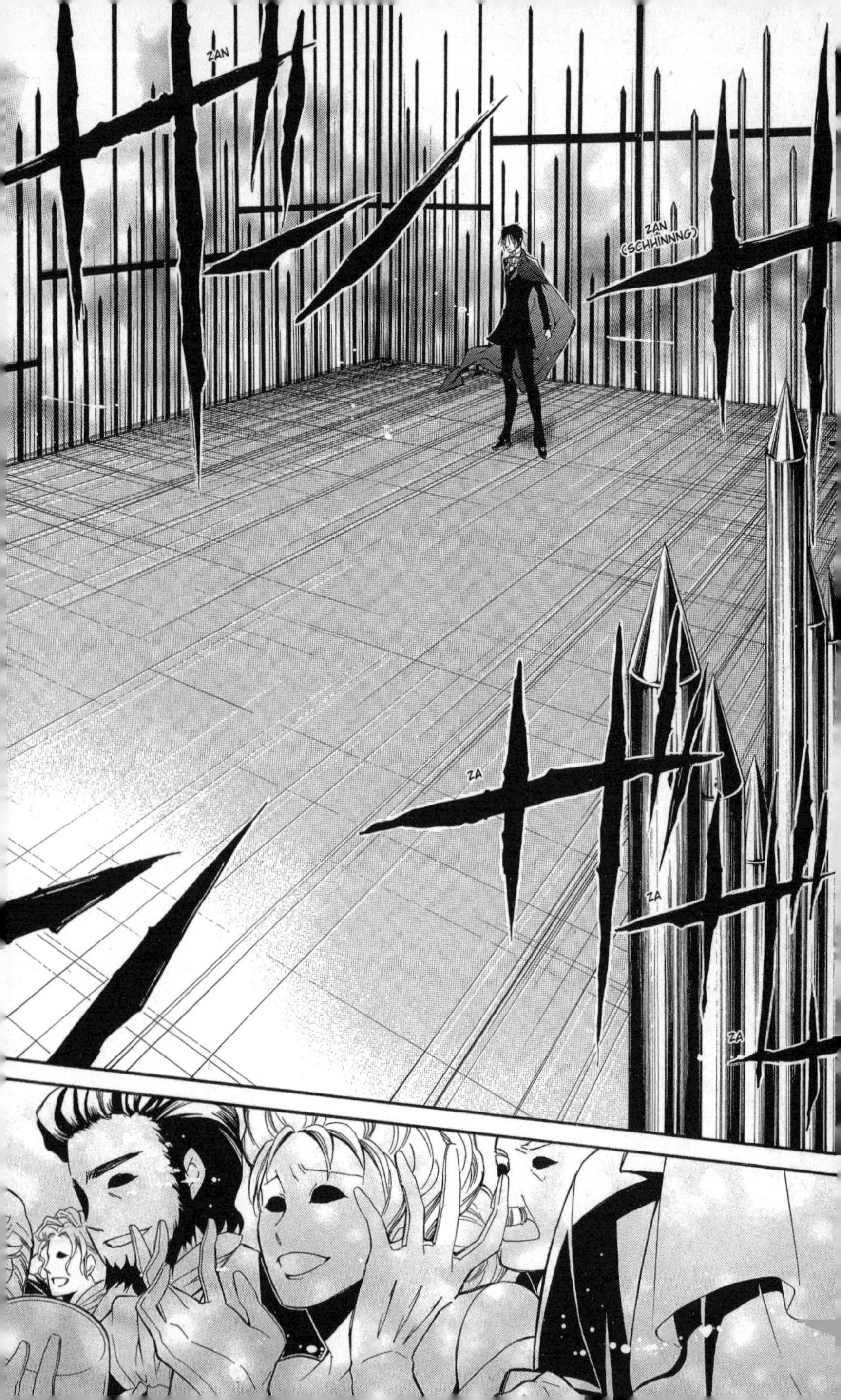
ZAN (SCHHINNNG)
ZAN
ZA
ZA
ZA

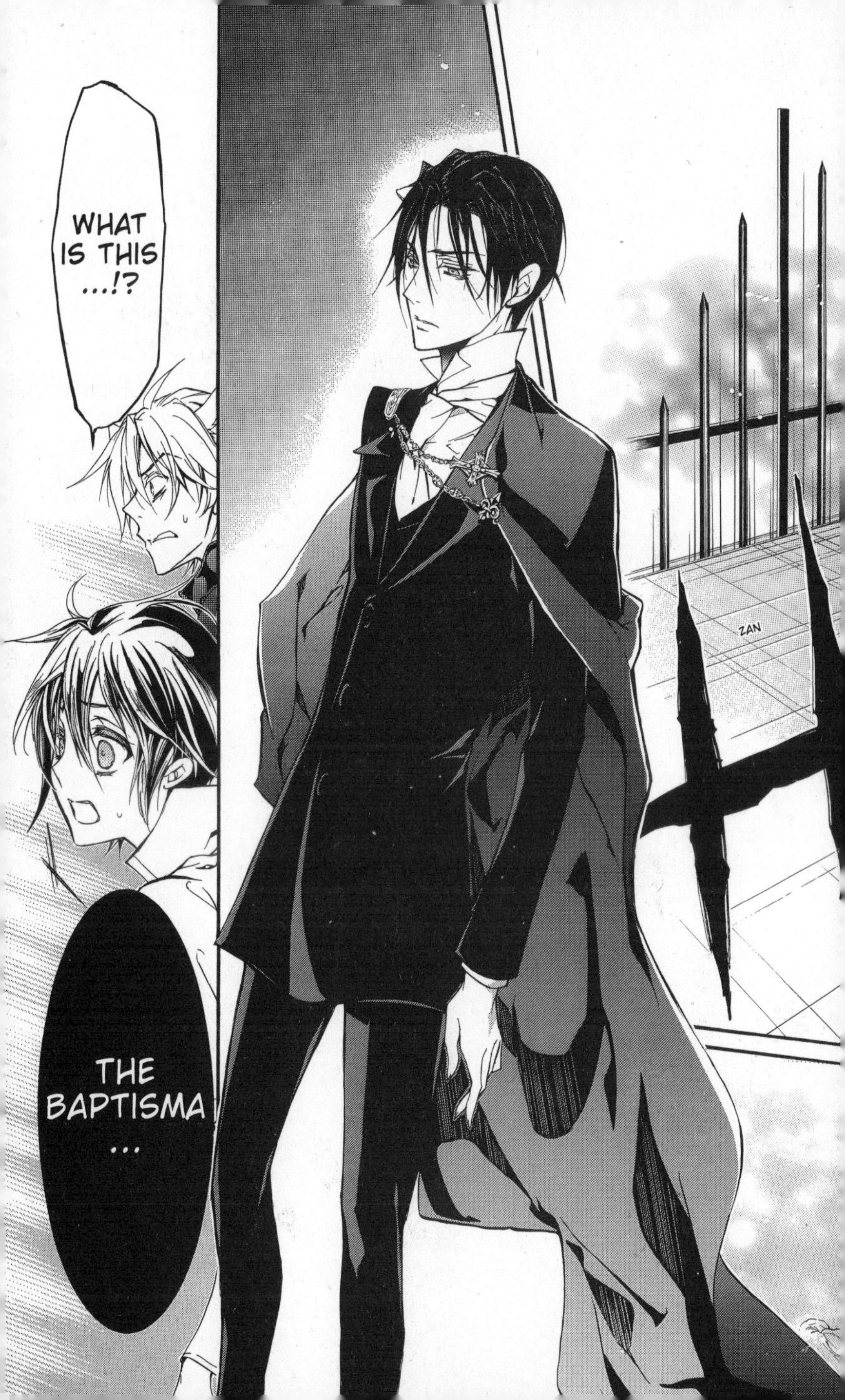
ZAN
WHAT IS THIS ...!?
THE BAPTISMA ...

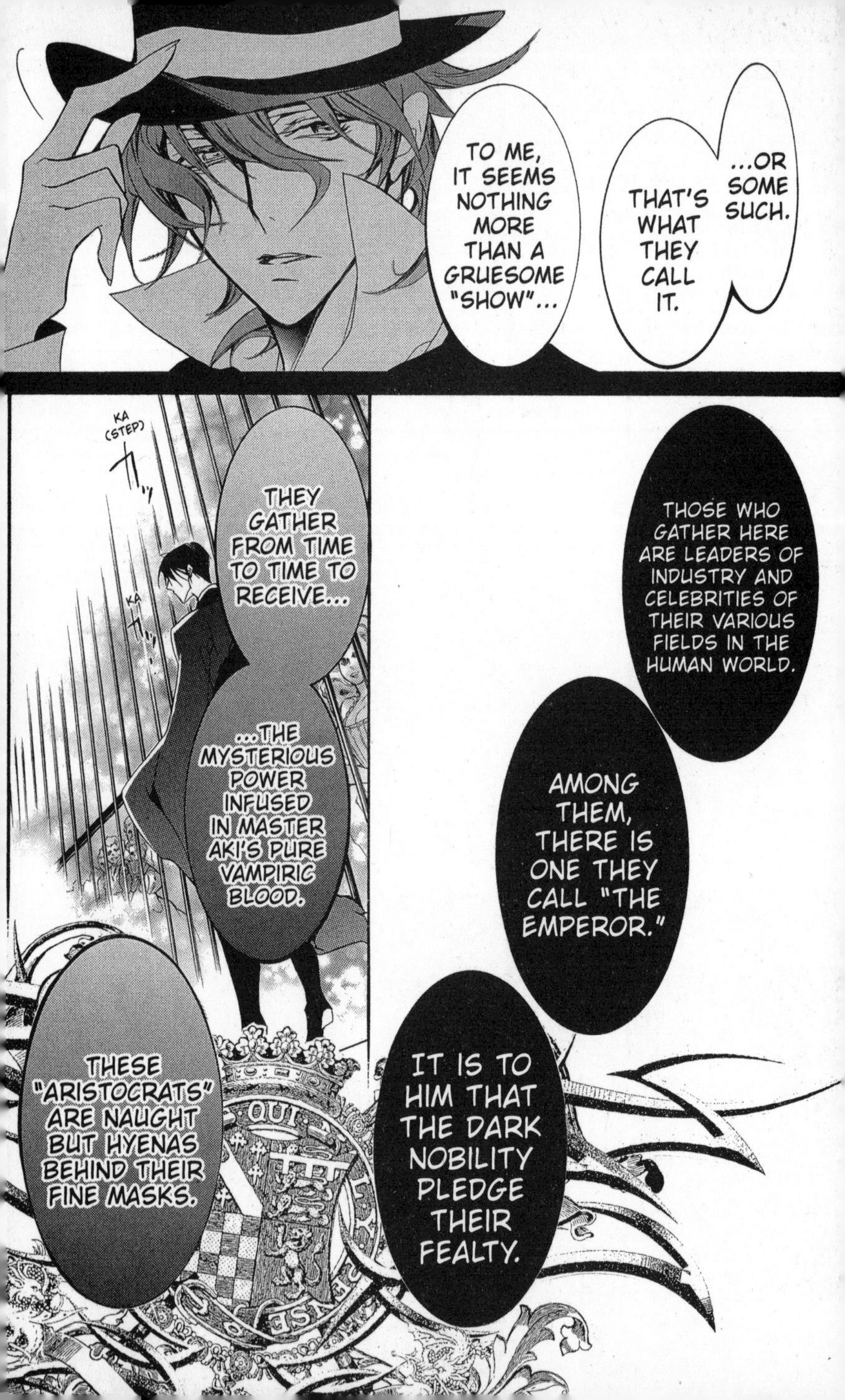
TO ME, IT SEEMS NOTHING MORE THAN A GRUESOME "SHOW"...
THAT'S WHAT THEY CALL IT.
...OR SOME SUCH.
THOSE WHO GATHER HERE ARE LEADERS OF INDUSTRY AND CELEBRITIES OF THEIR VARIOUS FIELDS IN THE HUMAN WORLD.
AMONG THEM, THERE IS ONE THEY CALL "THE EMPEROR."
IT IS TO HIM THAT THE DARK NOBILITY PLEDGE THEIR FEALTY.
KA (STEP)
KA
THEY GATHER FROM TIME TO TIME TO RECEIVE...
...THE MYSTERIOUS POWER INFUSED IN MASTER AKI'S PURE VAMPIRIC BLOOD.
THESE "ARISTOCRATS" ARE NAUGHT BUT HYENAS BEHIND THEIR FINE MASKS.

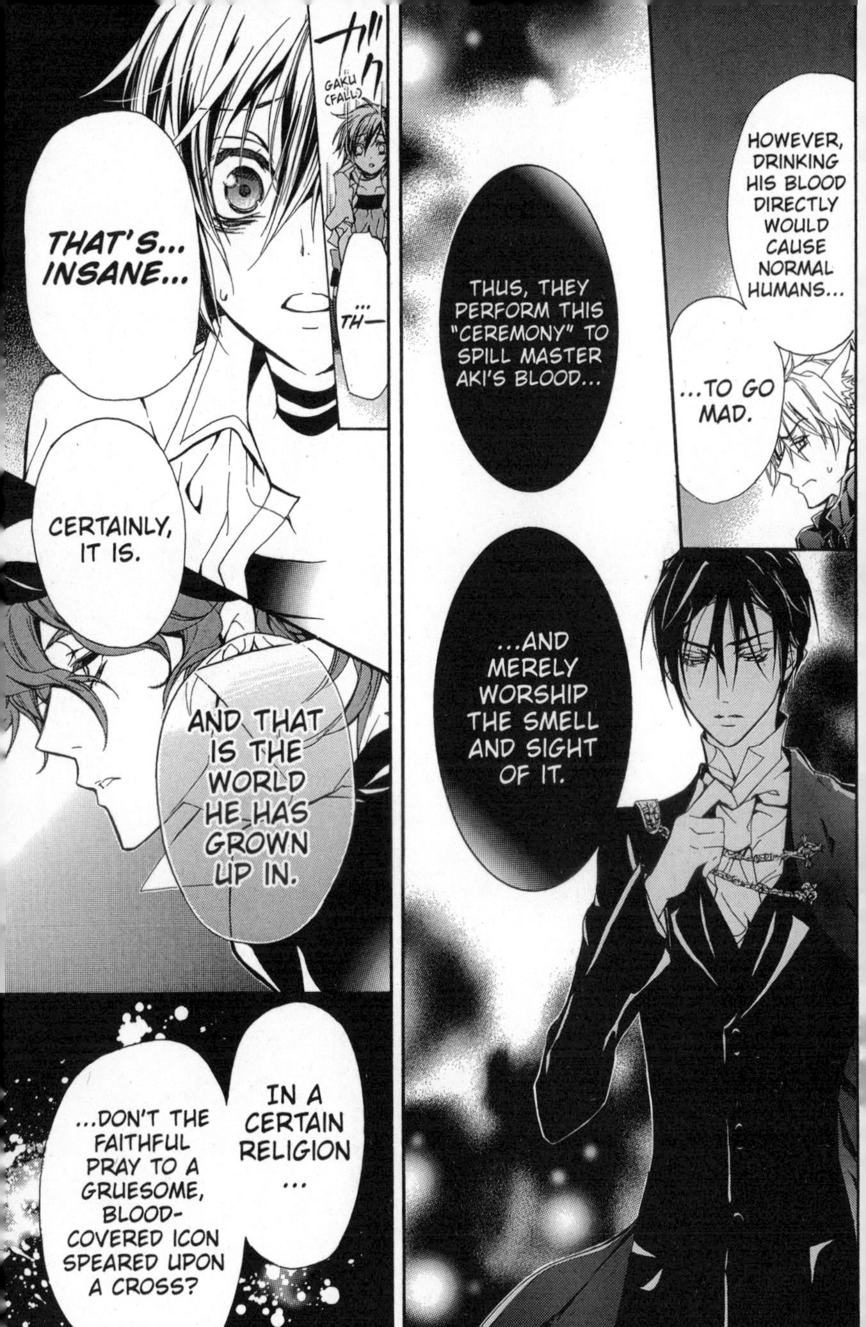
HOWEVER, DRINKING HIS BLOOD DIRECTLY WOULD CAUSE NORMAL HUMANS...
...TO GO MAD.
THUS, THEY PERFORM THIS "CEREMONY" TO SPILL MASTER AKI'S BLOOD...
...AND MERELY WORSHIP THE SMELL AND SIGHT OF IT.
GAKU (FALL)
...TH—
THAT'S... INSANE...
CERTAINLY, IT IS.
AND THAT IS THE WORLD HE HAS GROWN UP IN.
IN A CERTAIN RELIGION...
...DON'T THE FAITHFUL PRAY TO A GRUESOME, BLOOD-COVERED ICON SPEARED UPON A CROSS?

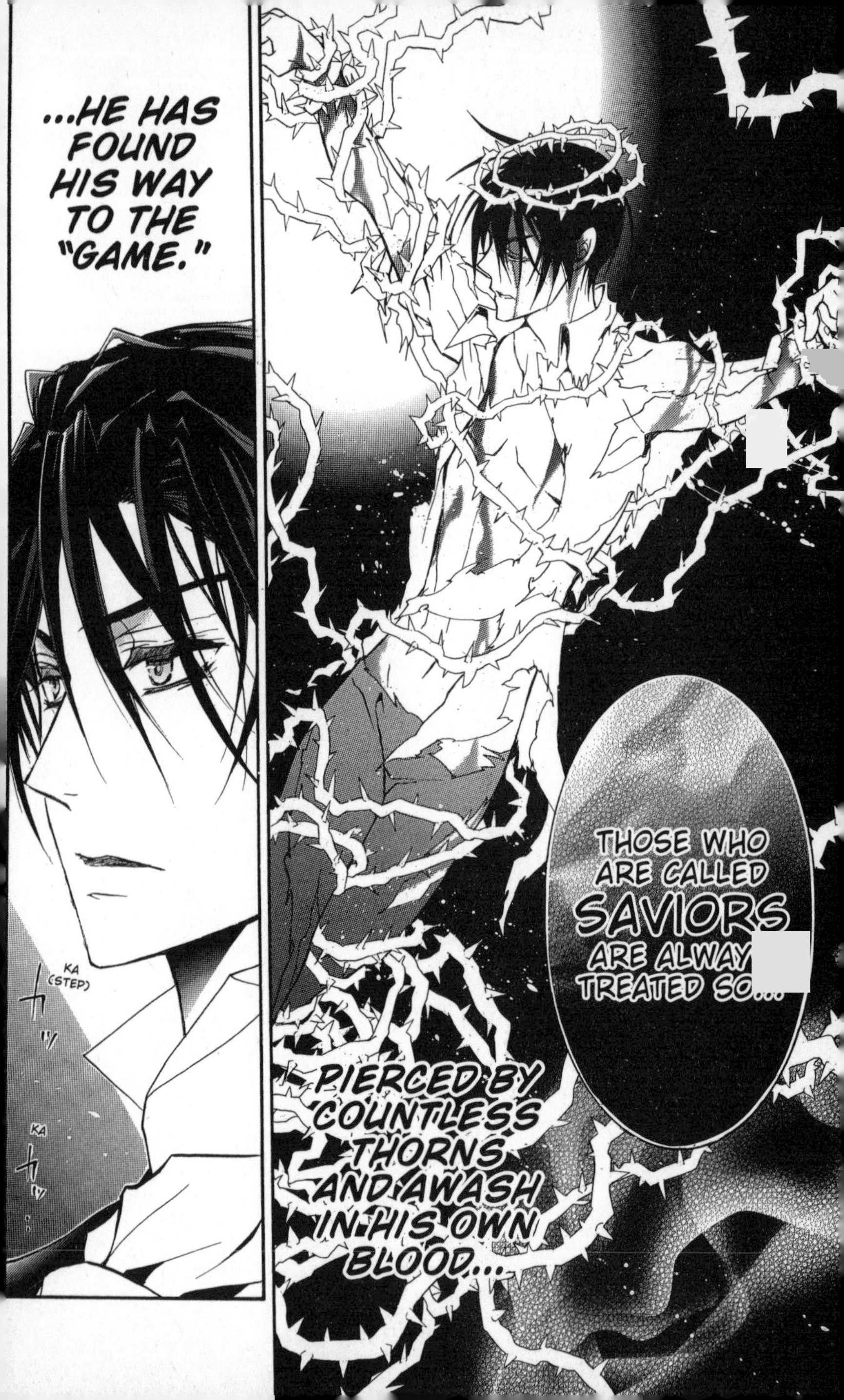
THOSE WHO ARE CALLED SAVIORS ARE ALWAY TREATED SO...
PIERCED BY COUNTLESS THORNS AND AWASH IN HIS OWN BLOOD...
...HE HAS FOUND HIS WAY TO THE "GAME."
KA (STEP)
KA

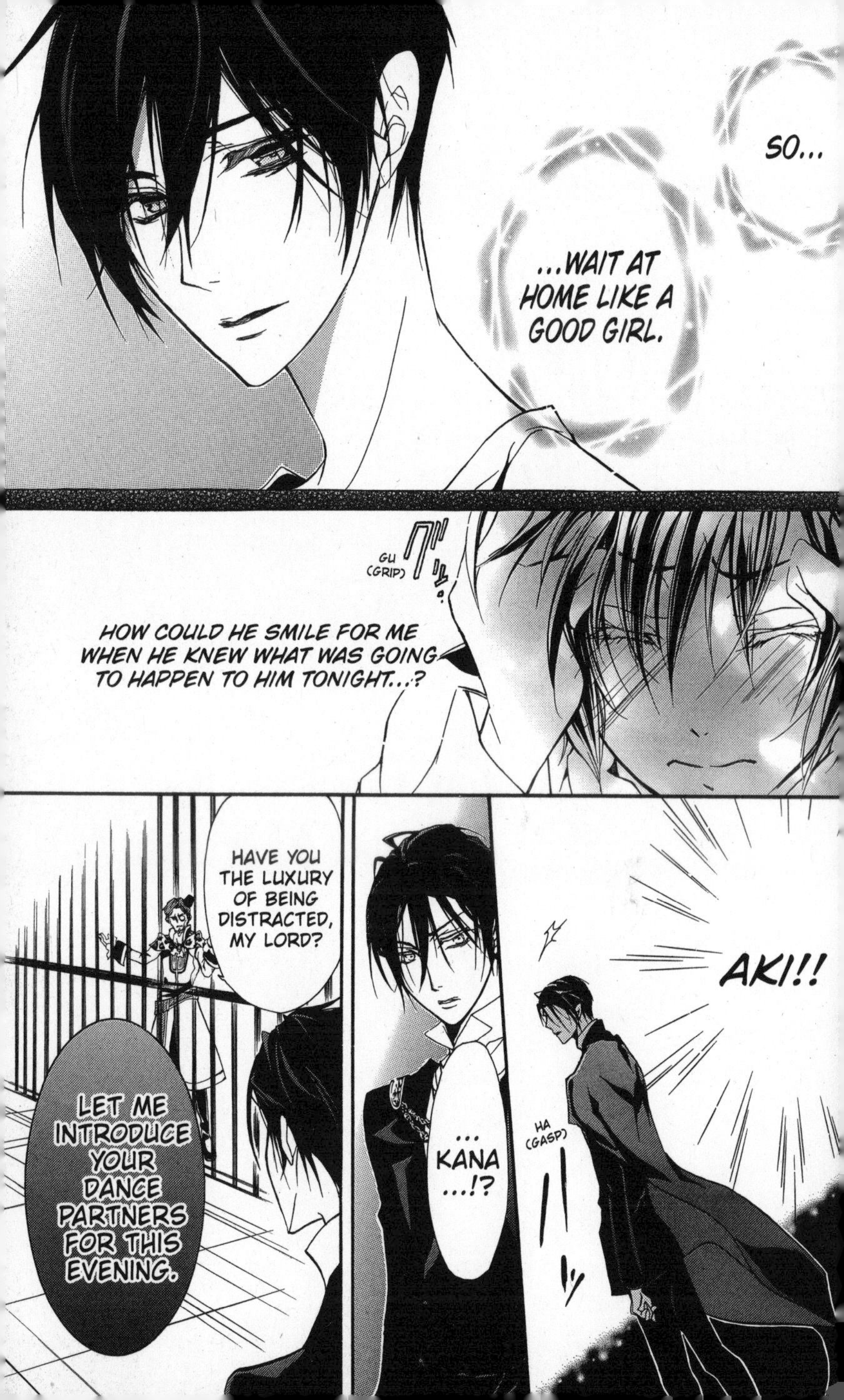
SO...
...WAIT AT HOME LIKE A GOOD GIRL.
GU (GRIP)
HOW COULD HE SMILE FOR ME WHEN HE KNEW WHAT WAS GOING TO HAPPEN TO HIM TONIGHT...?
AKI!!
HA (GASP)
...KANA...!?
HAVE YOU THE LUXURY OF BEING DISTRACTED, MY LORD?
LET ME INTRODUCE YOUR DANCE PARTNERS FOR THIS EVENING.

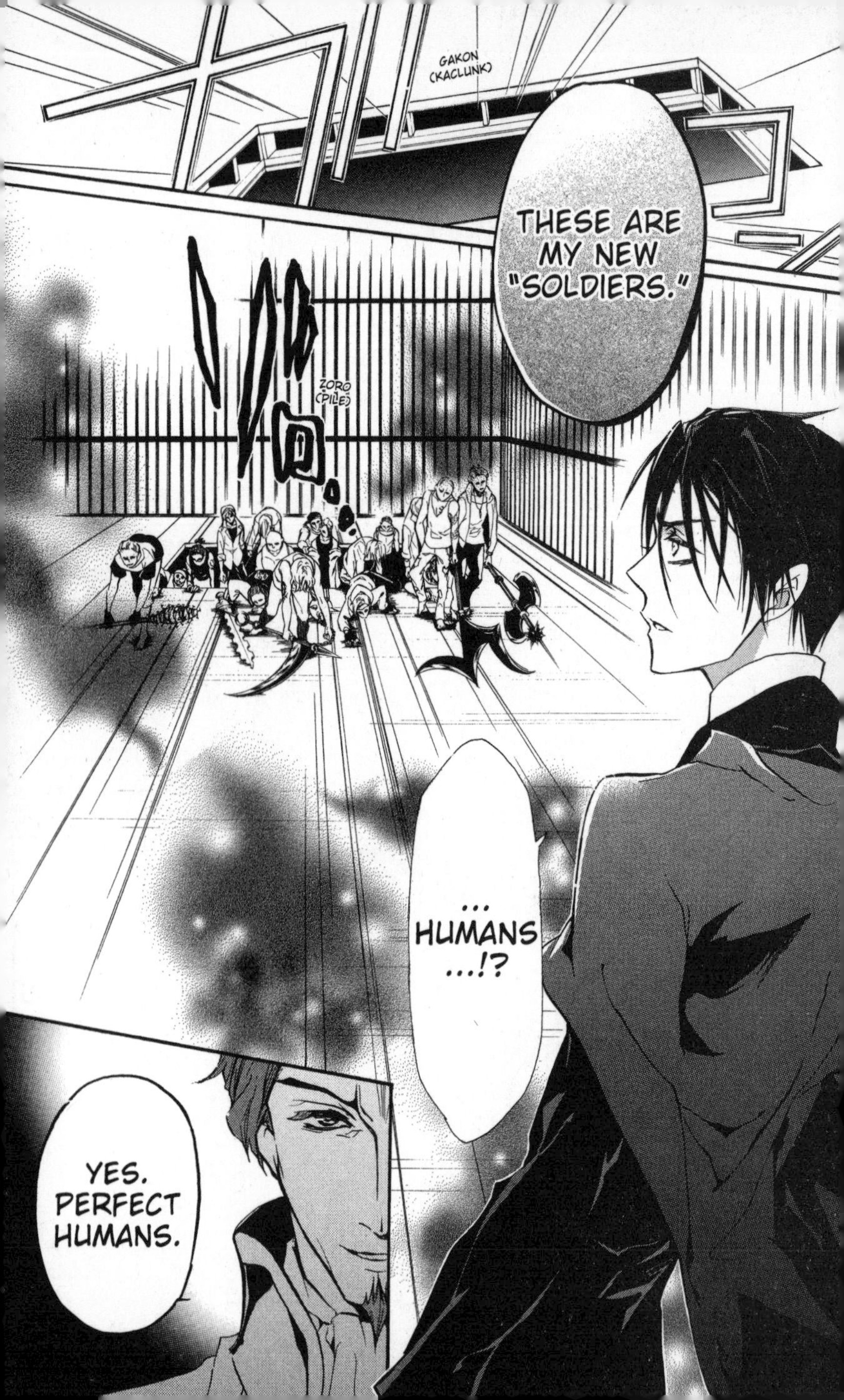
GAKON (KACLUNK)
THESE ARE MY NEW "SOLDIERS."
ZORO (PILE)
... HUMANS ...!?
YES. PERFECT HUMANS.

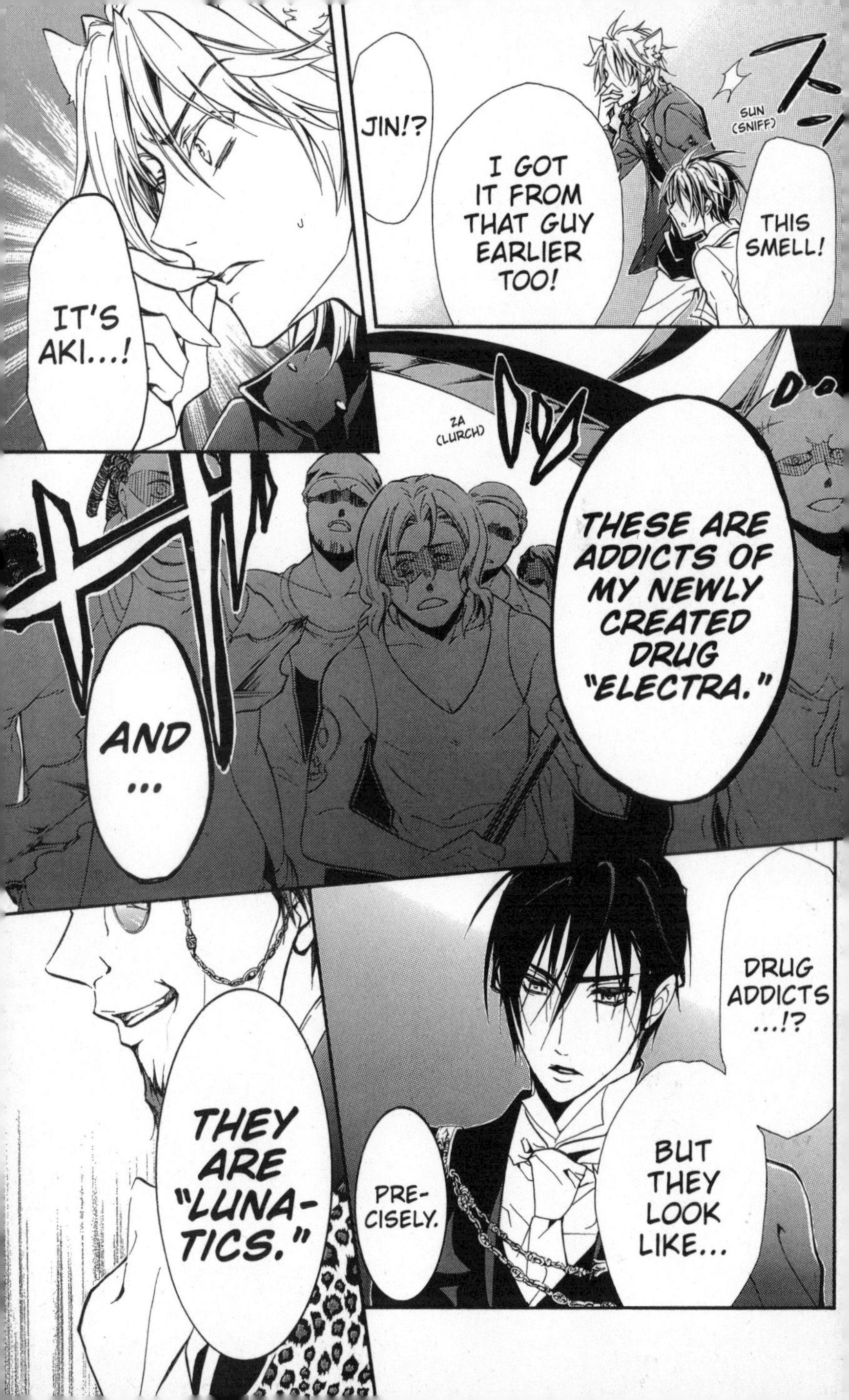
SUN (SNIFF)
THIS SMELL!
I GOT IT FROM THAT GUY EARLIER TOO!
JIN!?
IT'S AKI...!
ZA (LURCH)
THESE ARE ADDICTS OF MY NEWLY CREATED DRUG "ELECTRA."
AND ...
DRUG ADDICTS ...!?
BUT THEY LOOK LIKE...
PRE-CISELY.
THEY ARE "LUNA-TICS."

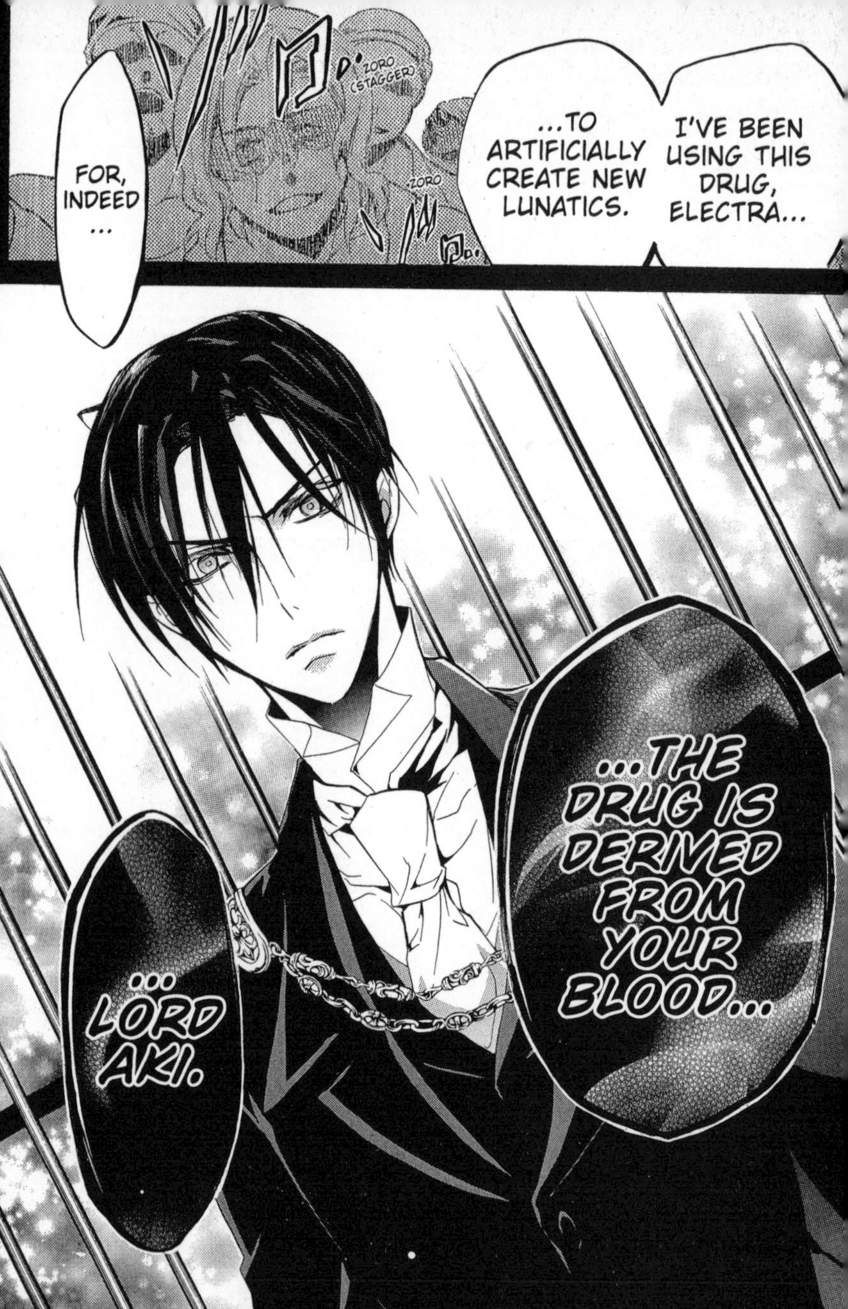
I'VE BEEN USING THIS DRUG, ELECTRA...
...TO ARTIFICIALLY CREATE NEW LUNATICS.
ZORO (STAGGER)
ZORO
FOR, INDEED ...
...THE DRUG IS DERIVED FROM YOUR BLOOD...
...LORD AKI.

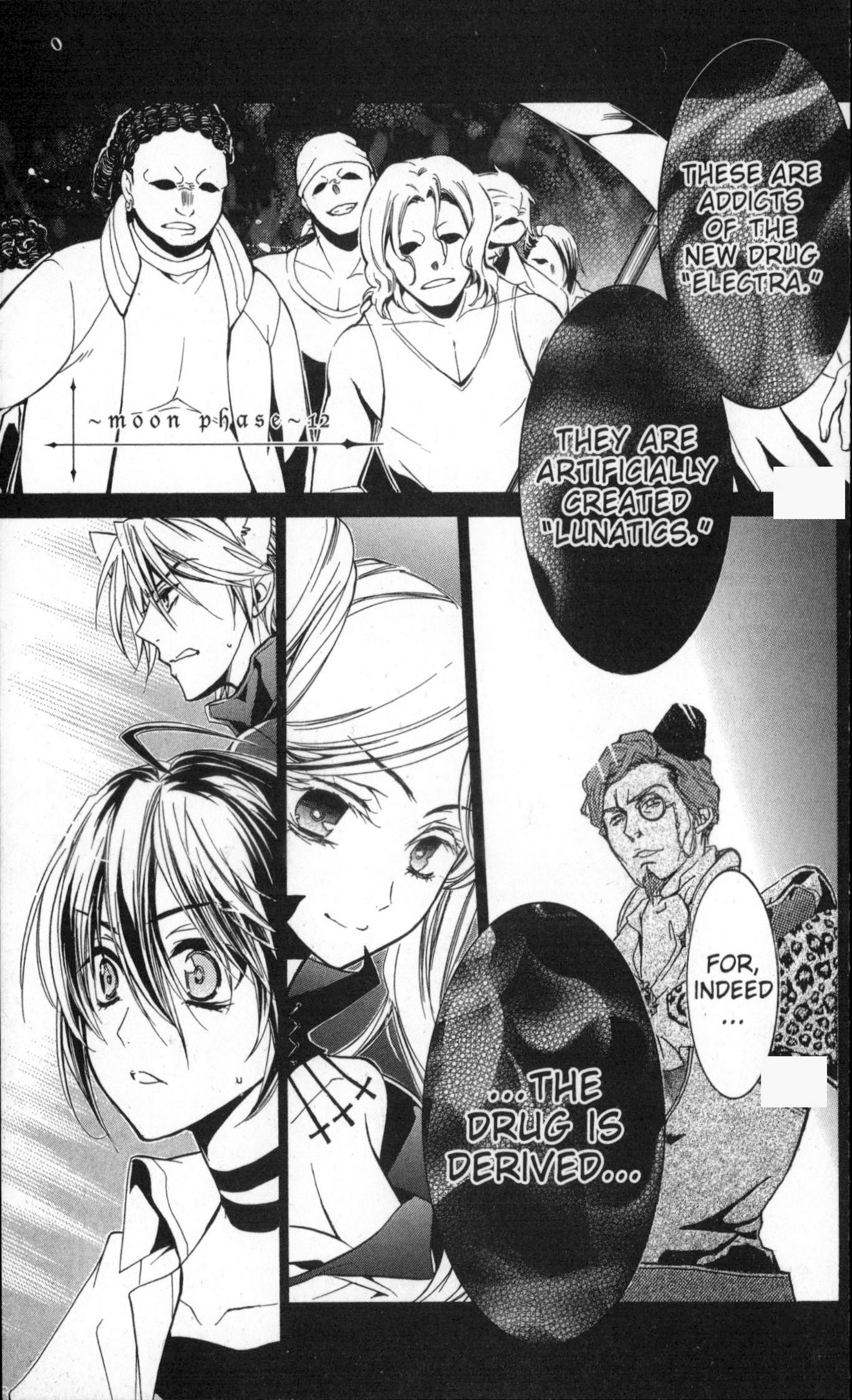
THESE ARE ADDICTS OF THE NEW DRUG "ELECTRA."
~moon phase~ 12
THEY ARE ARTIFICIALLY CREATED "LUNATICS."
FOR, INDEED ...
...THE DRUG IS DERIVED...

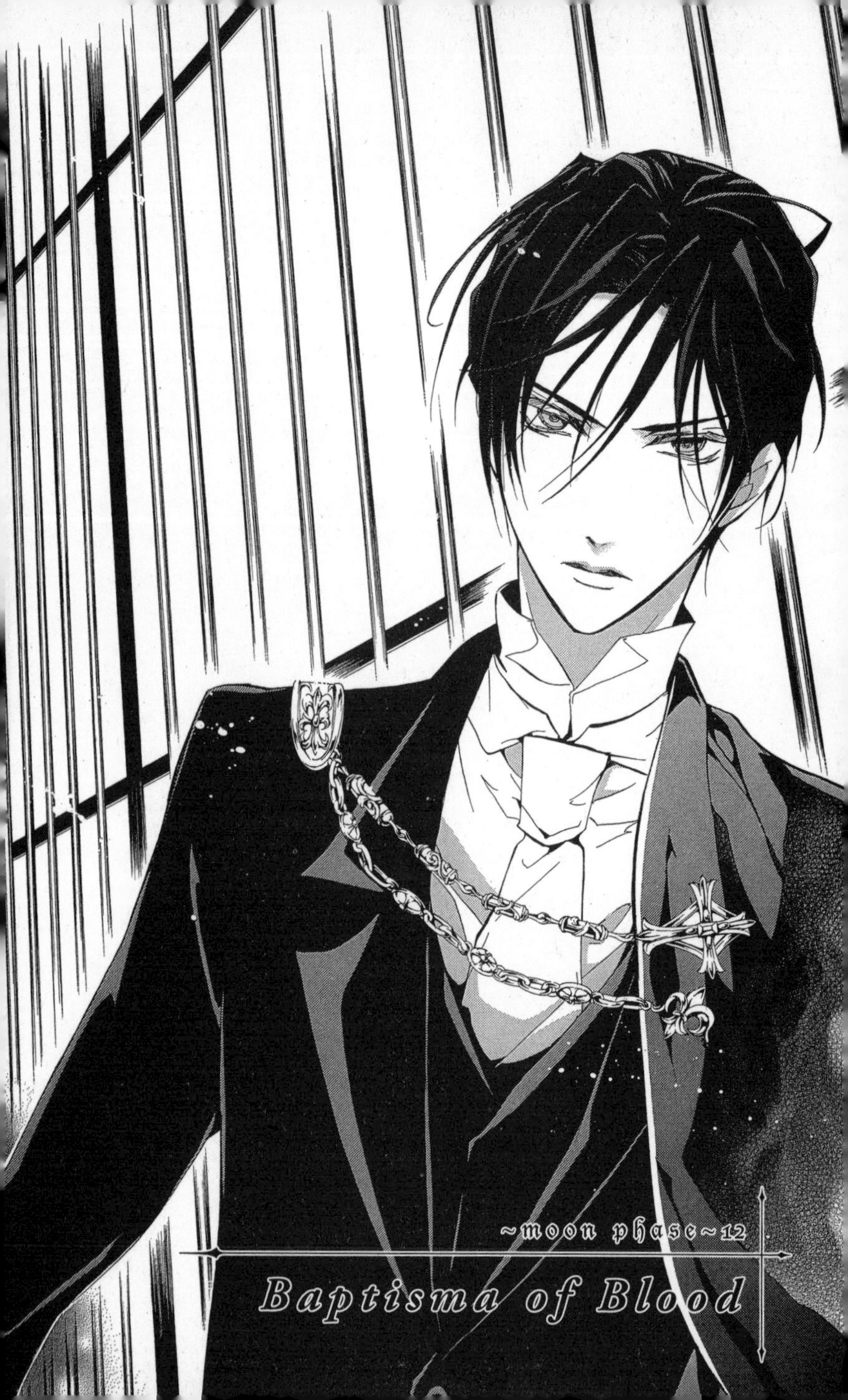
~moon phase~12
Baptisma of Blood

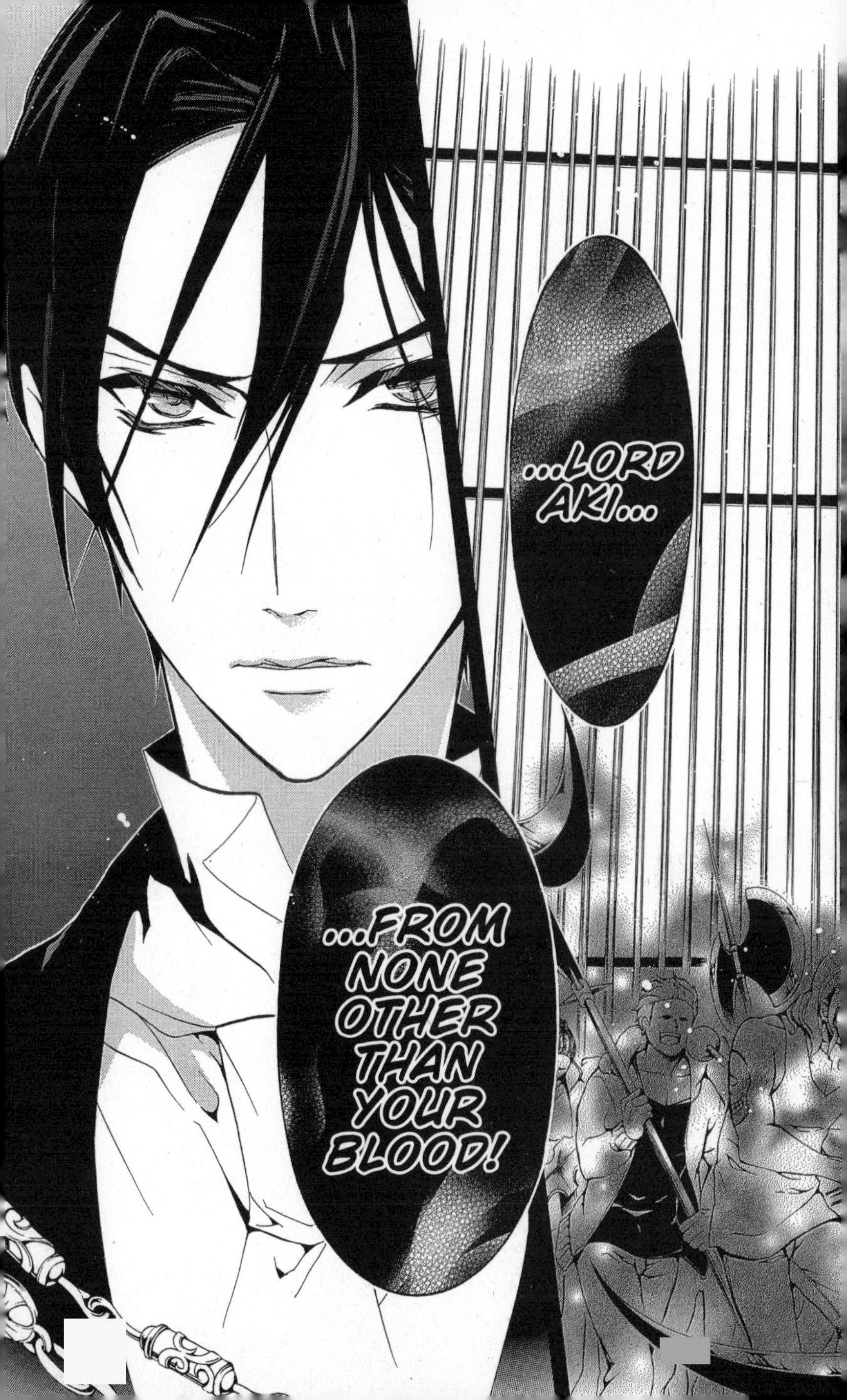
...LORD AKI...
...FROM NONE OTHER THAN YOUR BLOOD!

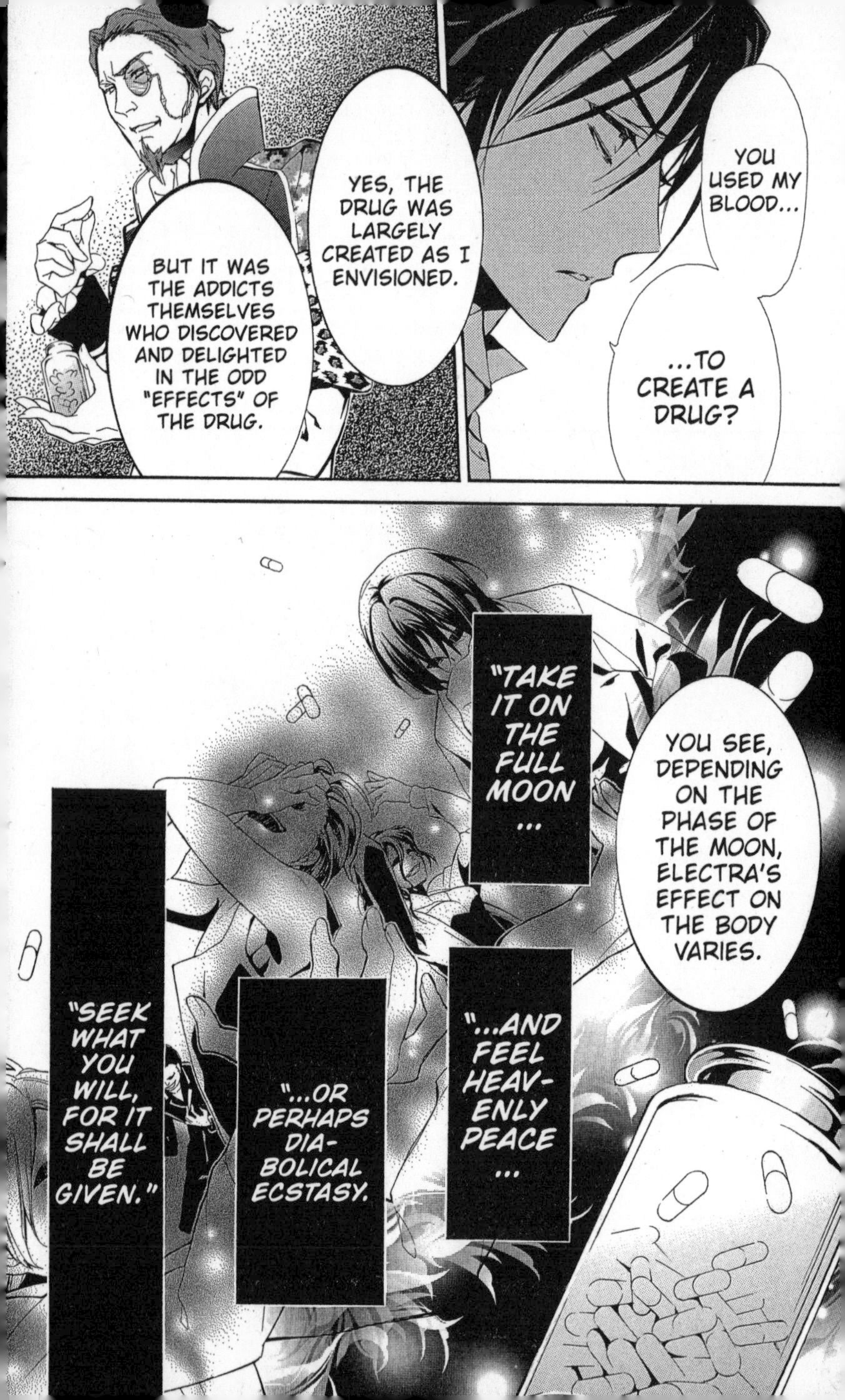
YOU USED MY BLOOD...
...TO CREATE A DRUG?
YES, THE DRUG WAS LARGELY CREATED AS I ENVISIONED.
BUT IT WAS THE ADDICTS THEMSELVES WHO DISCOVERED AND DELIGHTED IN THE ODD "EFFECTS" OF THE DRUG.
YOU SEE, DEPENDING ON THE PHASE OF THE MOON, ELECTRA'S EFFECT ON THE BODY VARIES.
"TAKE IT ON THE FULL MOON...
"...AND FEEL HEAVENLY PEACE...
"...OR PERHAPS DIABOLICAL ECSTASY.
"SEEK WHAT YOU WILL, FOR IT SHALL BE GIVEN."

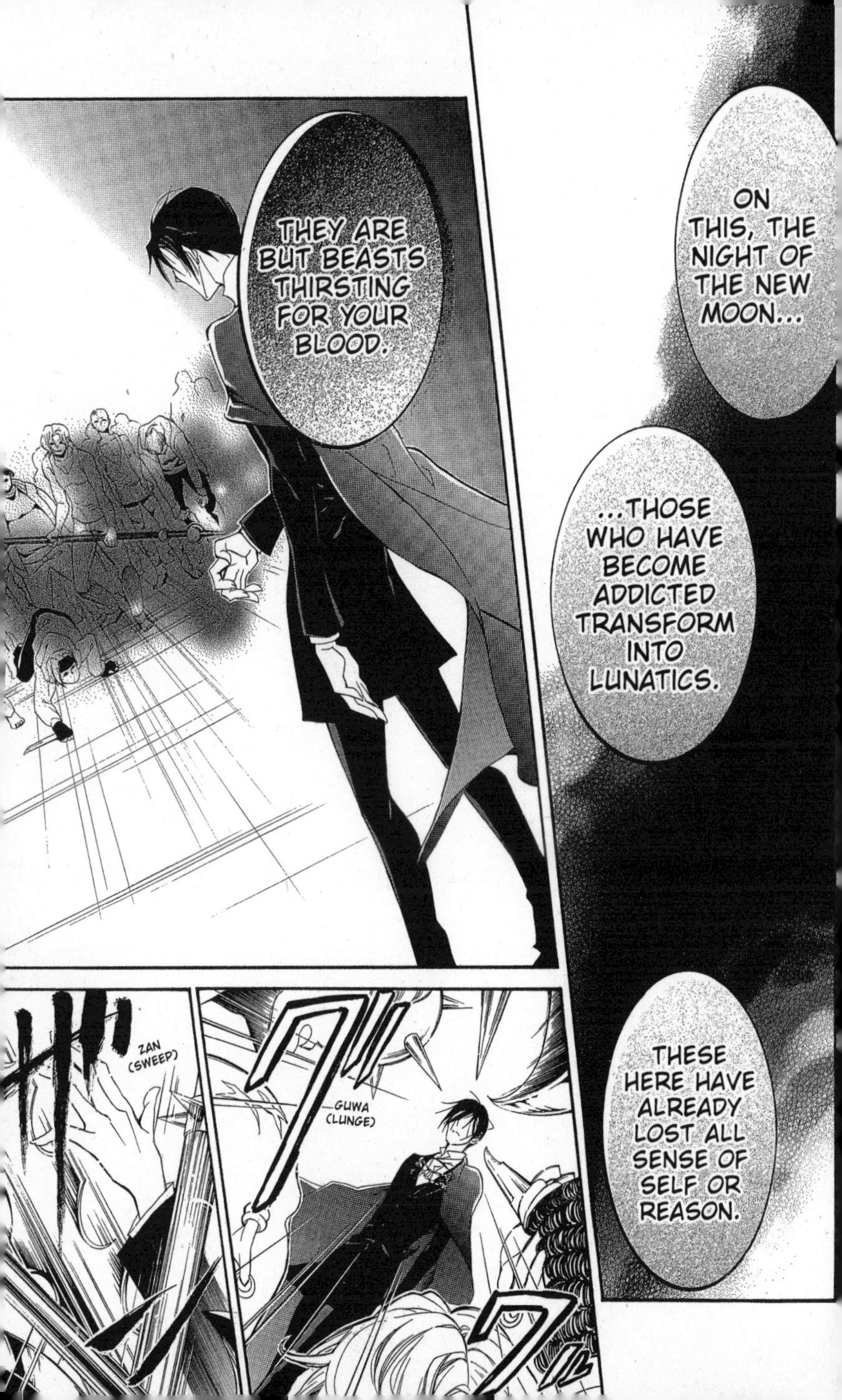
ON THIS, THE NIGHT OF THE NEW MOON...
...THOSE WHO HAVE BECOME ADDICTED TRANSFORM INTO LUNATICS.
THESE HERE HAVE ALREADY LOST ALL SENSE OF SELF OR REASON.
THEY ARE BUT BEASTS THIRSTING FOR YOUR BLOOD.
GUWA (LUNGE)
ZAN (SWEEP)

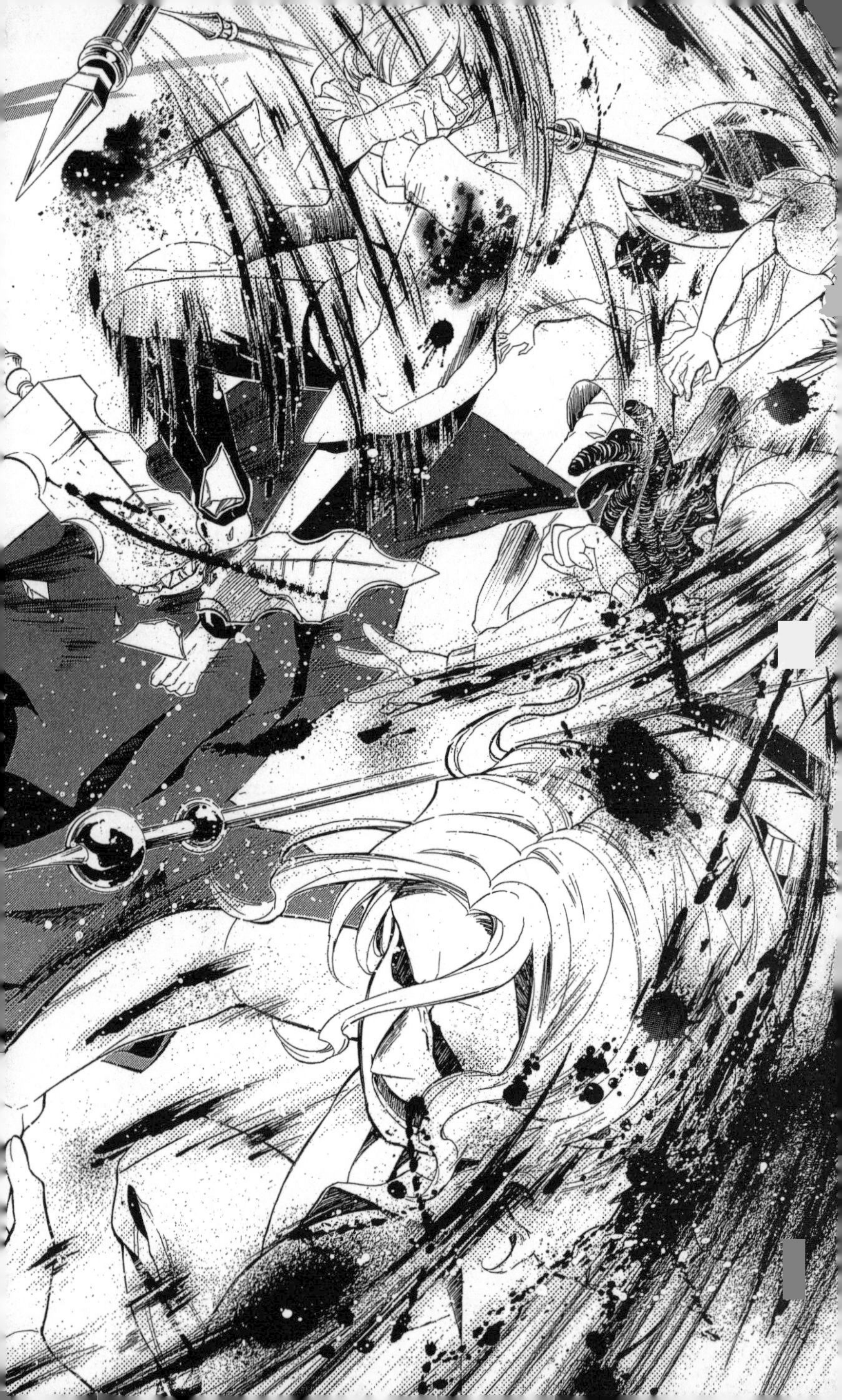

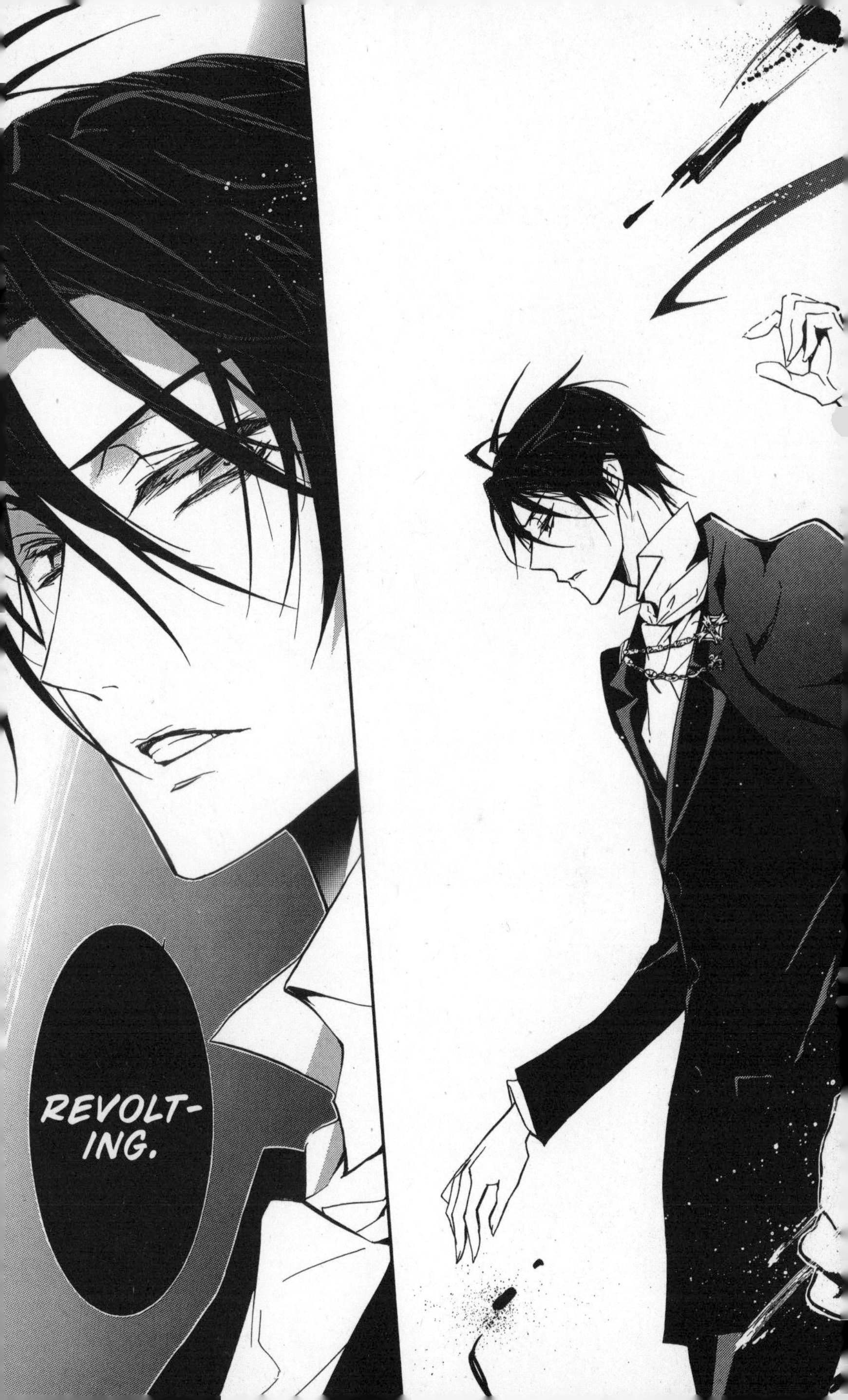
REVOLT-
ING.

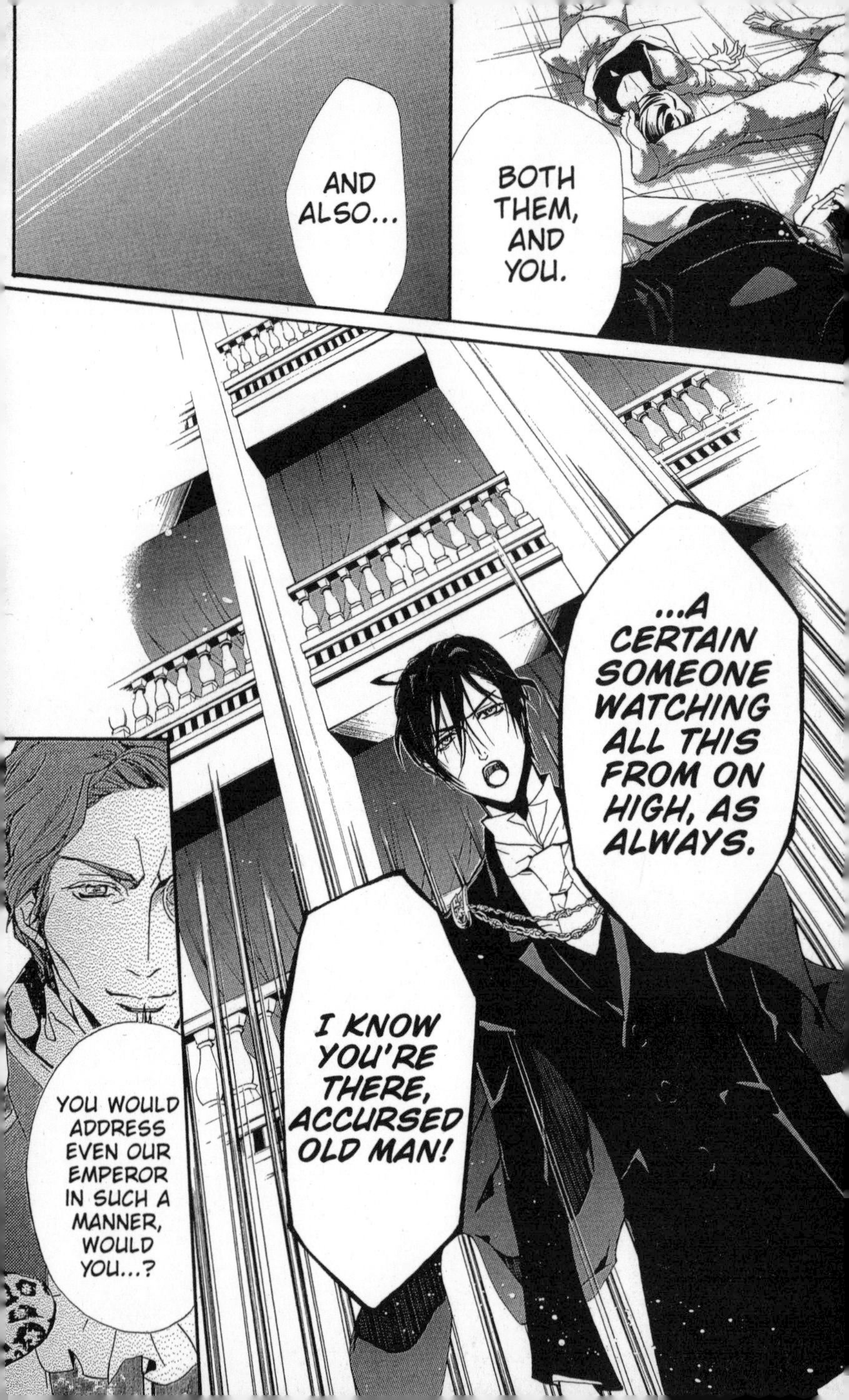
BOTH THEM, AND YOU.
AND ALSO...
...A CERTAIN SOMEONE WATCHING ALL THIS FROM ON HIGH, AS ALWAYS.
I KNOW YOU'RE THERE, ACCURSED OLD MAN!
YOU WOULD ADDRESS EVEN OUR EMPEROR IN SUCH A MANNER, WOULD YOU...?

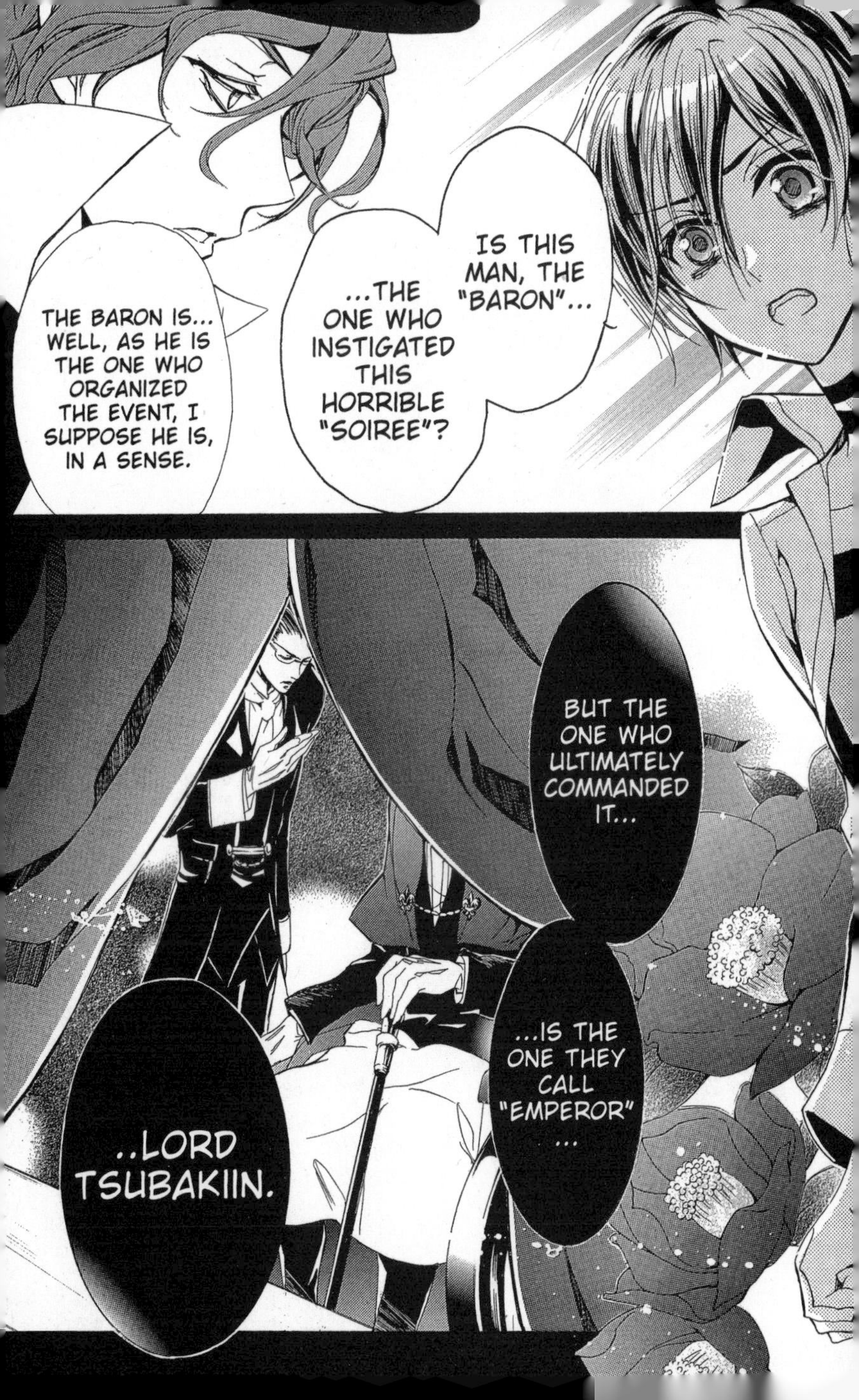
IS THIS MAN, THE "BARON"...
...THE ONE WHO INSTIGATED THIS HORRIBLE "SOIREE"?
THE BARON IS... WELL, AS HE IS THE ONE WHO ORGANIZED THE EVENT, I SUPPOSE HE IS, IN A SENSE.
BUT THE ONE WHO ULTIMATELY COMMANDED IT...
...IS THE ONE THEY CALL "EMPEROR" ...
..LORD TSUBAKIIN.

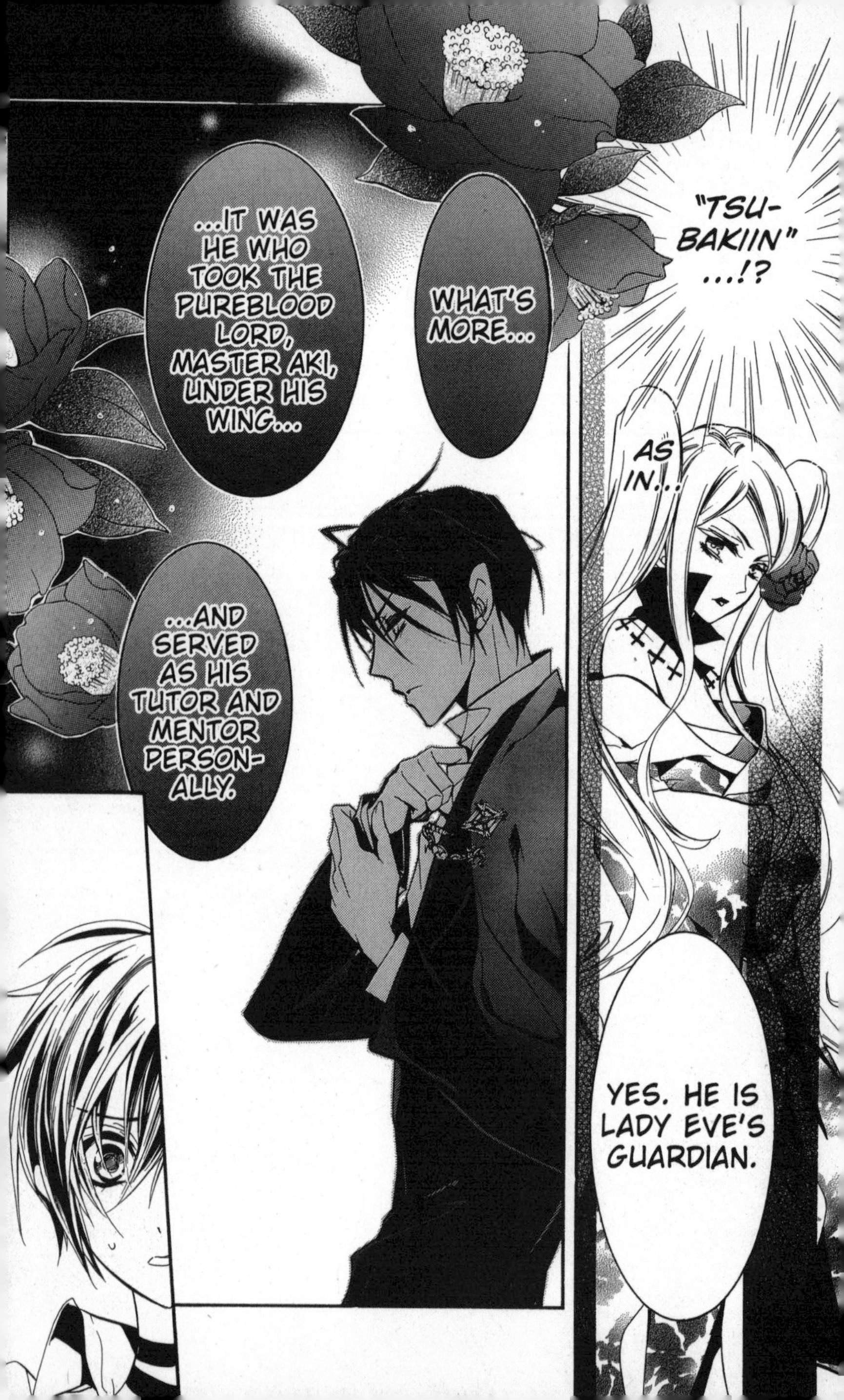
"TSU-BAKIIN" ...!?
AS IN...
YES. HE IS LADY EVE'S GUARDIAN.
WHAT'S MORE...
...IT WAS HE WHO TOOK THE PUREBLOOD LORD, MASTER AKI, UNDER HIS WING...
...AND SERVED AS HIS TUTOR AND MENTOR PERSON-ALLY.

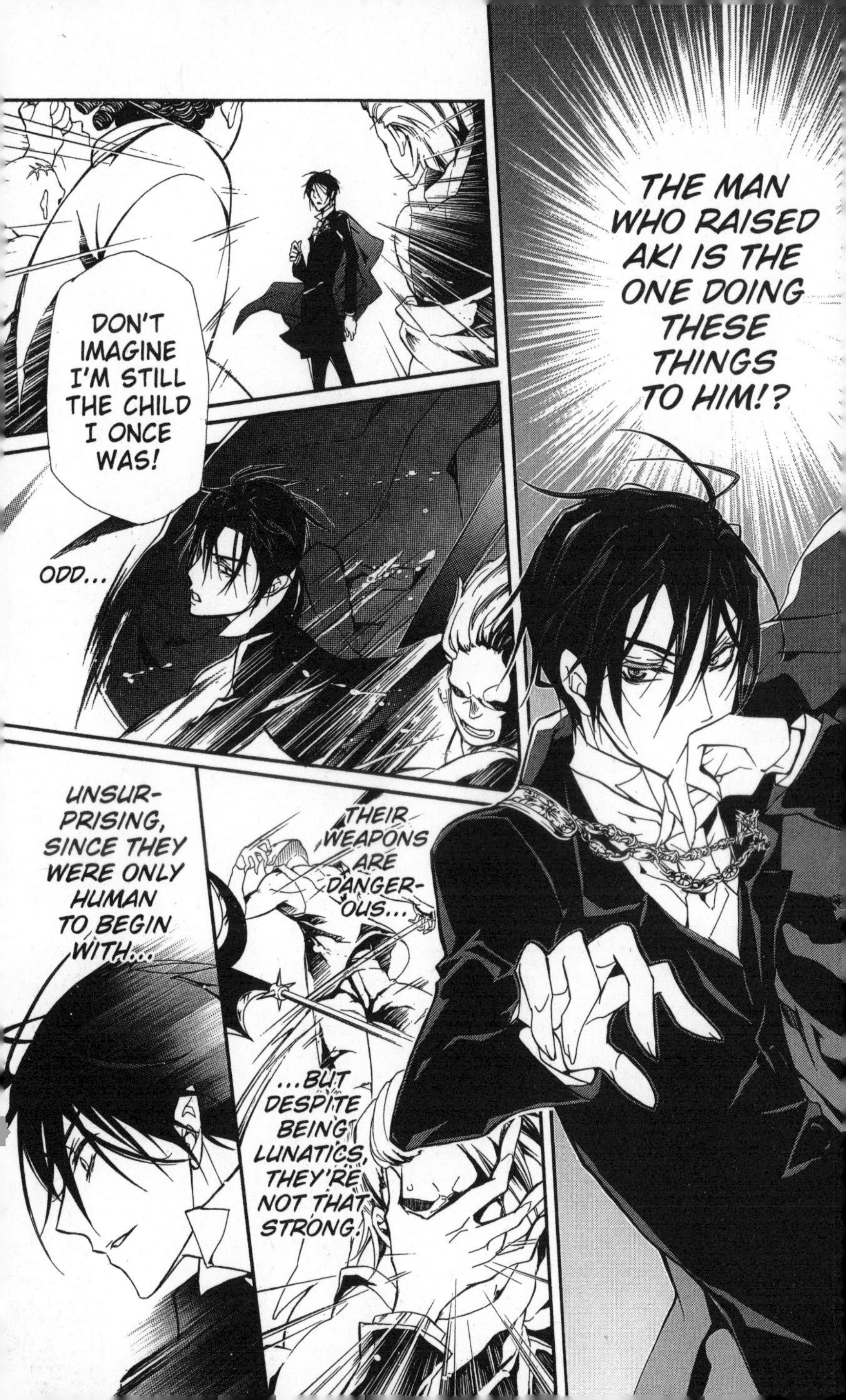
THE MAN WHO RAISED AKI IS THE ONE DOING THESE THINGS TO HIM!?
DON'T IMAGINE I'M STILL THE CHILD I ONCE WAS!
ODD...
THEIR WEAPONS ARE DANGER-OUS...
...BUT DESPITE BEING LUNATICS, THEY'RE NOT THAT STRONG.
UNSUR-PRISING, SINCE THEY WERE ONLY HUMAN TO BEGIN WITH...

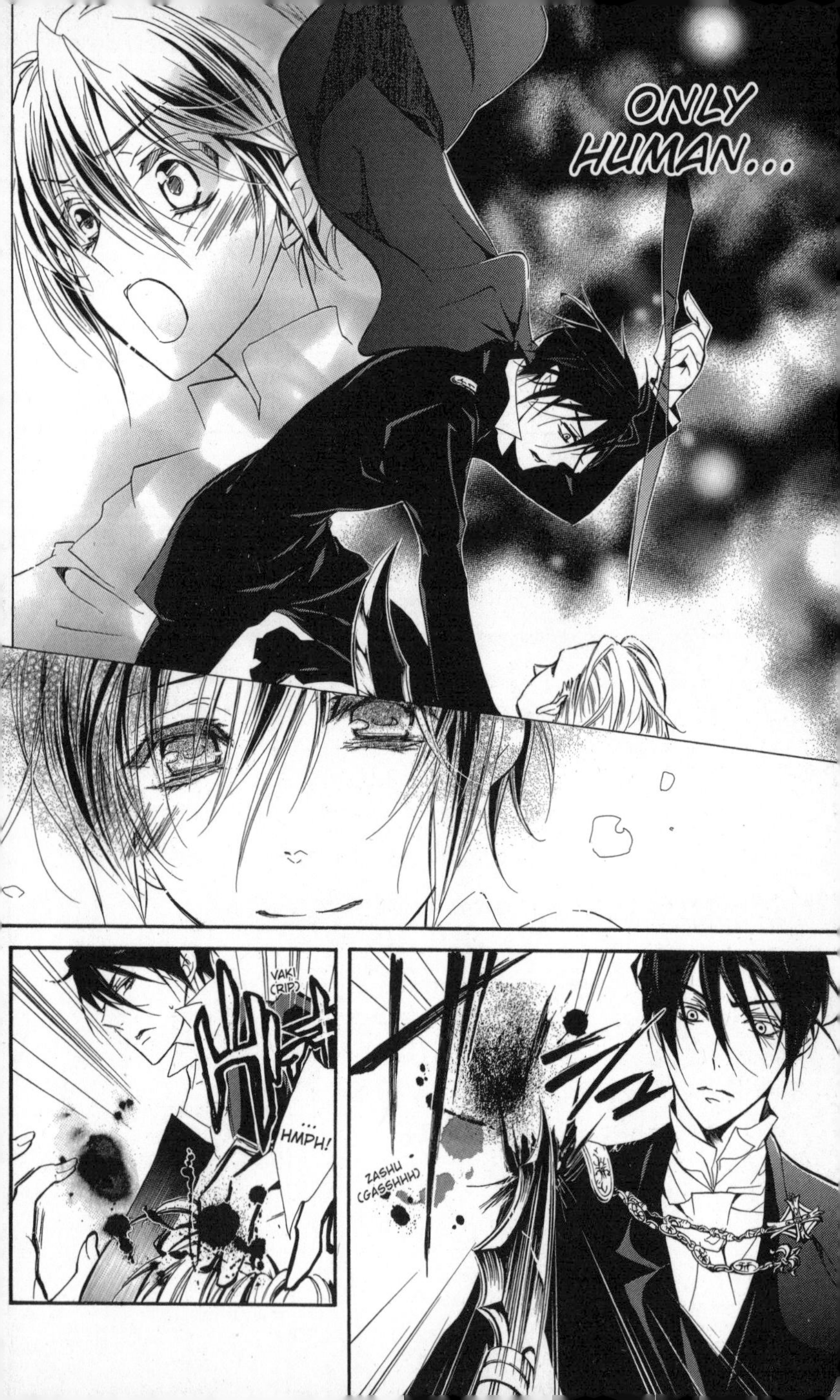
ONLY HUMAN...
ZASHU (GASSHHH)
VAK! (RIP)
...HMPH!

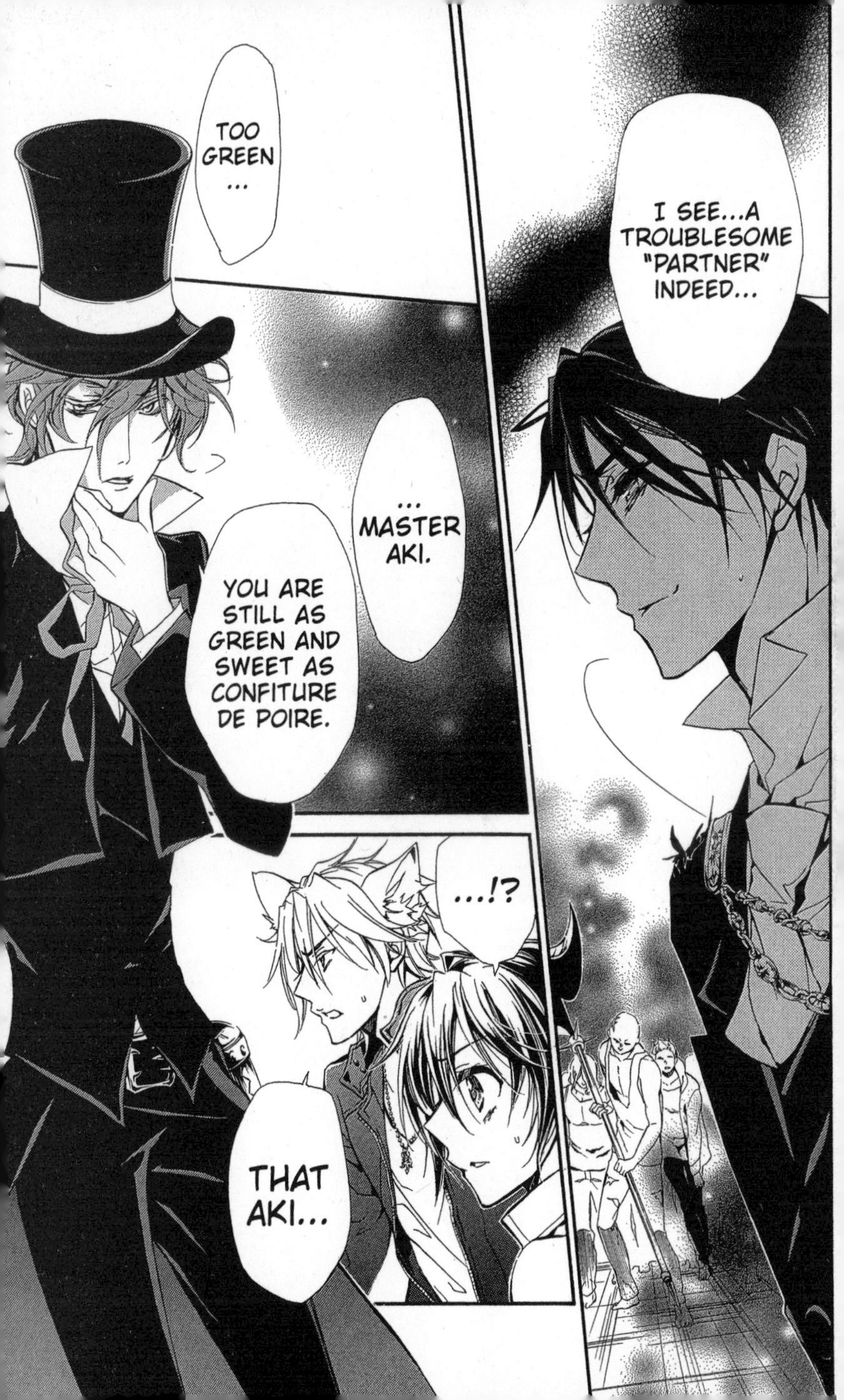

I SEE...A TROUBLESOME "PARTNER" INDEED...
TOO GREEN...
...MASTER AKI.
YOU ARE STILL AS GREEN AND SWEET AS CONFITURE DE POIRE.
...!?
THAT AKI...

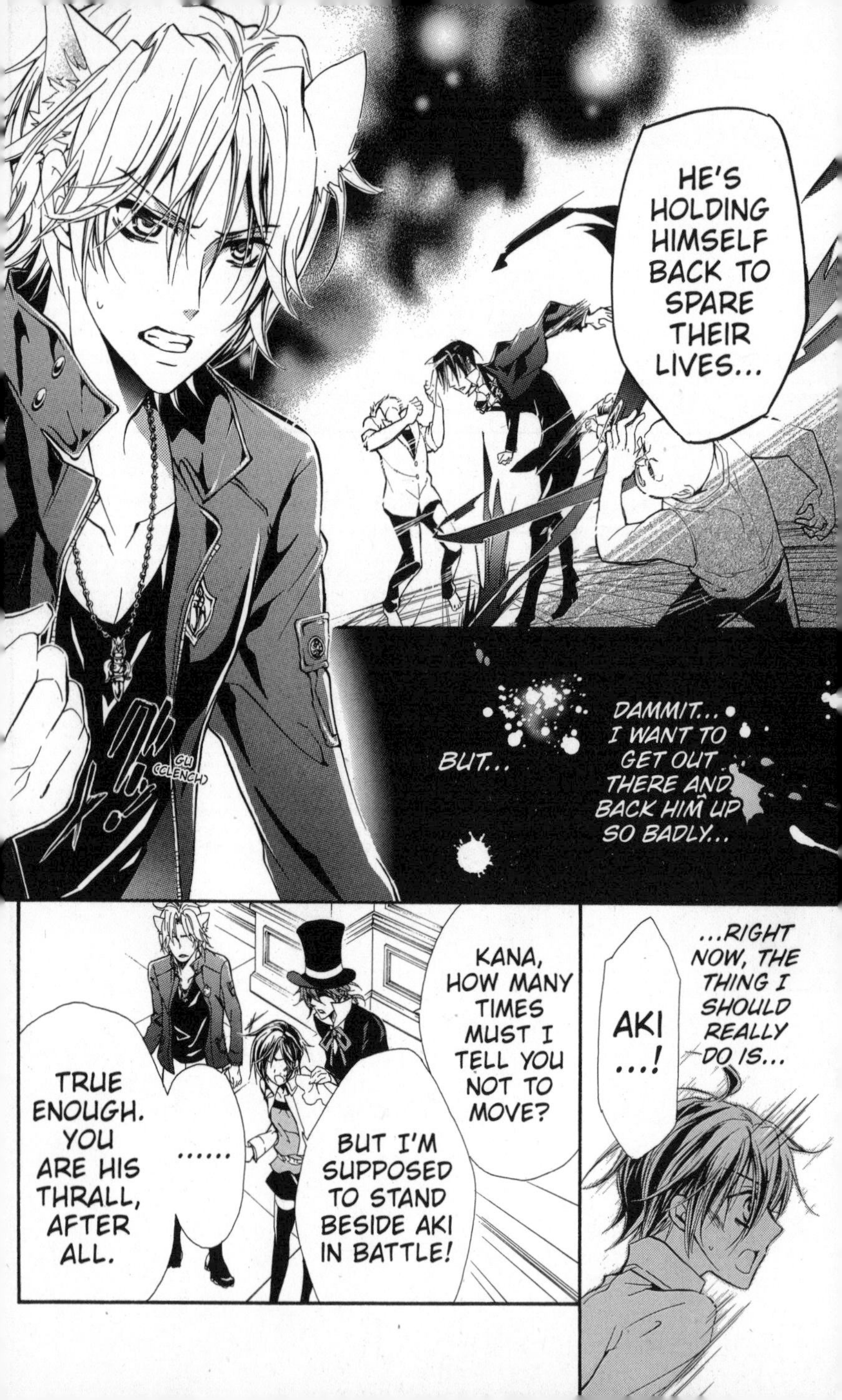
HE'S HOLDING HIMSELF BACK TO SPARE THEIR LIVES...
DAMMIT... I WANT TO GET OUT THERE AND BACK HIM UP SO BADLY...
BUT...
GU (CLENCH)
...RIGHT NOW, THE THING I SHOULD REALLY DO IS...
AKI ...!
KANA, HOW MANY TIMES MUST I TELL YOU NOT TO MOVE?
BUT I'M SUPPOSED TO STAND BESIDE AKI IN BATTLE!
......
TRUE ENOUGH. YOU ARE HIS THRALL, AFTER ALL.

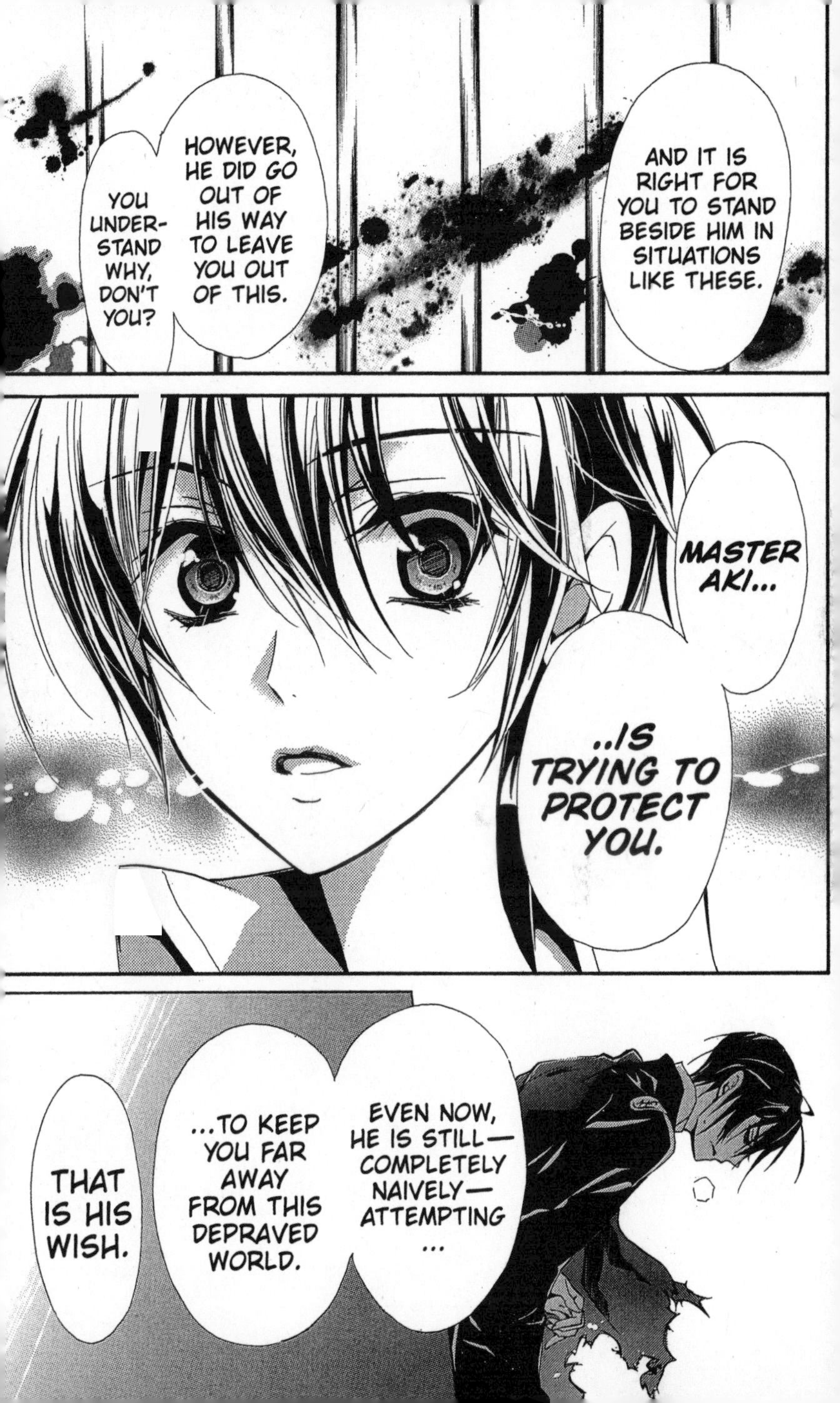

AND IT IS RIGHT FOR YOU TO STAND BESIDE HIM IN SITUATIONS LIKE THESE.
HOWEVER, HE DID GO OUT OF HIS WAY TO LEAVE YOU OUT OF THIS.
YOU UNDER-STAND WHY, DON'T YOU?
MASTER AKI...
..IS TRYING TO PROTECT YOU.
EVEN NOW, HE IS STILL—COMPLETELY NAIVELY—ATTEMPTING...
...TO KEEP YOU FAR AWAY FROM THIS DEPRAVED WORLD.
THAT IS HIS WISH.

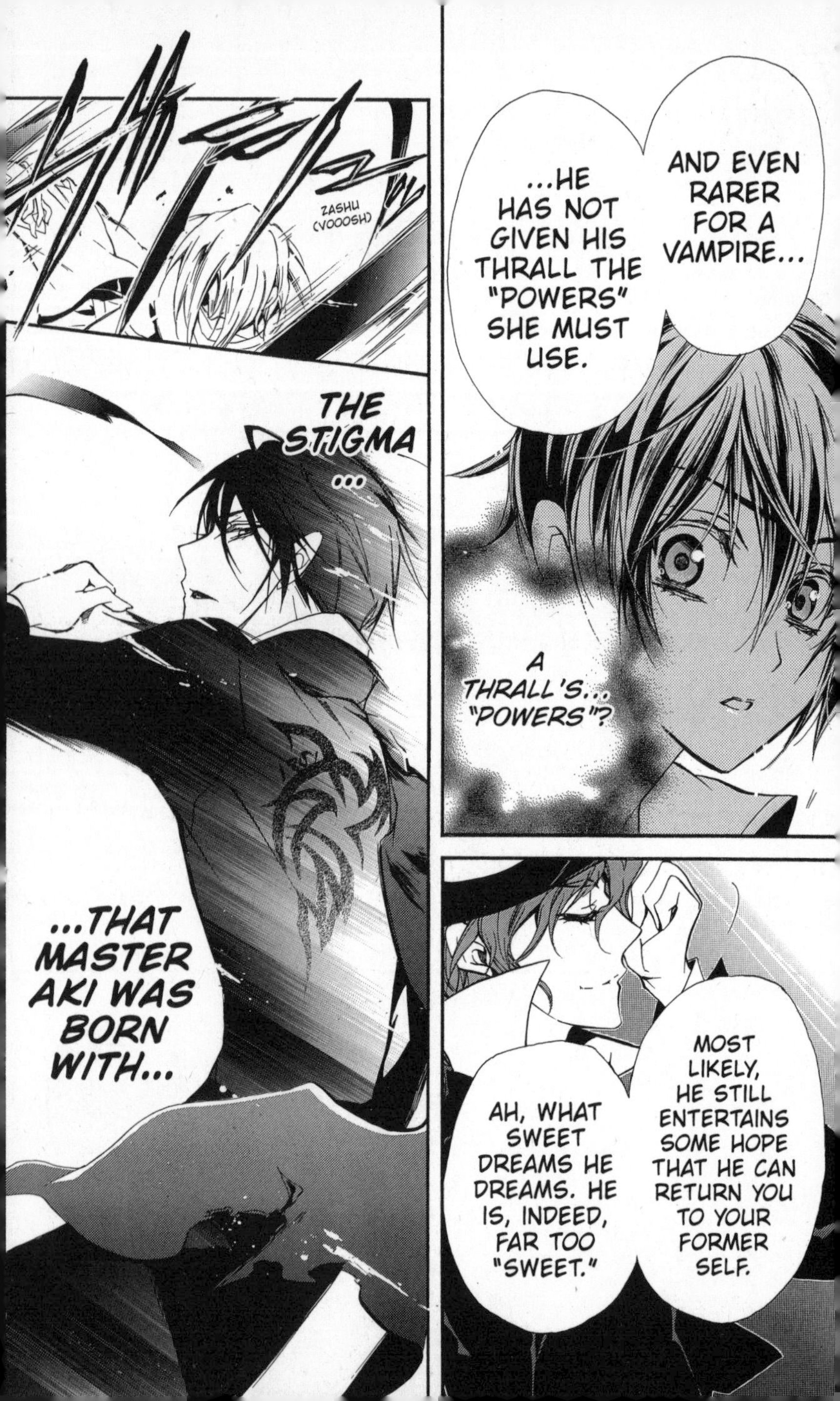
AND EVEN RARER FOR A VAMPIRE...
...HE HAS NOT GIVEN HIS THRALL THE "POWERS" SHE MUST USE.
A THRALL'S... "POWERS"?
MOST LIKELY, HE STILL ENTERTAINS SOME HOPE THAT HE CAN RETURN YOU TO YOUR FORMER SELF.
AH, WHAT SWEET DREAMS HE DREAMS. HE IS, INDEED, FAR TOO "SWEET."
ZASHU (VOOOSH)
THE STIGMA...
...THAT MASTER AKI WAS BORN WITH...

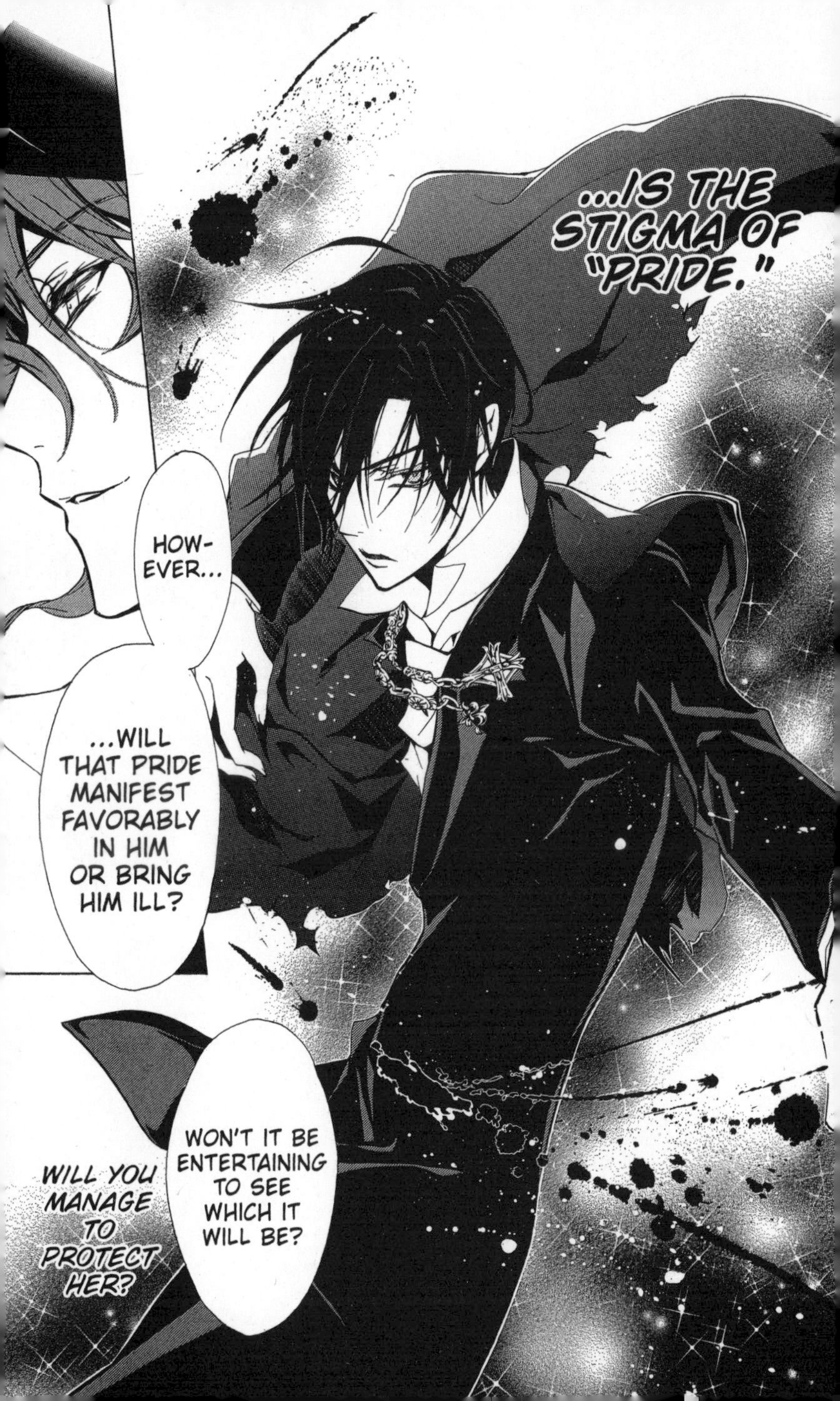
...IS THE STIGMA OF "PRIDE."
HOW-EVER...
...WILL THAT PRIDE MANIFEST FAVORABLY IN HIM OR BRING HIM ILL?
WON'T IT BE ENTERTAINING TO SEE WHICH IT WILL BE?
WILL YOU MANAGE TO PROTECT HER?

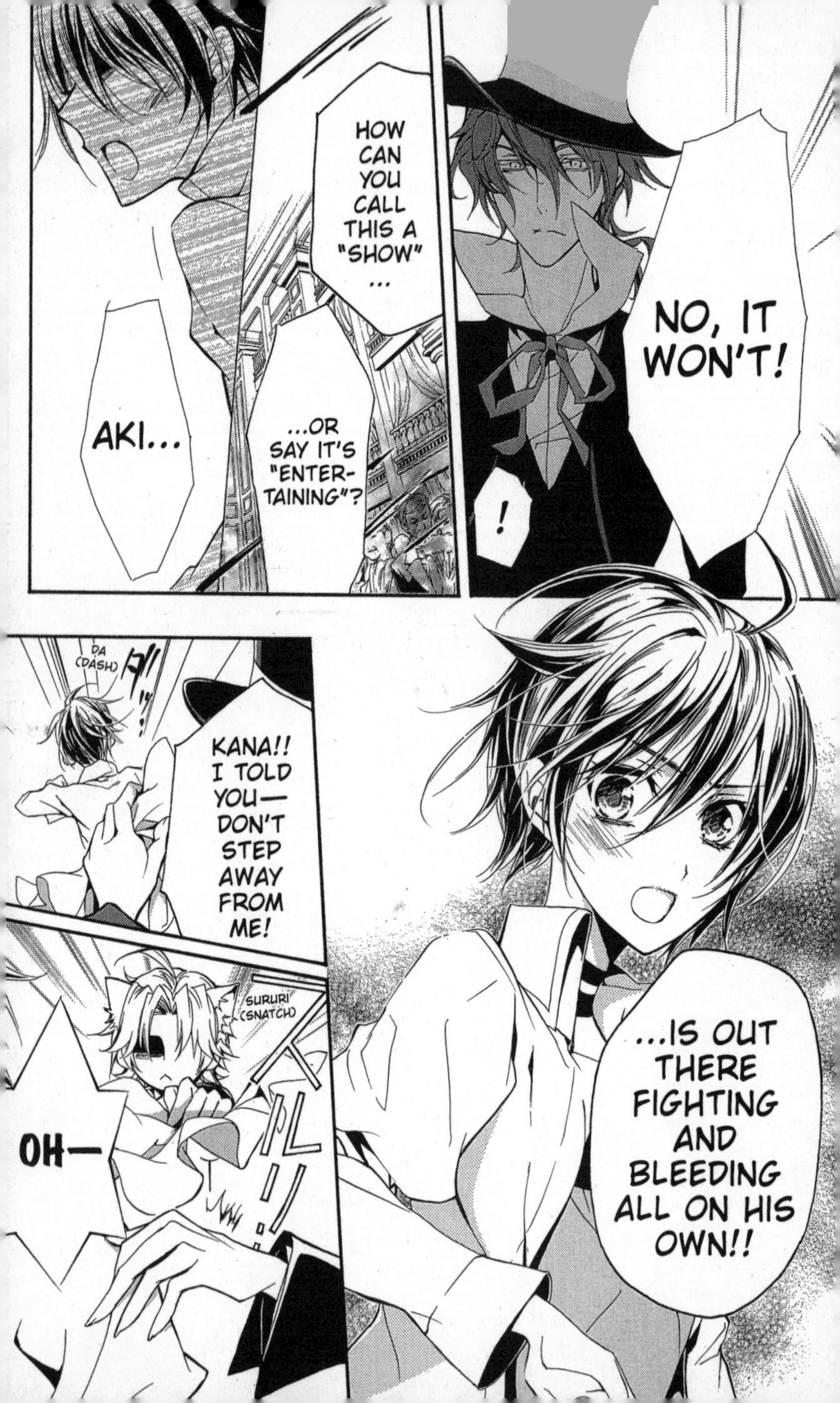
NO, IT WON'T!
!
HOW CAN YOU CALL THIS A "SHOW"...
...OR SAY IT'S "ENTER-TAINING"?
AKI...
...IS OUT THERE FIGHTING AND BLEEDING ALL ON HIS OWN!!
DA (DASH)
KANA!! I TOLD YOU— DON'T STEP AWAY FROM ME!
SURURI (SNATCH)
OH—

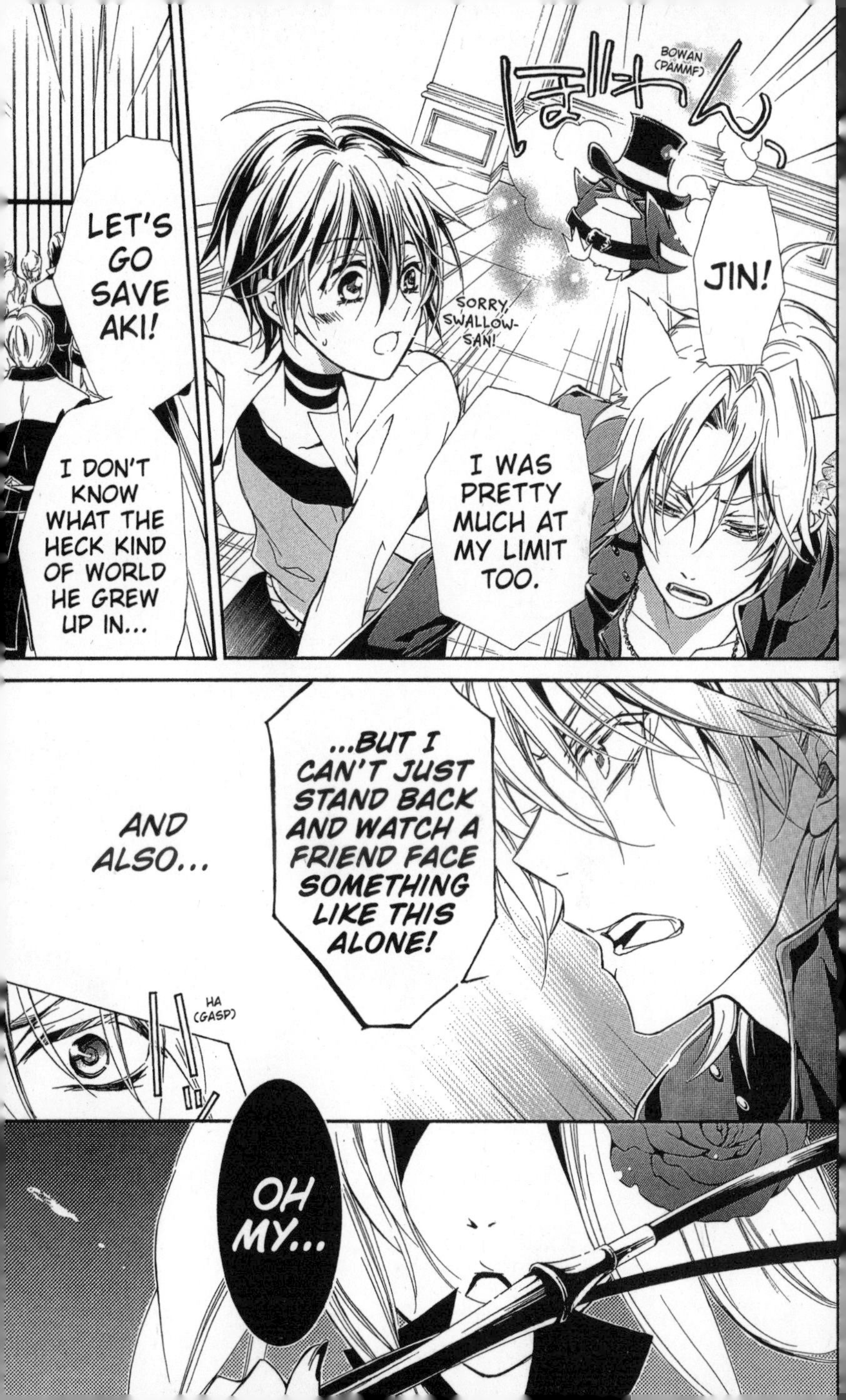
BOWAN (PAMMF)
JIN!
SORRY, SWALLOW-SAN!
I WAS PRETTY MUCH AT MY LIMIT TOO.
LET'S GO SAVE AKI!
I DON'T KNOW WHAT THE HECK KIND OF WORLD HE GREW UP IN...
...BUT I CAN'T JUST STAND BACK AND WATCH A FRIEND FACE SOMETHING LIKE THIS ALONE!
AND ALSO...
HA (GASP)
OH MY...

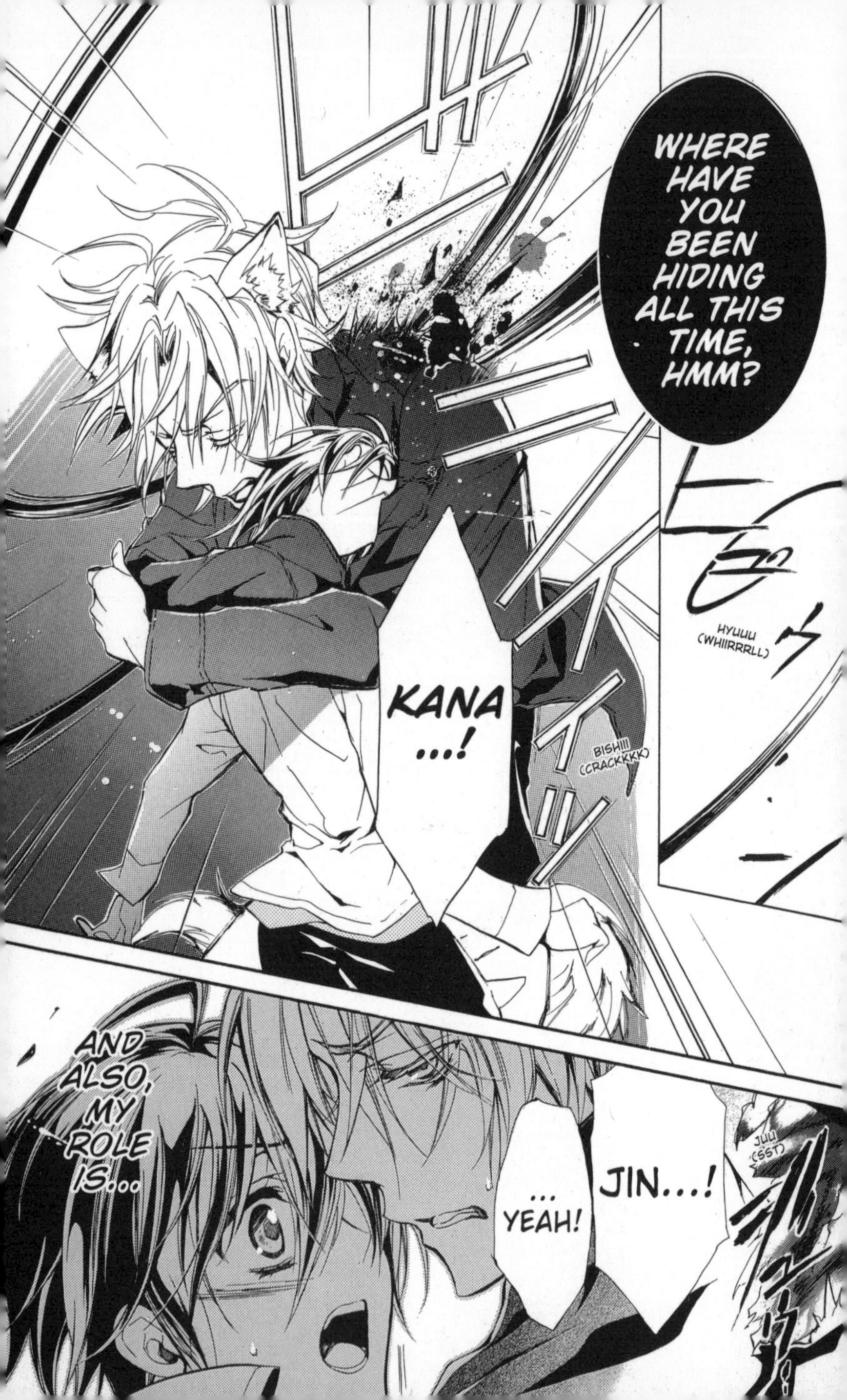
WHERE HAVE YOU BEEN HIDING ALL THIS TIME, HMM?
HYUUU (WHIIRRRLL)
BISHIII (CRACKKKK)
KANA ...!
JUU (SST)
JIN...!
... YEAH!
AND ALSO, MY ROLE IS...

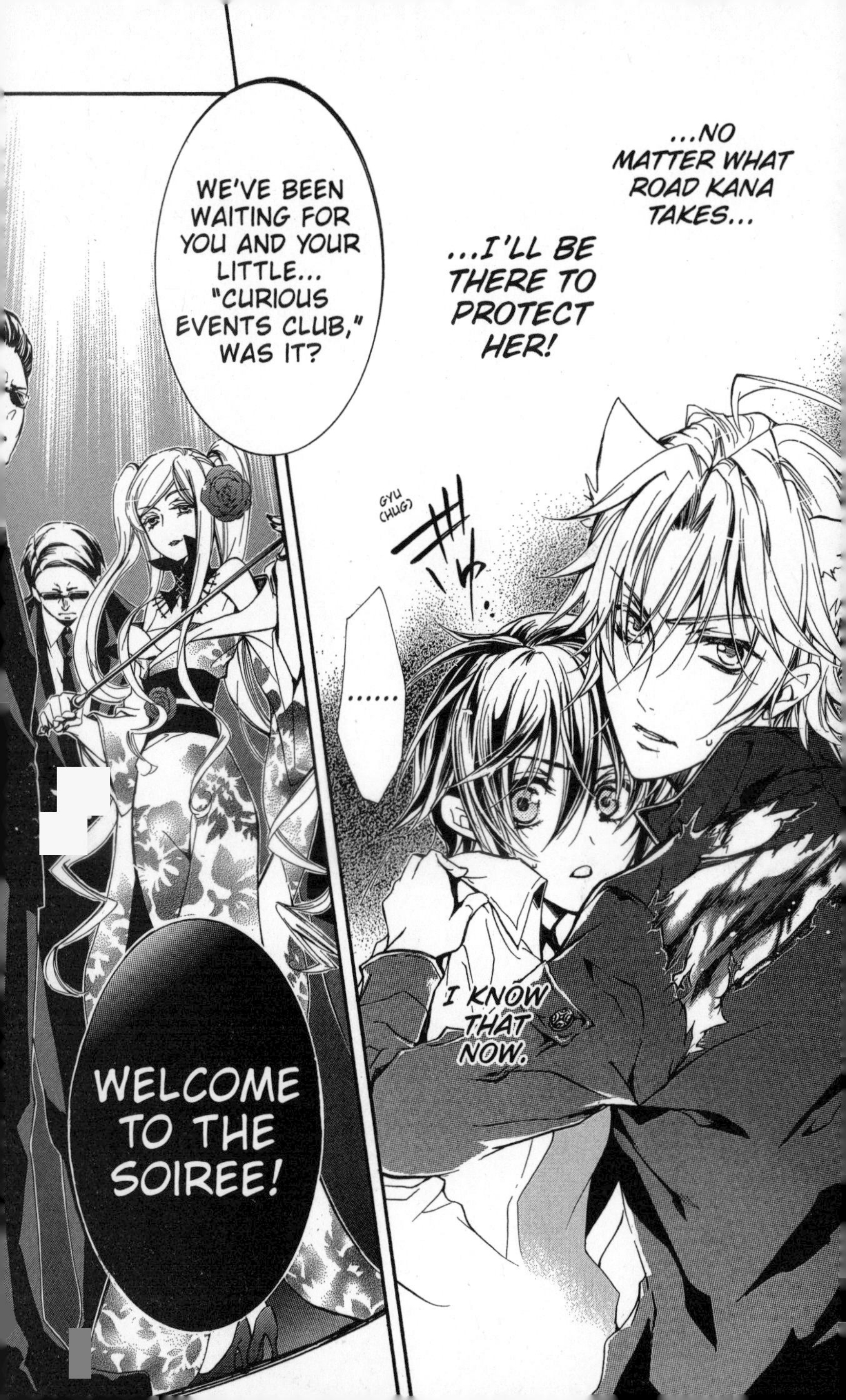
...NO MATTER WHAT ROAD KANA TAKES...
...I'LL BE THERE TO PROTECT HER!
GYU (HUG)
......
I KNOW THAT NOW.
WE'VE BEEN WAITING FOR YOU AND YOUR LITTLE... "CURIOUS EVENTS CLUB," WAS IT?
WELCOME TO THE SOIREE!

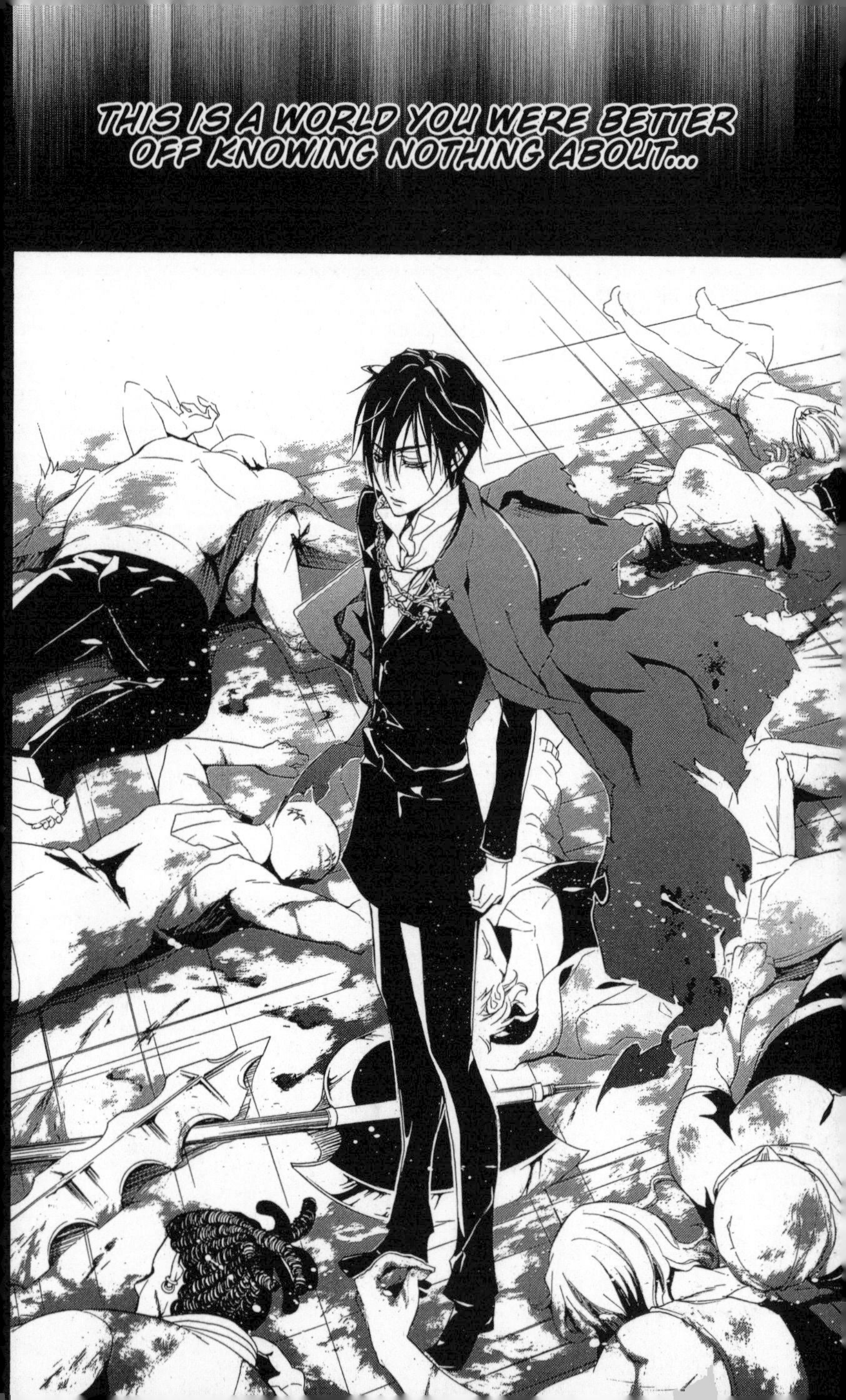
THIS IS A WORLD YOU WERE BETTER OFF KNOWING NOTHING ABOUT...

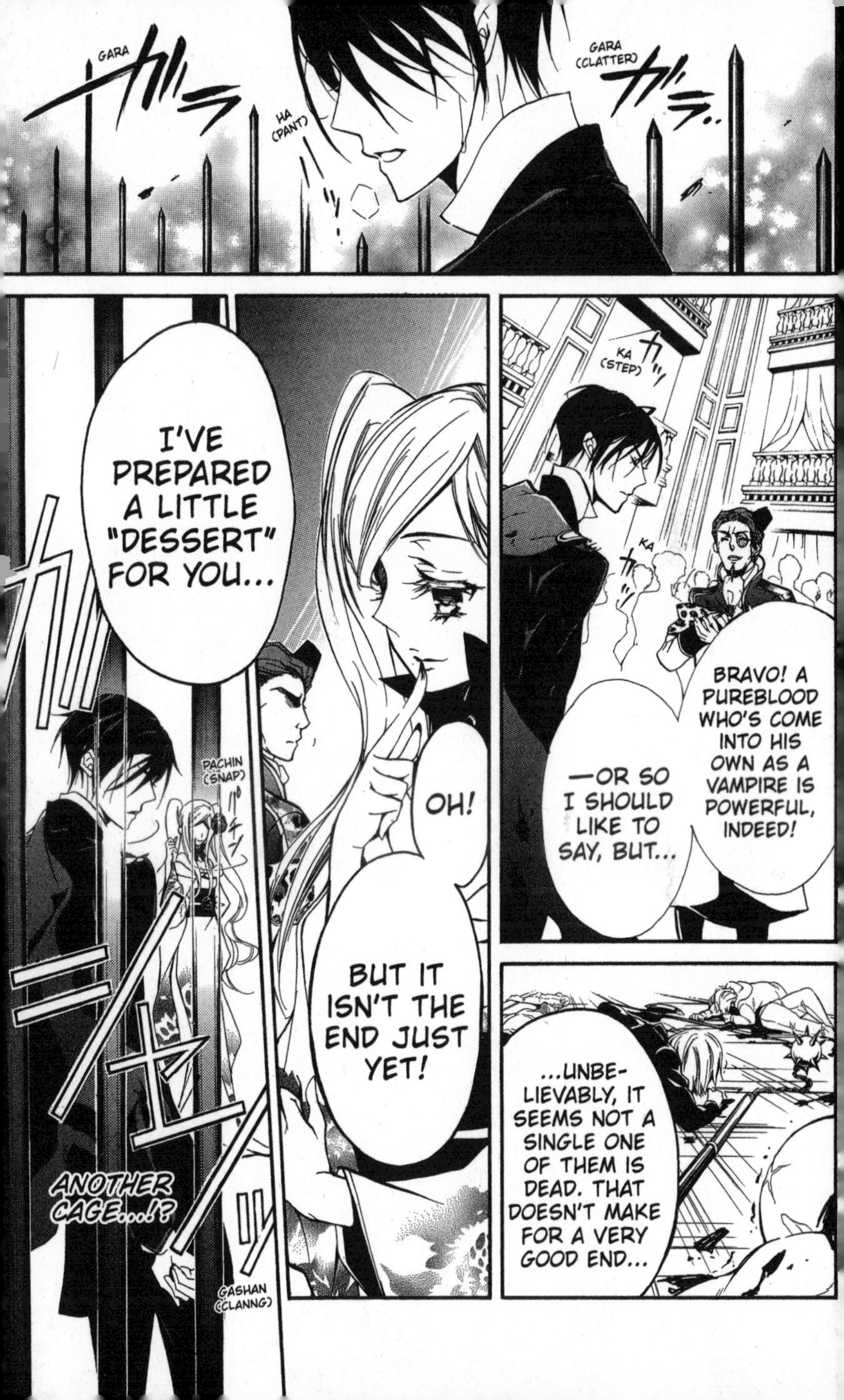
GARA (CLATTER)
HA (PANT)
GARA
KA (STEP)
KA
BRAVO! A PUREBLOOD WHO'S COME INTO HIS OWN AS A VAMPIRE IS POWERFUL, INDEED!
—OR SO I SHOULD LIKE TO SAY, BUT...
...UNBE-LIEVABLY, IT SEEMS NOT A SINGLE ONE OF THEM IS DEAD. THAT DOESN'T MAKE FOR A VERY GOOD END...
OH!
BUT IT ISN'T THE END JUST YET!
I'VE PREPARED A LITTLE "DESSERT" FOR YOU...
PACHIN (SNAP)
GASHAN (CLANNG)
ANOTHER CAGE...!?

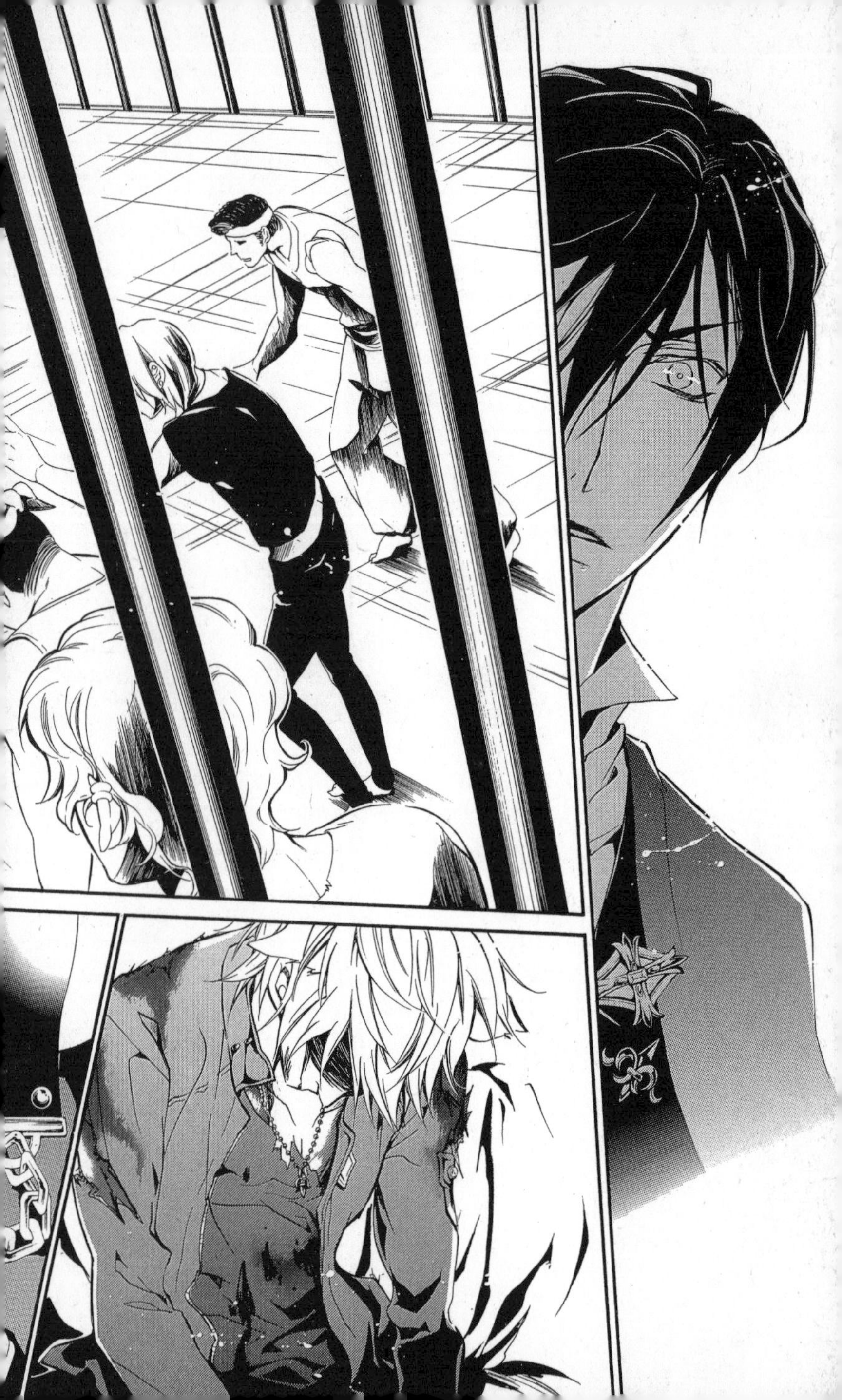

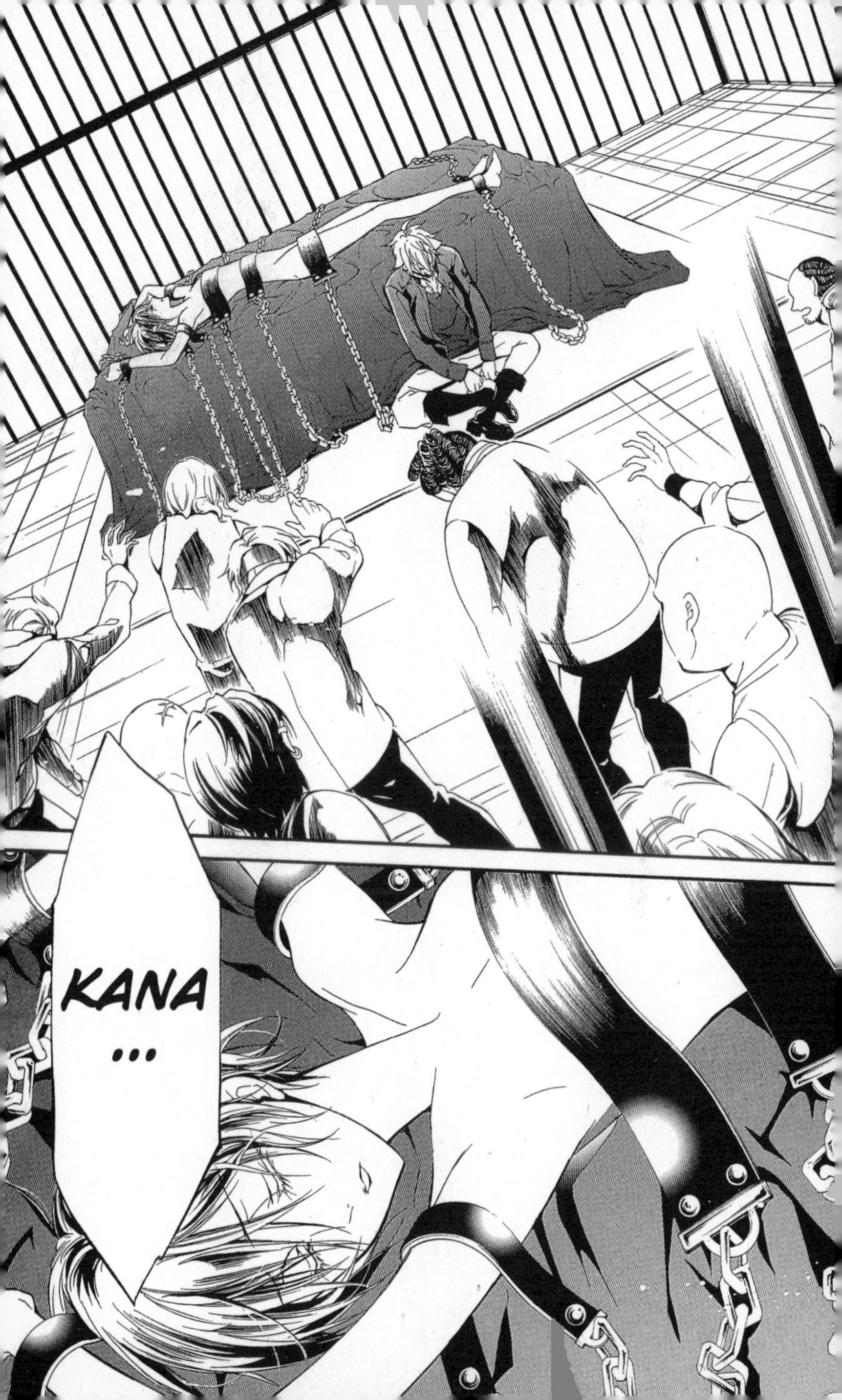
KANA ...

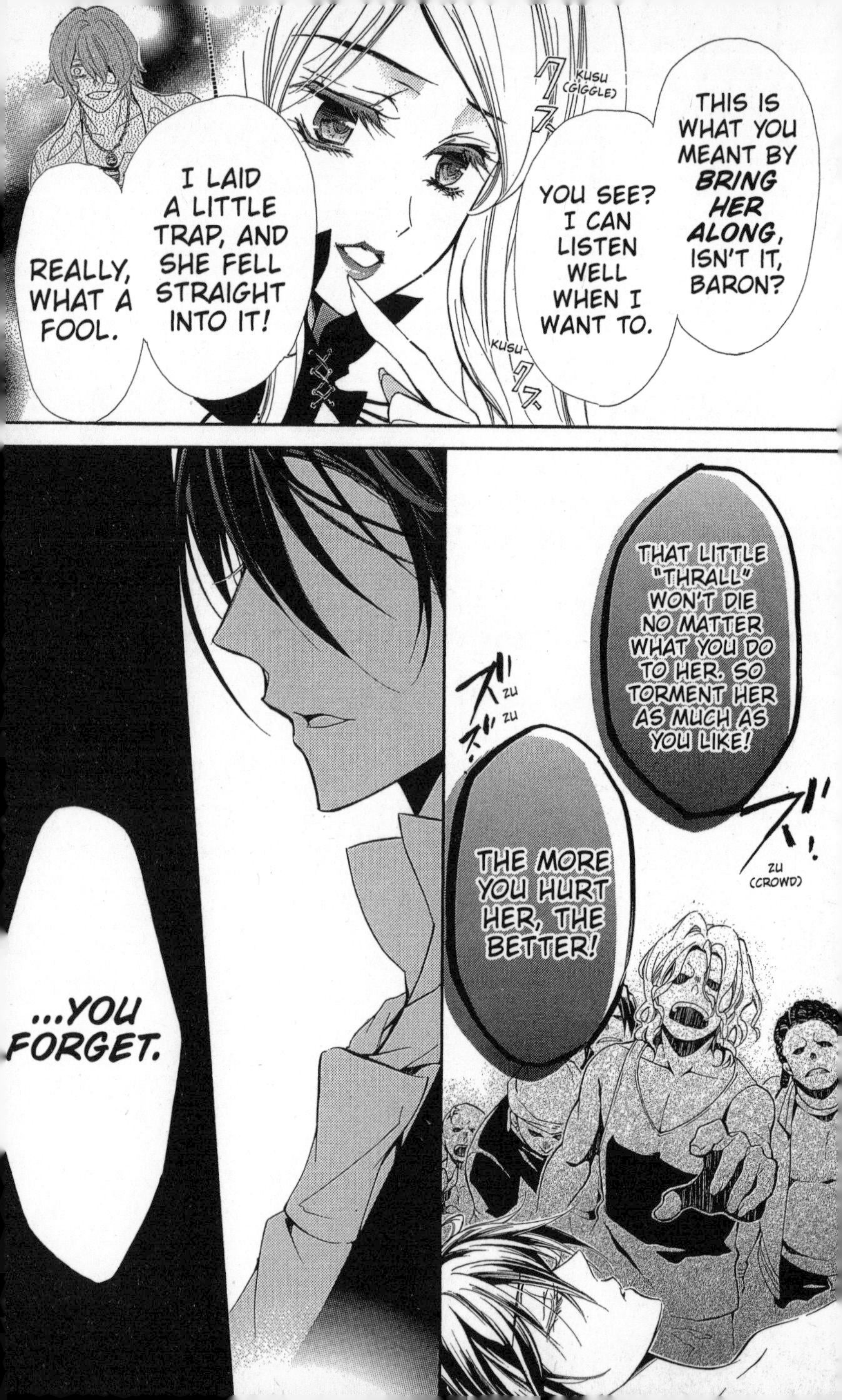
KUSU (GIGGLE)
THIS IS WHAT YOU MEANT BY BRING HER ALONG, ISN'T IT, BARON?
YOU SEE? I CAN LISTEN WELL WHEN I WANT TO.
KUSU-
I LAID A LITTLE TRAP, AND SHE FELL STRAIGHT INTO IT!
REALLY, WHAT A FOOL.
THAT LITTLE "THRALL" WON'T DIE NO MATTER WHAT YOU DO TO HER. SO TORMENT HER AS MUCH AS YOU LIKE!
ZU (CROWD)
ZU ZU
THE MORE YOU HURT HER, THE BETTER!
...YOU FORGET.

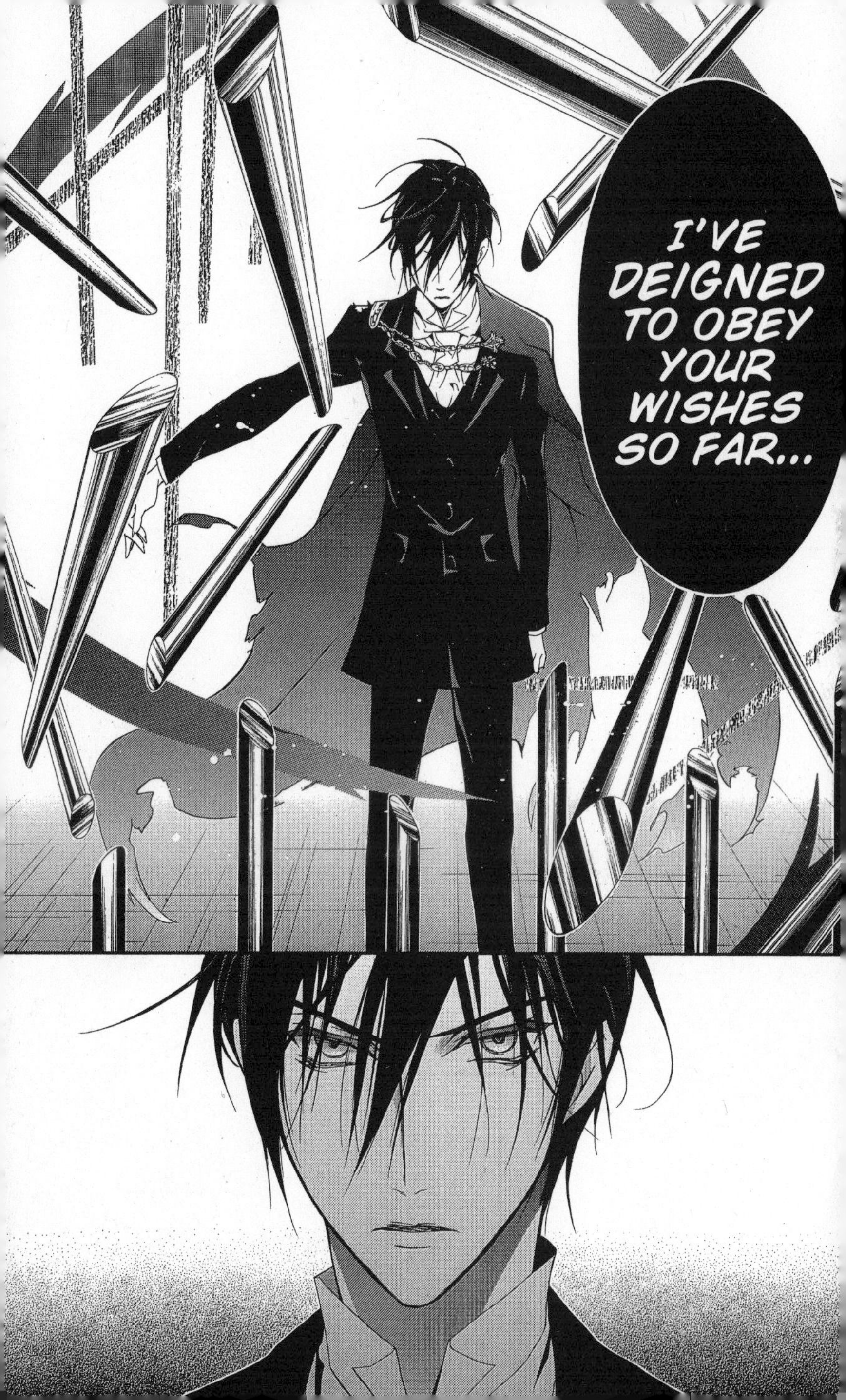
I'VE DEIGNED TO OBEY YOUR WISHES SO FAR...

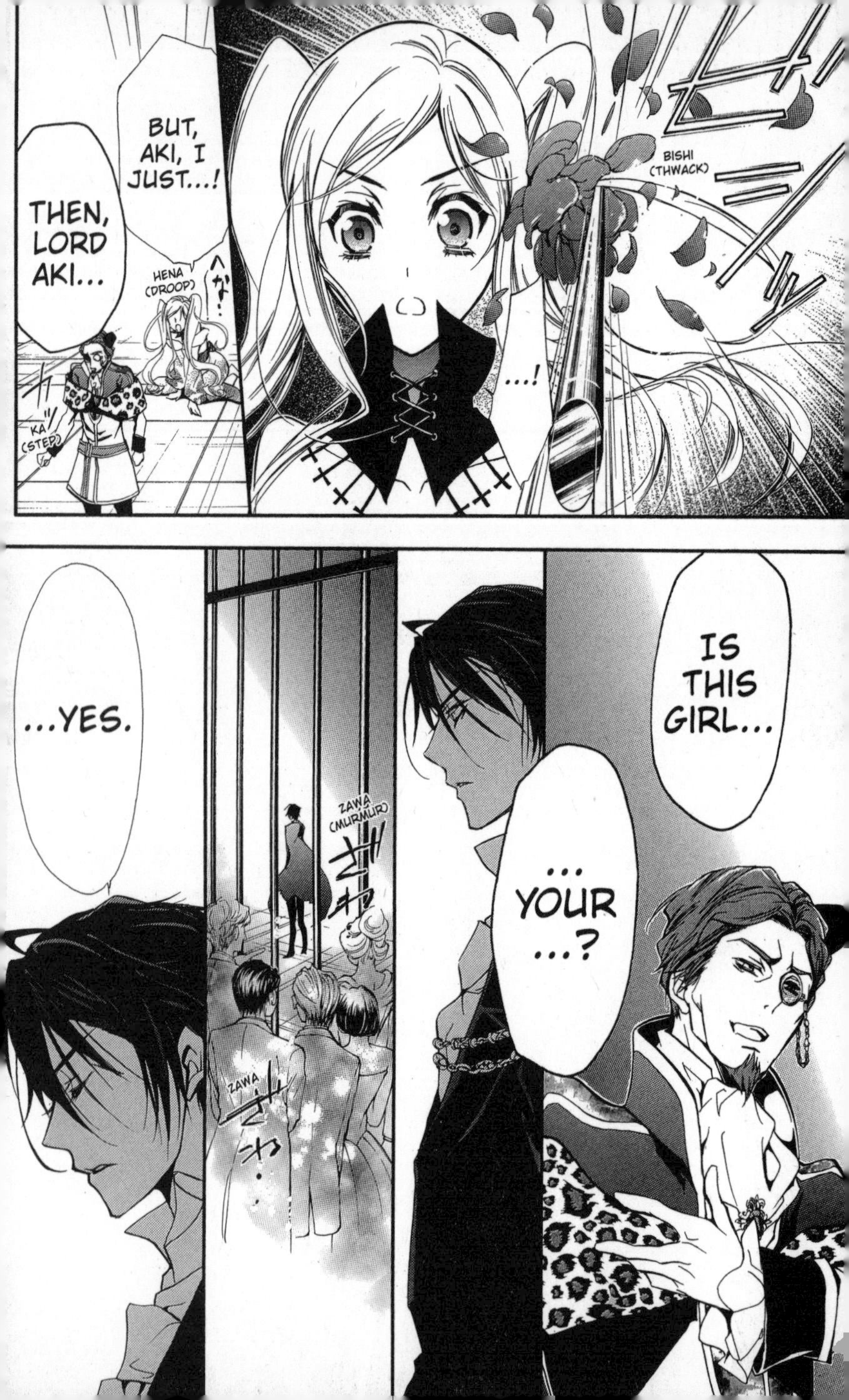
BISHI (THWACK)
...!
BUT, AKI, I JUST...!
HENA (DROOP)
THEN, LORD AKI...
KA (STEP)
IS THIS GIRL...
... YOUR ...?
ZAWA (MURMUR)
ZAWA
...YES.

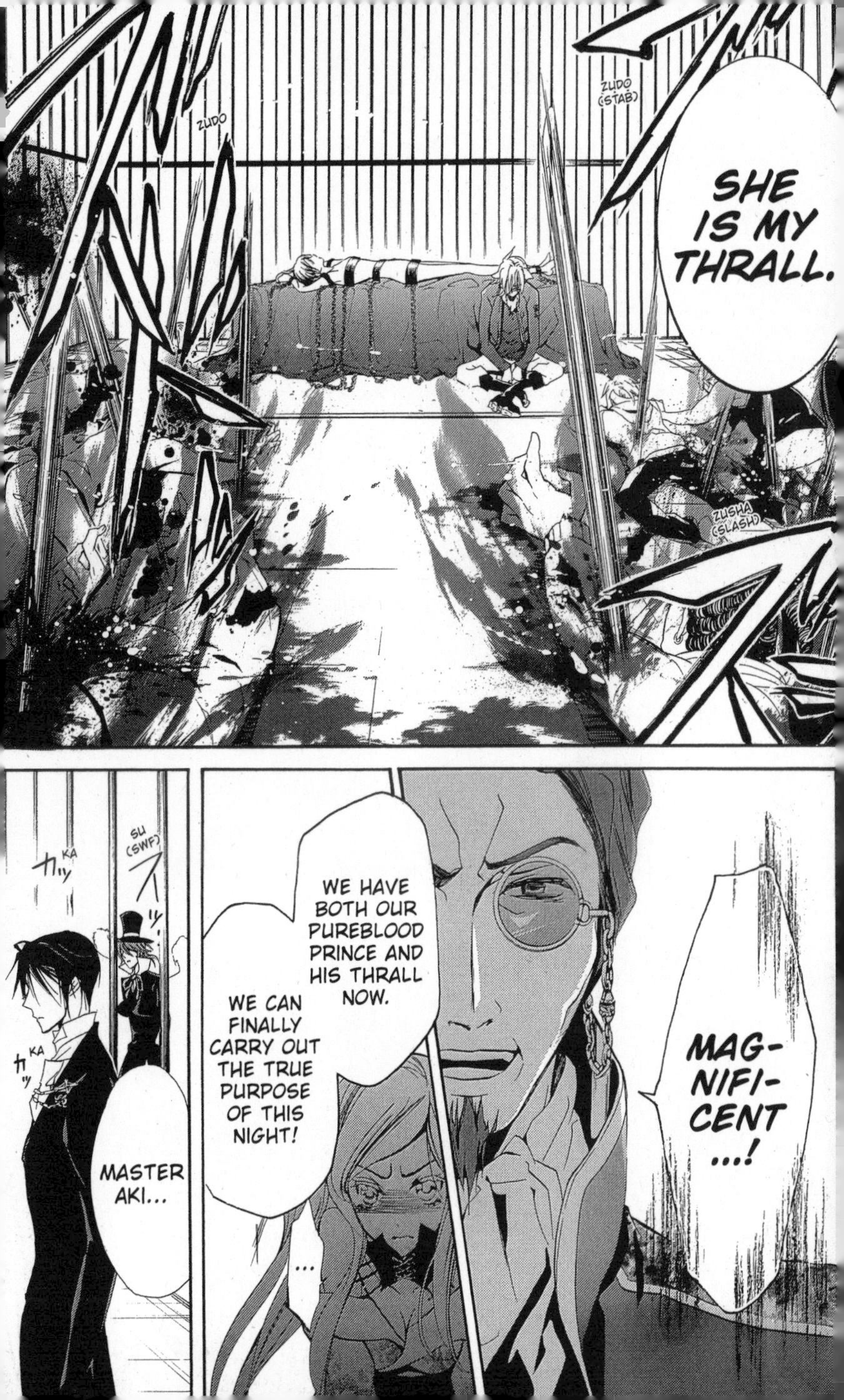
ZUDO (STAB)
SHE IS MY THRALL.
ZUDO
ZUSHA (SLASH)
MAG-NIFI-CENT ...!
WE HAVE BOTH OUR PUREBLOOD PRINCE AND HIS THRALL NOW.
WE CAN FINALLY CARRY OUT THE TRUE PURPOSE OF THIS NIGHT!
...
SU (SWF)
カッ KA
カッ KA
MASTER AKI...

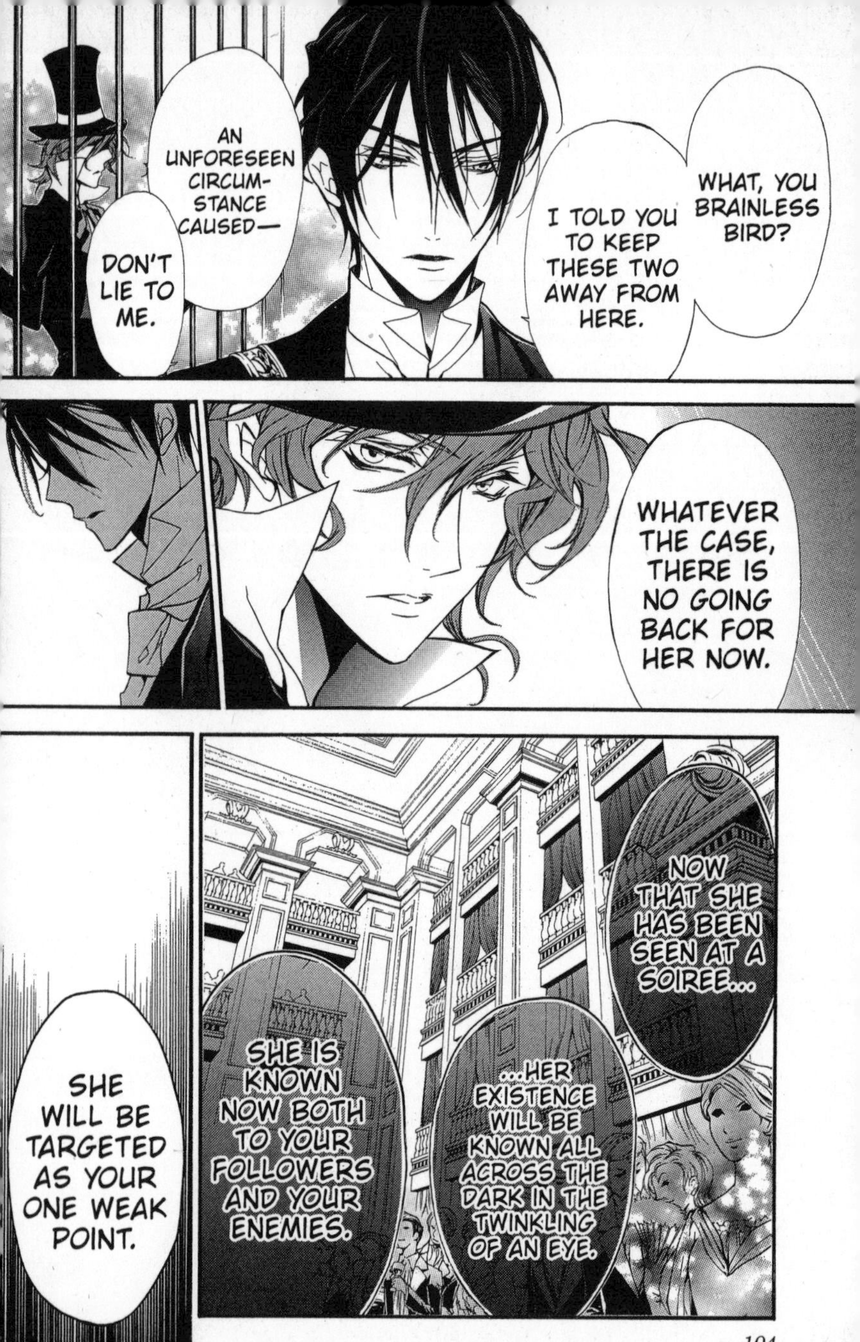
WHAT, YOU BRAINLESS BIRD?
I TOLD YOU TO KEEP THESE TWO AWAY FROM HERE.
AN UNFORESEEN CIRCUM-STANCE CAUSED—
DON'T LIE TO ME.
WHATEVER THE CASE, THERE IS NO GOING BACK FOR HER NOW.
NOW THAT SHE HAS BEEN SEEN AT A SOIREE...
...HER EXISTENCE WILL BE KNOWN ALL ACROSS THE DARK IN THE TWINKLING OF AN EYE.
SHE IS KNOWN NOW BOTH TO YOUR FOLLOWERS AND YOUR ENEMIES.
SHE WILL BE TARGETED AS YOUR ONE WEAK POINT.

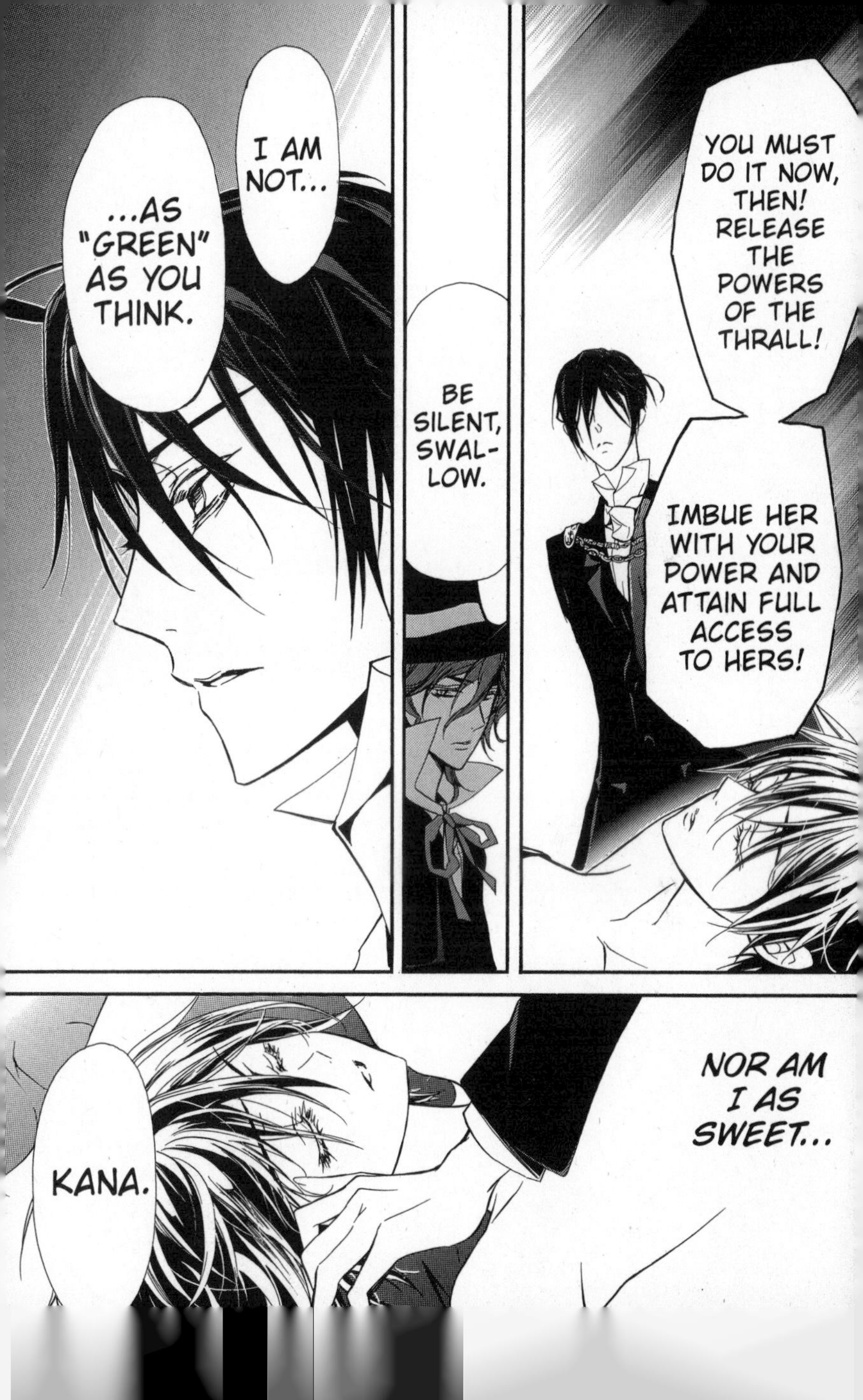
YOU MUST DO IT NOW, THEN! RELEASE THE POWERS OF THE THRALL!
IMBUE HER WITH YOUR POWER AND ATTAIN FULL ACCESS TO HERS!
BE SILENT, SWAL-LOW.
I AM NOT...
...AS "GREEN" AS YOU THINK.
NOR AM I AS SWEET...
KANA.

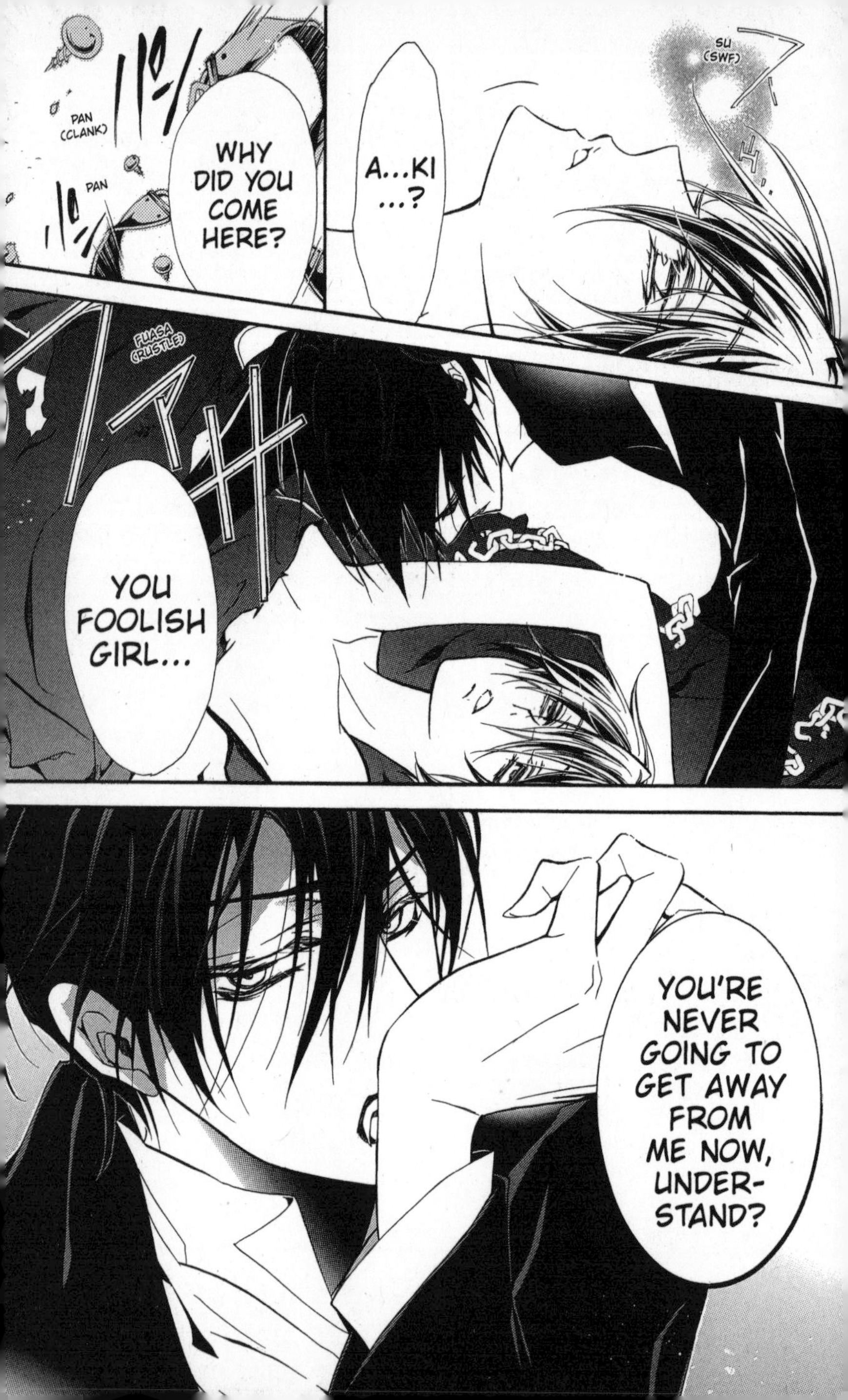
SU (SWF)
A...KI ...?
WHY DID YOU COME HERE?
PAN (CLANK)
PAN
FUASA (RUSTLE)
YOU FOOLISH GIRL...
YOU'RE NEVER GOING TO GET AWAY FROM ME NOW, UNDER-STAND?

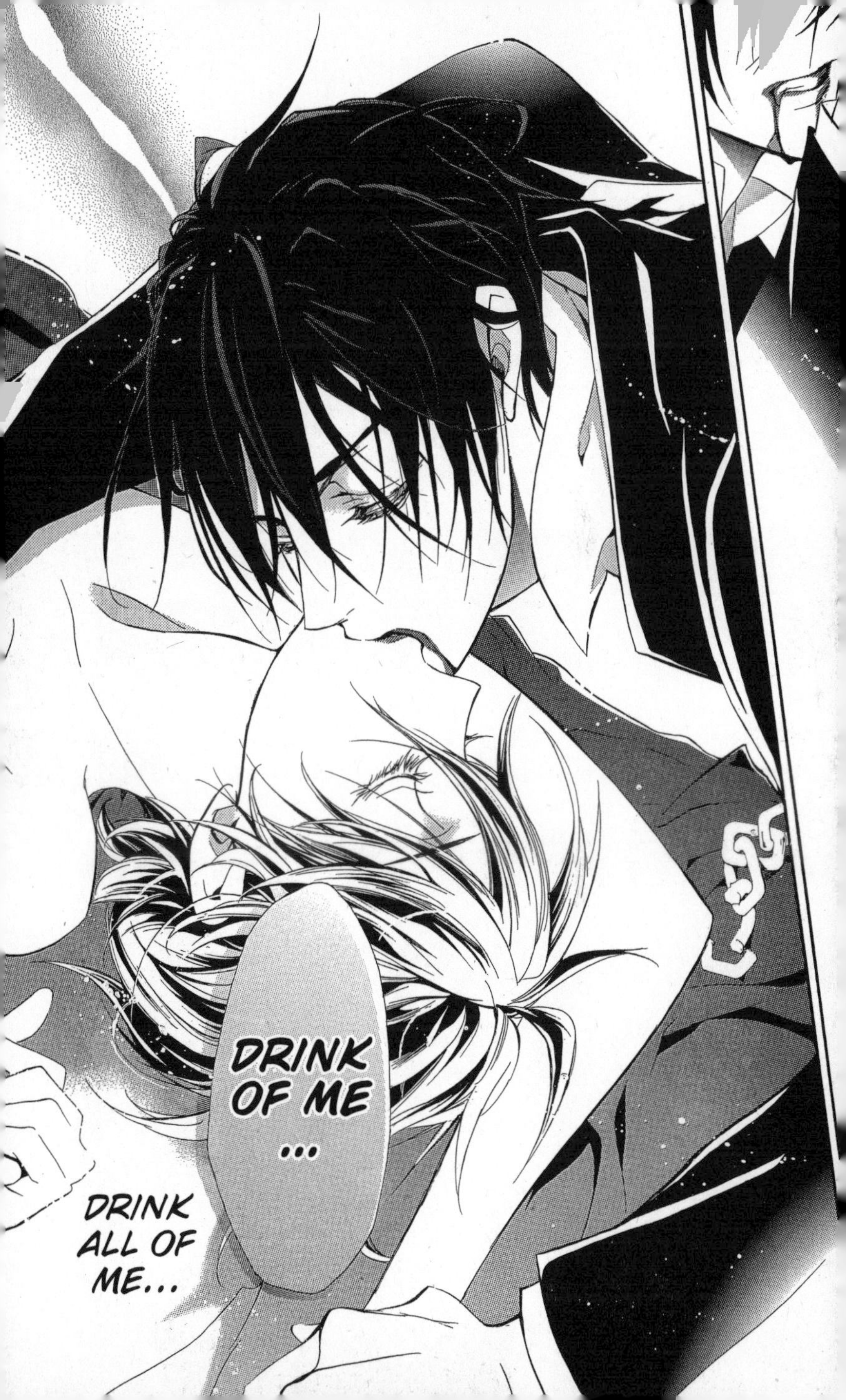
DRINK OF ME ...
DRINK ALL OF ME...

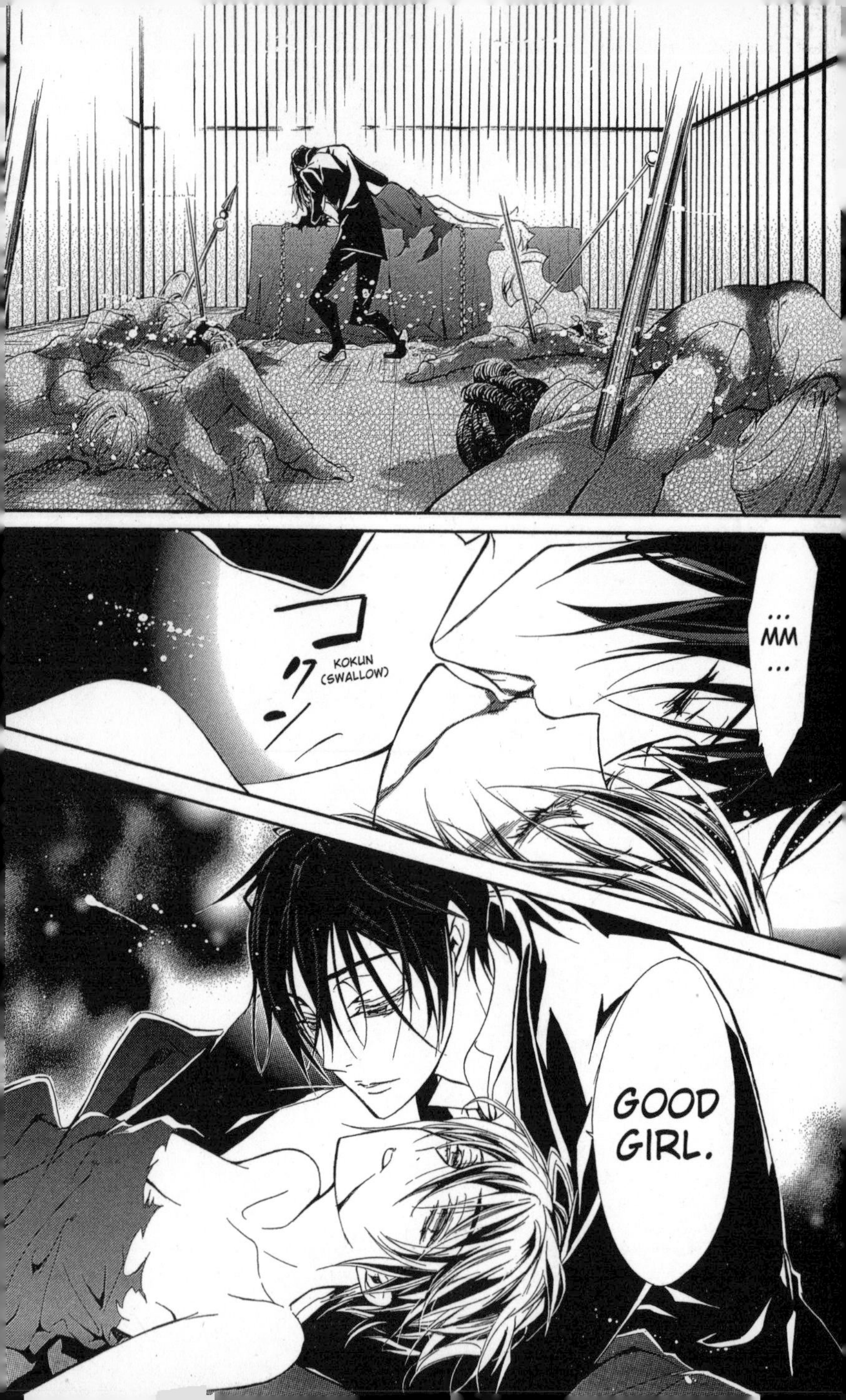
...MM...
KOKUN (SWALLOW)
GOOD GIRL.

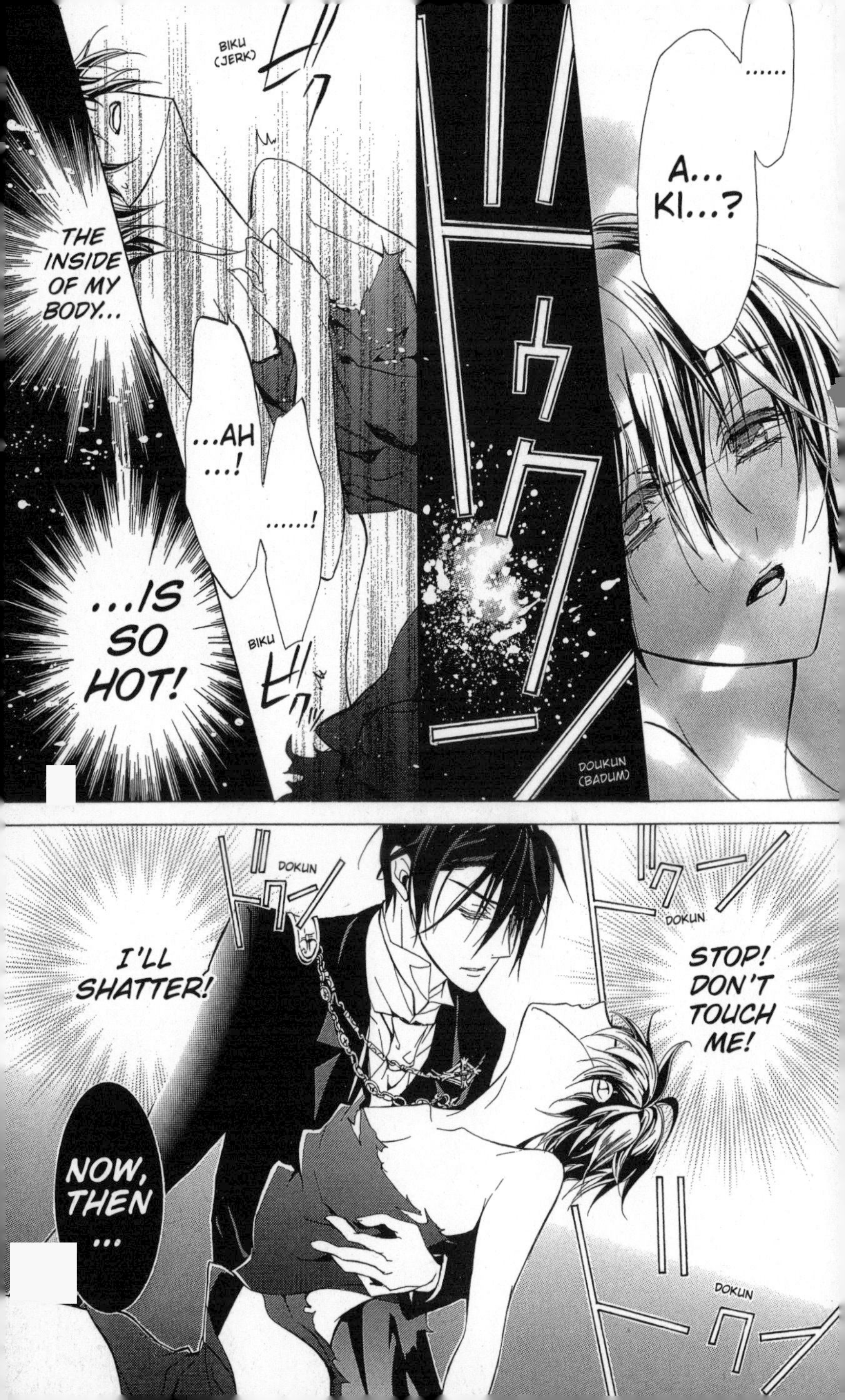
......
A... KI...?
DOUKUN (BADUM)
BIKU (JERK)
...AH ...!
......!
THE INSIDE OF MY BODY...
BIKU
...IS SO HOT!
DOKUN
STOP! DON'T TOUCH ME!
DOKUN
DOKUN
I'LL SHATTER!
NOW, THEN ...

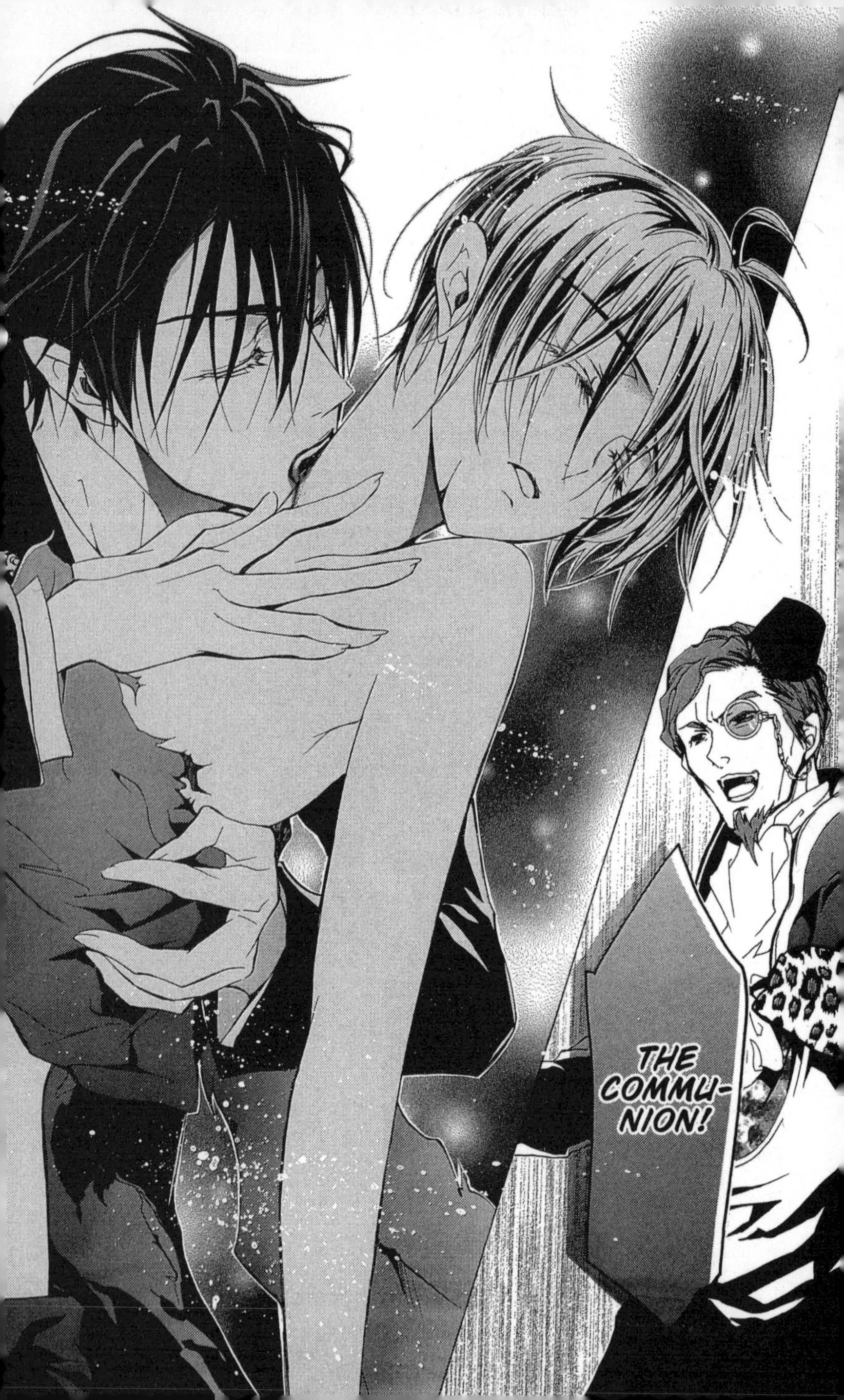
THE COMMU-NION!

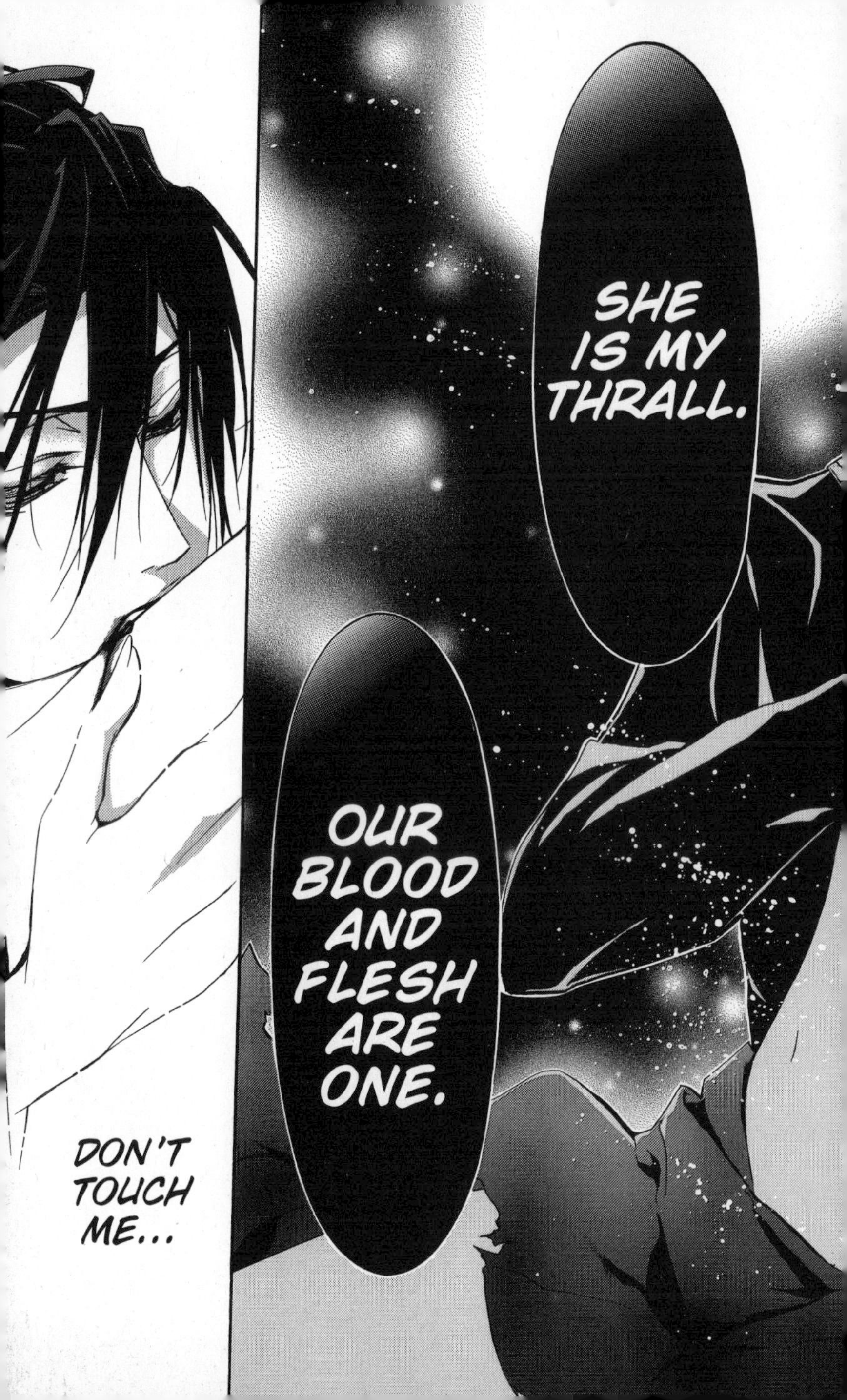
SHE IS MY THRALL.
OUR BLOOD AND FLESH ARE ONE.
DON'T TOUCH ME...

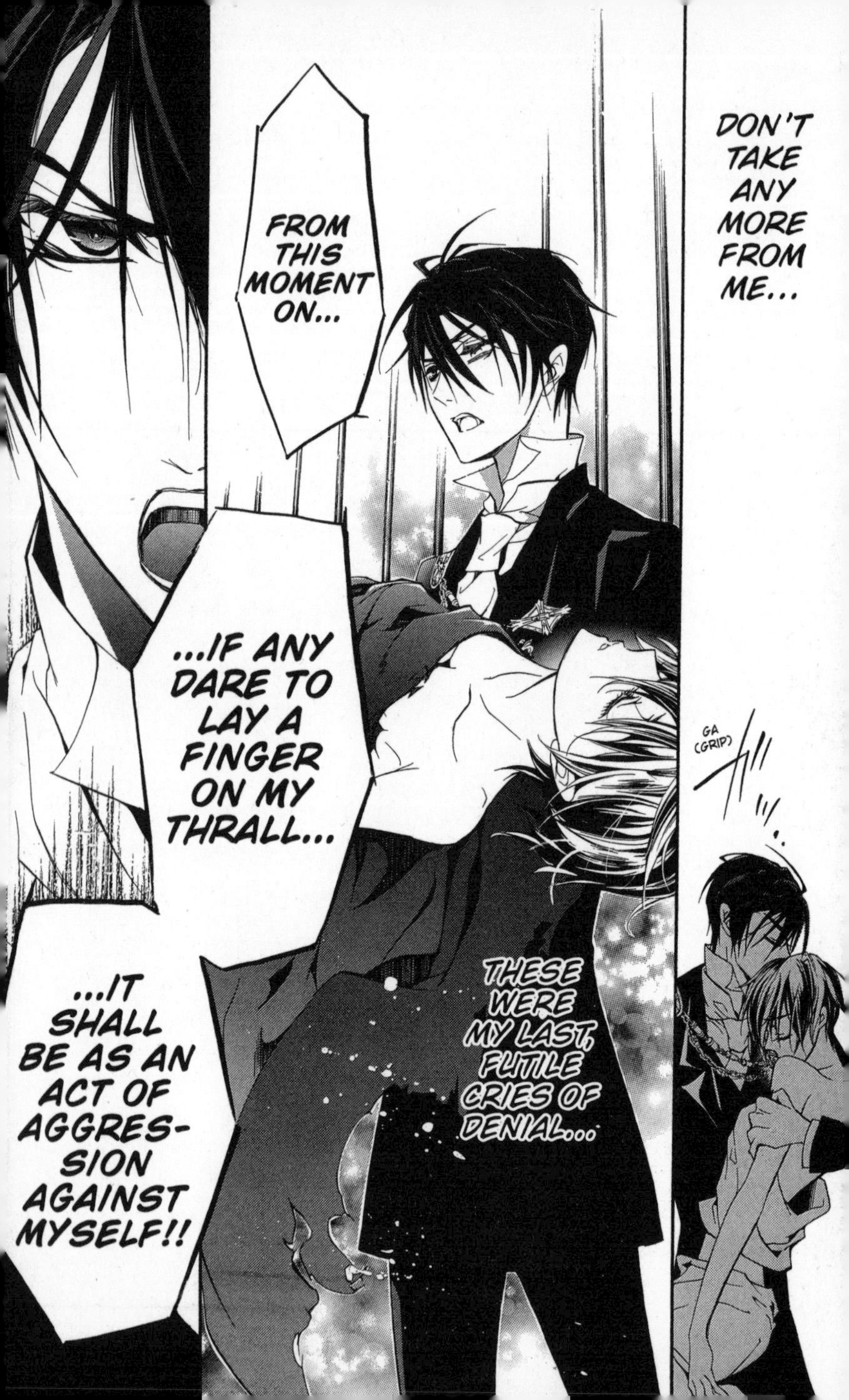
DON'T TAKE ANY MORE FROM ME...
GA (GRIP)
FROM THIS MOMENT ON...
...IF ANY DARE TO LAY A FINGER ON MY THRALL...
...IT SHALL BE AS AN ACT OF AGGRES-SION AGAINST MYSELF!!
THESE WERE MY LAST, FUTILE CRIES OF DENIAL...

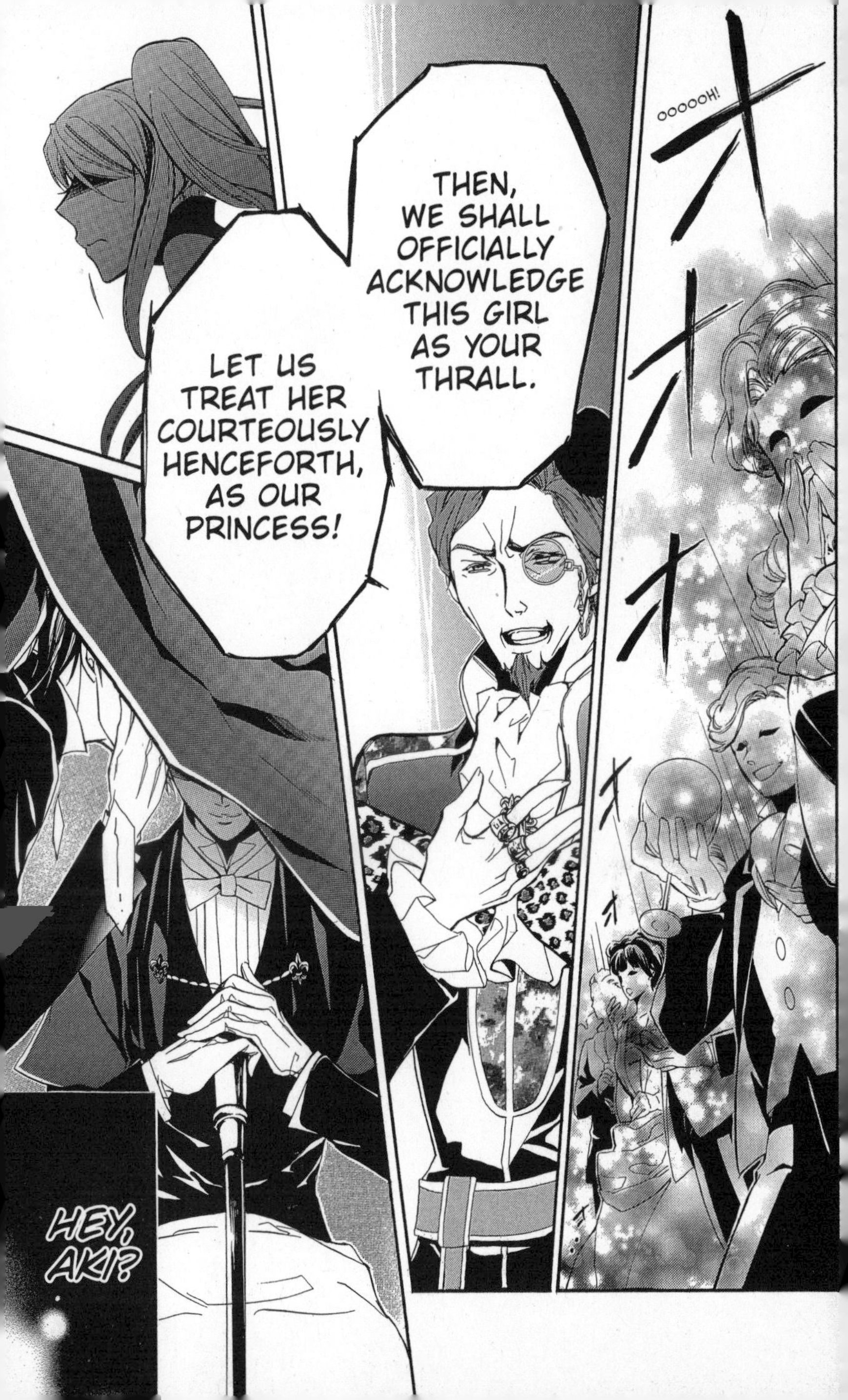
OOOOOH!
THEN, WE SHALL OFFICIALLY ACKNOWLEDGE THIS GIRL AS YOUR THRALL.
LET US TREAT HER COURTEOUSLY HENCEFORTH, AS OUR PRINCESS!
HEY, AKI?

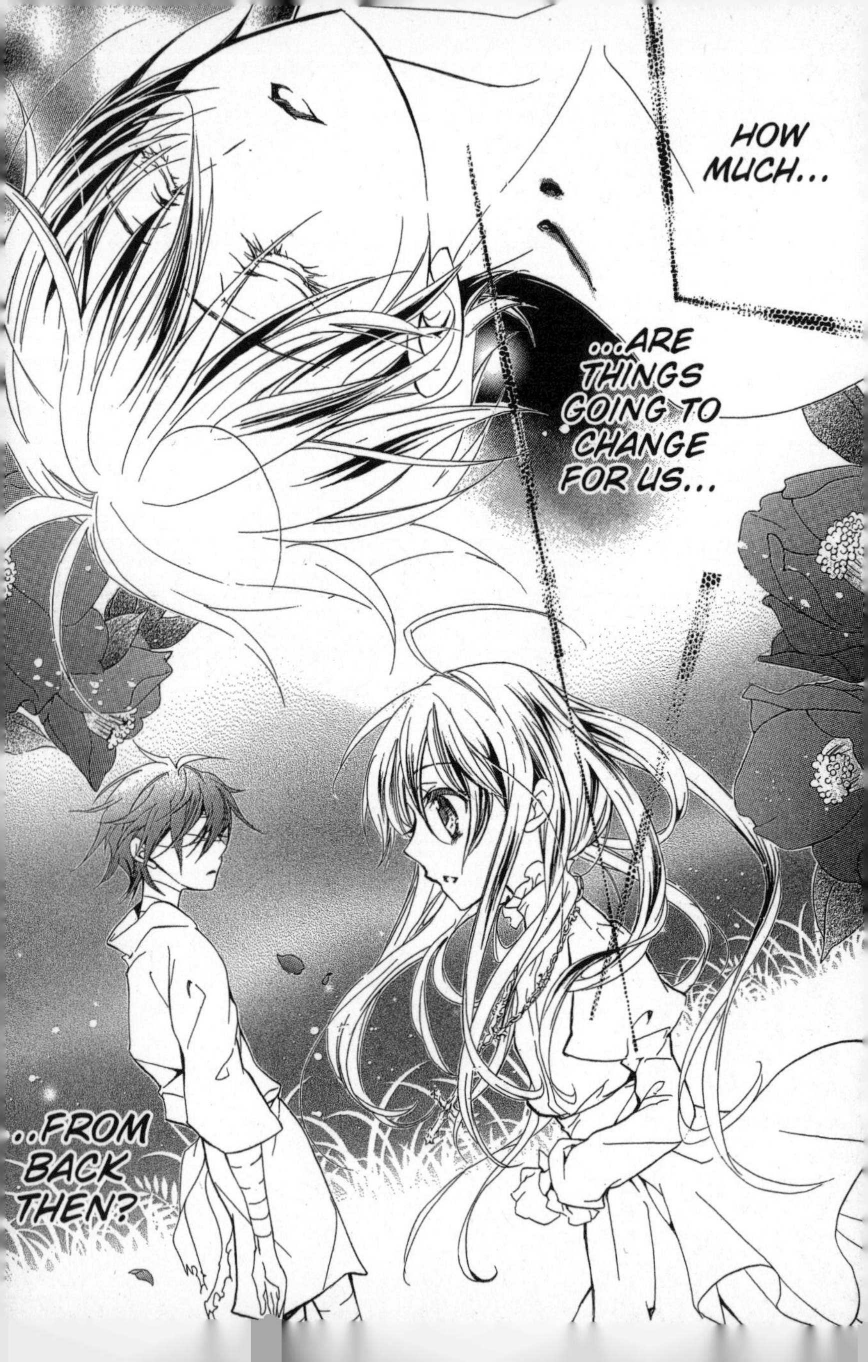
HOW MUCH...
...ARE THINGS GOING TO CHANGE FOR US...
..FROM BACK THEN?

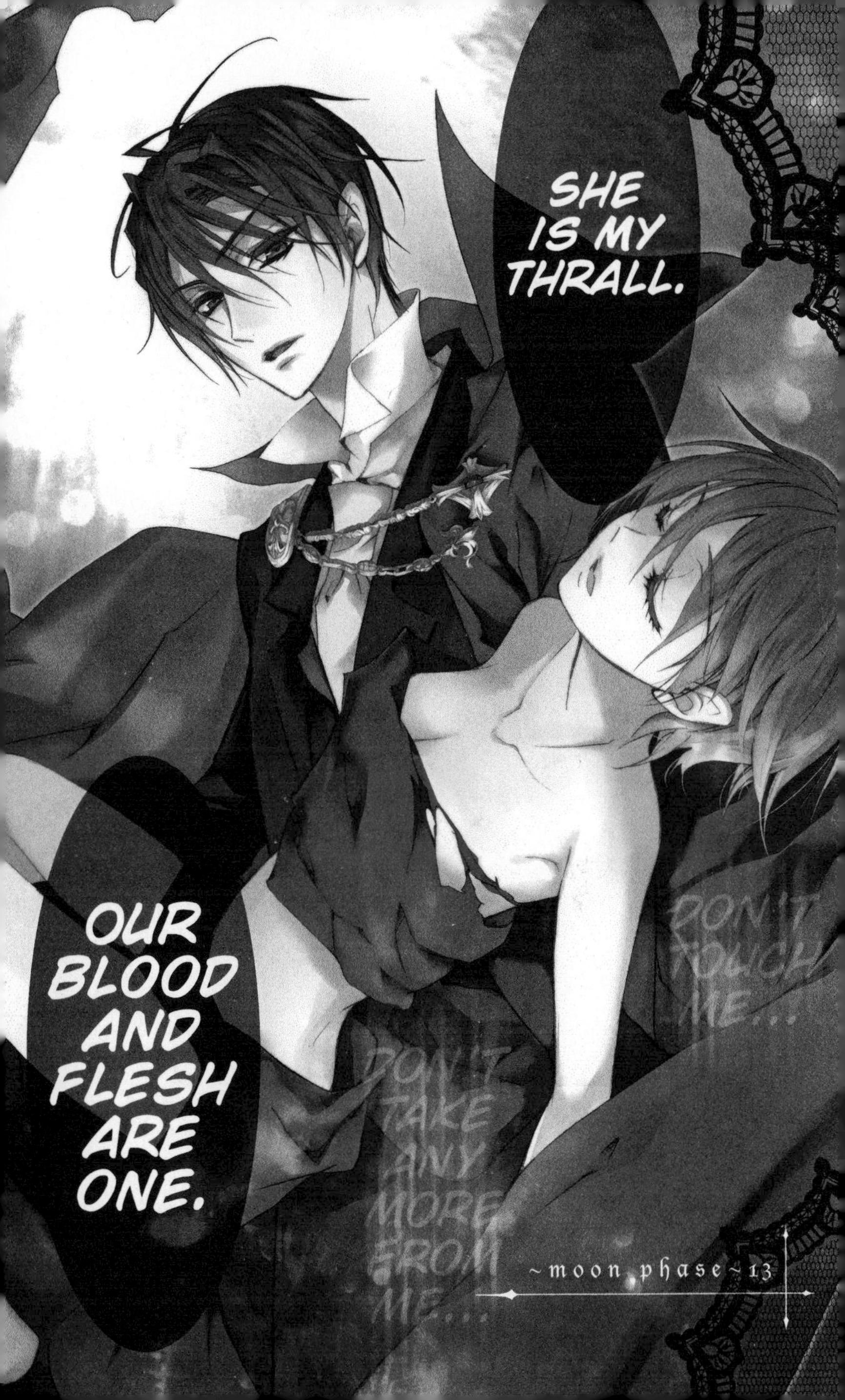
SHE IS MY THRALL.
DON'T TOUCH ME...
DON'T TAKE ANY MORE FROM ME...
OUR BLOOD AND FLESH ARE ONE.
~moon phase~13

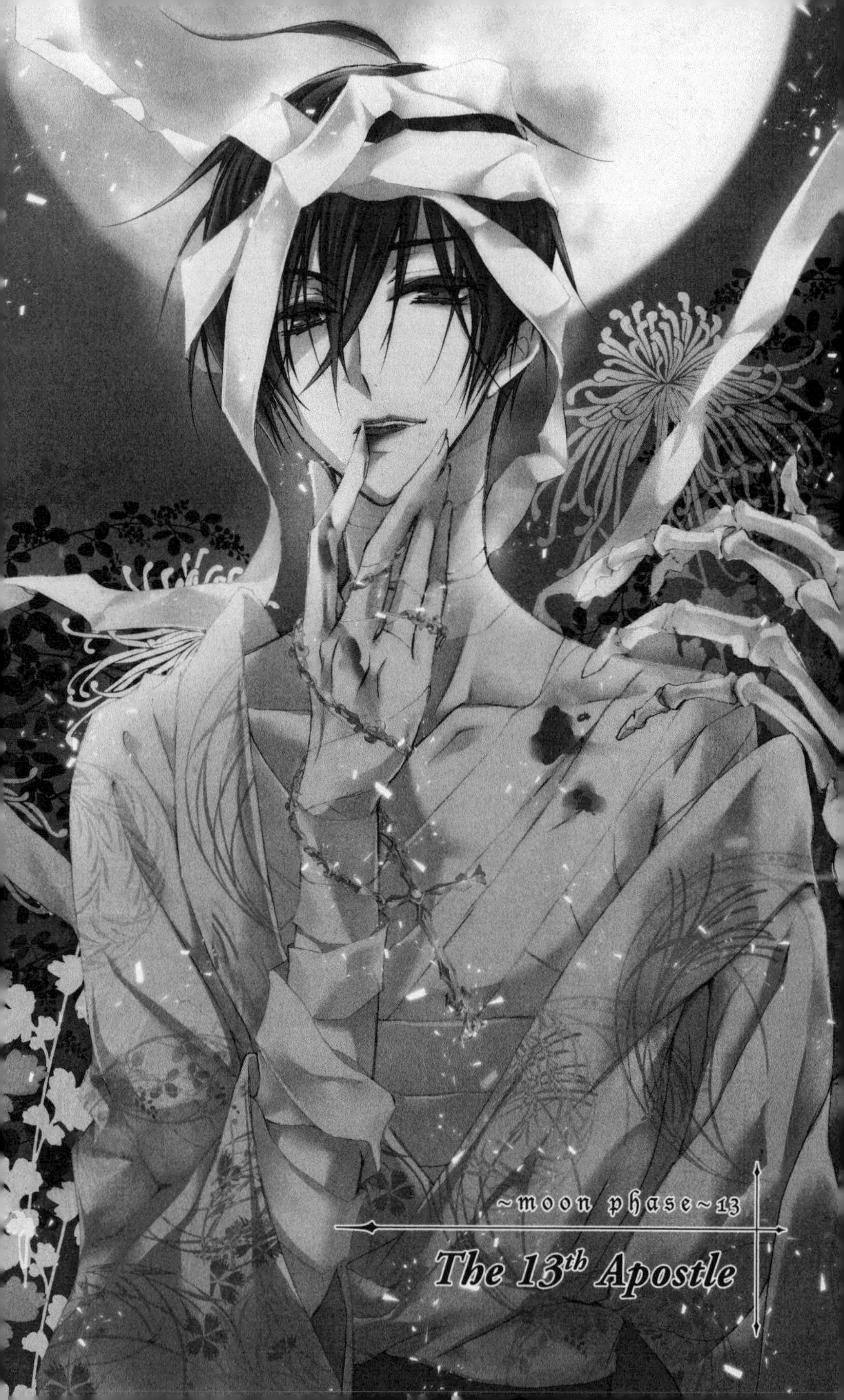
~moon phase~13
The 13th Apostle

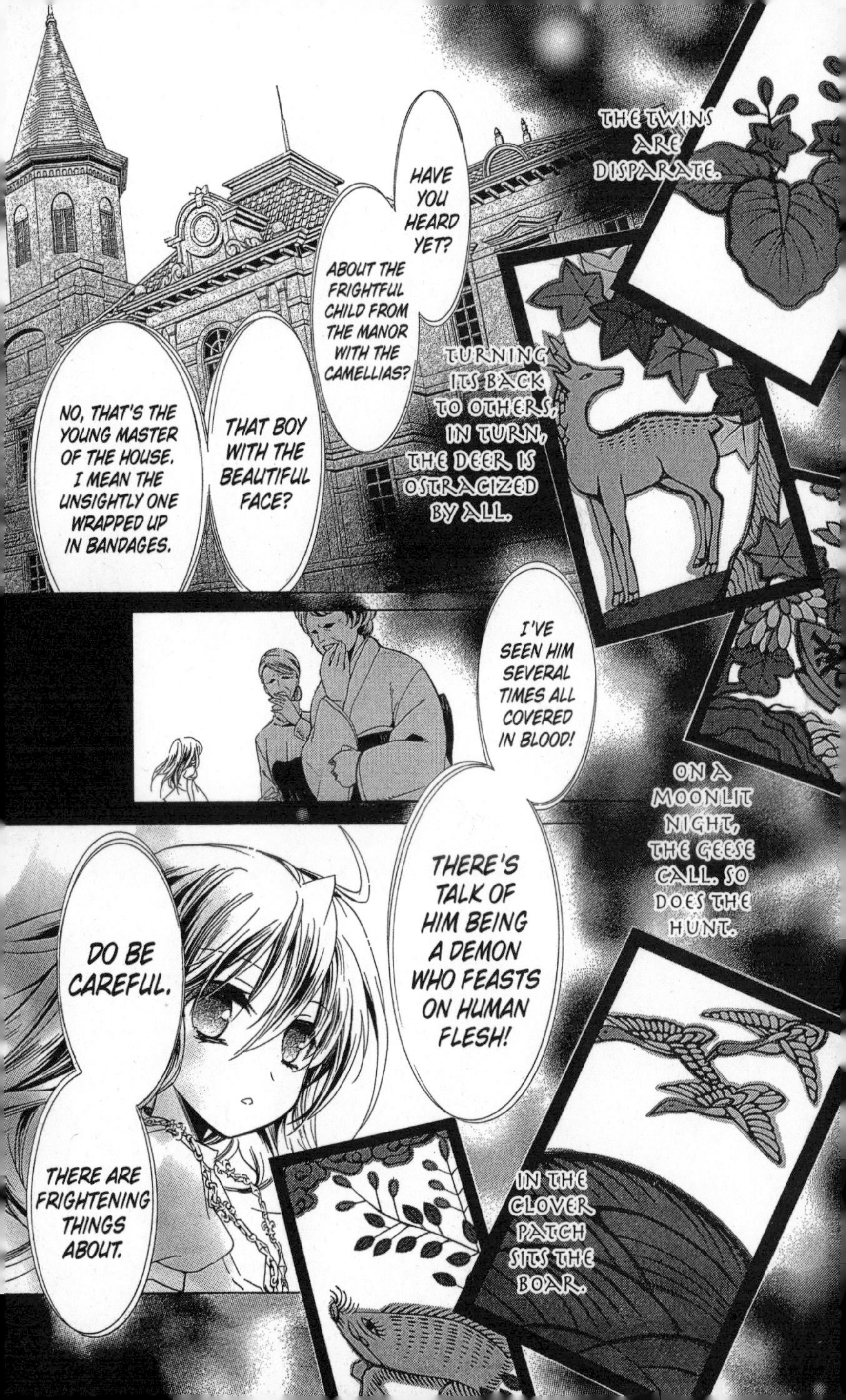
THE TWINS ARE DISPARATE.
HAVE YOU HEARD YET?
ABOUT THE FRIGHTFUL CHILD FROM THE MANOR WITH THE CAMELLIAS?
TURNING ITS BACK TO OTHERS, IN TURN, THE DEER IS OSTRACIZED BY ALL.
THAT BOY WITH THE BEAUTIFUL FACE?
NO, THAT'S THE YOUNG MASTER OF THE HOUSE. I MEAN THE UNSIGHTLY ONE WRAPPED UP IN BANDAGES.
I'VE SEEN HIM SEVERAL TIMES ALL COVERED IN BLOOD!
ON A MOONLIT NIGHT, THE GEESE CALL. SO DOES THE HUNT.
THERE'S TALK OF HIM BEING A DEMON WHO FEASTS ON HUMAN FLESH!
DO BE CAREFUL.
IN THE CLOVER PATCH SITS THE BOAR.
THERE ARE FRIGHTENING THINGS ABOUT.

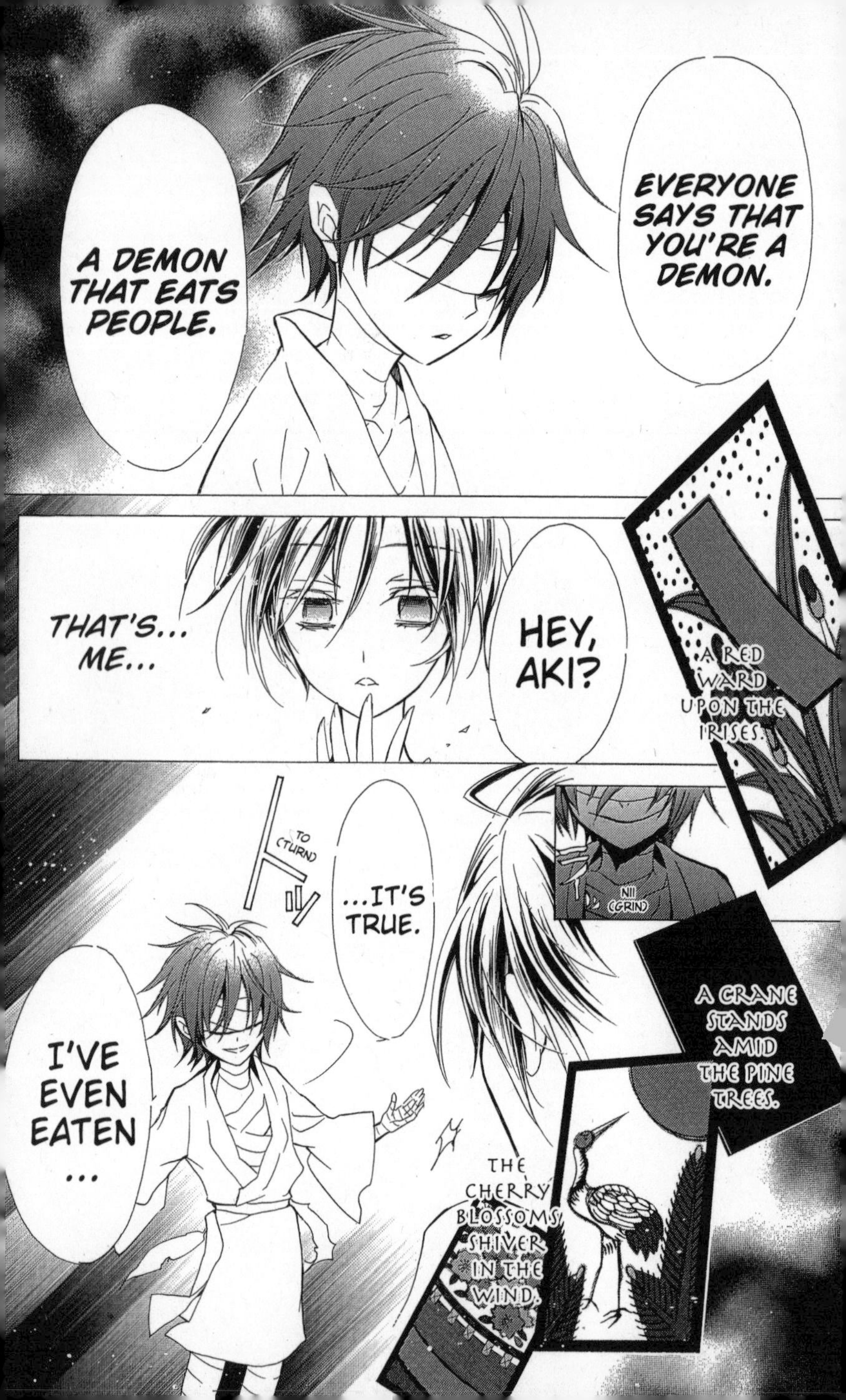
EVERYONE SAYS THAT YOU'RE A DEMON.
A DEMON THAT EATS PEOPLE.
A RED WARD UPON THE IRISES.
HEY, AKI?
THAT'S... ME...
NII (GRIN)
A CRANE STANDS AMID THE PINE TREES.
THE CHERRY BLOSSOMS SHIVER IN THE WIND.
...IT'S TRUE.
TO (TURN)
I'VE EVEN EATEN ...

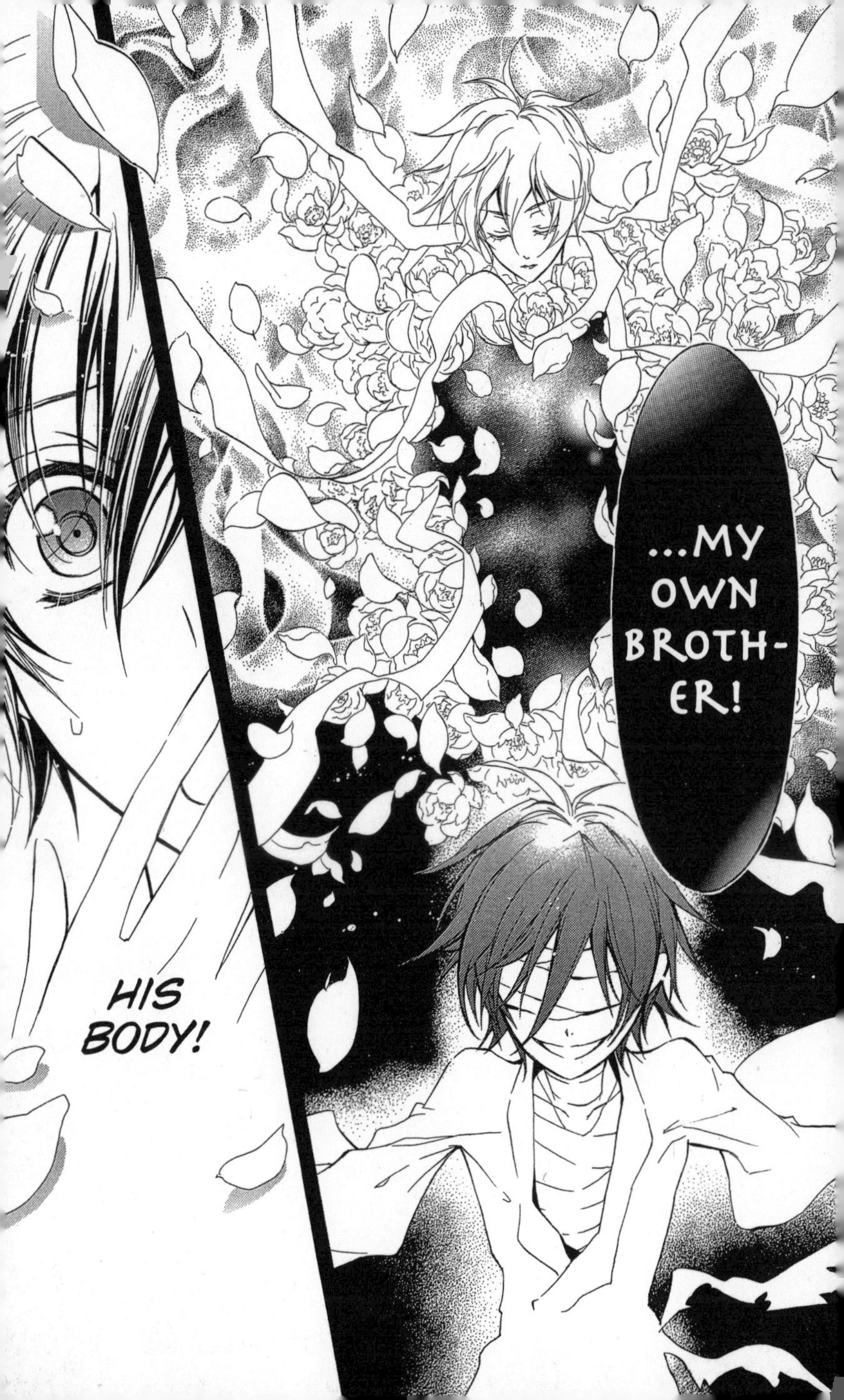
...MY OWN BROTHER!
HIS BODY!

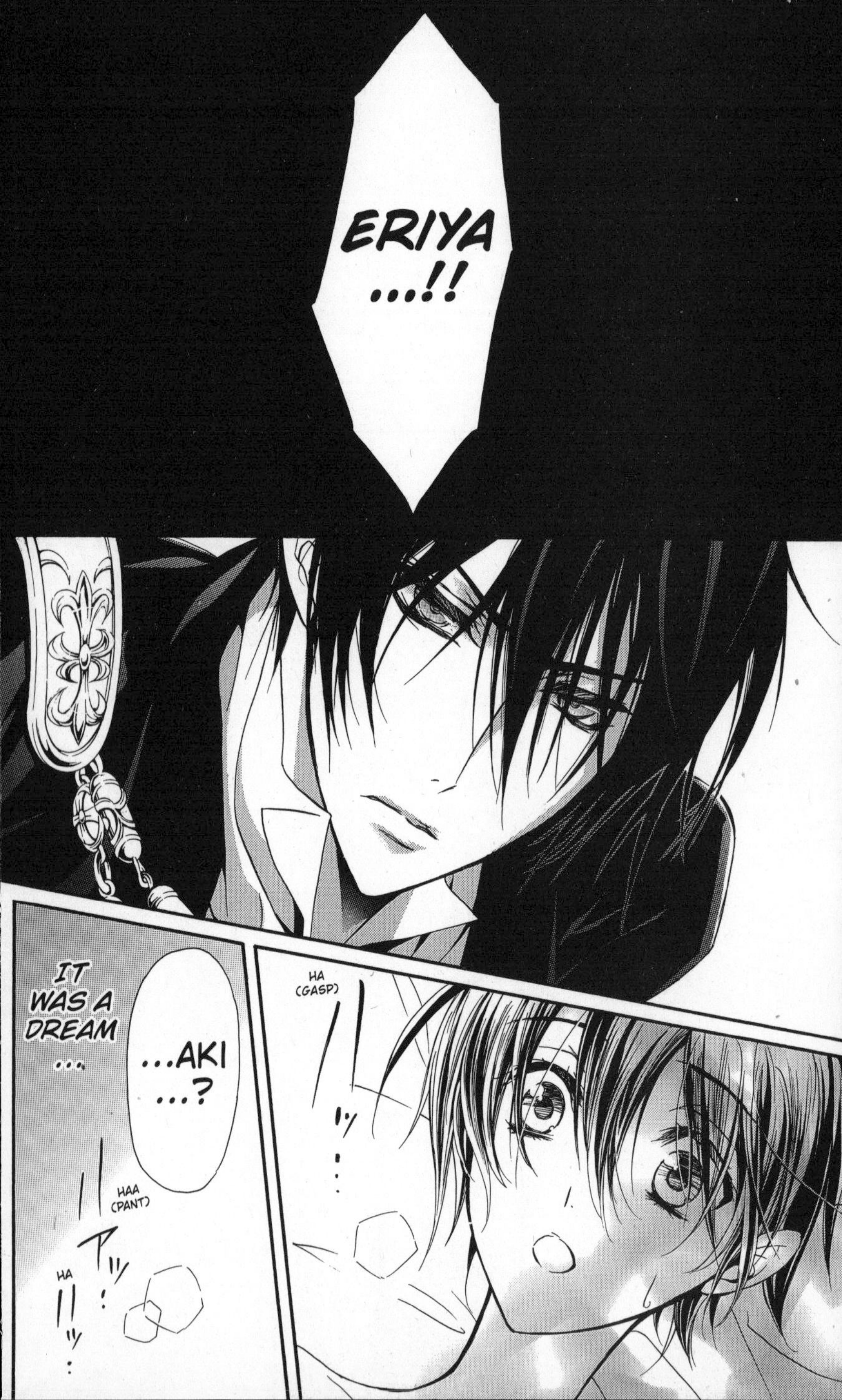
ERIYA ...!!
HA (GASP)
IT WAS A DREAM ...
...AKI ...?
HAA (PANT)
HA

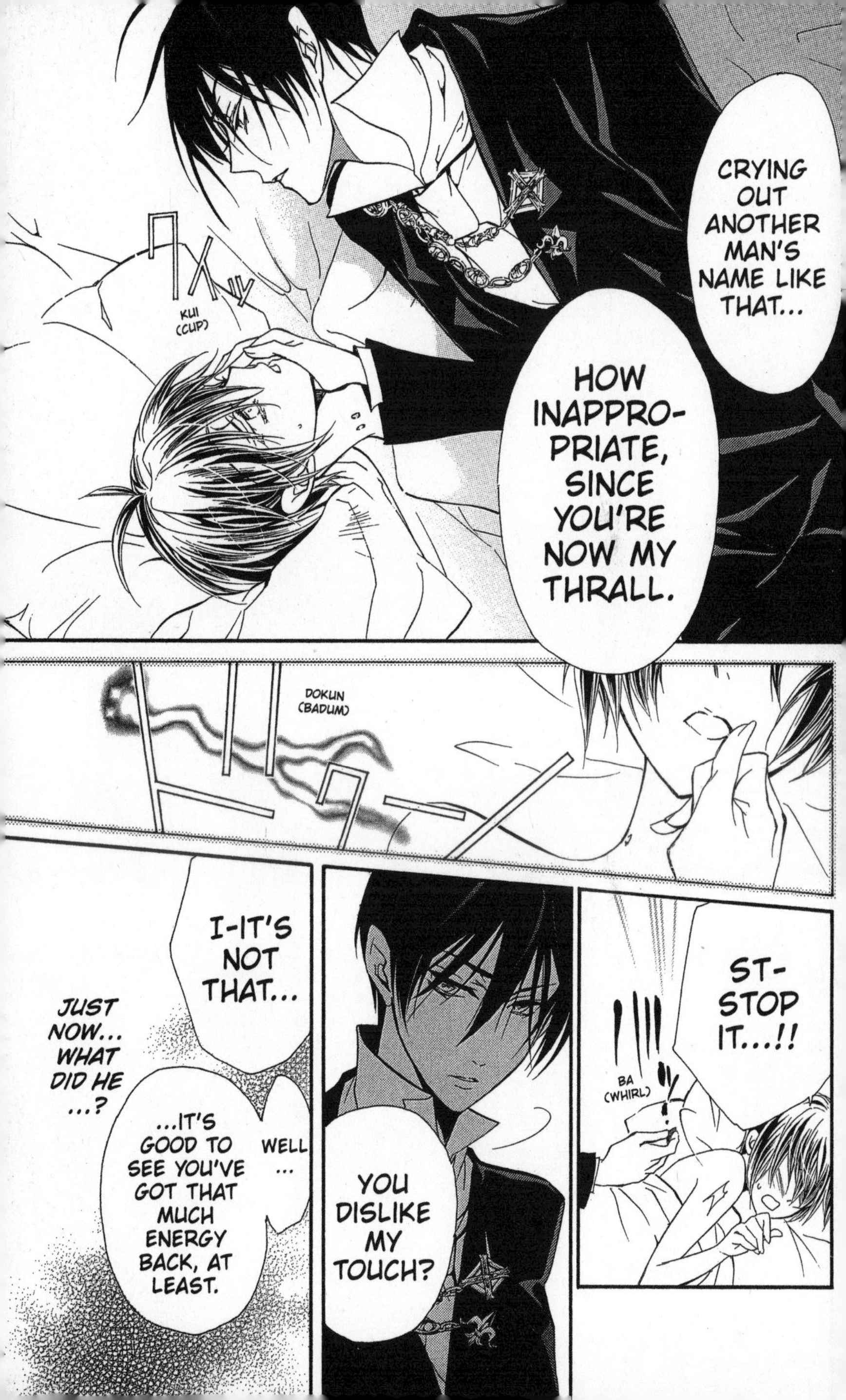
CRYING OUT ANOTHER MAN'S NAME LIKE THAT...
HOW INAPPROPRIATE, SINCE YOU'RE NOW MY THRALL.
KUI (CUP)
DOKUN (BADUM)
ST-STOP IT...!!
BA (WHIRL)
YOU DISLIKE MY TOUCH?
I-IT'S NOT THAT...
JUST NOW... WHAT DID HE ...?
WELL ...
...IT'S GOOD TO SEE YOU'VE GOT THAT MUCH ENERGY BACK, AT LEAST.

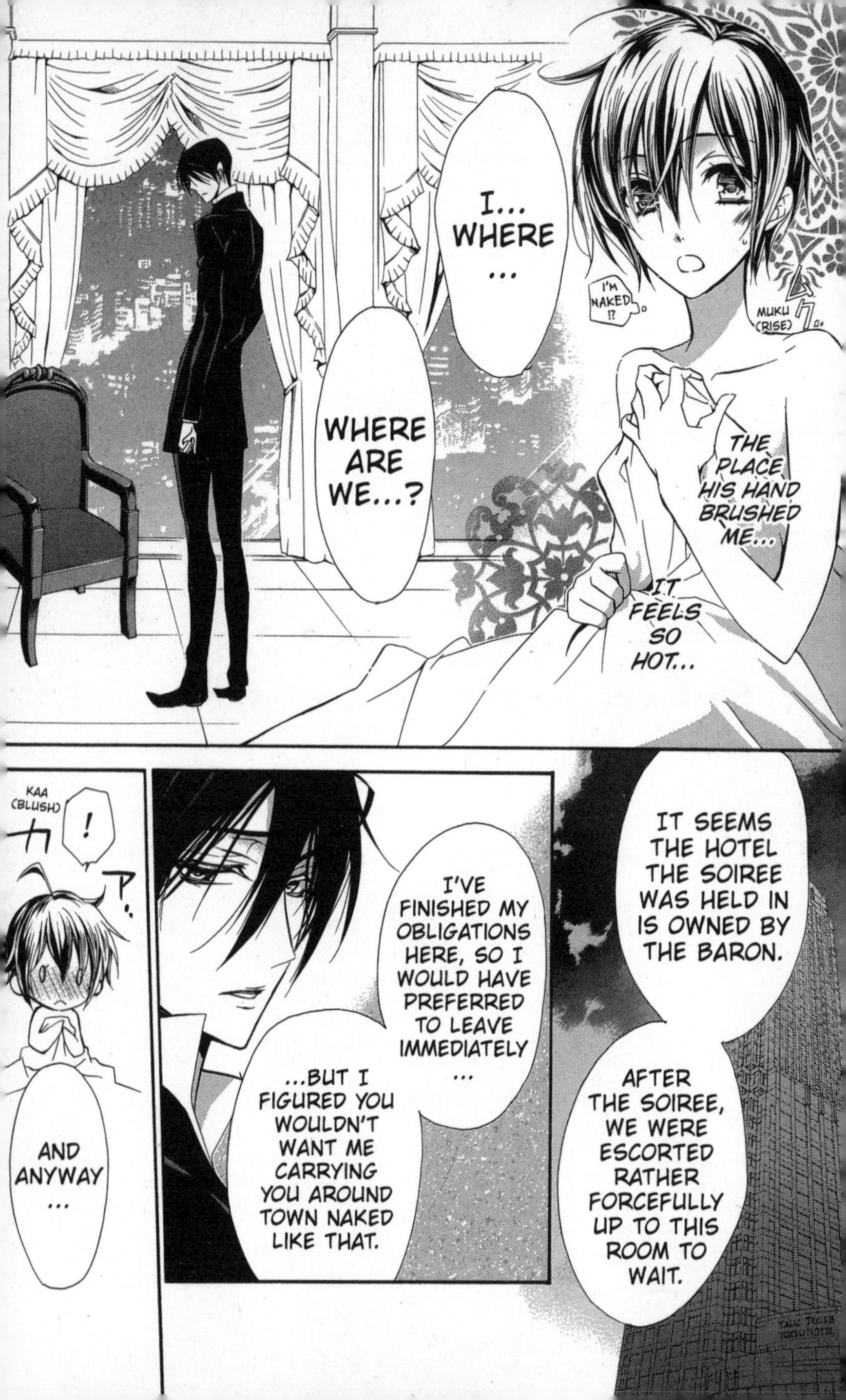
I... WHERE ...
WHERE ARE WE...?
MUKU (RISE)
I'M NAKED !?
THE PLACE HIS HAND BRUSHED ME...
IT FEELS SO HOT...
IT SEEMS THE HOTEL THE SOIREE WAS HELD IN IS OWNED BY THE BARON.
AFTER THE SOIREE, WE WERE ESCORTED RATHER FORCEFULLY UP TO THIS ROOM TO WAIT.
I'VE FINISHED MY OBLIGATIONS HERE, SO I WOULD HAVE PREFERRED TO LEAVE IMMEDIATELY ...
...BUT I FIGURED YOU WOULDN'T WANT ME CARRYING YOU AROUND TOWN NAKED LIKE THAT.
KAA (BLUSH)
!
AND ANYWAY ...

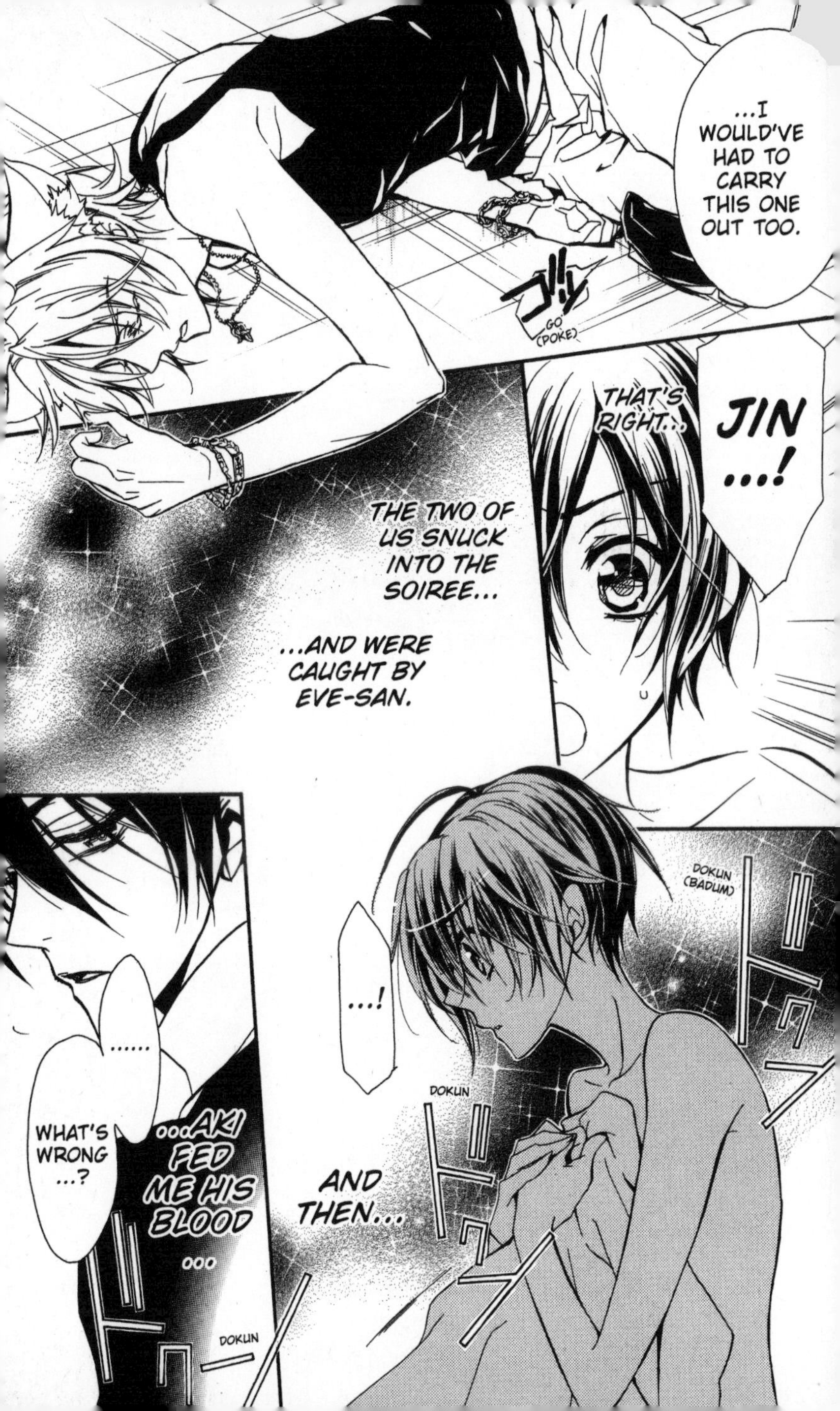
...I WOULD'VE HAD TO CARRY THIS ONE OUT TOO.
GO (POKE)
JIN ...!
THAT'S RIGHT...
THE TWO OF US SNUCK INTO THE SOIREE...
...AND WERE CAUGHT BY EVE-SAN.
DOKUN (BADUM)
...!
DOKUN
AND THEN...
......
WHAT'S WRONG ...?
...AKI FED ME HIS BLOOD ...
DOKUN

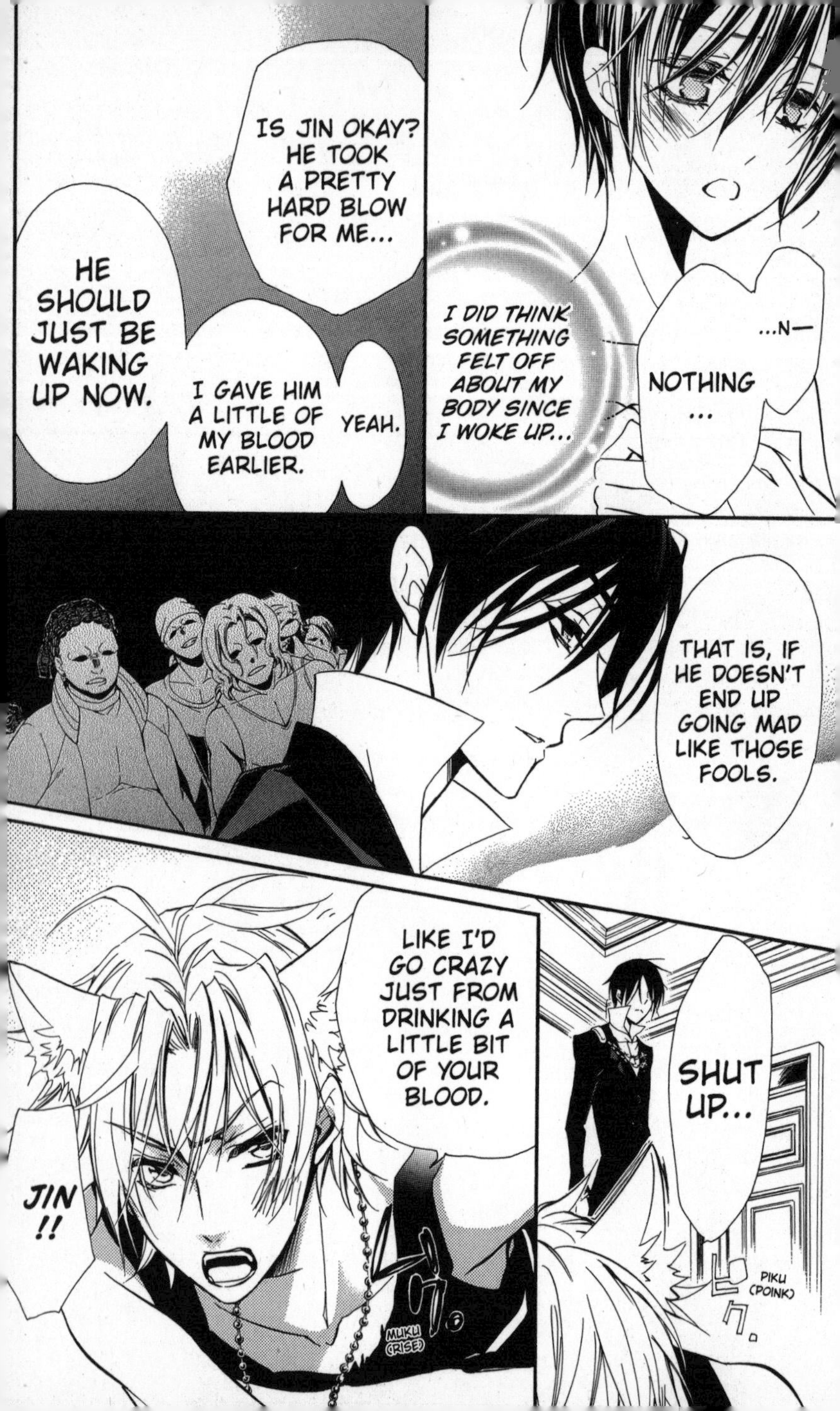
...N—
NOTHING ...
I DID THINK SOMETHING FELT OFF ABOUT MY BODY SINCE I WOKE UP...
IS JIN OKAY? HE TOOK A PRETTY HARD BLOW FOR ME...
YEAH.
I GAVE HIM A LITTLE OF MY BLOOD EARLIER.
HE SHOULD JUST BE WAKING UP NOW.
THAT IS, IF HE DOESN'T END UP GOING MAD LIKE THOSE FOOLS.
SHUT UP...
PIKU (POINK)
LIKE I'D GO CRAZY JUST FROM DRINKING A LITTLE BIT OF YOUR BLOOD.
JIN !!
MUKU (RISE)

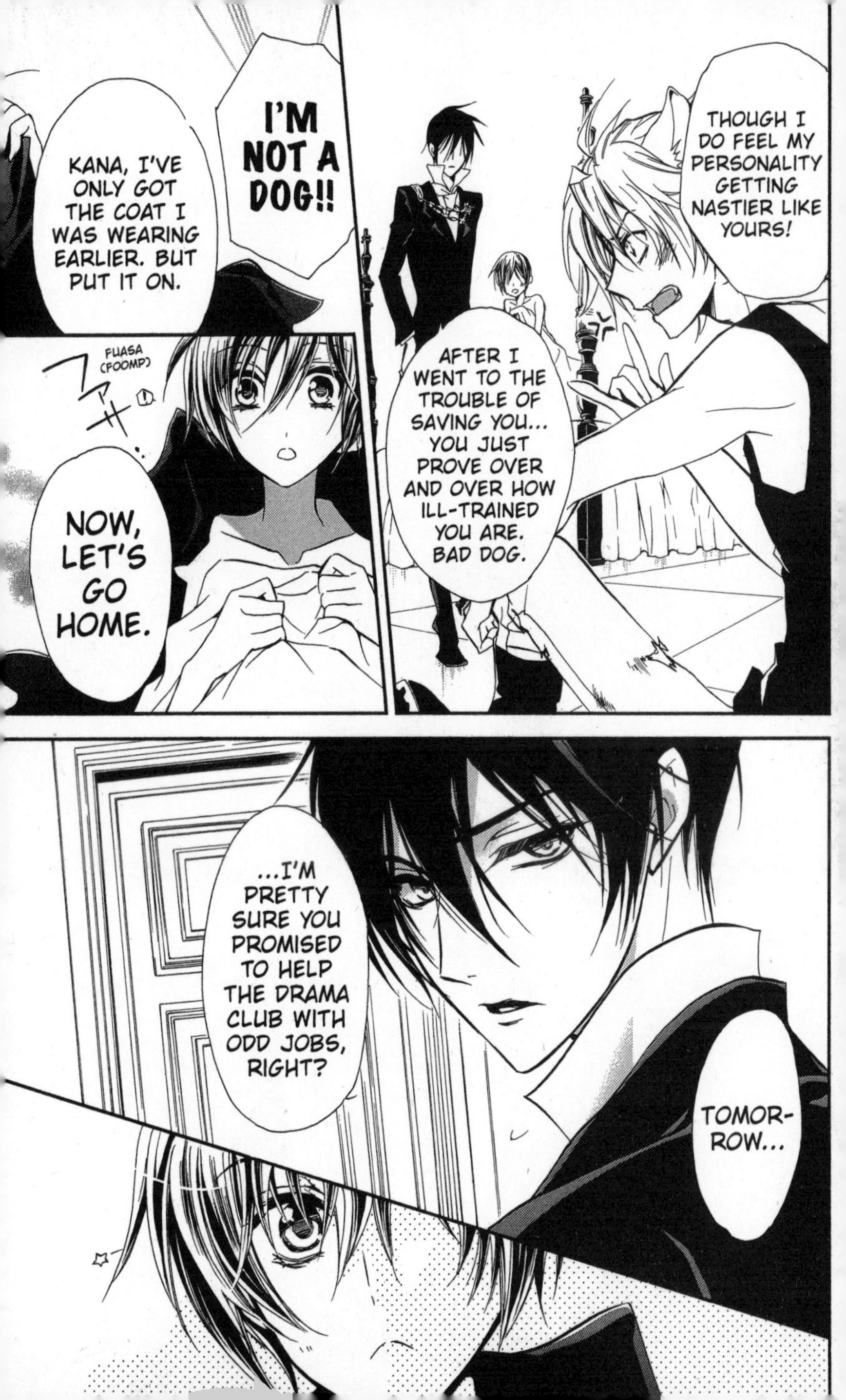
THOUGH I DO FEEL MY PERSONALITY GETTING NASTIER LIKE YOURS!
AFTER I WENT TO THE TROUBLE OF SAVING YOU... YOU JUST PROVE OVER AND OVER HOW ILL-TRAINED YOU ARE. BAD DOG.
I'M NOT A DOG!!
KANA, I'VE ONLY GOT THE COAT I WAS WEARING EARLIER. BUT PUT IT ON.
FUASA (FOOMP)
NOW, LET'S GO HOME.
TOMOR-ROW...
...I'M PRETTY SURE YOU PROMISED TO HELP THE DRAMA CLUB WITH ODD JOBS, RIGHT?

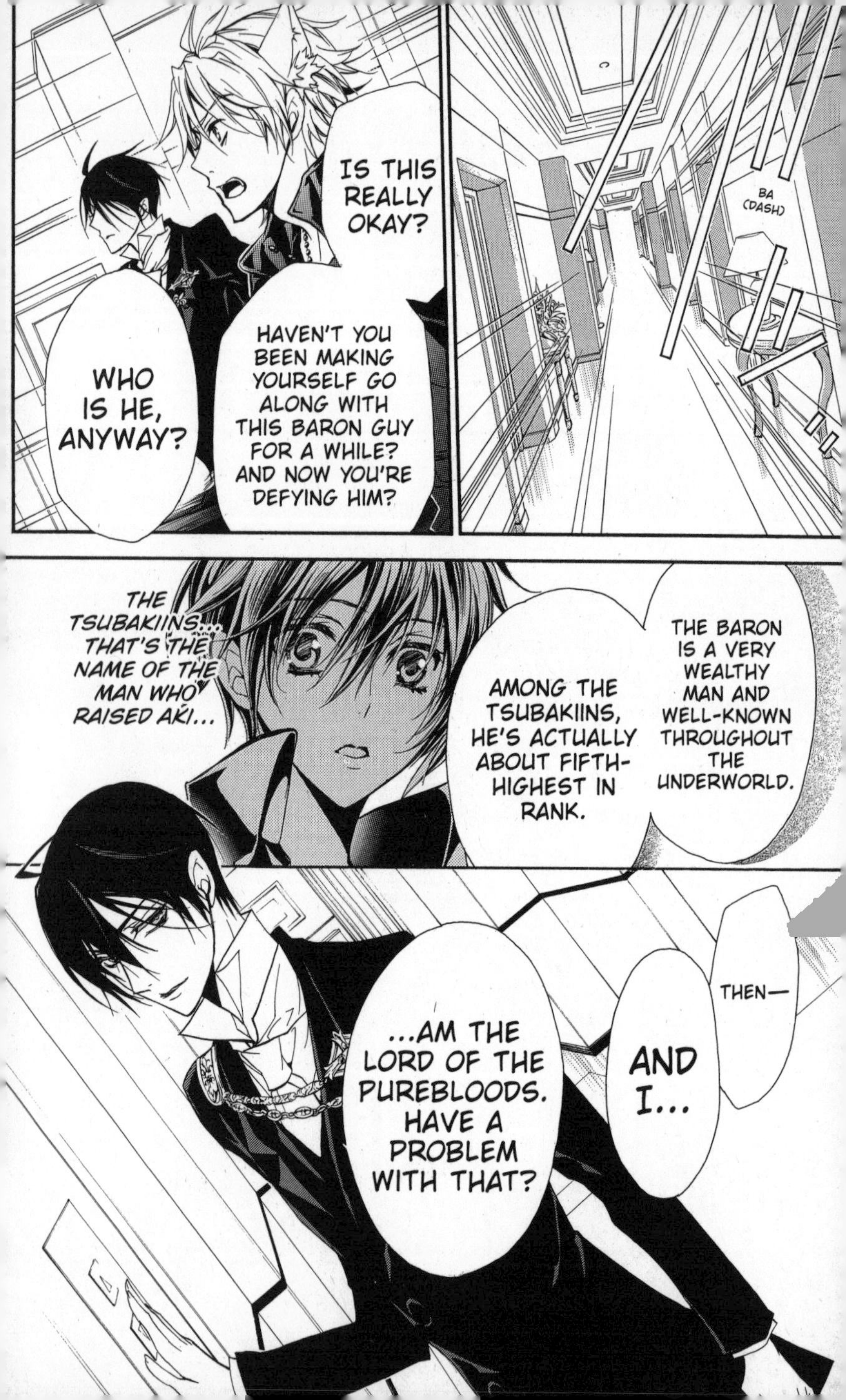
BA (DASH)
IS THIS REALLY OKAY?
HAVEN'T YOU BEEN MAKING YOURSELF GO ALONG WITH THIS BARON GUY FOR A WHILE? AND NOW YOU'RE DEFYING HIM?
WHO IS HE, ANYWAY?
THE BARON IS A VERY WEALTHY MAN AND WELL-KNOWN THROUGHOUT THE UNDERWORLD.
AMONG THE TSUBAKIINS, HE'S ACTUALLY ABOUT FIFTH-HIGHEST IN RANK.
THE TSUBAKIINS... THAT'S THE NAME OF THE MAN WHO RAISED AKI...
THEN—
AND I...
...AM THE LORD OF THE PUREBLOODS. HAVE A PROBLEM WITH THAT?

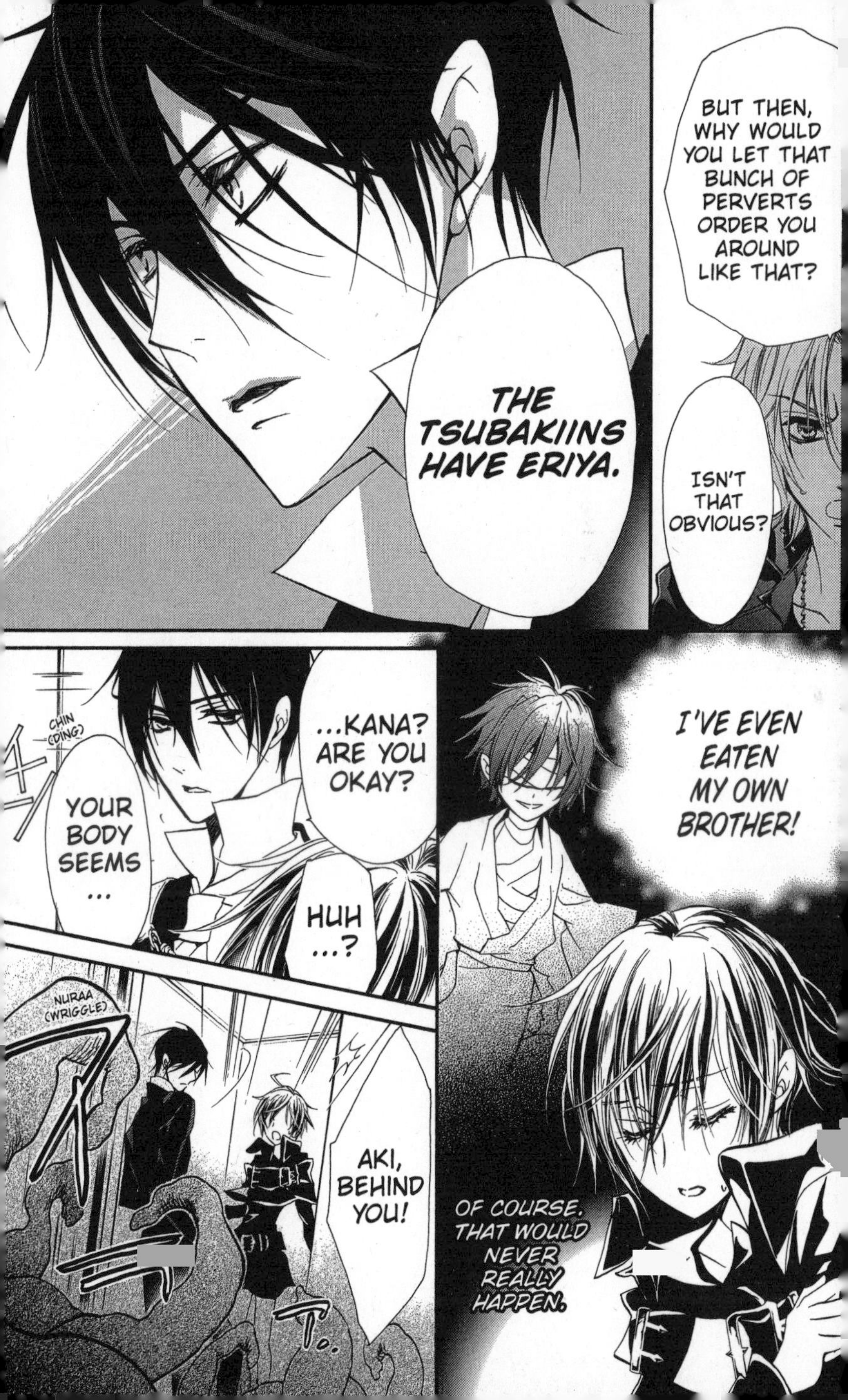
BUT THEN, WHY WOULD YOU LET THAT BUNCH OF PERVERTS ORDER YOU AROUND LIKE THAT?
ISN'T THAT OBVIOUS?
THE TSUBAKIINS HAVE ERIYA.
I'VE EVEN EATEN MY OWN BROTHER!
OF COURSE. THAT WOULD NEVER REALLY HAPPEN.
...KANA? ARE YOU OKAY?
CHIN (DING)
YOUR BODY SEEMS ...
HUH ...?
AKI, BEHIND YOU!
NURAA (WRIGGLE)

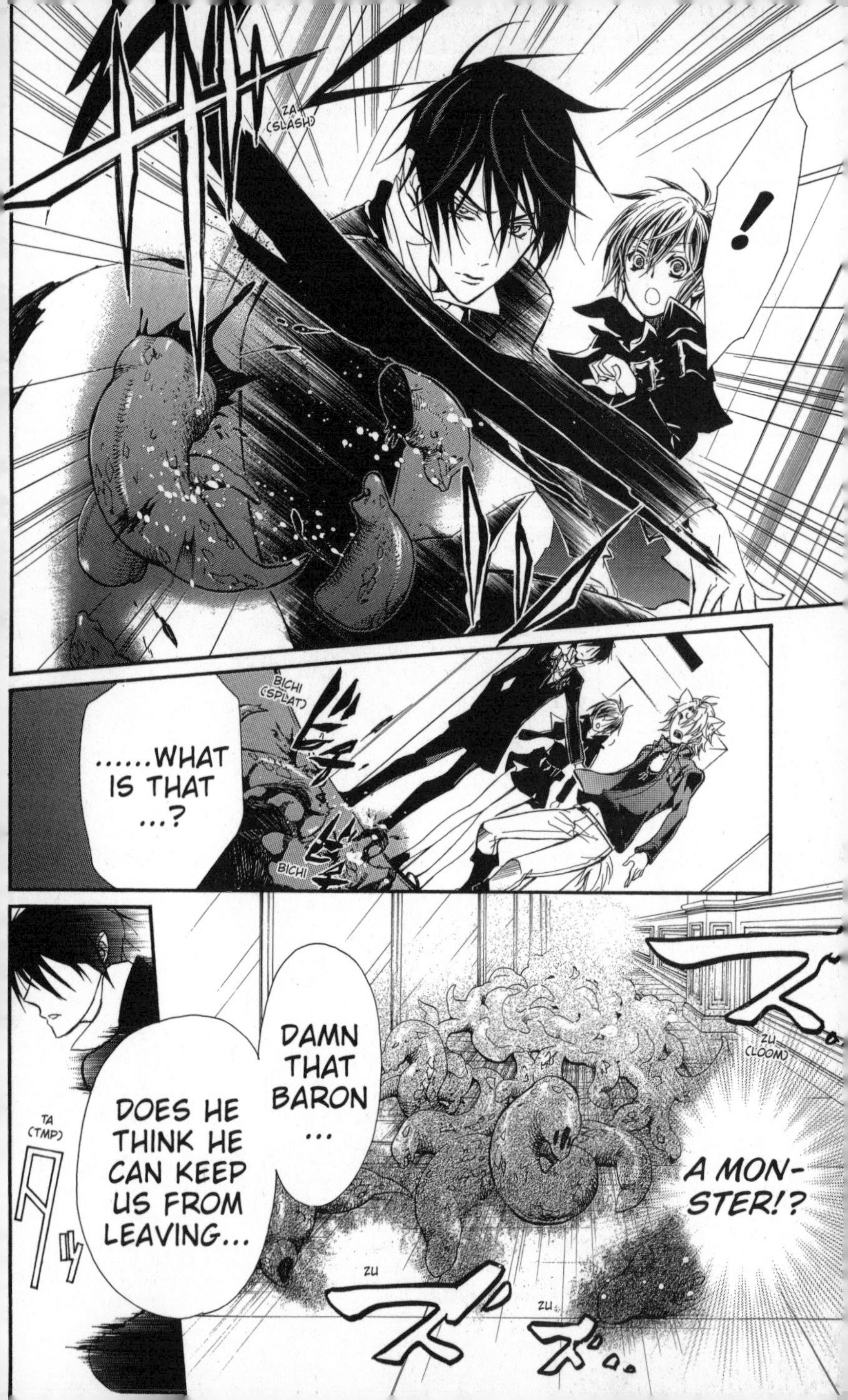
!
ZA (SLASH)
BICHI (SPLAT)
......WHAT IS THAT ...?
BICHI
ZU (LOOM)
A MON-STER!?
DAMN THAT BARON ...
DOES HE THINK HE CAN KEEP US FROM LEAVING...
TA (TMP)
ZU
ZU

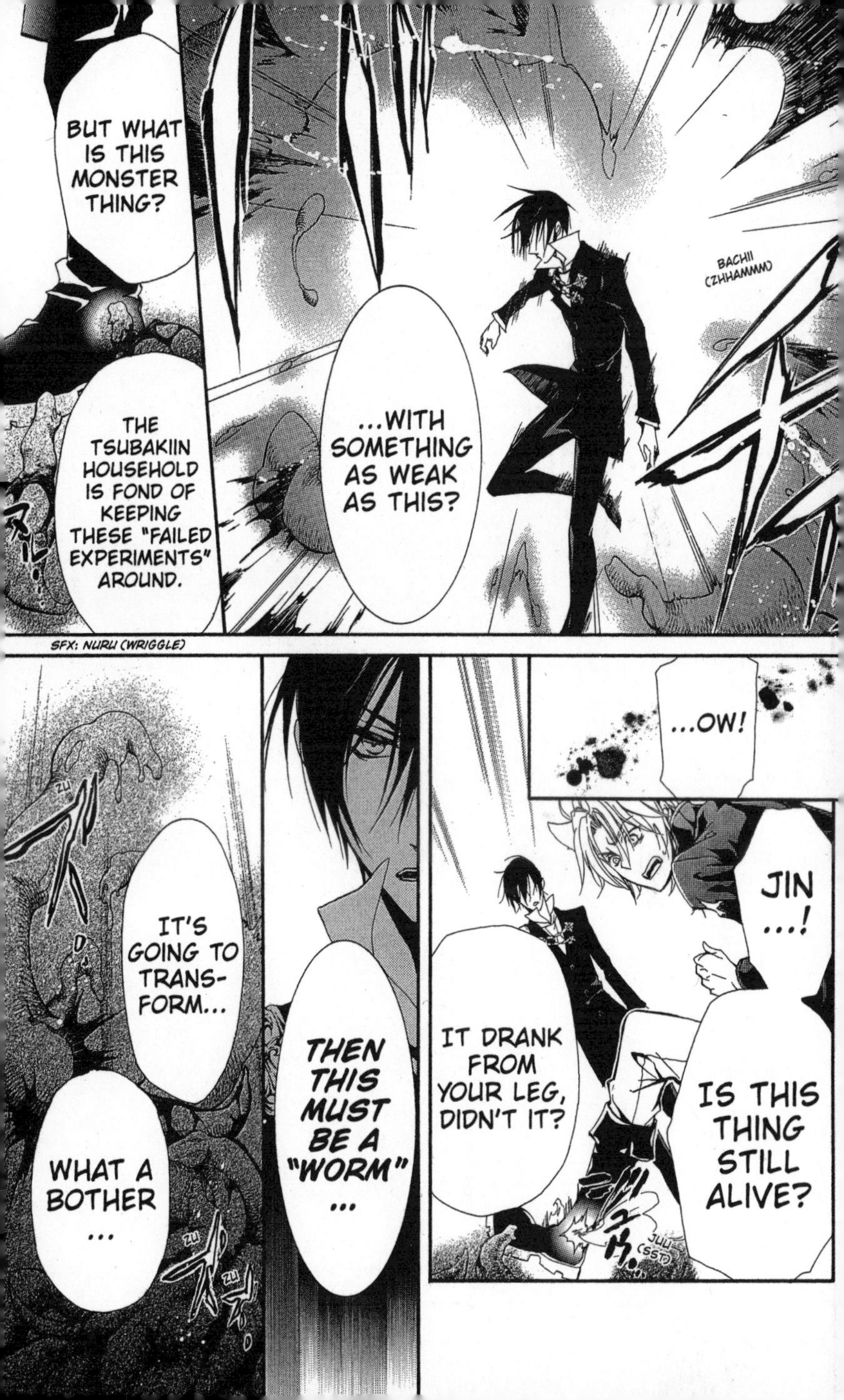
BACHII (ZHHAMMM)
...WITH SOMETHING AS WEAK AS THIS?
BUT WHAT IS THIS MONSTER THING?
THE TSUBAKIIN HOUSEHOLD IS FOND OF KEEPING THESE "FAILED EXPERIMENTS" AROUND.
SFX: NURU (WRIGGLE)
...OW!
JIN ...!
IS THIS THING STILL ALIVE?
IT DRANK FROM YOUR LEG, DIDN'T IT?
JUU (SST)
THEN THIS MUST BE A "WORM" ...
ZU
IT'S GOING TO TRANS-FORM...
WHAT A BOTHER ...
ZU
ZU

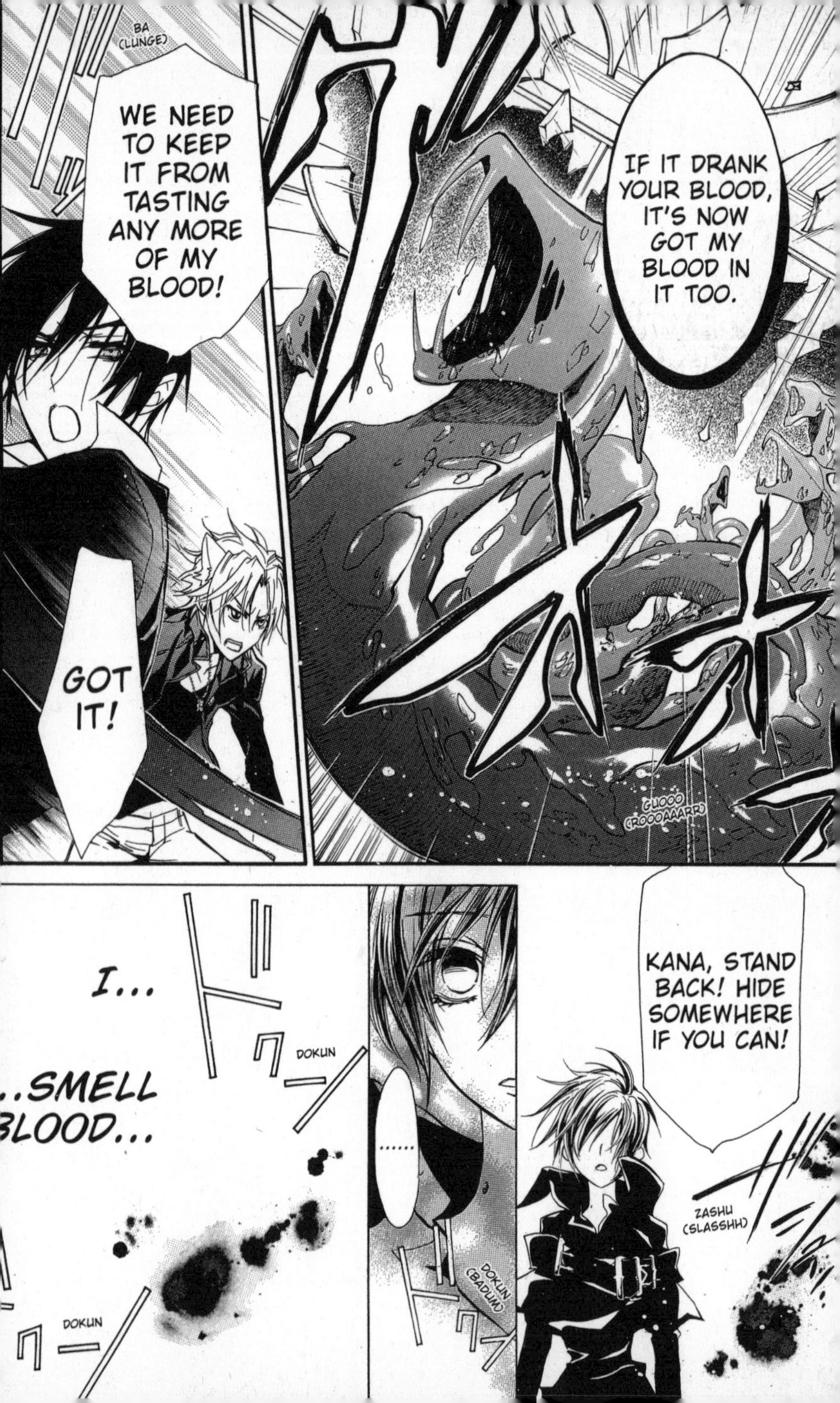
IF IT DRANK YOUR BLOOD, IT'S NOW GOT MY BLOOD IN IT TOO.
GUOOO (ROOOAAARR)
BA (LUNGE)
WE NEED TO KEEP IT FROM TASTING ANY MORE OF MY BLOOD!
GOT IT!
KANA, STAND BACK! HIDE SOMEWHERE IF YOU CAN!
ZASHU (SLASSHH)
......
DOKUN (BADUM)
I...
DOKUN
...SMELL BLOOD...
DOKUN

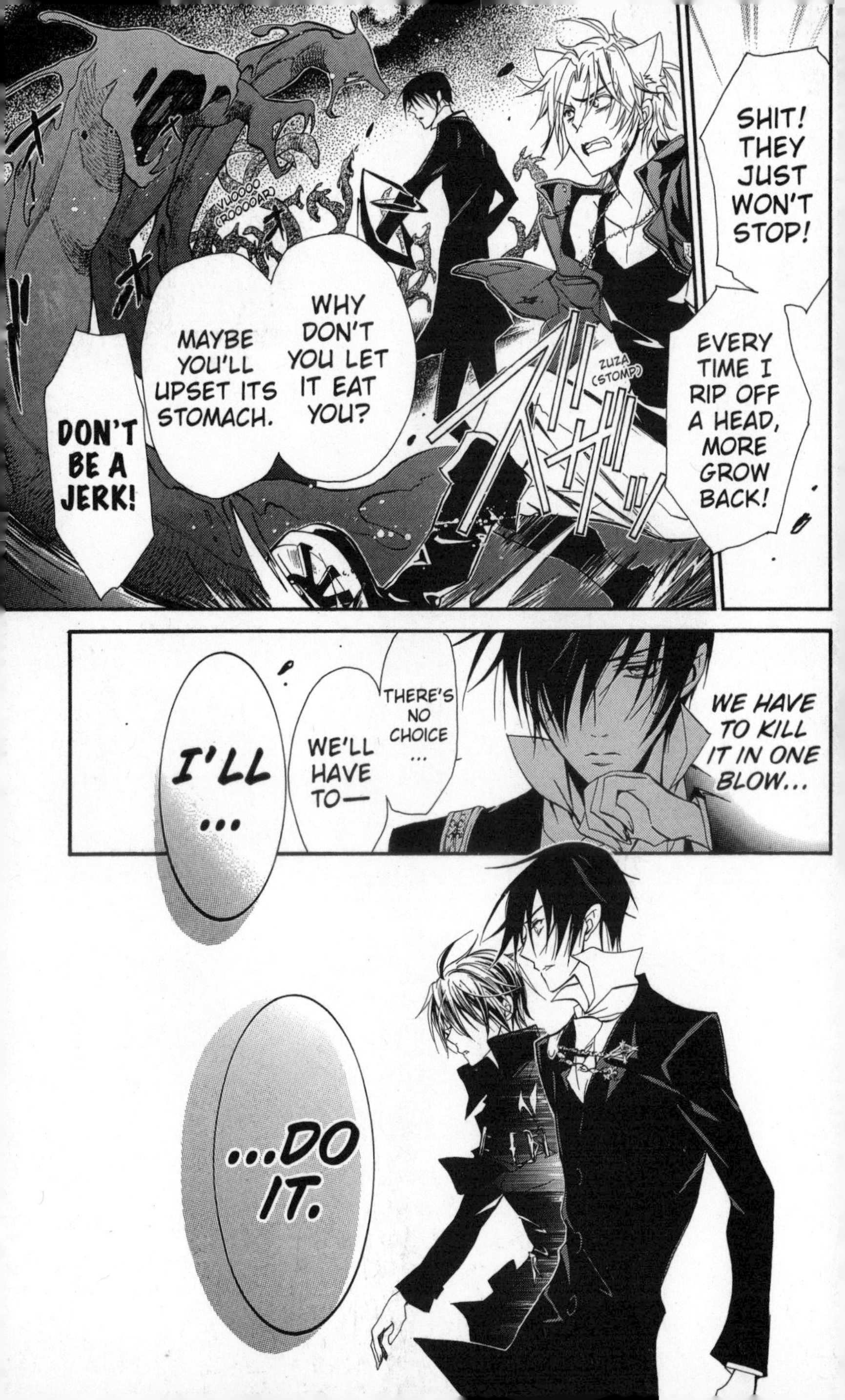

SHIT! THEY JUST WON'T STOP!
EVERY TIME I RIP OFF A HEAD, MORE GROW BACK!
VUOOOO (ROOOOAR)
ZUZA (STOMP)
WHY DON'T YOU LET IT EAT YOU?
MAYBE YOU'LL UPSET ITS STOMACH.
DON'T BE A JERK!
WE HAVE TO KILL IT IN ONE BLOW...
THERE'S NO CHOICE...
WE'LL HAVE TO—
I'LL...
...DO IT.

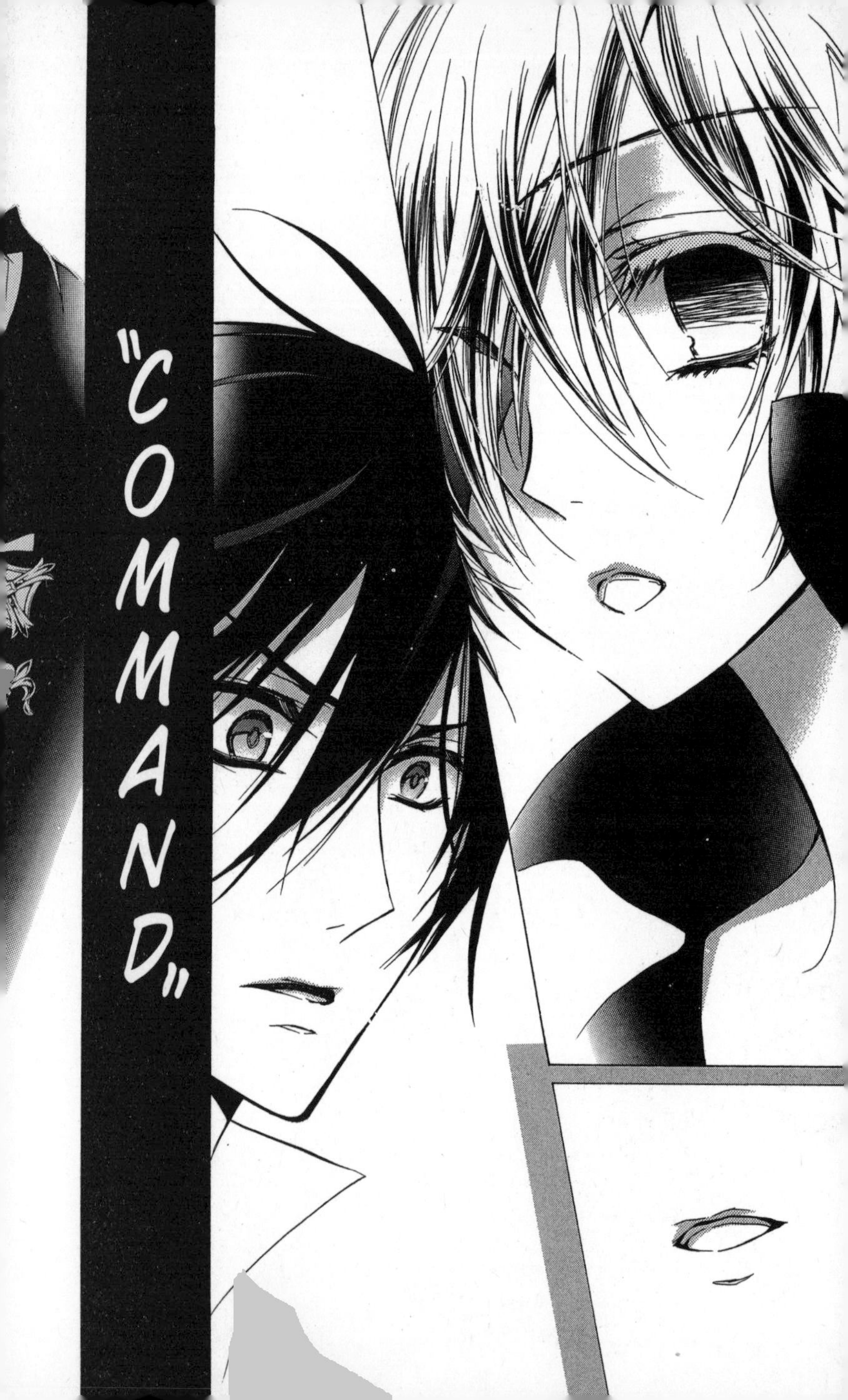
"COMMAND"

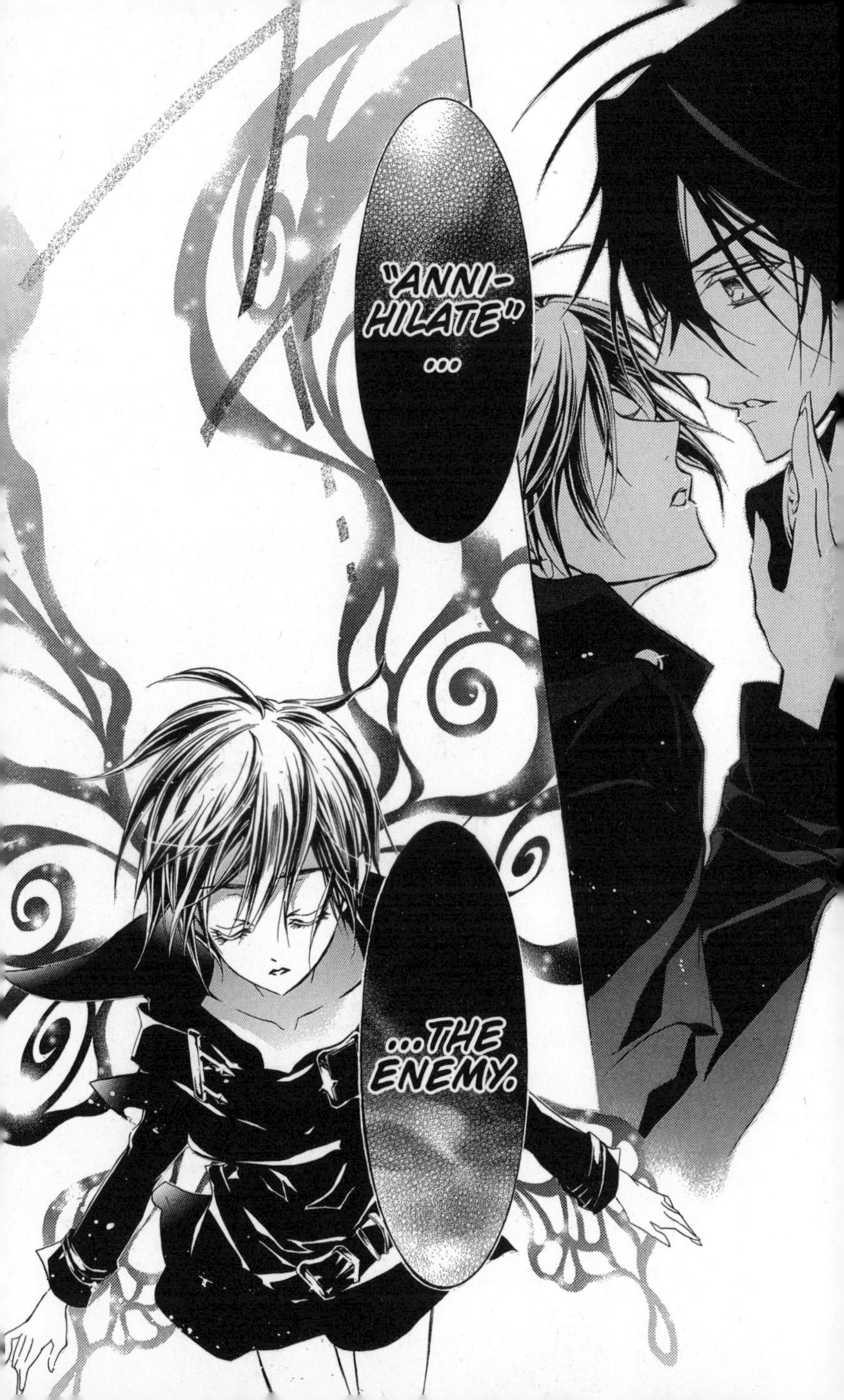
"ANNI-HILATE"...
...THE ENEMY.

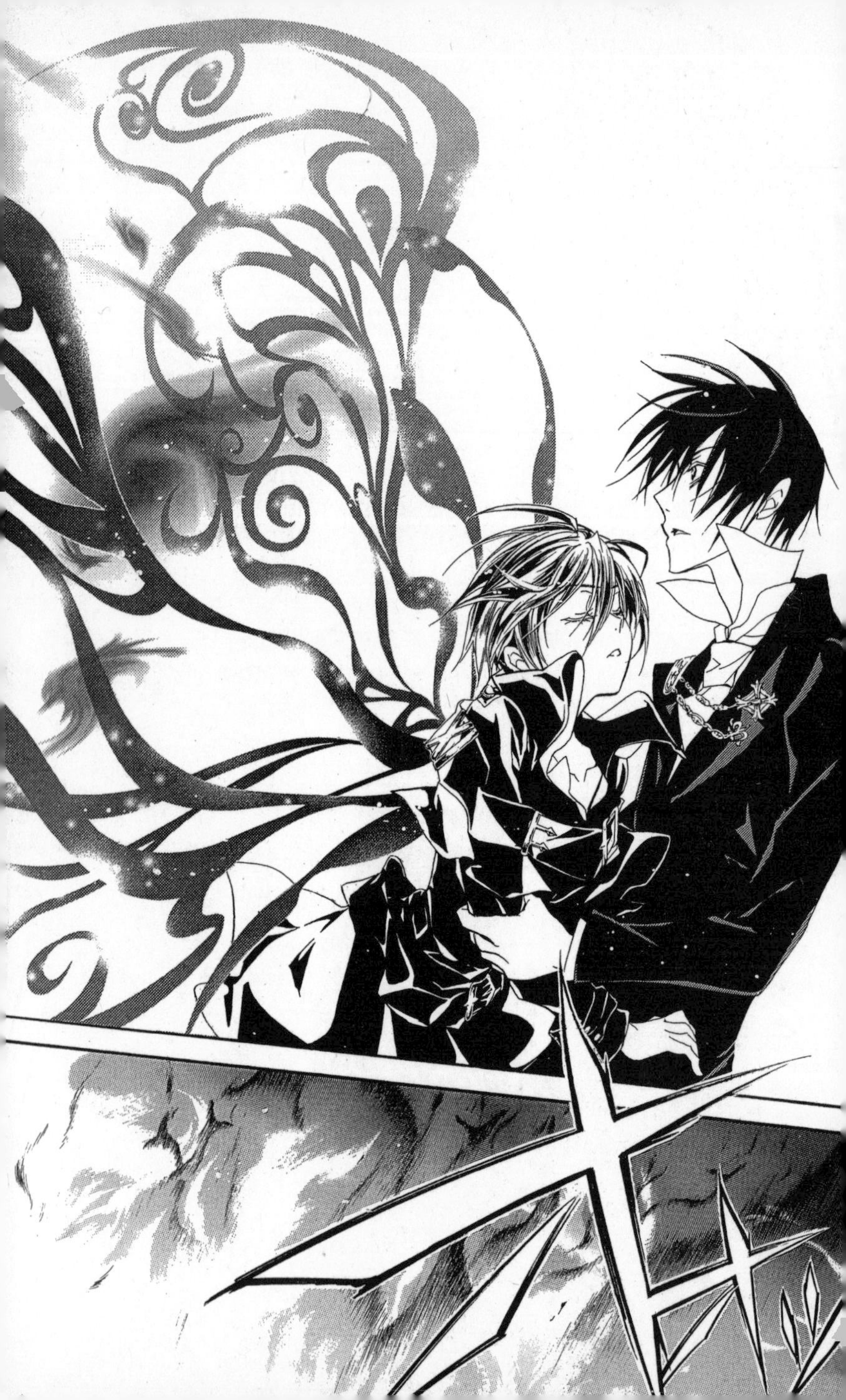

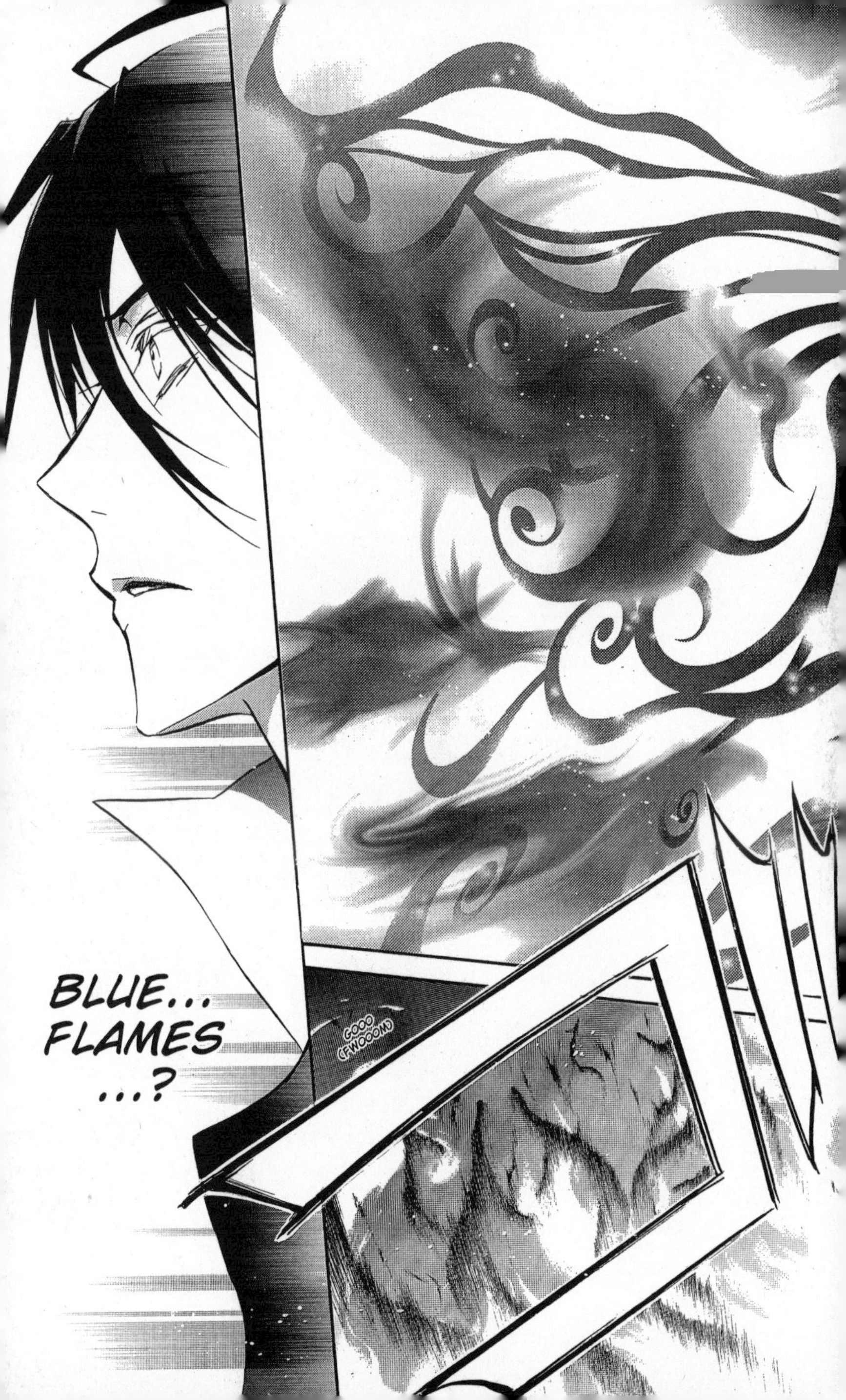
GOOO (FWOOOM)
BLUE... FLAMES ...?

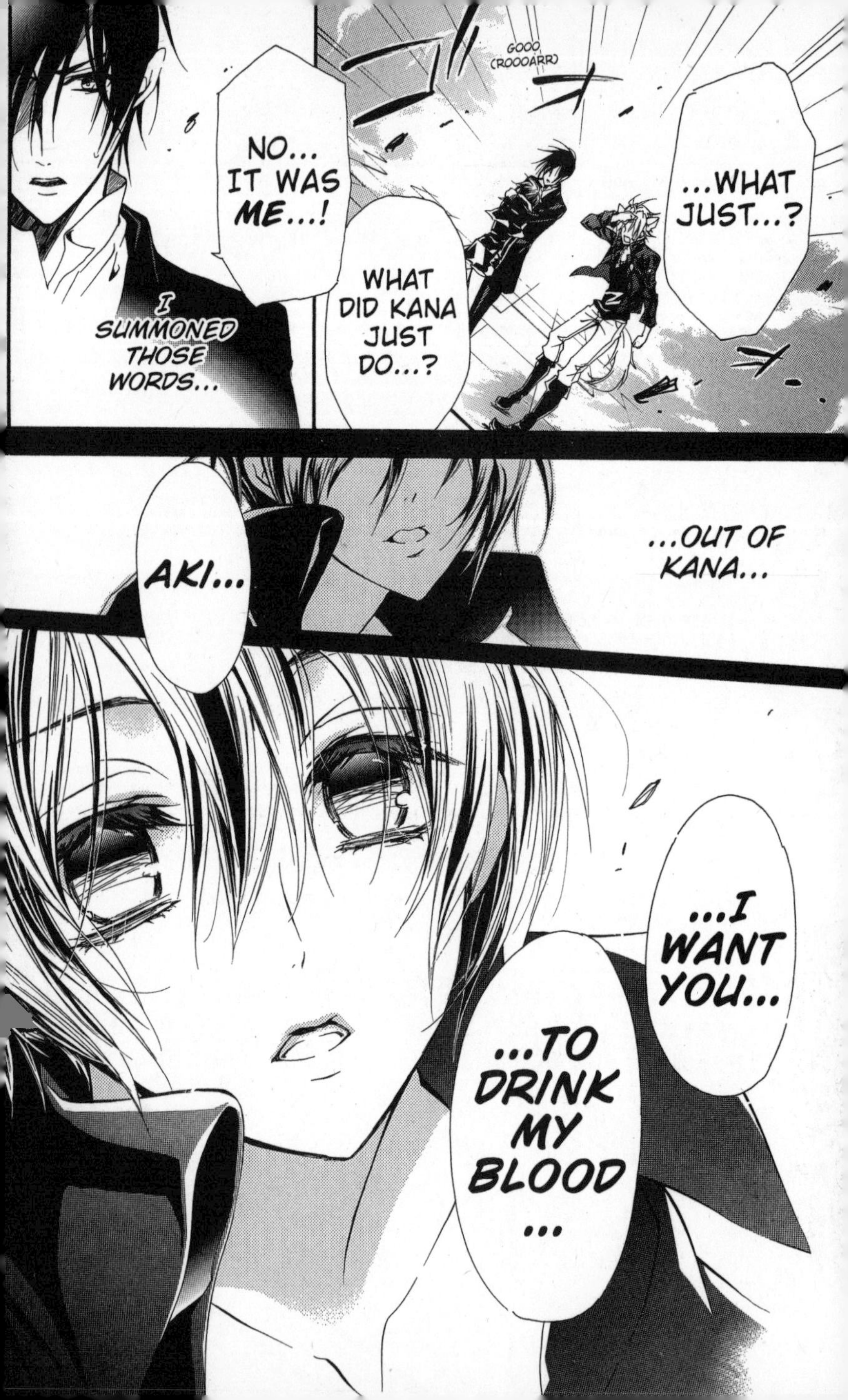
GOOO (ROOOARR)
...WHAT JUST...?
WHAT DID KANA JUST DO...?
NO... IT WAS ME...!
I SUMMONED THOSE WORDS...
...OUT OF KANA...
AKI...
...I WANT YOU...
...TO DRINK MY BLOOD ...

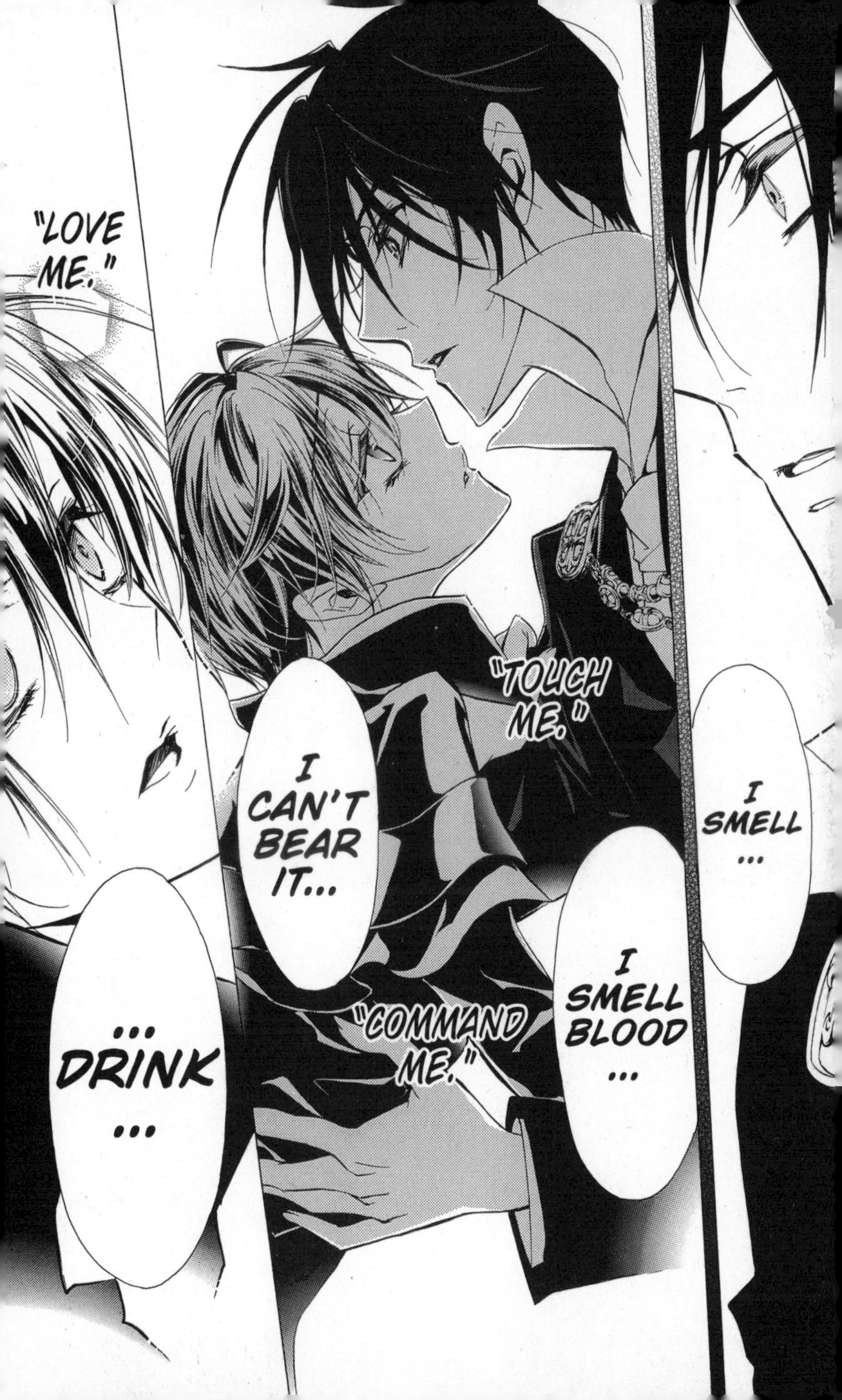

I SMELL ...
I SMELL BLOOD ...
"TOUCH ME."
I CAN'T BEAR IT...
"COMMAND ME."
"LOVE ME."
... DRINK ...

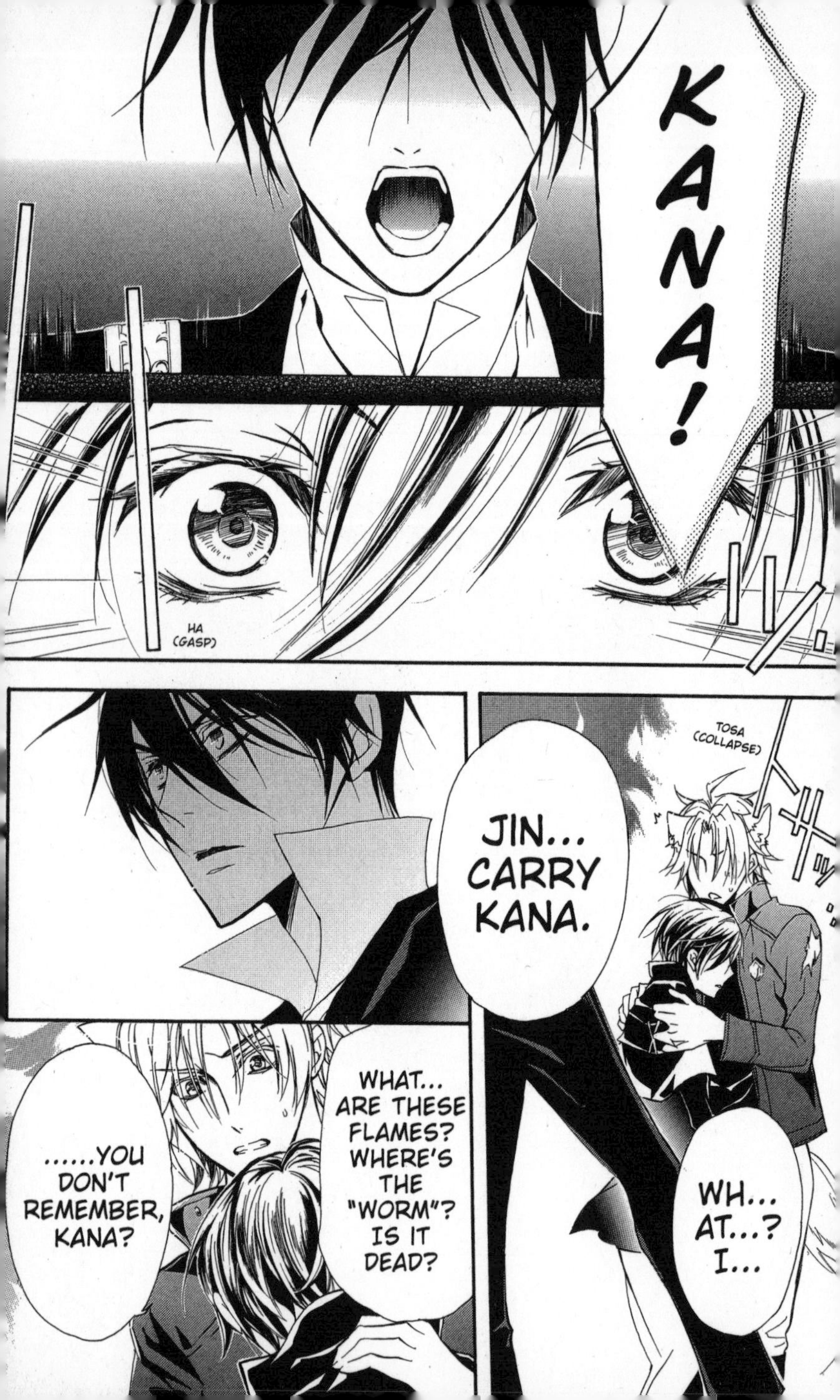
KANA!
HA (GASP)
TOSA (COLLAPSE)
JIN... CARRY KANA.
WH... AT...? I...
WHAT... ARE THESE FLAMES? WHERE'S THE "WORM"? IS IT DEAD?
......YOU DON'T REMEMBER, KANA?

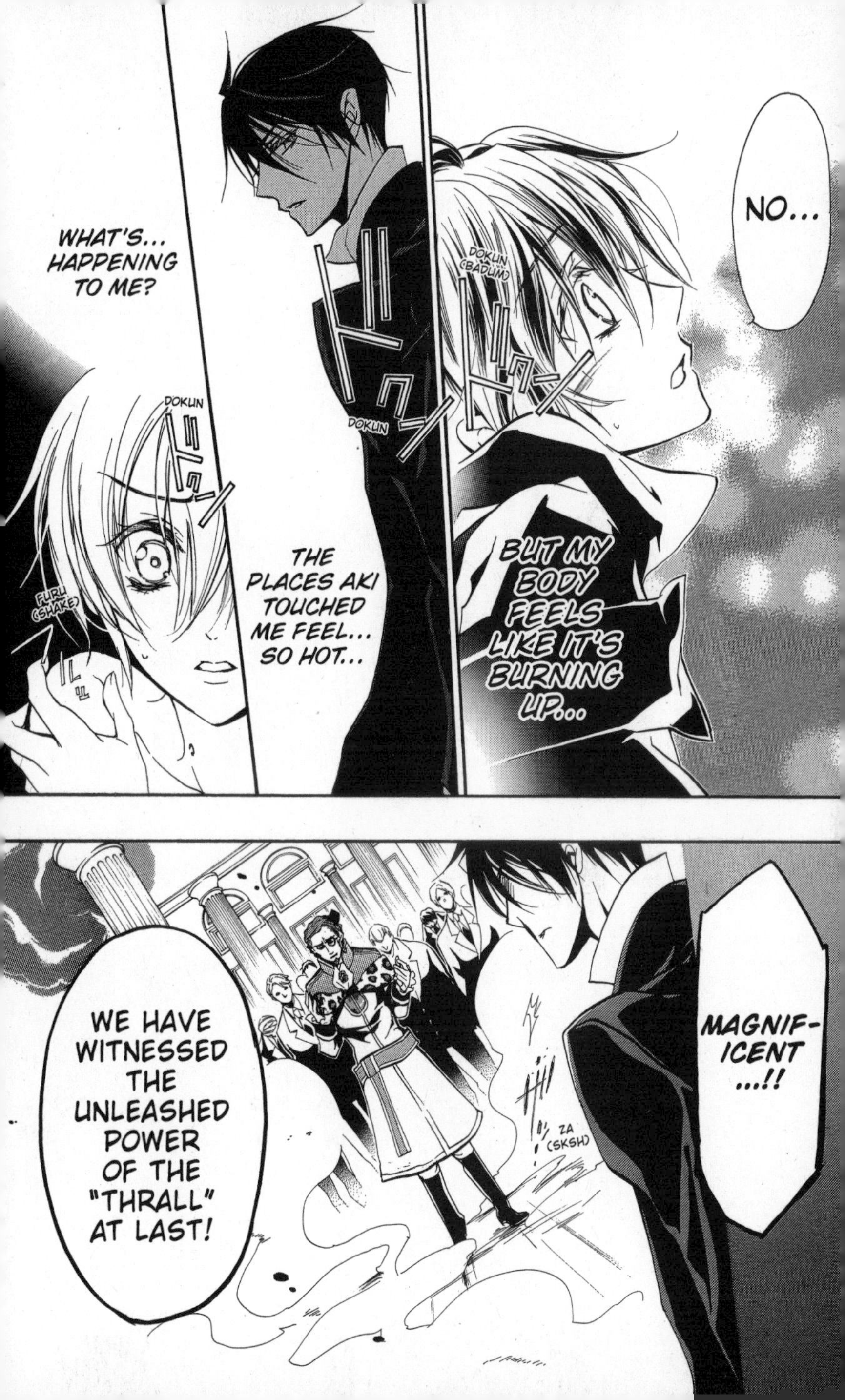
NO...
DOKUN (BADUM)
BUT MY BODY FEELS LIKE IT'S BURNING UP...
DOKUN
THE PLACES AKI TOUCHED ME FEEL... SO HOT...
WHAT'S... HAPPENING TO ME?
DOKUN
FURU (SHAKE)
MAGNIF-ICENT ...!!
ZA (SKSH)
WE HAVE WITNESSED THE UNLEASHED POWER OF THE "THRALL" AT LAST!

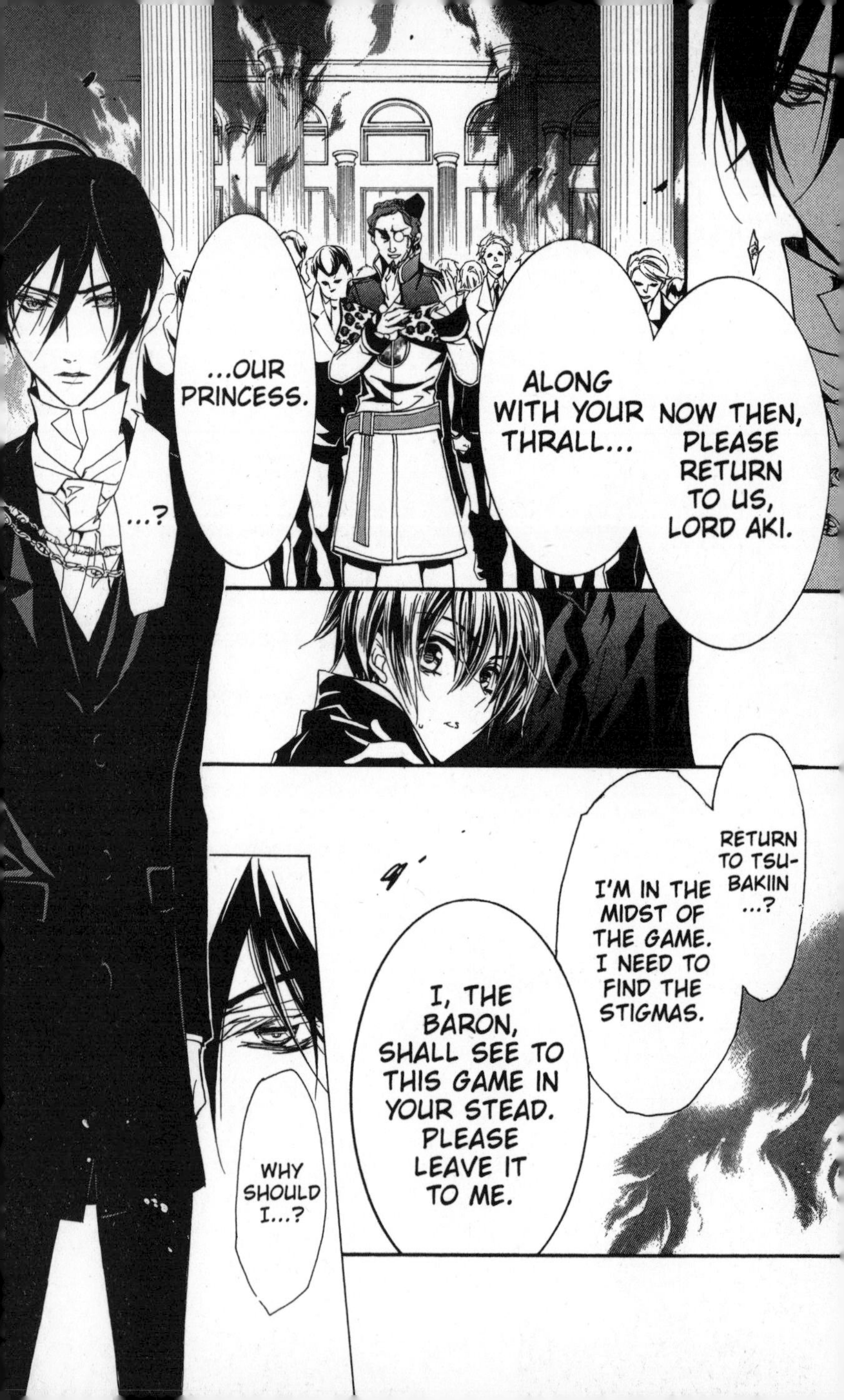
NOW THEN, PLEASE RETURN TO US, LORD AKI.
ALONG WITH YOUR THRALL...
...OUR PRINCESS.
...?
RETURN TO TSU-BAKIIN ...?
I'M IN THE MIDST OF THE GAME. I NEED TO FIND THE STIGMAS.
I, THE BARON, SHALL SEE TO THIS GAME IN YOUR STEAD. PLEASE LEAVE IT TO ME.
WHY SHOULD I...?

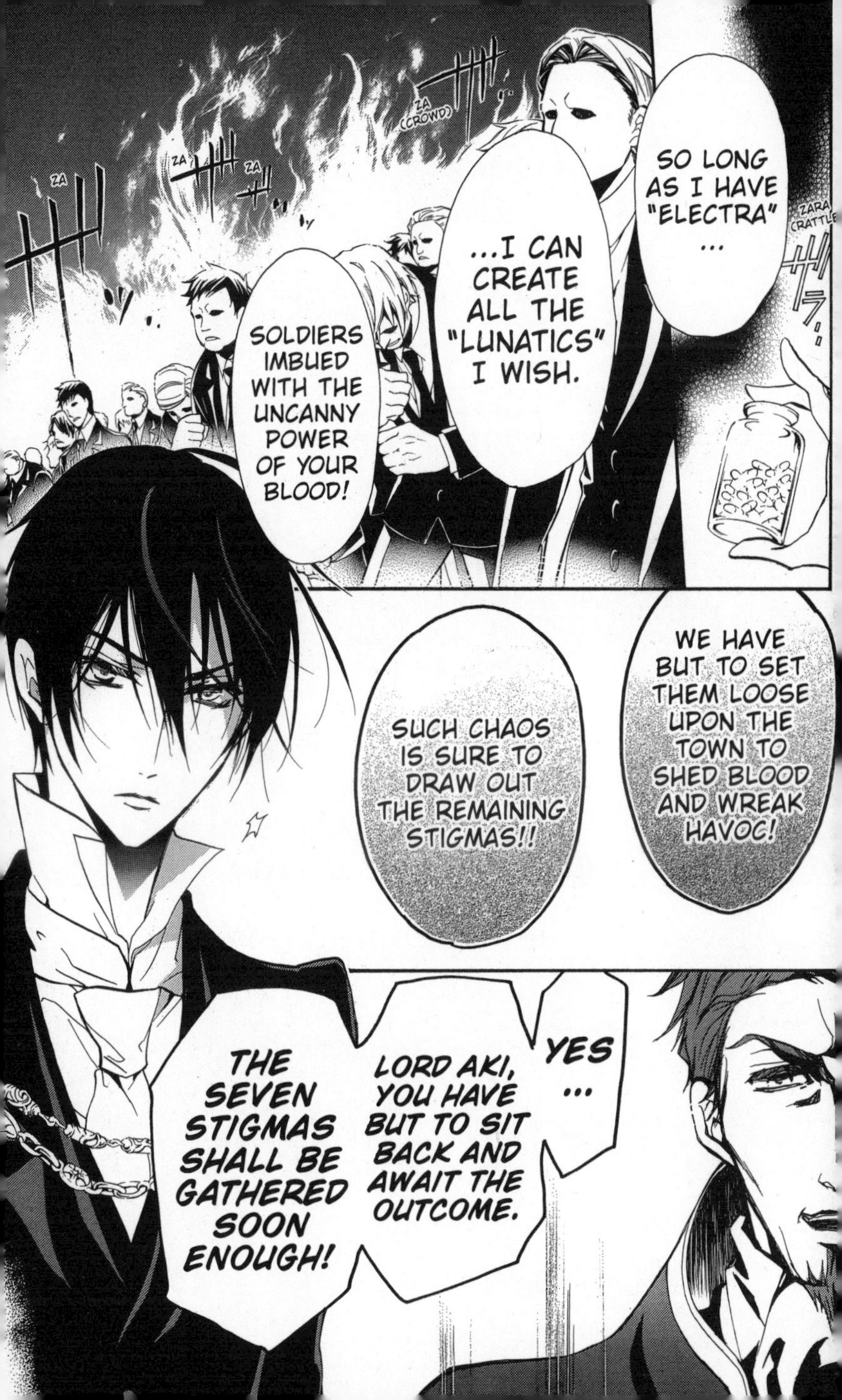
ZARA (RATTLE)
SO LONG AS I HAVE "ELECTRA" ...
ZA (CROWD)
...I CAN CREATE ALL THE "LUNATICS" I WISH.
ZA
ZA
ZA
SOLDIERS IMBUED WITH THE UNCANNY POWER OF YOUR BLOOD!
WE HAVE BUT TO SET THEM LOOSE UPON THE TOWN TO SHED BLOOD AND WREAK HAVOC!
SUCH CHAOS IS SURE TO DRAW OUT THE REMAINING STIGMAS!!
YES ...
LORD AKI, YOU HAVE BUT TO SIT BACK AND AWAIT THE OUTCOME.
THE SEVEN STIGMAS SHALL BE GATHERED SOON ENOUGH!

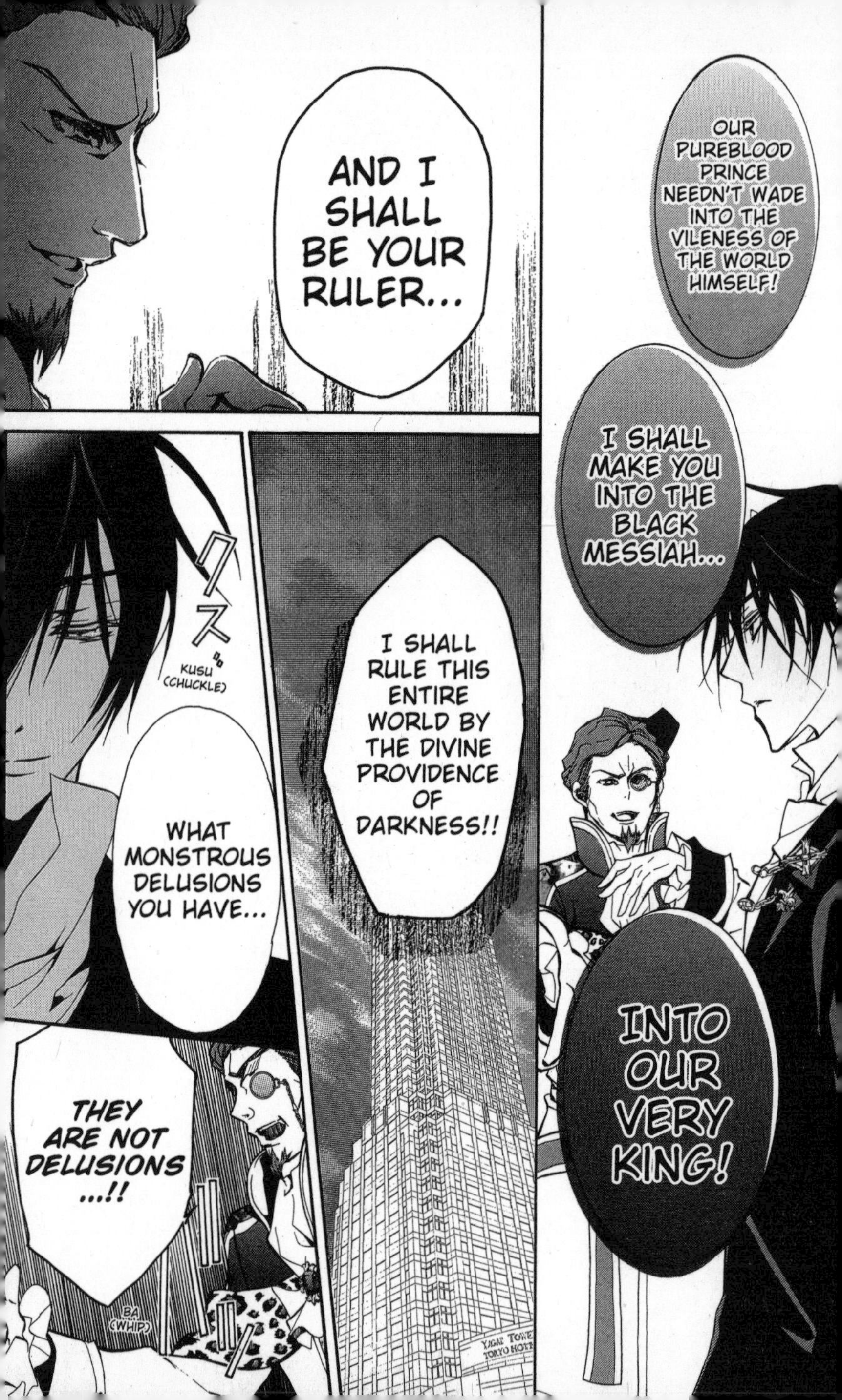

OUR PUREBLOOD PRINCE NEEDN'T WADE INTO THE VILENESS OF THE WORLD HIMSELF!
I SHALL MAKE YOU INTO THE BLACK MESSIAH...
INTO OUR VERY KING!
AND I SHALL BE YOUR RULER...
I SHALL RULE THIS ENTIRE WORLD BY THE DIVINE PROVIDENCE OF DARKNESS!!
クス
KUSU (CHUCKLE)
WHAT MONSTROUS DELUSIONS YOU HAVE...
THEY ARE NOT DELUSIONS ...!!
BA (WHIP)

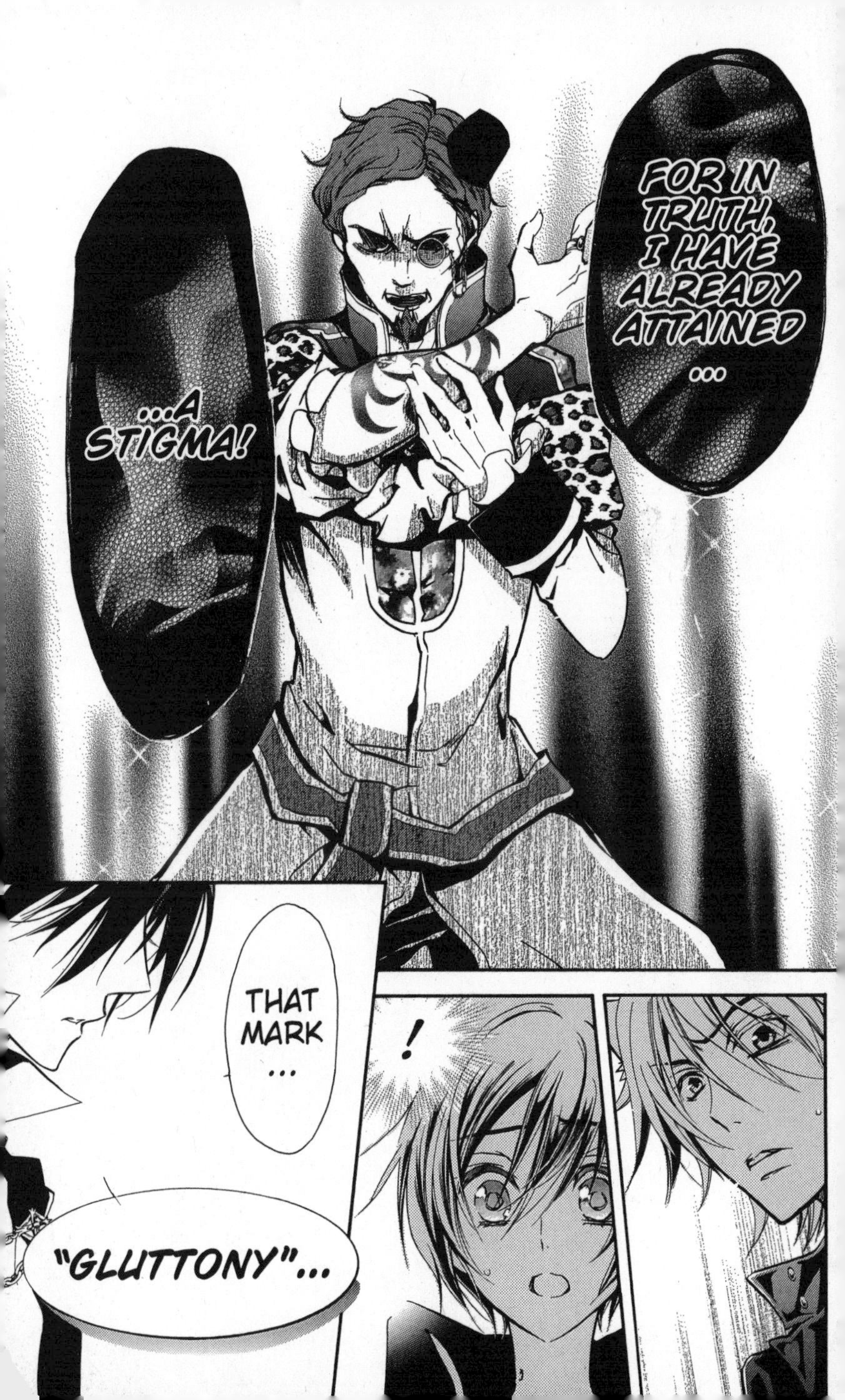
FOR IN TRUTH, I HAVE ALREADY ATTAINED ...
...A STIGMA!
!
THAT MARK ...
"GLUTTONY"...

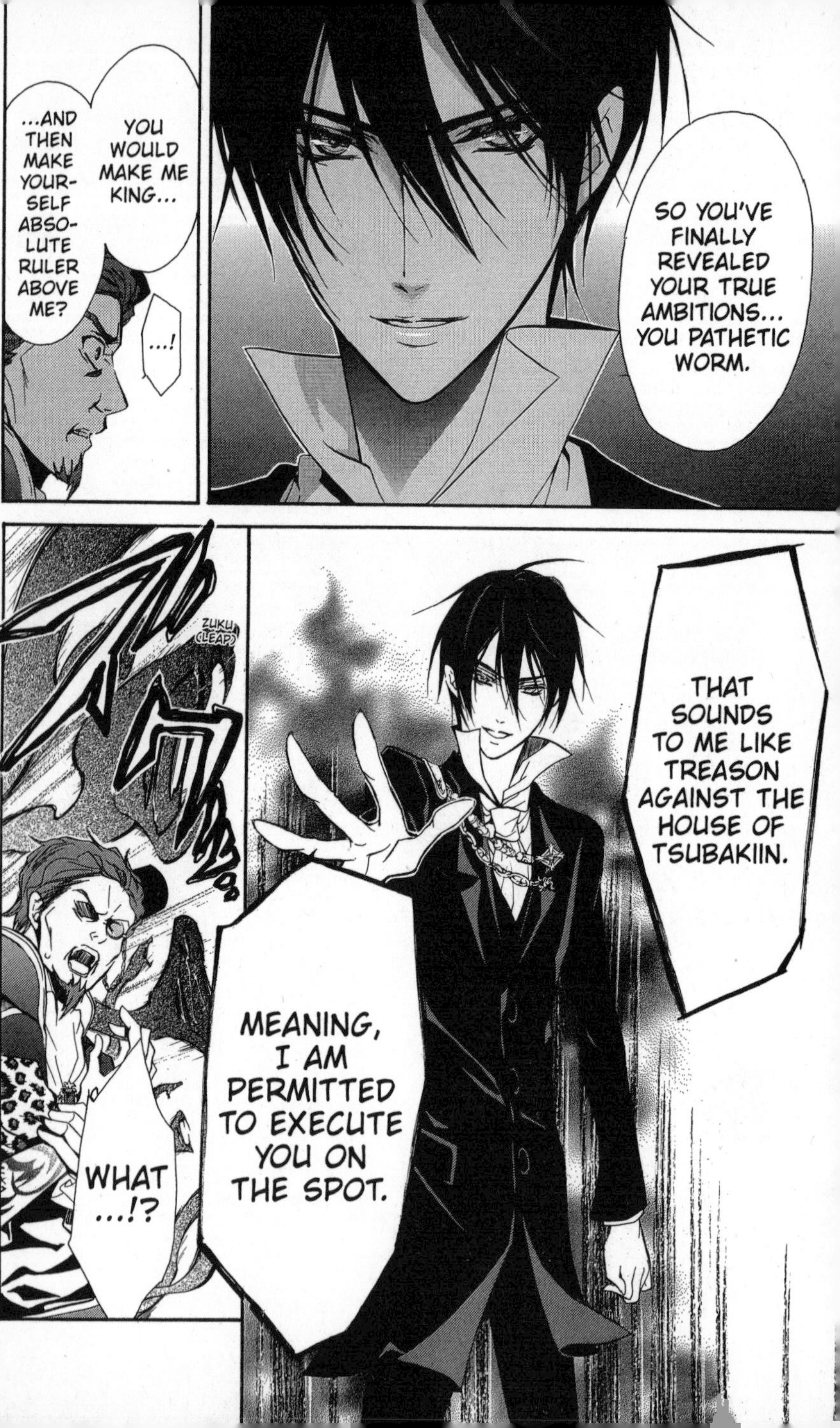
SO YOU'VE FINALLY REVEALED YOUR TRUE AMBITIONS... YOU PATHETIC WORM.
YOU WOULD MAKE ME KING...
...AND THEN MAKE YOUR-SELF ABSO-LUTE RULER ABOVE ME?
...!
THAT SOUNDS TO ME LIKE TREASON AGAINST THE HOUSE OF TSUBAKIIN.
MEANING, I AM PERMITTED TO EXECUTE YOU ON THE SPOT.
ZUKU (LEAP)
WHAT ...!?

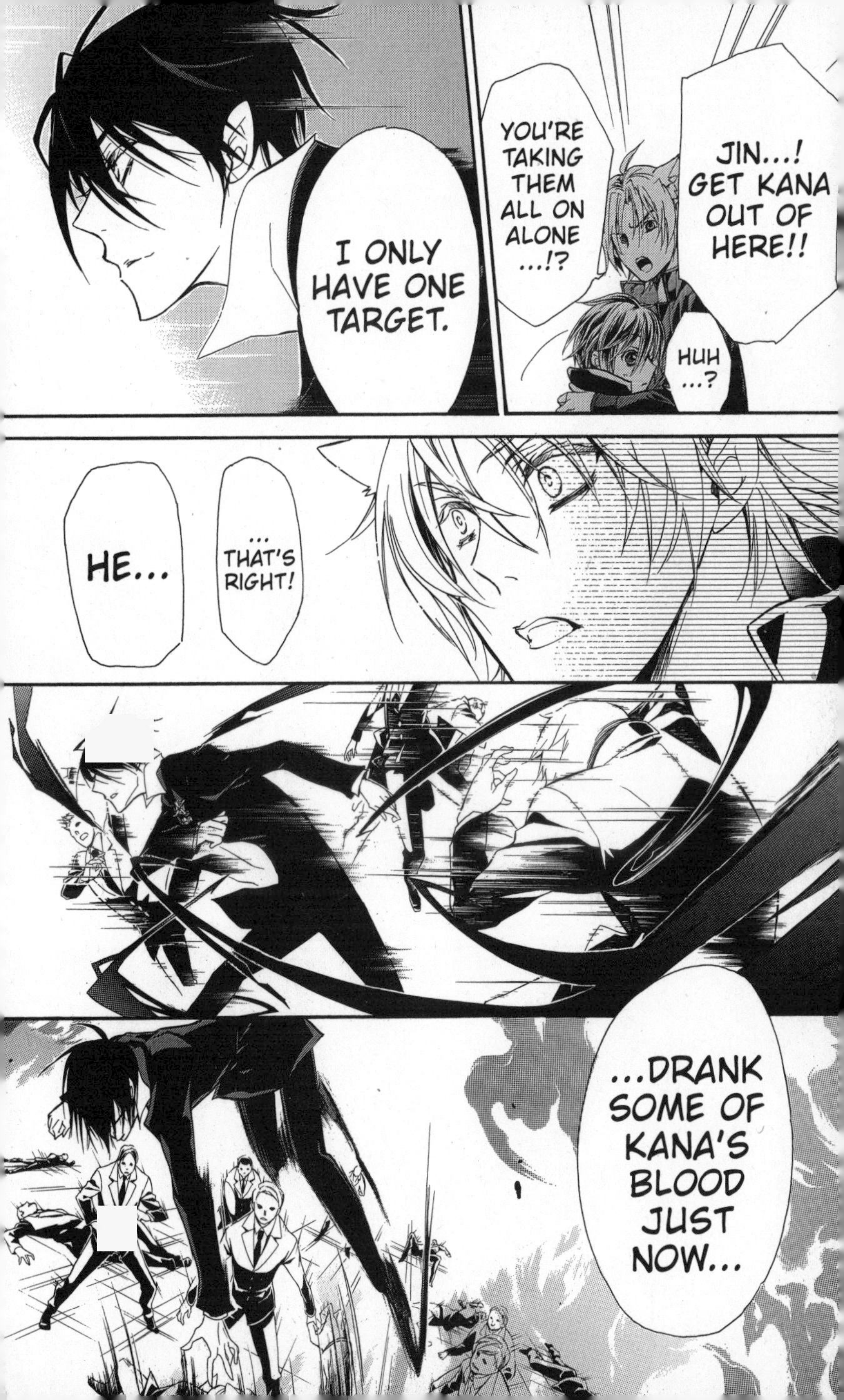
JIN...! GET KANA OUT OF HERE!!
HUH ...?
YOU'RE TAKING THEM ALL ON ALONE ...!?
I ONLY HAVE ONE TARGET.
... THAT'S RIGHT!
HE...
...DRANK SOME OF KANA'S BLOOD JUST NOW...

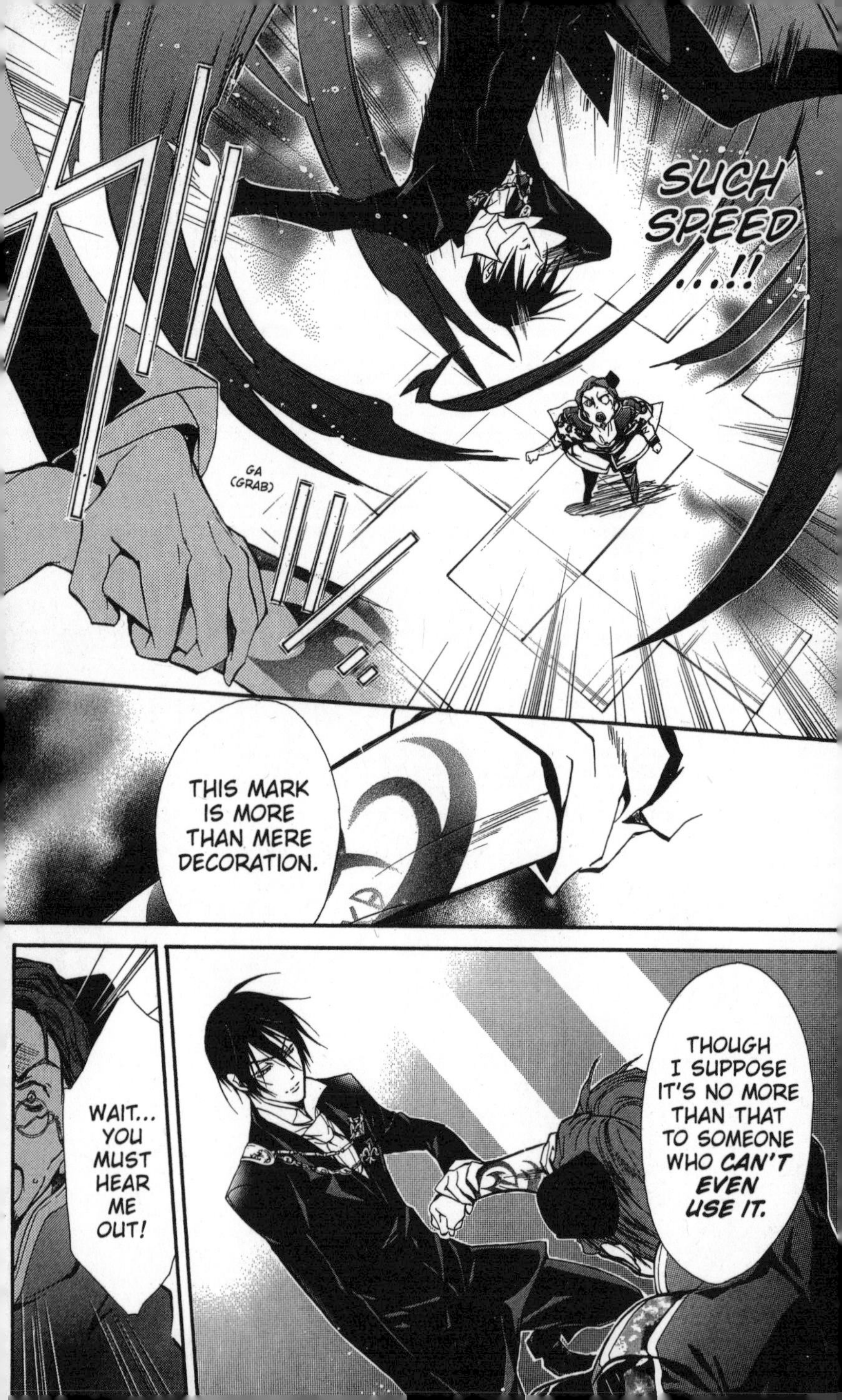
SUCH SPEED ...!!
GA (GRAB)
THIS MARK IS MORE THAN MERE DECORATION.
THOUGH I SUPPOSE IT'S NO MORE THAN THAT TO SOMEONE WHO **CAN'T EVEN USE IT.**
WAIT... YOU MUST HEAR ME OUT!

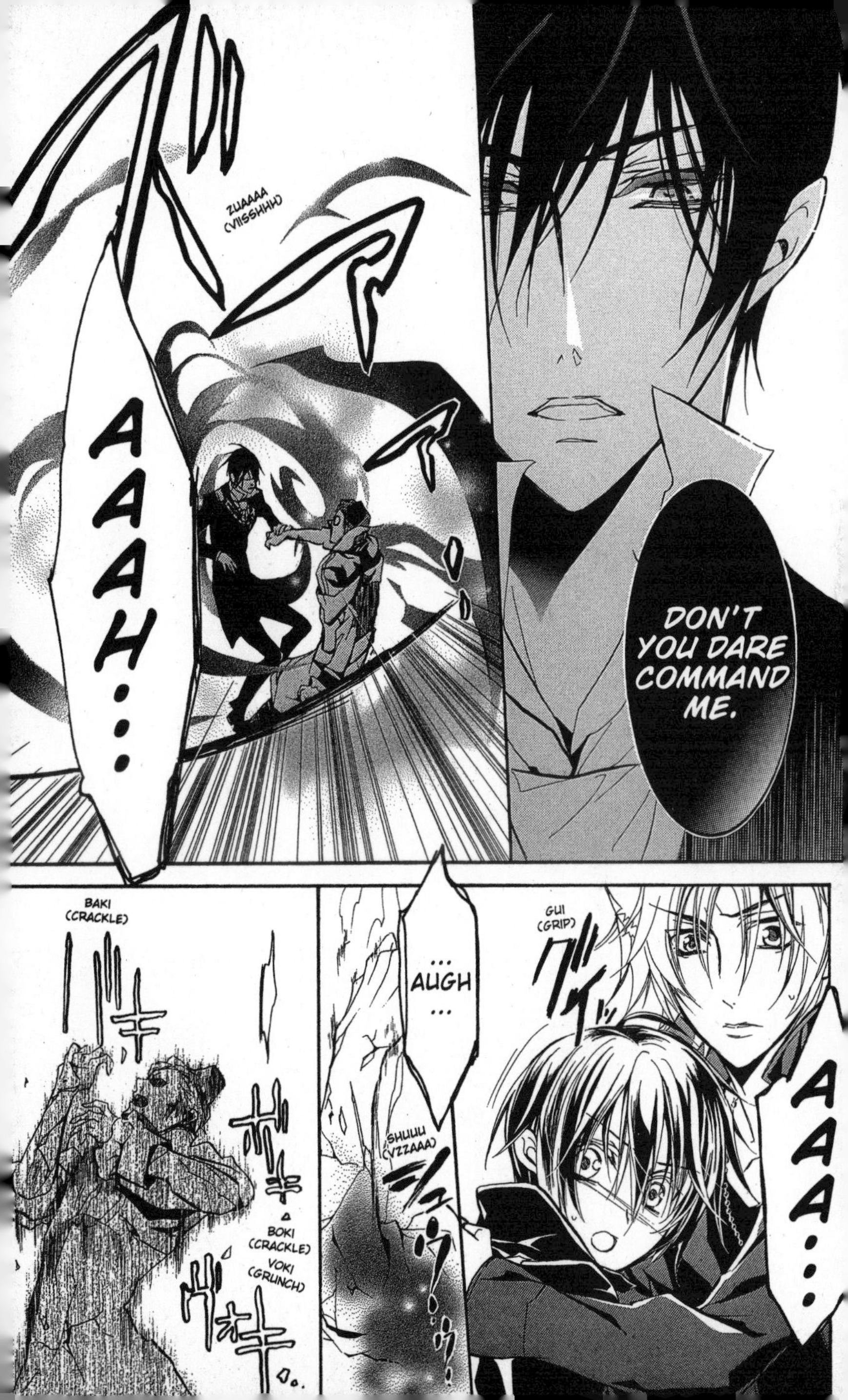
DON'T YOU DARE COMMAND ME.
ZUAAAA (VIISSHHH)
AAAAH...
GUI (GRIP)
...AUGH...
AAA...
SHUUU (VZZAAA)
BAKI (CRACKLE)
BOKI (CRACKLE)
VOKI (GRUNCH)

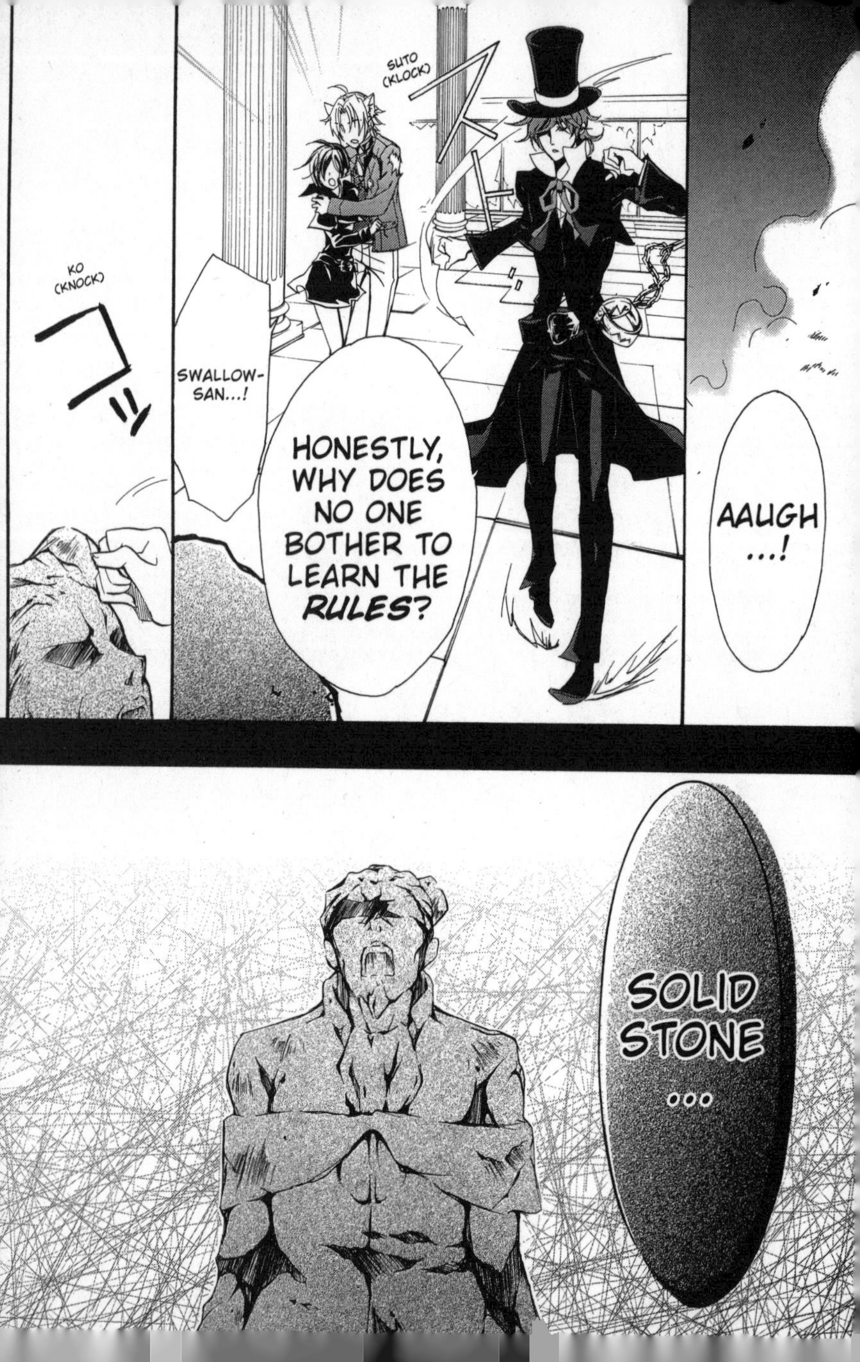
AAUGH ...!
SUTO (KLOCK)
HONESTLY, WHY DOES NO ONE BOTHER TO LEARN THE *RULES*?
SWALLOW-SAN...!
KO (KNOCK)
SOLID STONE ...

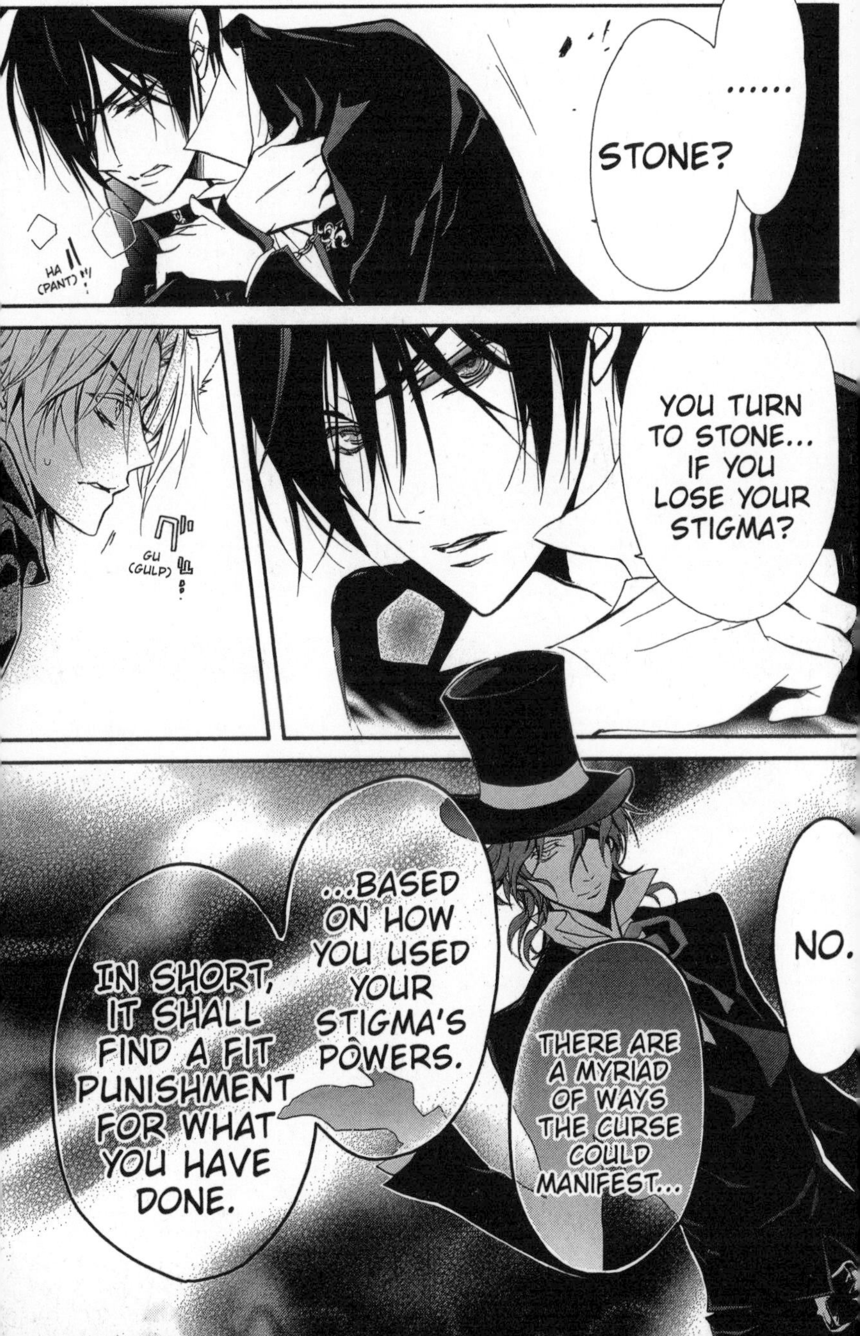
......
STONE?
HA (PANT)
YOU TURN TO STONE... IF YOU LOSE YOUR STIGMA?
GU (GULP)
NO.
THERE ARE A MYRIAD OF WAYS THE CURSE COULD MANIFEST...
...BASED ON HOW YOU USED YOUR STIGMA'S POWERS.
IN SHORT, IT SHALL FIND A FIT PUNISHMENT FOR WHAT YOU HAVE DONE.

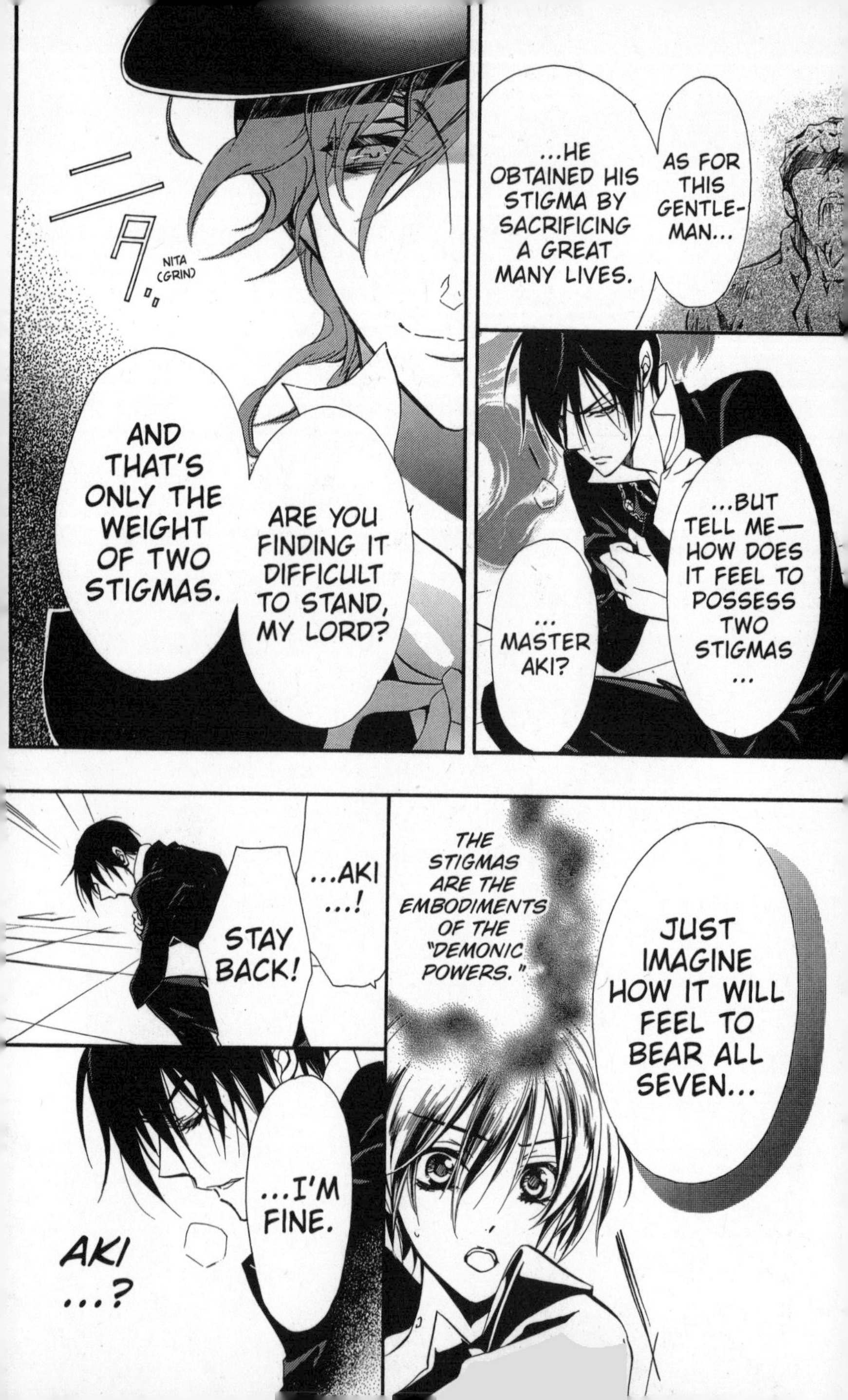
AS FOR THIS GENTLEMAN...
...HE OBTAINED HIS STIGMA BY SACRIFICING A GREAT MANY LIVES.
...BUT TELL ME—HOW DOES IT FEEL TO POSSESS TWO STIGMAS...
...MASTER AKI?
NITA (GRIN)
ARE YOU FINDING IT DIFFICULT TO STAND, MY LORD?
AND THAT'S ONLY THE WEIGHT OF TWO STIGMAS.
JUST IMAGINE HOW IT WILL FEEL TO BEAR ALL SEVEN...
THE STIGMAS ARE THE EMBODIMENTS OF THE "DEMONIC POWERS."
...AKI ...!
STAY BACK!
...I'M FINE.
AKI ...?

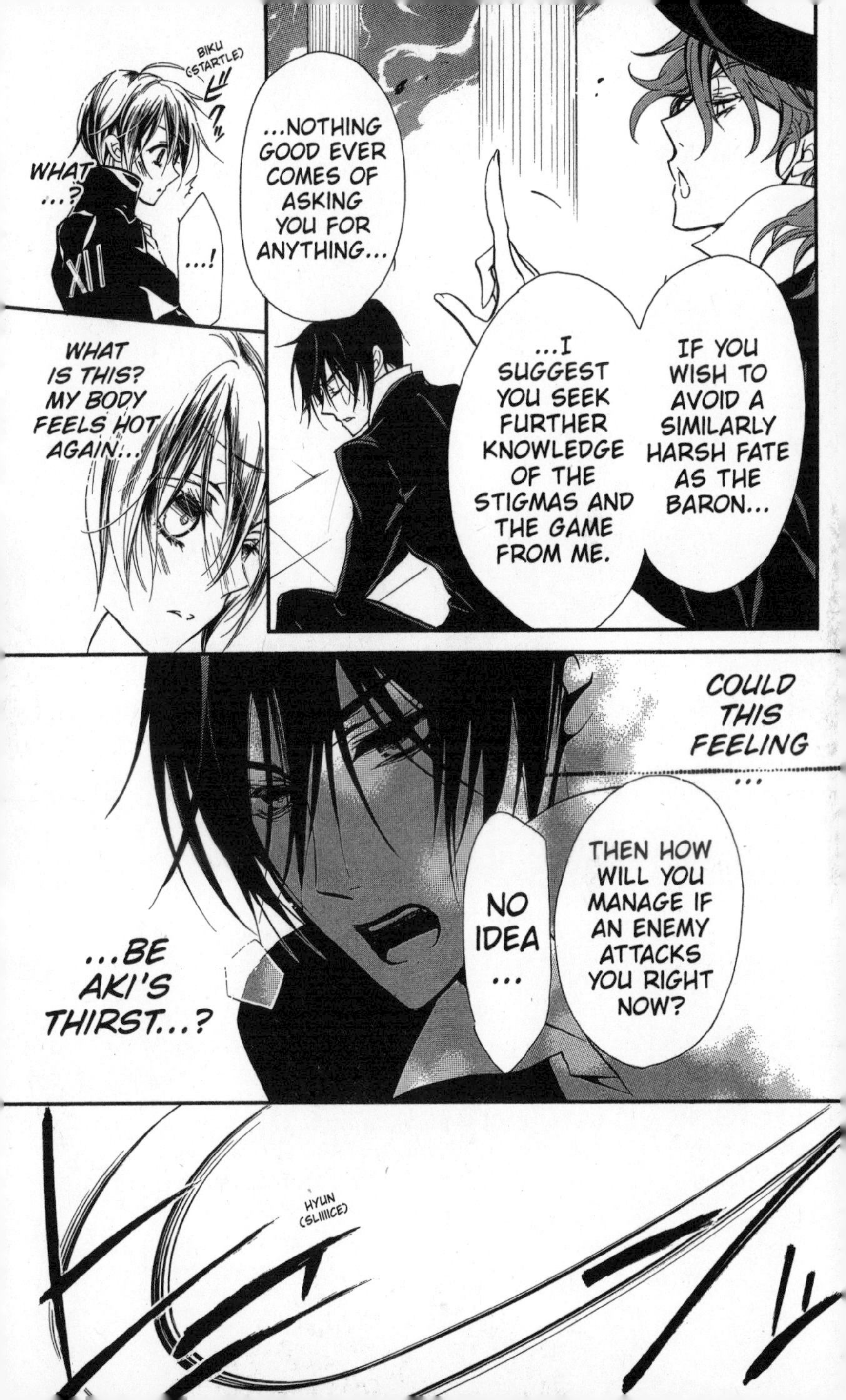
...NOTHING GOOD EVER COMES OF ASKING YOU FOR ANYTHING...
IF YOU WISH TO AVOID A SIMILARLY HARSH FATE AS THE BARON...
...I SUGGEST YOU SEEK FURTHER KNOWLEDGE OF THE STIGMAS AND THE GAME FROM ME.
BIKU (STARTLE)
WHAT ...?
...!
WHAT IS THIS? MY BODY FEELS HOT AGAIN...
COULD THIS FEELING ...
THEN HOW WILL YOU MANAGE IF AN ENEMY ATTACKS YOU RIGHT NOW?
NO IDEA ...
...BE AKI'S THIRST...?
HYUN (SLIIIICE)

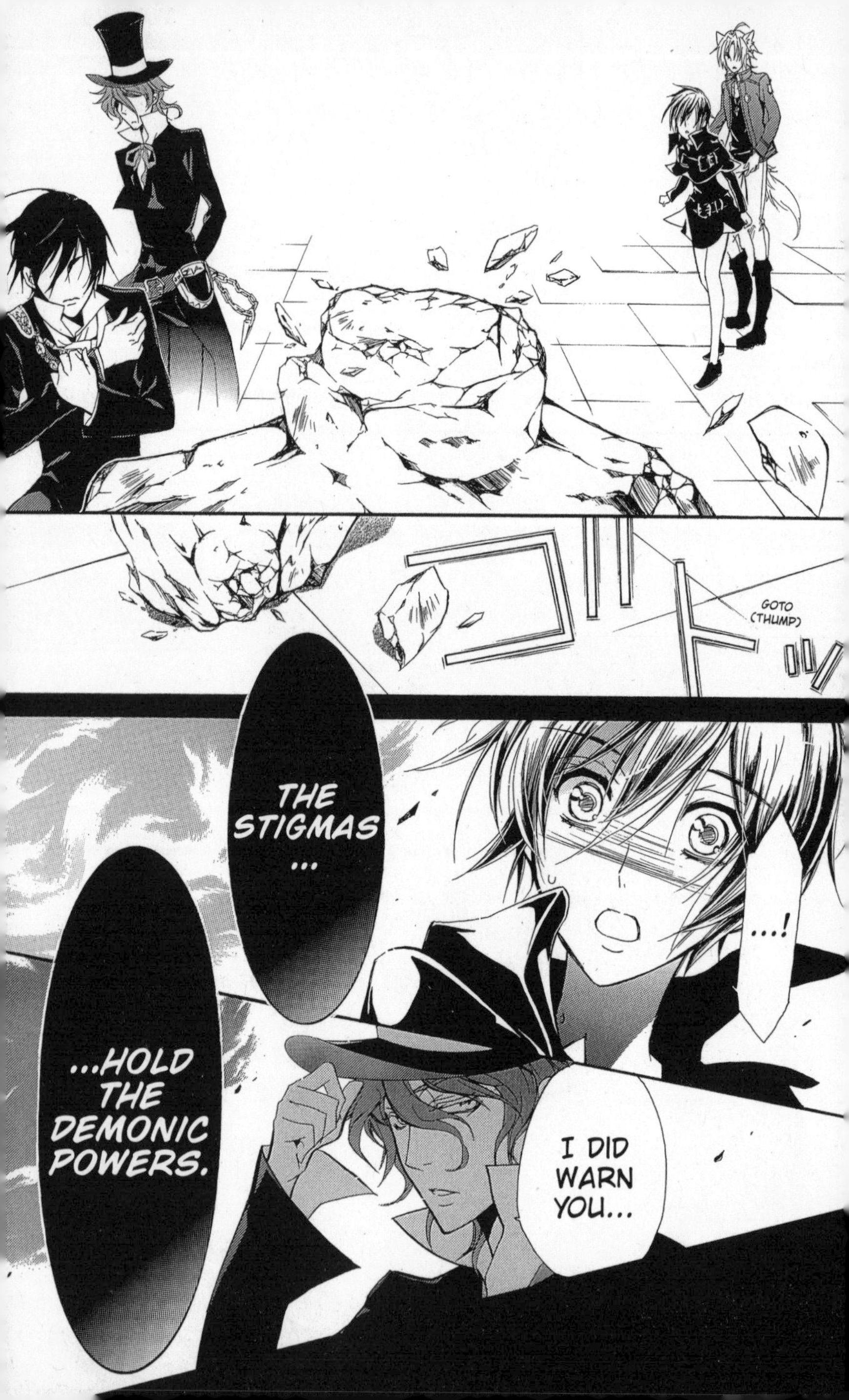
GOTO
(THUMP)
...!
I DID WARN YOU...
THE STIGMAS...
...HOLD THE DEMONIC POWERS.

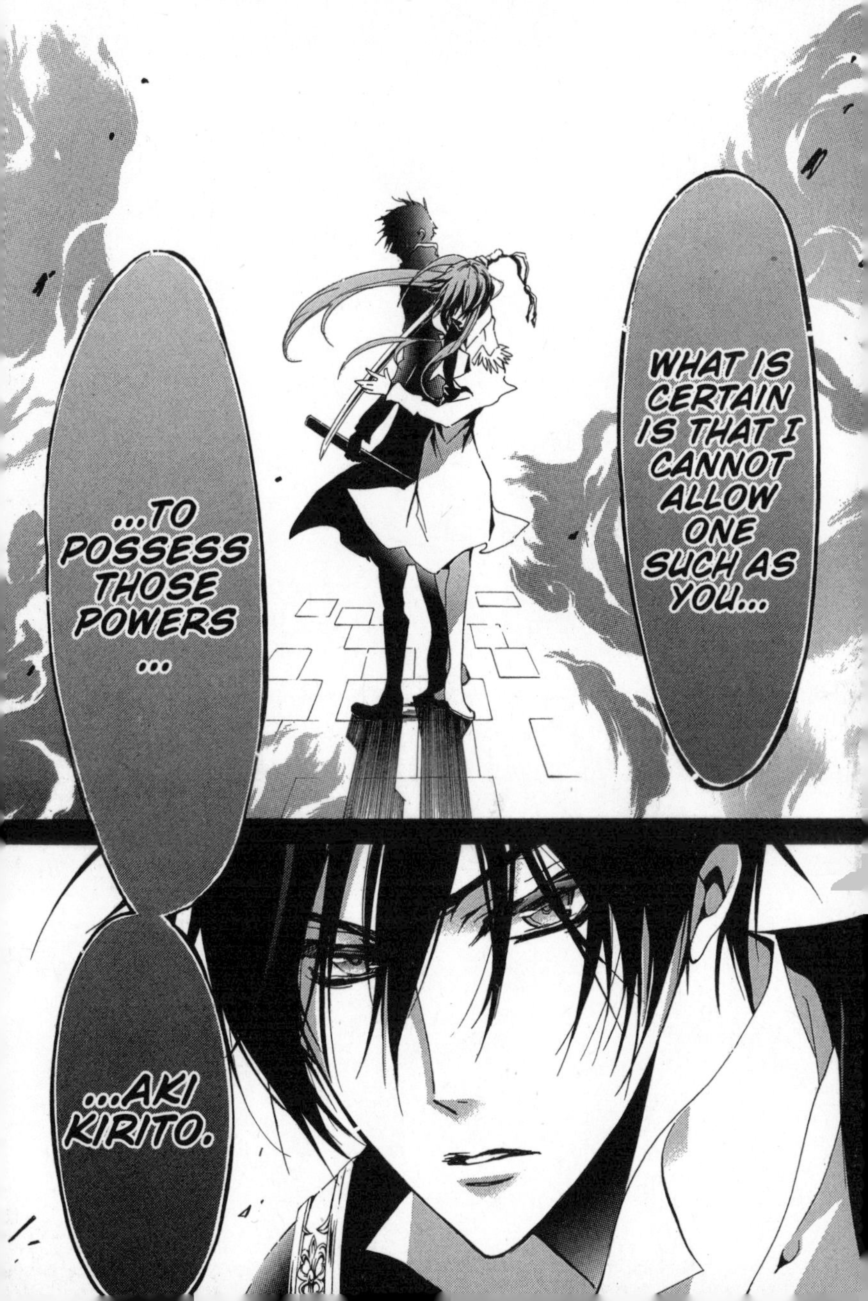
WHAT IS CERTAIN IS THAT I CANNOT ALLOW ONE SUCH AS YOU...
...TO POSSESS THOSE POWERS...
...AKI KIRITO.

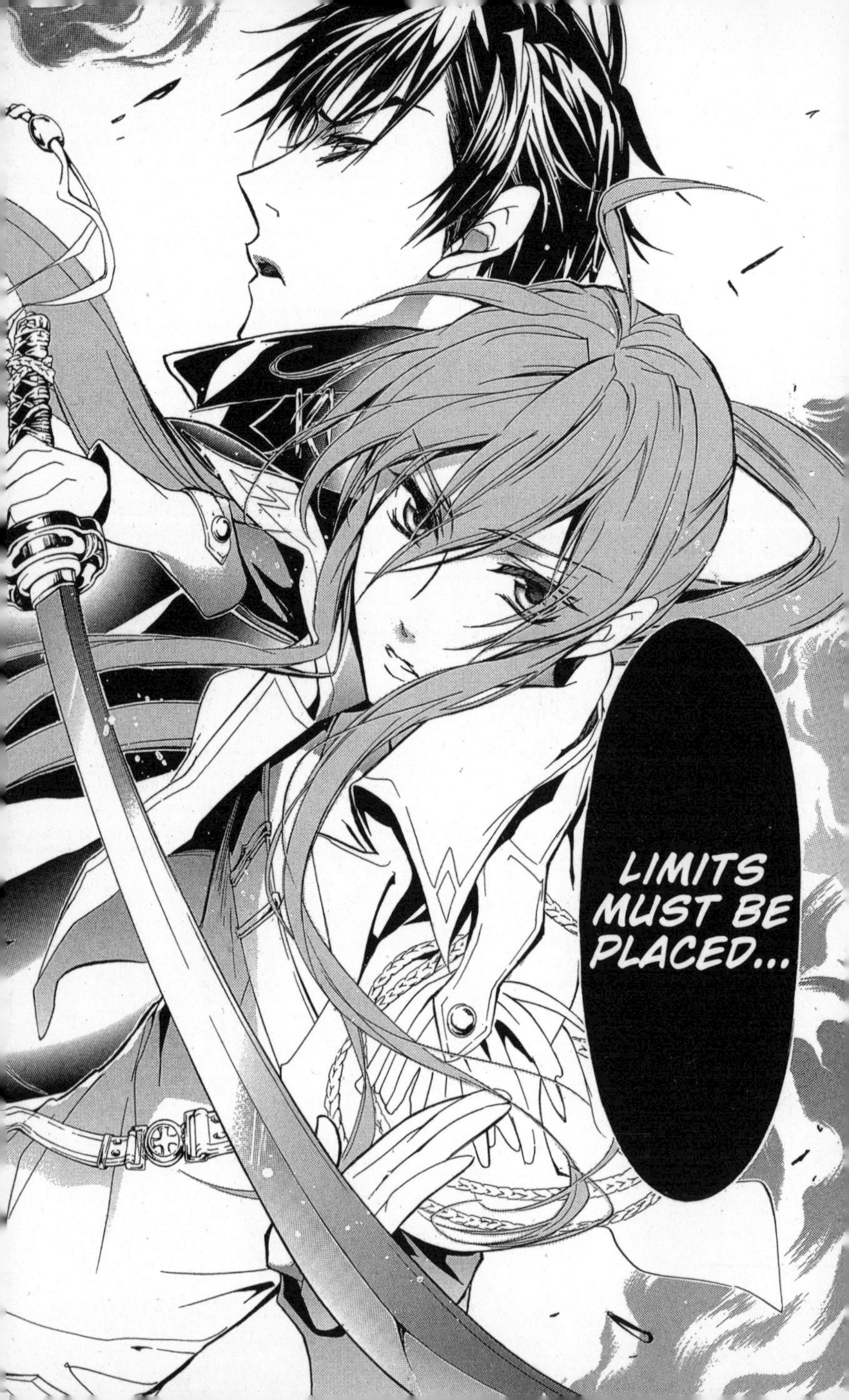
LIMITS MUST BE PLACED...

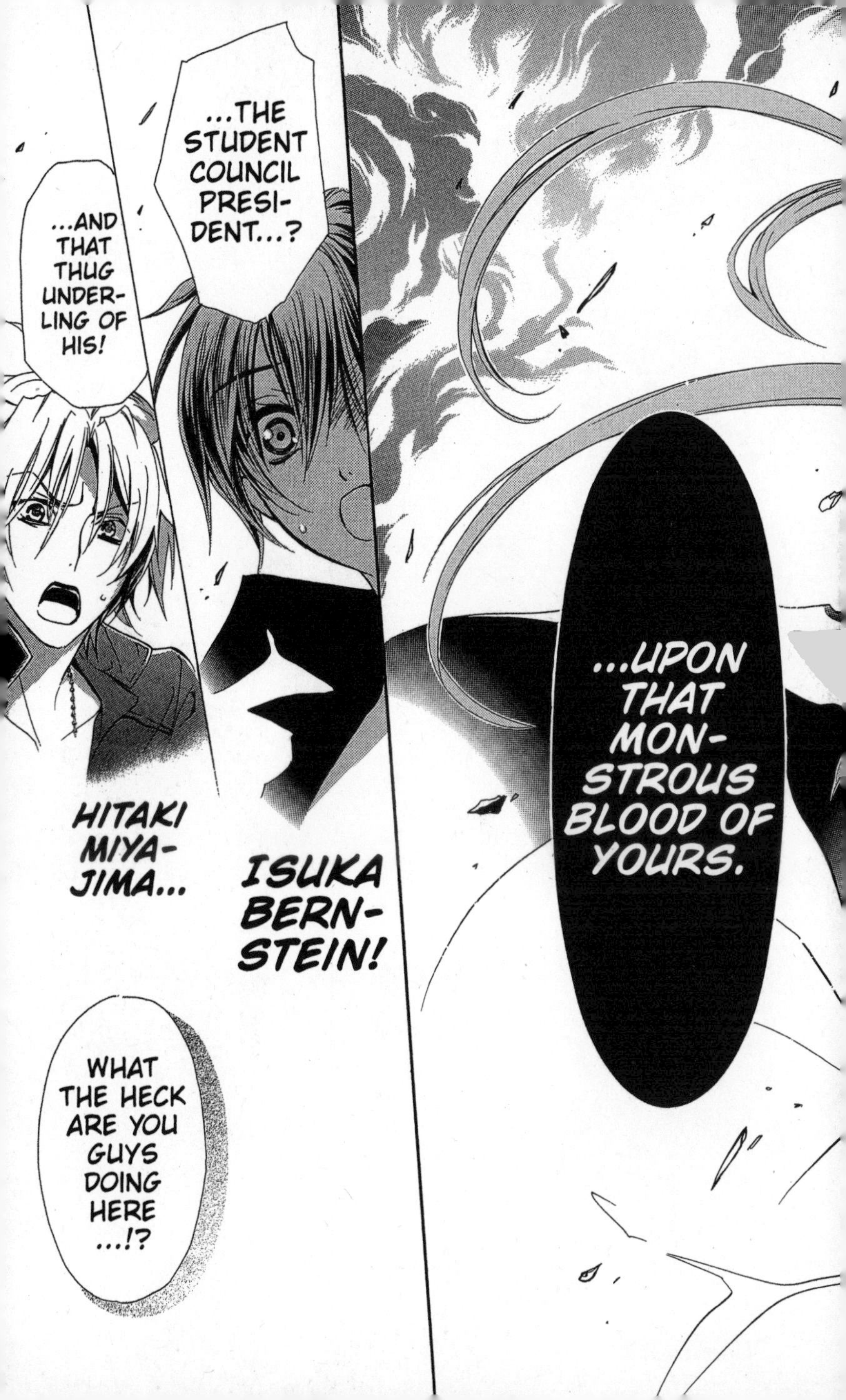
...UPON THAT MONSTROUS BLOOD OF YOURS.
...THE STUDENT COUNCIL PRESIDENT...?
...AND THAT THUG UNDERLING OF HIS!
ISUKA BERNSTEIN!
HITAKI MIYAJIMA...
WHAT THE HECK ARE YOU GUYS DOING HERE ...!?

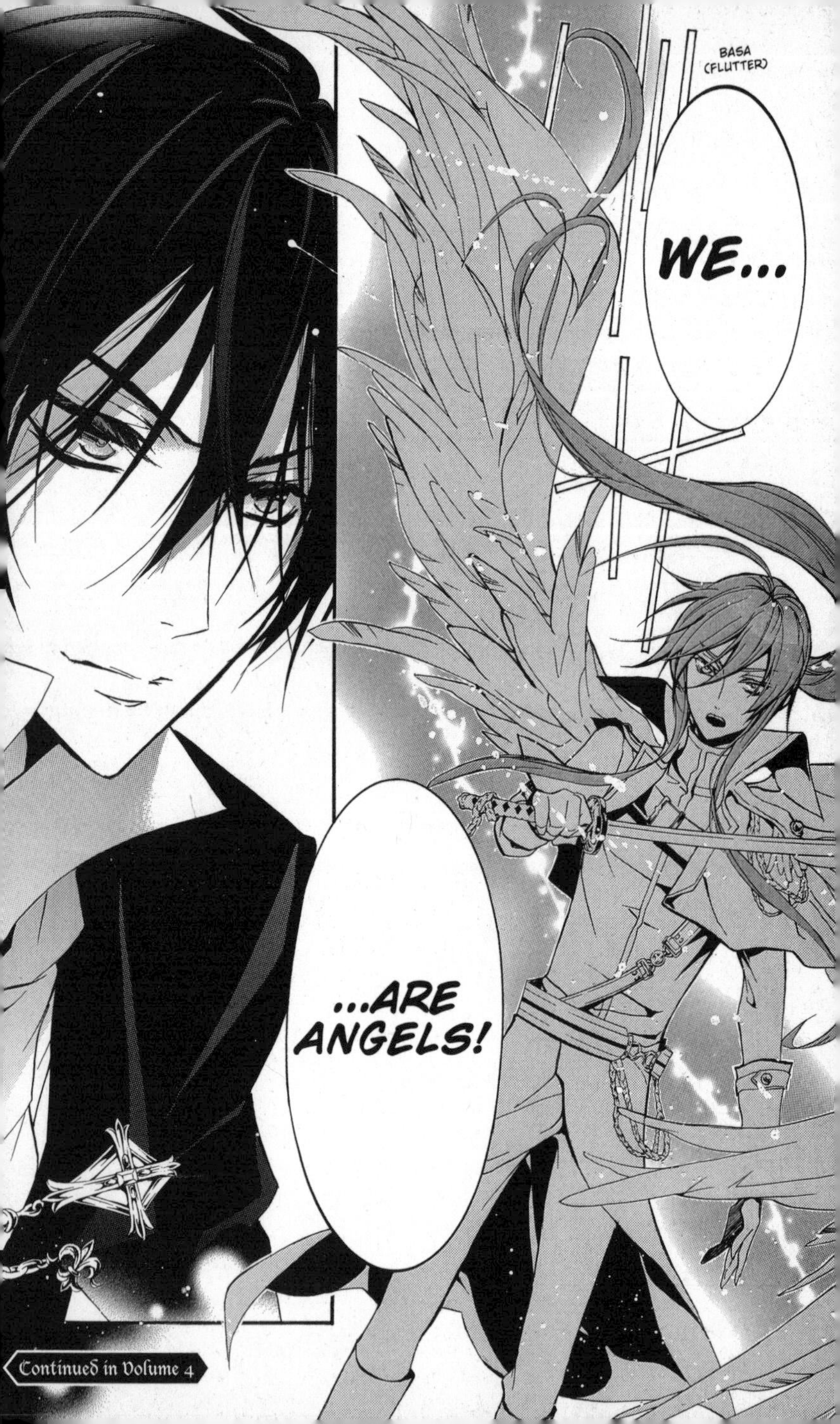
BASA (FLUTTER)
WE...
...ARE ANGELS!
Continued in Volume 4

He's my only vampire
Aya Shouoto

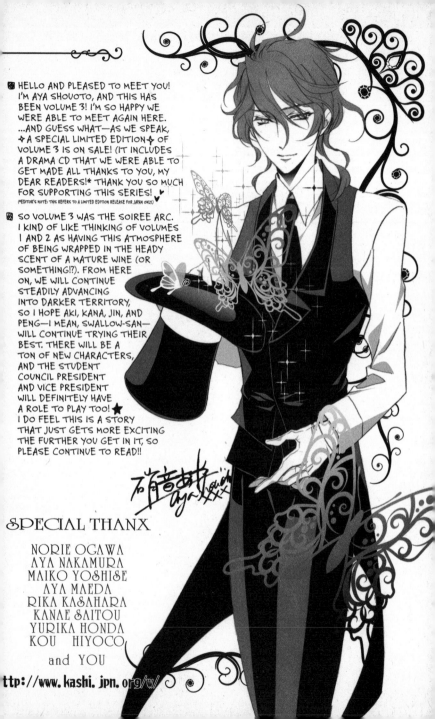

HELLO AND PLEASED TO MEET YOU! I'M AYA SHOUOTO, AND THIS HAS BEEN VOLUME 3! I'M SO HAPPY WE WERE ABLE TO MEET AGAIN HERE. ...AND GUESS WHAT—AS WE SPEAK, ✧A SPECIAL LIMITED EDITION✧ OF VOLUME 3 IS ON SALE! (IT INCLUDES A DRAMA CD THAT WE WERE ABLE TO GET MADE ALL THANKS TO YOU, MY DEAR READERS!* THANK YOU SO MUCH FOR SUPPORTING THIS SERIES! ♥

(*EDITOR'S NOTE: THIS REFERS TO A LIMITED EDITION RELEASE FOR JAPAN ONLY.)

SO VOLUME 3 WAS THE SOIREE ARC. I KIND OF LIKE THINKING OF VOLUMES 1 AND 2 AS HAVING THIS ATMOSPHERE OF BEING WRAPPED IN THE HEADY SCENT OF A MATURE WINE (OR SOMETHING!?). FROM HERE ON, WE WILL CONTINUE STEADILY ADVANCING INTO DARKER TERRITORY, SO I HOPE AKI, KANA, JIN, AND PENG—I MEAN, SWALLOW-SAN—WILL CONTINUE TRYING THEIR BEST. THERE WILL BE A TON OF NEW CHARACTERS, AND THE STUDENT COUNCIL PRESIDENT AND VICE PRESIDENT WILL DEFINITELY HAVE A ROLE TO PLAY TOO! ★ I DO FEEL THIS IS A STORY THAT JUST GETS MORE EXCITING THE FURTHER YOU GET IN IT, SO PLEASE CONTINUE TO READ!!

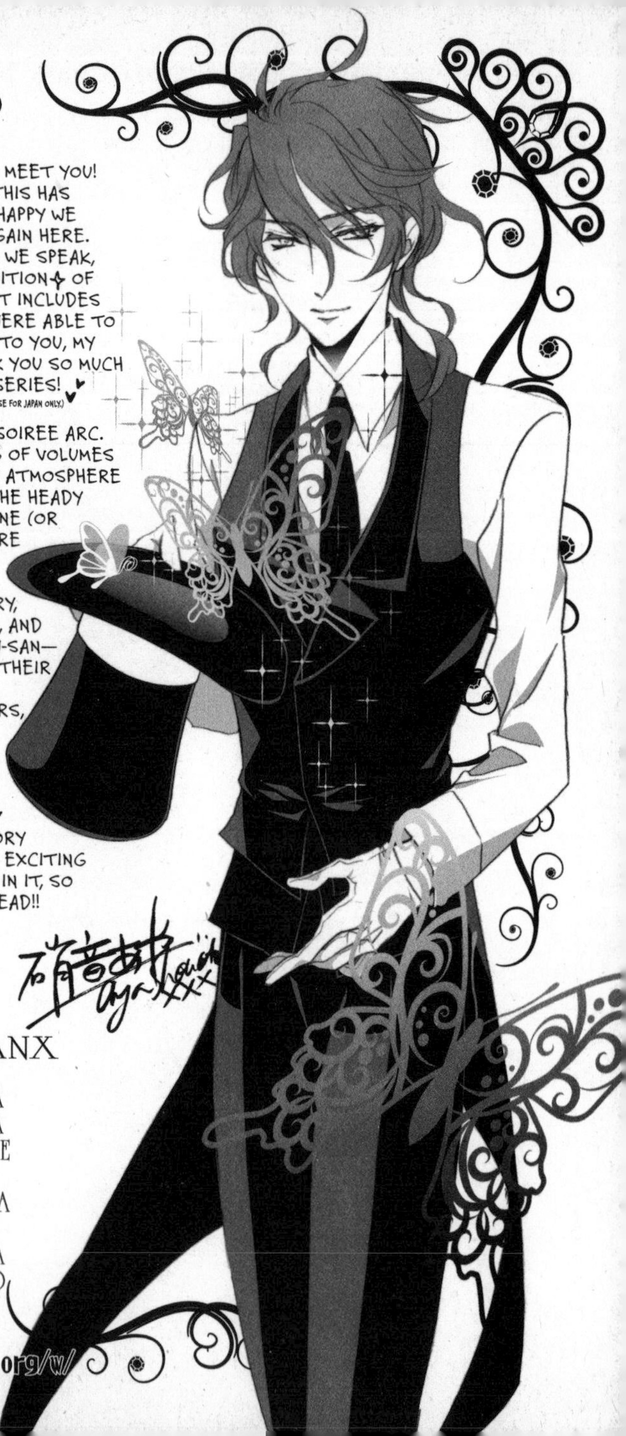

SPECIAL THANX

NORIE OGAWA
AYA NAKAMURA
MAIKO YOSHISE
AYA MAEDA
RIKA KASAHARA
KANAE SAITOU
YURIKA HONDA
KOU HIYOCO

and YOU

ttp://www.kashi.jpn.org/w/

Pure Blood Boyfriend In The House

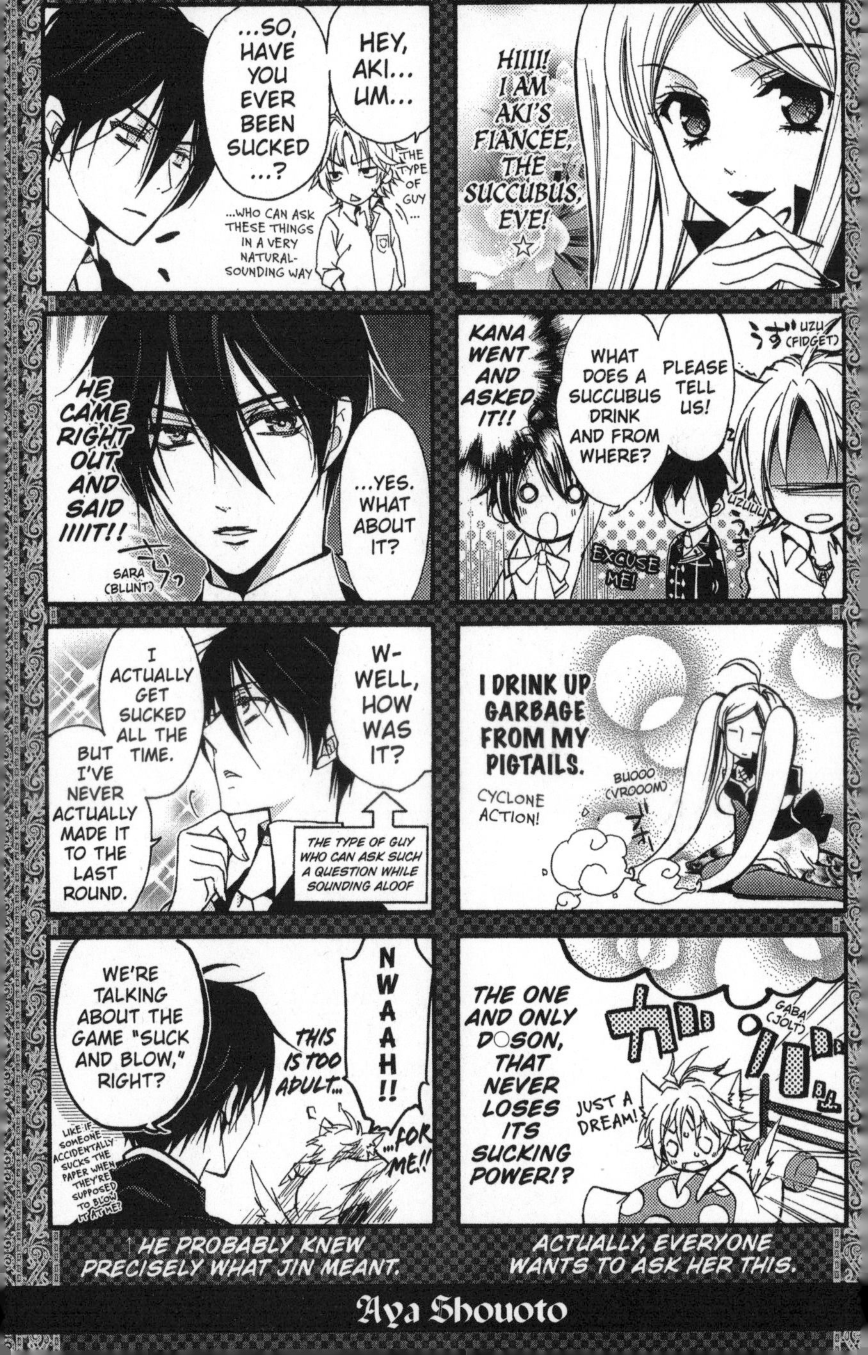
HIIII! I AM AKI'S FIANCÉE, THE SUCCUBUS, EVE! ☆
UZU (FIDGET)
PLEASE TELL US!
WHAT DOES A SUCCUBUS DRINK AND FROM WHERE?
KANA WENT AND ASKED IT!!
UZUUU
EXCUSE ME!
I DRINK UP GARBAGE FROM MY PIGTAILS.
BUOOO (VROOOM)
CYCLONE ACTION!
GABA (JOLT)
THE ONE AND ONLY D○SON, THAT NEVER LOSES ITS SUCKING POWER!?
JUST A DREAM!
HEY, AKI... UM...
...SO, HAVE YOU EVER BEEN SUCKED ...?
THE TYPE OF GUY ...
...WHO CAN ASK THESE THINGS IN A VERY NATURAL-SOUNDING WAY
...YES. WHAT ABOUT IT?
HE CAME RIGHT OUT AND SAID IIIIT!!
SARA (BLUNT)
W-WELL, HOW WAS IT?
I ACTUALLY GET SUCKED ALL THE TIME.
BUT I'VE NEVER ACTUALLY MADE IT TO THE LAST ROUND.
THE TYPE OF GUY WHO CAN ASK SUCH A QUESTION WHILE SOUNDING ALOOF
NWAAAH!!
THIS IS TOO ADULT...
...FOR ME!!
WE'RE TALKING ABOUT THE GAME "SUCK AND BLOW," RIGHT?
LIKE IF SOMEONE ACCIDENTALLY SUCKS THE PAPER WHEN THEY'RE SUPPOSED TO BLOW IT AT ME?

ACTUALLY, EVERYONE WANTS TO ASK HER THIS.

↑HE PROBABLY KNEW PRECISELY WHAT JIN MEANT.

Aya Shouoto

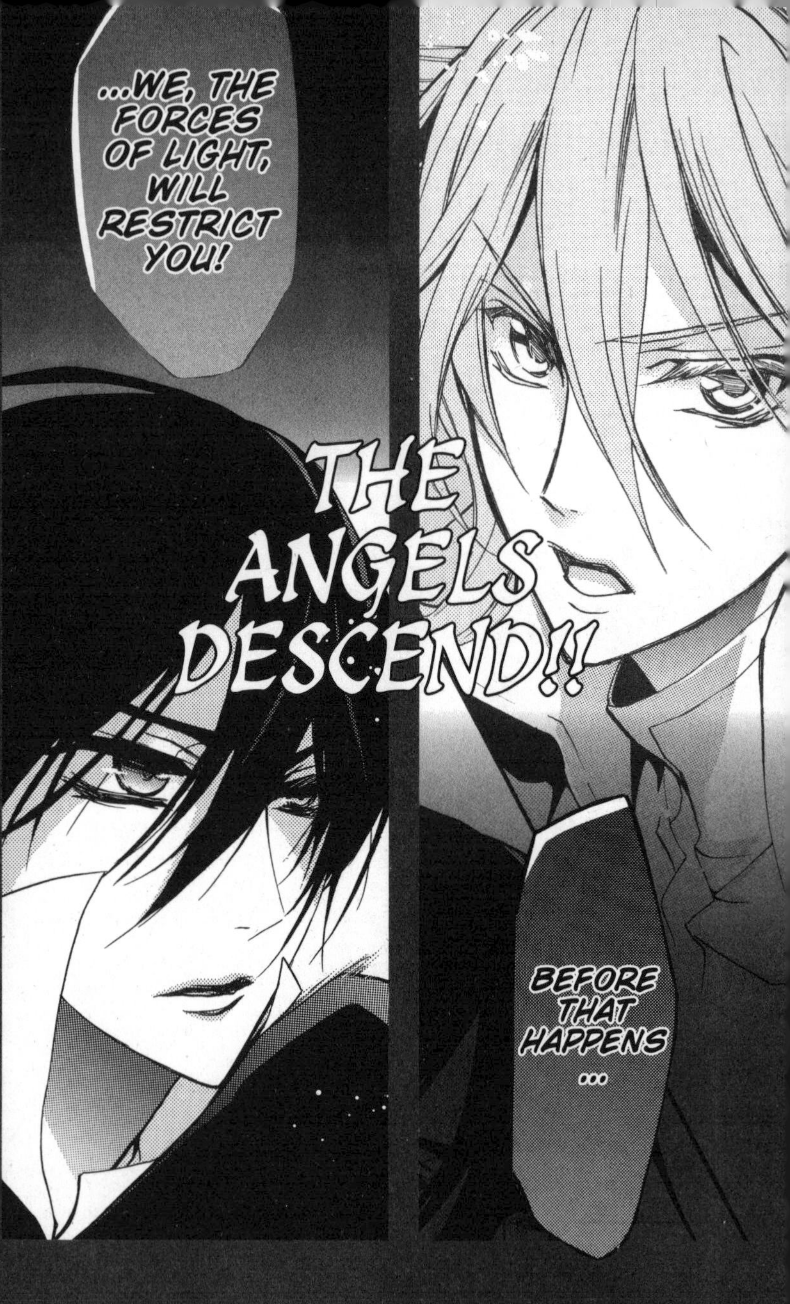
BEFORE THAT HAPPENS ...
...WE, THE FORCES OF LIGHT, WILL RESTRICT YOU!
THE ANGELS DESCEND!!

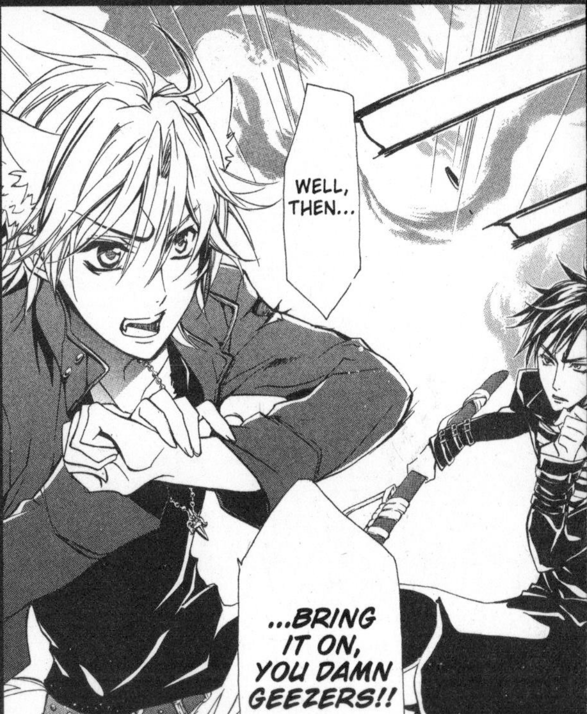
WELL, THEN...
...BRING IT ON, YOU DAMN GEEZERS!!

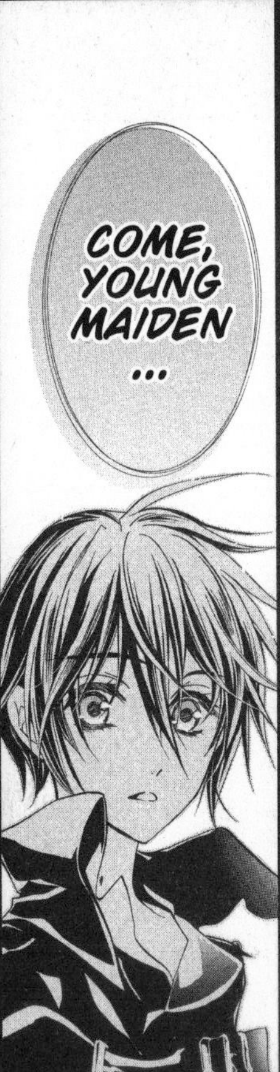
COME, YOUNG MAIDEN ...

"WE ARE ANGELS"—HAVING SPOKEN THOSE WORDS, ISUKA AND HITAKI TAKE UP THEIR SWORDS, ARMED WITH THE RIGHTEOUSNESS OF JUSTICE! IN AKI'S HOUR OF NEED, WHAT WILL KANA DO!?

He's My Only Vampire 4

A NEW SHADOW STIRS IN THE DARKNESS...

He's My Only Vampire 3

Aya Shouoto

Translation: Su Mon Han † Lettering: Alexis Eckerman

HE'S MY ONLY VAMPIRE Volume 3 © 2011 Aya Shouoto. All
rights reserved. First published in Japan in 2011 by Kodansha
Ltd., Tokyo. Publication rights for this English edition arranged
through Kodansha Ltd., Tokyo.

English translation © 2015 by Yen Press, LLC

Yen Press
1290 Avenue of the Americas
New York, NY 10104

Visit us at yenpress.com † facebook.com/yenpress †
twitter.com/yenpress † yenpress.tumblr.com †
instagram.com/yenpress

First Yen Press Edition: June 2015

Yen Press is an imprint of Yen Press, LLC.
The Yen Press name and logo are trademarks of Yen Press, LLC.

Library of Congress Control Number: 2014504630

ISBN: 978-0-316-26055-8

10 9 8 7 6 5 4 3

BVG

Printed in the United States of America